Praise for Marion Lennox

“With some books, I can’t get past [the conventions] but with others, I hardly notice because I’m so interested in the characters, or the setting or the story. Or, as in the case here, [illegible] can’t wait for the next [illegible]

[illegible] *[illegible]k Rescuer*, [illegible]nded Read

“Humor, str[illegible] make this a story [illegible]

—*RT Book [illegible]* on *Crowned: The Palace Nanny*

“Lennox takes an overused premise and makes it her own with a couple of inspired twists. The characters are marvelous too, and there’s a real spark between them.”

—*RT Book Reviews* on *Claimed: Secret Royal Son*

“A sweet, involving story with fabulous characters. Sentimental but also often hilarious, it’s a keeper.”

—*RT Book Reviews* on *His Miracle Bride*

“Vintage Lennox, combining a fairy-tale holiday setting and story with a likable, no-nonsense heroine and a sympathetic, aristocratic hero.... The relationships feel real, and...she manages to balance the sweetness with a few down-to-earth characters.”

—*Dear Author* on *Christmas at the Castle*, Recommended Read

Marion Lennox has written more than a hundred romances and is published in over a hundred countries and thirty languages. Her multiple awards include the prestigious RITA® Award (twice), and the *RT Book Reviews* Career Achievement Award for "a body of work that makes us laugh and teaches us about love." Marion adores her family, her kayak, her dog and lying on the beach with a book someone else has written. Heaven!

Books by Marion Lennox

Harlequin Romance

Sparks Fly with the Billionaire
Christmas at the Castle
Christmas Where They Belong
The Earl's Convenient Wife
His Cinderella Heiress
Stepping into the Prince's World
Stranded with the Secret Billionaire

Visit the Author Profile page
at Harlequin.com for more titles.

An Unlikely Match

Marion Lennox

Previously published as *Nikki and the Lone Wolf* and *Misty and the Single Dad*

ISBN-13: 978-1-335-69086-9

An Unlikely Match

First published as Nikki and the Lone Wolf by Harlequin Books in 2011 and Misty and the Single Dad by Harlequin Books in 2011.

This edition published by arrangement with Harlequin Books S.A.

For questions and comments about the quality of this book, please contact us at CustomerService@Harlequin.com.

Printed in U.S.A.

CONTENTS

NIKKI AND THE LONE WOLF

To Gail and to Charles, for Bob,
a gentle giant with a heart as big as he was.

Chapter 1

A wolf was at her door.

Okay, maybe it wasn't quite at her door, Nikki conceded, as she came back to earth. Or back to the sofa. The howl was close, though. Her hair felt as if it was spiking straight up, and for good reason.

It was the most appalling, desolate sound she could imagine—and she wasn't imagining it.

She set her china teacup onto the coffee table with care, absurdly pleased she hadn't spilled it. She was a country girl now. Country girls didn't get spooked by wolves.

Yes, they did.

She fought for logic. Wolves didn't exist in Banksia Bay. This was the north coast of New South Wales.

Was it a dingo?

Her landlord hadn't mentioned dingoes.

He wouldn't, she thought bitterly. Gabe Carver was one of the most taciturn men she'd ever met. He spoke in monosyllabic grunts. 'Sign here. Rent first Tuesday of the month. Any problems, talk to Joe down at the wharf. He's the handyman. Welcome to Banksia Bay.'

Even his welcome had seemed grudging.

Was he at home?

She peered nervously out into the night and was absurdly comforted to see lights on next door. Actually, it wasn't even next door. This was a huge old house on the headland at the edge of town. Three rooms had been split from the rest of the house and a kitchen installed to make her lovely apartment.

Her landlord was thus right through the wall. They shared the entrance porch. Taciturn or not, the thought that he was at home was reassuring. The burly seaman seemed tough, capable, powerful—even vaguely scary. If the wolf came in…

This was crazy. Nothing was coming in. Her door was locked. And it couldn't be a wolf. It was…

The howl came again, long, low and filling the night with despair.

Despair?

What would she know?

It was just a dog, howling at the moon.

It didn't sound like…just a howl.

She peered out again, then tugged the curtains closed. Logical or not, this was scary. Barricade the door and go to bed. It was the only logical thing to do.

Another howl.

Pain.

Desolation.

Did pain and desolation make any kind of sense?

Step away from the window, Nikkita, she told herself. This is nothing to do with you. This is weird country stuff.

'I'm a country girl.' She said it out loud.

'Um, no,' she corrected herself. 'You're not. You're a city girl who's lived in Banksia Bay for all of three weeks. You ran here because your low-life boss broke your heart. It was a dumb, irrational move. You know nothing about country living.'

But her landlord was right next door. Dogs? Wolves? Whatever it was, he'd be hearing it. He could deal with it himself or he could call Joe.

She was going to bed.

The howl filled the night, echoing round and round the big old house.

There was a dog out there, in trouble.

It was not Gabe's problem. Not.

The howl came again, mournful as death, filling his head with its misery. If Jem had been here she'd be off to investigate.

He missed Jem so much it was as if he'd lost a part of him.

He was settled in his armchair by the fire. Things were as they'd always been, but the place at his feet was empty.

He'd found Jem sixteen years ago, a scrappy, half grown collie, skin and bones. She was attacking a rotting fish on the beach.

He'd lifted her away, half expecting the starved pup to growl or snap, but she'd turned and licked his face with her disgusting tongue—and sealed a friendship for life.

She passed away in her sleep, three months back. He still put his hand down, expecting the warmth of her rough coat. Expecting her to be…there.

The howl cut across his thoughts. Impossible to ignore.

He swore.

Okay, he didn't want to get involved—when had he ever?—but he couldn't bear this. The howl was coming from the beach. If a dog was trapped down there… The tide was on its way in.

Why would a dog be trapped on the beach?

Why would a dog be on the beach?

The howl…again.

He sighed. Abandoned his book. Hauled on the battered sou'wester that, as a professional fisherman, was his second skin. Tugged on his boots and headed for the door.

There wasn't a lot of use staring at the fire anyway. He'd made a conscious decision when his wife walked away to never live with anyone again. Emotional connection spelled disaster.

That didn't mean he had to like his solitary life. With Jem it had been just okay.

Not any more.

Her silk pyjamas were laid out on her pretty pink quilt, waiting for her to climb into her brand new single bed. But the howling went on.

She couldn't bear it.

She might not be a country girl but she'd figured

whatever was out there was distressed, not threatening. The howl contained all the misery in the world.

Her landlord lived next door. He should fix it, but would he?

The first day she'd been here she'd worried about pipes gurgling in her antiquated bathroom. The bathroom was vast, the bathtub was huge, and the plumbing looked as if it had come from a medieval castle. The gurgling had her thinking there was no way she was using the bath.

Gabe had been outside, chopping wood. She'd hesitated to approach, intimidated by his gruffness—and also the size, the sense of innate power, the sheer masculinity of the man. Chopping wood…he'd looked quite something.

Actually…he'd been stripped to the waist and he'd looked *really* something.

She was being stupid. Hormonal. Dumb. She'd plucked up courage and approached, feeling like Oliver Twist asking for more gruel. 'Please sir, could you fix my pipes?'

'See Joe,' he'd muttered and promptly disappeared.

She'd been disconcerted for days.

She'd seethed for a bit, tried to ignore the gurgling for a few days, had showers, and finally gone to find Joe.

Joe was an ancient ex-fisherman living on a dilapidated schooner that looked as if it hadn't been to sea for years. He'd promised to fix the gurgling that afternoon. He did—sort of—thumping the pipes with a spanner—but while she'd been explaining the problem, a fishing boat swept past. Huge. Freshly painted.

Gleaming clean and white. The deck was stacked with cray-pots. The superstructure was strung with scores of lanterns that Joe explained were to attract squid.

Her landlord had been at the wheel.

Still disconcerting. Big, weathered, powerful.

Still capable of doing things to her hormones just by…being.

‘Turns his hand to anything, that one,’ Joe told her as they watched Gabe go past. ‘Some of the guys here just fish for squid. Or crays. Or tuna. Then there’s a drop in numbers, or sales go off and they’re in trouble. I’ve been a fisherman all my life and I’ve seen so many go to the wall. Gabe just buys ’em out and keeps going. He went away for a while, but came back when things got bad. Bailed us out. Six of the boats here are his.’

At the wheel of his boat, Gabe looked an imposing figure. His sou’wester might have once been yellow, but that time was long past. He wore oversized waterproof trousers with braces, rubber boots and a faded checked shirt rolled up to reveal arms maybe four times the width of hers. His eyes were creased against the elements, and his face looked almost grim.

After days at sea, his stubble was almost a beard. His thick black hair—in need of a cut—was stiff with salt.

His boat passed within yards of Joe’s, and he gave Joe a salute. No smile, though.

He didn’t look as if he ever smiled.

He bought up other fishermen when they went broke? He made money out of other people’s misery?

Her hormones needed to find someone else to fantasise about, fast.

'I'd guess he's not popular,' she'd ventured, but Joe had looked at her as if she was crazy.

'Are you kidding? Without Gabe, the fishing industry here'd be bust. He buys out the guys who go broke, gives 'em a fair price, then employs 'em to keep working. He's got thirty men and women working for him now, all making a better living than they ever did solo, and there's not one but who'd lay down their lives for him. Not that he'd ask. Never asks anything of anyone. Never lets anyone close. If anyone's in trouble Gabe's first on hand, doing what needs doing, whatever the cost. But he doesn't want thanks. Backs off a mile if you try and give it. He keeps to himself, our Gabe. Apart from that one disaster of a marriage, he always has and he always will. The town respects that. We'd be nuts not to.'

He paused, watching as Gabe expertly manoeuvred his boat into a berth that seemed way too small to take her. He did it as if he was parking a Mini Minor in a paddock, as if he had all the room in the world. 'But now his dog's died,' Joe said slowly, reflectively. 'I dunno… We've never seen him without her; not since he was a lad, and how he's handling it…' He broke off and shook his head. 'Yeah, well, about those pipes…'

That was two weeks ago.

Another howl jerked her back to the present. A dog in trouble.

Desolation?

She had to do something.

There was nothing she could do. This was something her landlord had to cope with.

The howl came again, long, low and dreadful.

She'd tugged on her pyjama top. Almost defiantly.

Another howl.

She paused, torn.

What if her landlord wasn't at home? What if he'd left the light on and was gone?

There was a dog out there in trouble.

Not your problem. NYP. NYP. NYP.

She closed her eyes.

Another howl.

She hauled off her pyjamas and tugged on jeans. Designer jeans. She should do something about her clothes.

She should do something about a dog.

Where was a torch?

What if it was a dingo?

She grabbed her mobile phone. Checked reception. Checked she had the emergency services number on speed dial.

There was a heavy metal poker by the fireside. So far she hadn't lit the fire—or she had once but it had smoked and what did you do about a fire that smoked?

You bought a nice clean electric fire.

Another howl—they were now almost continuous.

Enough.

Poker in one hand, torch in the other, country-girl Nikki—or not—went to see.

The beach beneath the headland was bushland almost to the water's edge. Gabe strode down the darkened track with ease. He'd lived here all his life—he practically knew each twig. He didn't need a torch. In moonlight, torchlight stopped you seeing the big picture.

He reached the beach and looked out to the water's edge. Following the howl.

A huge dog. Skinny. Really skinny. Standing in the shallows, howling with all the misery in the world.

Gabe walked steadily forward, not wanting to startle it, walking as if he was strolling slowly along the beach and hadn't even noticed the dog.

The dog saw him. It stopped howling and backed further into the water. Obviously terrified.

A wolfhound? A wolfhound mixed with something else. Black and shaggy and desolate.

'It's okay.' He was still twenty yards away. 'Hey, boy, it's fine. You going to tell me what's the matter?'

The dog stilled.

It was seriously big. And seriously skinny. And very, very wet.

Had it come off a boat?

He thought suddenly of Jem, shivering on the beach sixteen years back. Jem, breaking his heart.

This dog was nothing to do with him. *This was not another Jem.*

He couldn't leave it, though. Could he entice it up the cliff? If he could get it into his truck he'd take it to Henrietta who ran the local Animal Welfare shelter.

That was the extent of his involvement. Dogs broke your heart almost worse than people.

'I'm not going to hurt you.' He should have brought some steak, something to coax him. 'You want to come home and get a feed? Here, boy?'

The dog backed still further. For whatever reason, this dog didn't want company. He looked a great galumphing frame of terror.

It'd have to be steak. There was no way he'd catch him without.

'Stay here,' he told the dog. 'Two minutes tops and I'll be back with supper. You like rump steak?'

The dog was almost haunch-deep in water. Was he dumb or just past acting rationally?

'Two minutes,' he promised. 'Don't go away.'

The dog was on the beach. As soon as she walked out of the front door she figured it out. The house was on the headland and the howls were echoing straight up.

Should she knock on her landlord's side of the house?

If he was home he must be hearing this, she thought, and if he'd heard it and done nothing, then no amount of pleading would make a difference. Joe said he helped people. Ha!

He must have heard and decided to ignore it. He was like Joe said, a loner.

Knock and see?

What was worse, the Hound of the Baskervilles or her landlord?

Don't be stupid. Knock.

She knocked.

Nothing.

She didn't know whether to be relieved or not.

Another howl.

What next? Ring the police?

What would she say? Excuse me but there's a dog on the beach. What sort of wimpy statement was that?

She needed to see what was happening.

Cautiously.

There was a narrow track from the house to the beach but she'd only been on it a couple of times. It was a private track, practically overgrown. Where did the track start?

She searched the edge of the overgrown garden with the torch but she couldn't find it.

So was she going to bush-bash her way down to the cove?

This was nuts. Dangerous nuts.

Only it wasn't dangerous. There was only about fifty yards of bush-land between the house and the beach. The bush wasn't so thick she couldn't push through.

And that howl was doing things to her insides. It sounded like she imagined the Hound of the Baskervilles would sound, howling ghostly anguish over the moors. Or over her beach.

The animal must be stuck in a trap or something.

If it was stuck, what could she do?

Go to the beach, figure what's wrong and then ring for help.

You can do this. You're a big girl. A country girl. Or not.

She wanted, suddenly and desperately, to be back home in Sydney. In her lovely life she'd walked away from.

Face that tomorrow, she told herself harshly. For tonight…go fix a howl.

He was striding up the track, moving swiftly. With a slab of meat in his hand he could approach the dog slowly, letting it smell the meat before it smelled him. He'd intended to have the steak for breakfast—he needed a decent meal before heading to sea again—but he could cope with eggs.

Don't get sucked in.

'I'm not getting sucked in,' he told himself. 'I'm hauling the thing out of the water, feeding it and handing it over to Henrietta. End of story.'

It was dark.

The bush was really thick. Her torch wasn't strong enough.

She was out of her mind.

The howls stopped.

Why?

The silence made it worse. Where had the howls been coming from? Where were the howls now?

Anything could be in here. Bunyips. Neanderthals. The odd rapist.

She was losing her mind, and she was going home now! She turned, pushed forward, and a branch slapped her forehead with a swish of leaves. She almost screamed. She was absurdly pleased that she didn't.

But still no howl.

Where was it?

She was going back to the house. There was no way she was going one inch further.

Where was the thing behind the howl?

She shoved her way around the next bush, pushing herself against the thick foliage. Suddenly the foliage gave way and she almost tumbled out onto the track.

Hands grabbed her shoulders—and held.

She screamed and jerked back.

She raised her poker and she hit.

Chapter 2

She'd killed him.

He went down like felled timber, crumpling from the knees, pitching sideways onto the leaf-littered track.

She had just enough courage not to run; to shine the torch at what she'd hit.

She'd hit someone—not something. She didn't believe in werewolves. Therefore…

Sanity returned with terrifying speed. She had it figured almost before she got the torchlight on his face, and what she saw confirmed it.

She whimpered. There seemed no other option.

This was ghastly on so many levels her head felt it might explode.

She'd knocked out her landlord.

The howling started up again just through the trees, and she jumped higher than the first time she'd heard it.

A lesser woman would run.

There wasn't room for her to be a lesser woman.

She knelt, shining the torchlight closer to see the damage.

Gabe's dark face was thick with stubble, harsh and angular. A thin trickle of blood was oozing down the side of his cheek. A bruise with a split at its centre was rising above his eye.

He seemed totally unconscious.

To say her heart sank was an understatement. Her heart was below her ankles. It was threatening to abandon her body entirely.

But then… He stirred and groaned and his fingers moved towards his head.

Conscious. That had to be good.

What to do? Deep breath. This was no time for hysterics. He looked as if he was trying to focus.

She placed the poker behind her. Out of sight.

'Are you… Are you okay?' she managed.

He groaned. He closed his eyes and appeared to think about it.

'No,' he managed at last. 'I'm not.'

'I'll find a doctor.' Her voice wobbled to the point of ridiculous. 'An ambulance.'

He opened his eyes again, touched his head, winced, closed his eyes again. 'No.'

'You need help.' She was gabbling. 'Someone.' She went to touch his face and then thought better of it. She definitely needed help. Someone who knew what they were doing. She reached inside her jacket for her cellphone.

His eyes flew open, he grabbed her wrist and he held like a vice.

'What did you hit me with?' His voice was a slurred growl.

'A…a poker.' His voice was deep. In contrast, her voice was practically a squeak.

'A poker,' he said, almost conversationally. 'Of course. And now what?'

'S…sorry?'

'You have a gun in your jacket? Or is only your poker loaded?'

Her breath came out in a rush. If he was making stupid jokes, maybe she hadn't done deathly damage.

'There's not…that's not funny,' she managed. 'You scared the daylights out of me.'

'You *hit* the daylights out of me.'

Reaction was making her shake. 'You snuck up.' Her voice was getting higher. 'You grabbed me.'

'Snuck up…' He sounded flabbergasted. 'I believe,' he said through gritted teeth, 'that I was running up the track. On *my* land. Back to *my* house. And you burst out of the undergrowth. Bearing poker.'

He had a point, she conceded. She'd almost fallen as she lurched onto the cleared track. She might indeed have fallen into his path.

It might even have been reasonable for him to grab her to stop them both falling.

And he was her landlord. Hitting someone was bad enough, but to hit Gabe…

It hadn't been easy to find decent rental accommodation in Banksia Bay and she'd been really lucky to find this apartment. Apart from howling dogs, it had everything she needed. 'Just be nice to your landlord and respect his privacy,' the woman in the rental agency had advised. 'He's a bit of a loner. You leave Gabe in peace and you'll get along fine.'

Leaving him in peace wouldn't include hitting him, she conceded. Mentally she was already packing.

'I need steak,' he said across her thoughts.

She blinked. 'Steak?' She groped for basic first aid; thought of something she'd once read. 'To stop the swelling?' She tried to look wise. Tried to stop gibbering. 'I don't… I don't have steak but I'll get ice.'

'For the dog, dummy.' He'd raised his head but now he set it down again, staying flat on the leaf litter. Gingerly fingering the bruise. 'The dog needs help. There's steak in my fridge. Fetch it.'

'I can't…'

'Just fetch it,' he snapped and closed his eyes. 'If you run round in the middle of the night with pokers, you face the consequences. Get the steak.'

'I can't leave you,' she said miserably, and he opened one eye and looked at her. Flinching.

'Turn the torch around,' he said, and she realised that just possibly she was blinding him as well as hitting him.

'Sorry.' She swivelled the light so it was shining harmlessly into the bush.

'No, onto you.'

He reached out, grabbed the flashlight and turned it onto her face. Then he surveyed her while she thought ouch, having a flashlight in her eyes hurt.

'There's no need to be scared,' he said.

'I'm not scared.' But then the dog howled again and she jumped. Okay, maybe she was.

'You can't afford to be,' he said, and she could tell by the strain in his voice that he was hurting. 'Because the dog needs help. I don't know what's wrong with him. He's standing on the beach howling. You were heading down with a poker. I, on the other hand, intend to try steak. I believe my method is more humane. It might take me a few moments to stop seeing stars, however, so you fetch it.'

'Are you really seeing stars?'

'Yes.' Then he relented. 'It's night. There are stars. Yes, I'm dizzy, but I'll get over it. I won't die while you're away, but I do need a minute to stop things spinning. My door's open. Kitchen's at the back. Steak's in the paper parcel in the fridge. Chop it into bite sized pieces. I'll lie here and count stars till you come back. Real ones.'

'I can't leave you. I need to call for help.'

'I'm fine,' he said with exaggerated patience. 'I've had worse bumps than this and lived. Just do what I ask like a good girl and give me space to recover.'

'You lost consciousness. I can't…'

'If I did it was momentary and I don't need anyone to hold my hand,' he snapped. 'Neither do you. You're wasting time, woman. Go.'

She went. Feeling dreadful.

She tracked the path with her torch, trying to run. She couldn't. The path was a mass of tree roots. If Gabe had been running he must know the path by heart.

She didn't have the right shoes for running either.

She didn't have the right shoes at all, she thought. She was wearing Gucci loafers. They worked beautifully for wandering the Botanic Gardens in Sydney after a Sunday morning latte. They didn't work so well here.

She wanted so much to be back in her lovely apartment overlooking Sydney Harbour. Back in her beautifully contained life, her wonderful job, her friends, the lovely parties, the coffee haunts, control.

Jon's fabulous apartment. A job in a lovely office right next to Jon's. A career that paid…extraordinarily. A career with Jon. Friends she shared with Jon. Coffee haunts where people greeted Jon before they greeted her.

Jon's life. Or half of Jon's life. She'd thought she had the perfect life and it had been based on a lie.

What to do when your world crumbled?

Run. She'd run to here.

'Don't think about it.' She said it to herself as a mantra, over and over, as she headed up the track as fast as she could in her stupid shoes. There'd been enough self-pity. This was her new life. Wandering around in the dark, coshing her landlord, looking for steak for the Hound of the Baskervilles?

It was her new life until tomorrow, she thought miserably. Tomorrow Gabe would ask her to leave.

Another city might be more sensible than moving back to Sydney. But it was probably time she faced the fact that moving to the coast had been a romantic notion, a dignified way she could explain her escape to friends.

'I can't stand the rat race any longer. I can deal with my clients through the Internet and the occasional city visit. I see myself in a lovely little house overlooking the sea, just me and my work and time to think.'

Her friends—Jon's friends—thought she was nuts, but then they didn't know the truth about Jon.

Scumbag.

She'd walked away from a scumbag. Now she'd hit her landlord.

Men! Where was a nice convent when a girl needed one? A cloistered convent where no man set foot. Ever.

There seemed to be a dearth of convents on her way back to the house.

Steak.

She reached the house, and headed through the porch they shared, where two opposite doors delineated His and Hers.

She'd never been in His. She opened his door cautiously as if there might be a Hound or two in there as well.

No Hounds. The sitting room looked old and faded and comfy, warmed by a gorgeous open fire. There was one big armchair by the fire. A half-empty beer glass. Books scattered—lots of books. Masculine, unfussed, messy.

All this she saw at a glance as she headed towards the kitchen, but strangely...here was the hormone thing again. She was distracted by the sheer masculinity of the place.

As she was...distracted...by the sheer masculinity of her landlord.

Stupid. Get on with it, she told herself crossly, and she did.

His fridge held more than hers. Meat, vegetables, fruit, sauces—interesting stuff that said when he was at home he cooked.

She needed to learn, she thought suddenly, as she caught the whiff of meals past and glanced at the big old firestove that was the centrepiece of the kitchen. Enough with 'Waistline Cuisine'.

It was hardly the time to be thinking cooking classes now, though. Or hormones.

Steak.

She had it. A solid lump, enough for a team of Hounds. She sliced it into chunks in seconds, then opened the freezer and grabbed a packet of frozen peas as well.

First aid and Hound meat, coming up.

Men and dogs. She could cope.

She had no choice. Convents had to wait.

What did you do with hormones in convents?

He'd terrified her.

Gabe lay back and looked at the sky and let his head clear. She'd packed a huge punch, but any anger he felt had been wiped by the look on her face. She'd looked sicker than he felt.

What was he about, letting the place to a needy city woman?

It was the second time he'd let it. The first time he'd rented it to Mavis, a spinster with two dogs. The moment she'd moved in she decided he needed mothering. Finally, after six months of tuna bakes, her mother had 'a turn' and Mavis headed back to Sydney to take care of her. Gabe had been so relieved he'd waived the last month's rent.

And now this.

Dorothy in the letting agency had made this woman sound businesslike and sensible. Very different to Mavis.

'Nikkita Morrissy. Thirty years old. She designs air conditioning systems for big industrial projects. Her usual schedule is three weeks home, one week on site, often overseas. She's looking for a quiet place with a view, lots of natural light and nothing to disturb her.'

A woman who worked in industrial engineering. She sounded clever, efficient and non-needy.

His house was huge. He should move into town but he'd lived in this place all his life. *His mother was here.*

He'd lost his mother when he was eight years old, and this was all that was left. The garden she'd loved. The fence she'd almost finished. He walked outside sometimes and he could swear he saw her.

'I'll never leave you...'

People lied. He'd learned that early. Depend on no one. But here...in his mother's garden, looking out over the bay she'd loved, this was all that was left of a promise he'd desperately wanted to believe in.

Emotional nonsense? Of course it was, he knew it, but his childhood house was a good place to crash when he wasn't at sea. He had the money to keep it. If he could get a reasonable tenant for the apartment, then there'd be someone keeping the rooms warm, used.

Go ahead, he'd told Dorothy.

And then he'd met Nikkita. Briefly, the day she'd moved in.

She didn't look like an industrial engineer. She looked like someone in one of those glossy magazines Hattie kept leaving on the boat. She was tall, five nine or so, slim and pale-skinned, with huge eyes and professionally applied make-up—yes, he was a bachelor but that didn't mean he couldn't pick decent cosmetics a mile off. Her glossy black hair was cut into some sort of sculpted bob, dead straight, all fringe and sharp edges.

And her clothes… The day she'd arrived she'd been wearing a black tunic with a diagonal slash of crimson across the hips. She'd added loopy silver earrings, red tights and glossy black boots that were practically thigh high. Low heels though. It was her moving day. She'd obviously thought low heels were workmanlike.

Tonight she'd been wearing jeans. Skin-tight jeans and a soft pink sweater. She must be roughing it, he thought, and his thoughts were bitter.

His head was thumping. He was trying hard not to think critical thoughts about ditzy air conditioning engineers who bush-bashed through the night with pokers.

And suddenly she was back again—practically running, though if she'd tried to run in those shoes she would have run right out of them. She was panting. Her eyes were still huge and the sculpted hair was… well, a lot less sculpted. She had a twig stuck behind one ear. A big twig.

'Are you okay?' she demanded, breathless, as if she'd expected to find him dead.

'I'm fine,' he growled and struggled to stand. Enough of lying round feeling sorry for himself. He shook away the hand she proffered, pushed himself to his feet—and the world swayed. Not much, but enough for him to grab her hand to steady himself.

She was stronger than he thought. She grabbed his other hand and held, hard, waiting for him to steady.

'S…sorry.' For a moment he thought he might throw up. He concentrated for a bit and decided no, he might keep his dignity.

'Let me help you to the house.'

'Dog first,' he said.

'You first.'

'The dog's standing up to his hocks in the water, howling. I'm not even whinging. I'm prioritizing.' He made to haul his hands away but she still held.

He stopped pulling and let her hold.

Two reasons. One, he was still unsteady.

Two, it felt…not bad at all.

He worked with women. A good proportion of his fishing crews were female. They mostly smelled of, yeah, well, of fish. After a while, no matter how much washing, you didn't get the smell out.

Nikkita smelled of something citrussy and tangy and outright heady. It didn't make the dizziness worse, though. In truth it helped. He stood still, breathing in the scent of her, while the night settled around him.

She didn't speak. She simply held.

Two minutes. Three. She wasn't a talker, then. She'd figured he needed time to make the ground solid and she was giving it to him. It was the first decent thing he'd seen of her.

Maybe there were more decent things.

Her hands felt good. They were small hands for a tall woman. Soft…

Yeah, well, of course they'd be soft. For the last ten years any woman he'd ever gone out with was a local, one of the fishing crews, women who worked hard for a living. The only woman he'd ever gone out with who had soft hands…

Yeah. Lisbette. He'd married her.

So much for soft hands.

'I'm right now,' he said, finally, as another howl split the night. 'Dog.'

'Please let me take you home first.'

'Are you good with dogs?'

'Um…no.'

'Then we both do the dog,' he said. 'Sure, I'm unsteady, so you do what I tell you. Exactly what I tell you. After the poker, it's the least you can do.'

Was she out of her mind?

She was acting under orders.

Gabe was sitting in the shadows, watching, as she approached the dog with her hands full of steak. Upwind, according to Gabe's directions, so he could smell the meat.

The dog was huge. Soaking wet, its coat was clinging to its skinny frame, so it looked almost like a small black horse.

Talk gently, Gabe had said. Soft, unthreatening.

So… 'Hey, Horse, it's okay,' she told him. 'Come out of the water and have some steak. Gabe's gone to a lot of trouble to get it for you. The least you can do is eat it.'

Take one small step after another, Gabe had told her. Stop at the first hint of nervousness. Let the dog figure for himself that you're not a threat.

'Come on, boy. Hey, Horse, it's okay. It's fine. Come and tell me what your real name is.'

What was she doing, standing in the shallows with her hands full of raw meat? She'd tugged off her shoes but her jeans were soaked. To no avail. The dog was backing away, still twenty feet from her.

His coat was ragged, long and dripping. Fur was matted over his eyes.

He wasn't coming near.

If Gabe wasn't in the shadows watching she might have set the meat down on the sand and retreated.

But her landlord was expecting her to do this. He'd do it himself, only, despite what he told her, the thump on the head was making him nauseous. She knew it. He wasn't letting her call for help but she knew it went against the grain to let her approach the dog. Especially when she was so bad at it.

'Here, Horse. Here...'

A wave, bigger than the rest, came sideways instead of forward. It slapped into another wave, crested, hit her fair across the chest.

She yelped. She couldn't help herself.

The dog backed fast into the waves.

'It's okay,' she called and forgot to lower her voice.

The dog cast her a terrified glance and backed some more. The next wave knocked him sideways. He regained his footing and ran, like the horse he resembled. Along the line of the surf, away, around the bed in the headland and out of sight.

* * *

'It's okay.'

It wasn't, but she hadn't expected him to say it. She'd expected him to yell.

She'd coshed him. She'd scared the dog away.

A little voice at the back of her mind was saying, *At least the howling's stopped.*

NYP, the same little voice in the back of her head whispered. Not your problem. She could forget the dog.

Only… He'd looked tragic. Horse…

Gabe was sitting where the sand gave way to the grassy verge before the bush began. At least he looked okay. At least he was still conscious.

'You did the best you could.' *For a city girl.* It wasn't said. It didn't have to be said.

'Maybe he's gone home.'

'Does he look to you like he has a home?' He flicked his cellphone from his top pocket and punched in numbers. Then he glanced at her, sighed, and hit loudspeaker so she could hear who he was talking to.

A male voice. Authoritive. 'Banksia Bay Police,' the voice said.

'Raff?' Gabe's voice still wasn't completely steady and the policeman at the end of the line obviously heard it. Maybe he was used to people with unsteady voices calling. He also recognised the caller.

'Gabe? What's up?' She heard concern.

'No problem. Or not a major one. A stray dog.'

'Another one.' The policeman sighed.

'What are you talking about?' Gabe demanded.

'Henrietta's Animal Welfare van was involved in

an accident a few days back,' the policeman explained. 'We have stray dogs all over town. Describe this one.'

'Big, black and malnourished,' Gabe said. He was watching Nikki as he spoke. Nikki was trying to get the sand from between her toes before she put her shoes on. It wasn't working.

She was soaking. She sat and the sand stuck to her. Ugh.

She was also unashamedly listening.

'Like Great Dane big?'

'Yeah, but he's shaggy,' Gabe said. 'I'd guess Wolfhound with a few other breeds mixed in as well. And I don't have him. He was down the beach below the house. We tried to catch him with a lump of steak but he's headed round the headland to your side of town.'

'We?' Raff said.

'Yeah,' Gabe said dryly. 'My tenant's been helpful.'

'But the two of you can't catch him.'

'No,' Gabe said, and Nikki thought miserably that he sounded as if he could have done it if he was by himself. Maybe he could, but at least he didn't say so.

'I'll check from the headland in the morning,' Raff was saying. 'You okay? You sound odd.'

'Nothing I can't handle. If he comes back…you want me to take him to the shelter?'

'You might as well take him straight to the vet's,' Raff said. 'He was on his way there to be put down. If he's the one I think he is, someone threw him off a boat a couple of weeks back. We found him on the beach, starving. He's well past cute pup stage. He's huge and shabby. Old scars and not a lot of loveliness. He looks like he's been kicked and neglected. No one will re-house a dog like that, so Henrietta made the decision to get him put down. But if he doesn't come back to your beach it's not your worry, mate. Thanks for letting me know. 'Night.'

''Night.'

Gabe repocketed his phone.

Nikki flicked more sand away.

A starving dog. Kicked and neglected. Thrown from a boat. She hadn't even managed to give him a meal, and now he was lost again.

Plus a landlord who was still sounding shaken because she'd thumped him.

Was there a scale for feeling bad? Bad, terrible, appalling.

'Leave the steak just above the high tide mark,' Gabe said, his voice gentle. 'It's not your fault.'

'Nice of you to say so.'

'Yeah, well, the bang on the head was your fault,' he conceded, and he even managed a wry smile. 'But there's nothing more we can do for the dog. He's gone. If he smelled the steak he might come back, but he won't come near if he smells us. We've done all we can. Moving on, I need an aspirin. Do you have those toes sand-free yet?'

'I…yes.' No. She was crusted in sand but she stood up and prepared to move on.

She glanced along the beach, half hoping the dog would lope back.

Why would he?

'Raff'll find him,' Gabe said.

'He's the local cop?'

'Yes.'

'He won't look tonight?'

'There's no hope of finding him tonight. The beach around the headland is inaccessible at high tide. We'll find him tomorrow.'

'You'll look, too?'

'I'm leaving at dawn,' he said. 'I have fish to catch, but you're welcome to look all you want. Now, if you want to stay here you're also welcome, but I need my bed.'

She followed him up the track, feeling desolate. But Gabe must be feeling worse than she was. Maybe he was walking slowly to cater for her lack of sensible shoes, but she didn't think so. Once he stumbled and she put out a hand. He steadied, looked down at her hand and shook his head. And winced again.

'I hit you hard,' she muttered.

'Women aren't what they used to be,' he said. 'Whatever happened to a nice, tidy slap across the cheek? That's what they do in movies.'

'I'll remember it next time.'

'There won't be a next time,' he said, and she thought uh-oh, was her tenancy on the line?

'I'm not about to evict you,' he said wearily, and she flinched. Beside being clumsy and stupid, was she also transparent?

'I didn't think…'

'That I was about to evict you for hitting me? Good.'

'Thank you,' she said feebly and he went on concentrating on putting one foot in front of the other.

He didn't stop until they reached the house. The lights were still on. He stood back to let her precede him into the porch. Instead of going straight into her side of the house, she paused.

Under the porch-light he looked…ill. Yes, he still looked large, dark and dangerous, but he also looked pale under the weathering, and the thin trickle of blood was at the centre of a bruise that promised to be ugly.

He staggered a bit. She reached out instinctively but he grabbed the veranda post. Steadied.

She could have killed him. He looked so…so…

Male?

There was a sensible thought.

'You could have me arrested,' she managed. 'I'm so sorry.'

'But you weren't planning to hit the dog.' It wasn't a question.

'N…no.'

'That's why I won't have you arrested. You meant well.'

'You need to see a doctor.'

'I need to go to bed.'

'But what if it's terrible?' she said before she could stop herself. 'I've read about head wounds. People get hit on the head and go to bed and never wake up. You should get your pupils looked at. If one's bigger than the other…or is it if one doesn't move? I don't know, but I do know that you should get yourself checked. Please, can I drive you to the hospital?'

'No.' Flat. Inflexible. Non negotiable.

'Why not?'

'I've spent my life on boats. Believe it or not, I've been thumped a lot worse than this. I'm fine.'

'You should be checked.'

'You want to look at my pupils?'

'I wouldn't know what to look for. But if you go to bed now… It could be dangerous. Please…'

He was too close, she thought. He was too big. He smelled of the sea. But maybe it wasn't just the sea. He smelled of diesel oil, and fish, and salt, and other incredibly masculine smells she'd never smelled before.

The only man she'd been this close to in the last few years was Jon. Jon of the sleek business suits, of expensive aftershave, of cool, sleek, corporate style.

Compared to Jon, Gabe was another species. They both might be guys at the core, but externally Gabe had been left behind in the cave. Or at sea.

Beside Gabe she felt small and insignificant and stupid. And he made her feel…vulnerable? Maybe, but something more. Exposed. It was a feeling she couldn't explain and she didn't want to explain. All she knew was that she didn't want to be beside him one moment longer, but she was still worried about him. That worry wouldn't be ignored.

'You should be checked every couple of hours,' she said, doggedly now. Once upon a time, well before Jon, she'd dated a medical student. She knew this much.

'I'm fine.' He was getting irritated. 'In eight hours I'll be out at sea. I need to go to bed now. Goodnight.'

'At least let me check.'

'Check what?'

'Check you. All night.'

He stilled. They were far too close. The porch was far too small. Exposed? It was a dumb thought, but that was definitely how he made her feel. His face was lined, worn, craggy. He couldn't be much over thirty, she thought, but he looked as if life had been hard.

It could get harder if she didn't check him. If he was to die…

'What are you talking about?' he demanded.

'I need to check you every two hours,' she said miserably, knowing her conscience would let her off with nothing less. 'I'll come in and make sure you're conscious.'

'I won't be conscious. I'll be asleep.'

'Then I'll wake you and you can tell me your name and what day it is and then you can go back to sleep.'

'I won't know which day it is.'

'Then tell me how much you dislike the tenant next door,' she said, starting to feel desperate. 'For worrying. But I need to do this.' Deep breath. 'It's two-hour checks or I'll phone your friend, the cop, and I tell him how badly I hit you. I wouldn't be the least bit surprised if he's the kind of guy who'll be up here with sirens blazing making you see sense.'

Silence.

Her guess was right, she thought. In that one short phone conversation she'd sensed friendship between the two men, and maybe the unknown cop was as tough as the guy standing in front of her.

'I'm serious,' she said, jutting her jaw.

'I'll be on the boat at dawn. This is nonsense.'

'Being on the boat at dawn is nonsense. After a hit like that you should stay home.'

'Butt out of my life!' It was an explosion and she backed as far as the little porch allowed. Which wasn't far, but something must have shown in her face.

'Okay, sorry.' He raked his hand through his thatch of dark, unruly hair. He needed a haircut, Nikki thought inconsequentially. And then she thought, even more inconsequentially, what would he look like in a suit?

Like a caged tiger. This guy was not meant to be constrained.

That was what she was doing now, she thought. She was constraining him, but she wasn't backing down. There was no way she could calmly go to bed and leave him to die next door.

She met his gaze and jutted her chin some more and tried to look determined. She was determined.

'Every two hours or Raff,' she said.

'Fine.' He threw up his hands in defeat. 'Have it your way. You can sleep tomorrow; I can't. I'm going to bed. If you shine your torch in my eyes every two hours I might well tell you what I think of you.'

'Fine by me,' she said evenly. 'As long as you're alive.'

'Goodnight,' he snapped and turned away. But as he did she saw him wince again.

She really had hurt him.

She showered and tried not to think about dead landlords and starving dogs. What else?

Live landlords. Two-hourly checks. Pupil dilation?

Maybe not. Questions would have to do.

Her pipes gurgled.

She thought briefly about discussing antiquated pipes every two hours but decided, on balance, maybe not. Name and date. Keep it formal and brief.

She set her alarm for two hours on but she didn't sleep. Two hours later she tiptoed in next door.

She'd forgotten to ask which was his bedroom. It was a huge house.

There was a note on the floor in the passage, with an arrow pointing to the left.

'Florence Nightingale, this way.'

She managed a smile. Her first smile of the night. Okay, he'd accepted her help.

She tiptoed in.

He was sprawled on a big bed, the covers only to his waist. Face down, arms akimbo.

Bare back. Very bare back.

She was using her torch. She should quickly focus on his head, wake him, make sure he was coherent, then slip away.

Instead, she took just a moment to check out that body.

Wow.

Double wow.

His shoulders were twice the size of Jon's, but there was no hint of fat. This was pure muscle. A lifetime of pulling in nets, of hauling cray-pots, of hard manual labour, had tuned his body to…

Perfection.

It wasn't often that Nikki let herself look at a guy and think sheer physical perfection but she did now.

The weathering of the man…a life on the sea…

There was a scar on his shoulder, thin and white. She wanted, quite suddenly, to reach out and trace…

'I'm alive,' he snapped. 'Gabriel Carver, Tuesday the fourteenth. Go away.'

She almost yelped again. Habit-forming?

'Your...your head's hurting?'

'Not if I close my eyes and think of England. Instead of thinking of women with pokers. Go away.'

She went.

At least he was alive.

And at least she hadn't touched him. She hadn't traced that scar.

She still wanted to.

Nonsense.

She didn't sleep for another two hours. She checked again. He was sprawled on his back. He looked as if he'd been fighting with the bed.

He was deeply asleep this time, but he looked... done. The bruise on his face looked awful.

She couldn't see the scar on his back. All she could see was his face, exhaustion—pain?

Something inside her twisted. A giant of a man.

Just a little bit vulnerable?

He wouldn't thank her for thinking it but, stupid or not, the thought was there.

It was two in the morning. She glanced at his bedside clock. His alarm was set for four.

She hesitated. Then, carefully, she removed the clock, flicked the alarm off and slipped it in her pocket. His phone was on the bedside table. Why not go all the way? She pocketed that, too.

Then she touched his face. The good side.

His eyes opened. He looked a bit dazed, but he did focus. This was nothing more than someone waking from deep sleep.

'I'll live,' he said, slurred.

'Say something bitter.'

'I'm removing all fireside implements from rental properties.'

'That'll do,' she said and let him go back to sleep.

At four she checked him again. Another slurred response but just as together. Excellent. One more check would get her in the clear, she thought. No more inspections of semi-naked landlords.

She wasn't sure whether to be glad or sorry.

Glad, she told herself, astounded where her thoughts were taking her. Of course, glad.

She went back to bed. Tried not to think of half naked landlords.

Didn't succeed.

At five-thirty Gabe's phone rang. She was on her side of the wall with Gabe's phone beside her bed. She answered. A woman's voice. 'Gabe? Where are you?'

'Hi,' she said cautiously. 'This is Nikki, Gabe's next door neighbour.'

'The city chick,' the woman said blankly.

'That's me.'

'Where's Gabe?'

'I'm sorry, but Gabe had a bit of an accident last night. He won't be in this morning.'

'He won't be in…'

'He can't come to work.'

'What sort of an accident?'

'He fell. He almost knocked himself out. He's got a headache and a badly bruised face.' No need to mention he had the bruised face before he fell.

'Gabe turns up for work when he's half dead.' The woman sounded stunned. 'How bad is he?'

'Determined to come in but I've taken his alarm and his phone and he hasn't woken up.'

There was a moment's awed silence. Then… 'Well, good for you, love. You've got him in bed, you keep him there. When he wakes up, tell him Frank's rung in and his head cold's worse, so it would have only been me on board with him. The *Mariette*'s short a crew member as well, so I'll go on the *Mariette* and the *Lady Nell* can stay in port. That'll play into your hands as well. He no longer has a crew. You keep him in bed with my blessings, for as long as you want. Go for it, girl.'

She disconnected. Laughing.

Nikki stared at the phone as if it stung.

This was a small town. This'd be all over town in minutes.

How would Gabe react?

Um…what had she done?

Whatever. It was done now. She had an hour before the next check.

She really was incredibly tired.

She put her head on her pillow and closed her eyes.

She forgot to set the alarm.

Gabe woke and sunshine was flooding his bedroom. This on its own was a novelty. If the weather was decent he was out fishing, as simple as that.

He opened one eye and tried to figure it out. Why the sunbeams?

His head hurt a bit, not too much, just a dull ache.

If he lay still and only opened the one eye it didn't hurt at all.

The sun was streaming through his window. He felt…

Suddenly wide awake. He turned to the bedside table, looking for his clock in disbelief.

No clock.

He groped for his phone.

No phone.

What the…?

His watch.

It was eight o'clock. Eight! He'd slept for ten hours.

The boat. The crew. They'd be waiting.

Where were his…?

Nikkita.

Hitting him on the head was one thing; making him miss a day's fishing was another. She was so out of here.

He threw back the covers and headed for the door, thumping the wall as he went, just to make sure she was awake.

Anger didn't begin to describe what he was feeling. Women!

The thump on her bedroom wall was loud enough to wake the dead. She sat bolt upright. Stared at the clock.

Uh-oh. Uh-oh, uh-oh, uh-oh.

Eight o'clock. She might just have slept in.

She'd missed a check.

At least he wasn't dead, she thought. He should be grateful.

By the sound of the thump on her wall, he wasn't grateful.

By the sound of the thump, he wished for her undivided attention.

Her door was locked. A lesser woman might have tugged the duvet over her head and stayed where she was.

There were a lot of things a lesser woman might do. After today she was going right back to being a lesser woman, but right now…

There wasn't a lot of choice.

She grabbed her robe and headed next door to face Gabe.

She opened her door right as he opened his.

The dog was lying right across the porch.

Her Hound of the Baskervilles.

Horse.

Chapter 3

Nikki almost tripped and so did Gabe. They were focused on each other. Gabe's face was dark with anger, and Nikki was just plain terrified. Gabe was still only wearing boxers and that didn't help. Neither was looking at their feet and the dog was sprawled like a great wet floor mat.

Both of them stumbled and both had to grab the door jambs to keep their balance.

Both stared down in amazement.

The dog was even bigger than Nikki had thought last night. Four feet high? It was impossible to tell. All she knew was that, prone, he practically covered the small porch.

He was almost as flat as a doormat. He lay motionless, only the faint rise of his chest wall telling her he was alive.

'It's Horse,' she said blankly.

The big dog stirred at her voice. He hauled his great head off the floor, as if making a Herculean effort. He gazed up at her and all the misery of the world was in that gaze. It was a 'kill me now' look.

She didn't know a thing about dogs. If she'd been asked, she'd confess she probably didn't like them much. But that look…

Her heart twisted. In the face of that look, she forgot her landlord and she sank to her knees. 'Oh, my… Oh, Horse…'

'What do you think you're playing at?' Her landlord's voicc was like a whip above her. 'You've brought him in here…'

She wasn't listening. The big dog was so wet he couldn't get any wetter. While she watched, a shudder ran though his big frame and she thought…she thought…

She had to help. There was no way she could walk away. Not your problem? Ha.

'Hey, it's okay.' She ignored Gabe. She could only focus on the dog. She could only think about the dog.

'You caught him.' Gabe's voice had lost its edge as he took in Horse's condition.

'I didn't catch him. Maybe he found the meat and followed our scent. Pushed into the porch. Do you think he wants more?'

'Has he been here all night?'

'Are you nuts? Look at him. He's soaking. Why doesn't he move? Should we take him to the vet? Will you help me carry him to the car?'

'Fred will put him down,' Gable said bluntly.

'Fred?'

'The vet.'

That brought her up short. Last night's phone conversation was suddenly replaying in her head.

This dog had been on his way to be put down when he'd escaped. If they took him to the vet, that was what would happen.

'No,' she said. It was all she could think of to say.

'Do you want a dog?'

'I...'

She swallowed. Did she want a dog?

She didn't. She couldn't. But she wasn't thinking past now.

'I'll think about that later,' she said. 'He's not going anywhere until he's dry and warm and fed. Can you help me take him into my place?' She looked up at Gabe, and then she thought...

Anger. Uh-oh.

Maybe there were a few unresolved issues to be addressed before he'd help her.

She was aware again of his body. That chest. Those shoulders.

Hormones.

Anger.

'I slept,' he said, carefully neutral. 'Through my alarm. That might be because it was moved from my bedside table.'

'I slept through it too,' she confessed. 'That's because I forgot to set it.'

'My crew...'

Act efficient, she decided. Brisk. As if she knew what she was doing. 'Hattie's on the...let me think...

on the *Mariette*,' she told him. 'Because they're short a crew member. Frank called in sick so the *Lady Nell*'s staying in port. You have the day off.'

He didn't answer. He looked speechless.

'So can you help me with the dog?' she asked.

'You took my alarm.'

'You were sick. I thought I'd killed you. It was the least I could do.'

'You took my phone.'

'Yes, and I talked to Hattie. She agrees you need a day off.'

'It's not her business. It's not your business.'

'No,' she snapped. 'And neither is this dog but he's freezing. Get over it and help me.'

Her gaze locked with his. She could feel his anger, his frustration, his shock.

His body…

His body was almost enough to distract her from his anger, his frustration, his shock.

But she couldn't think of it now. She had the dog to think of. And, while she was chiding herself, Gabe stooped and touched the dog's face.

The dog tried to raise his head again. Failed.

'Don't think you've heard the last of this,' he said grimly. 'But this guy's done.'

'Done.' Nikki cringed. 'He's not dying.'

'Close to.' He'd moved on, she thought. All his attention was now on the dog. He seemed hesitant, as if he didn't want involvement, but the dog stirred and moaned, and something in Gabe's face changed. 'All right,' he said. 'If you're serious, let's get him into my place. The fire's going. Did you stoke it?'

'Yes. I did it for you.' Or not exactly. In her night-time prowls she'd tossed a couple of logs on the fire at each pass. It had seemed comforting. She'd been in need of comfort, and the thought of taking the dog in there now was a good one.

'Can you get up, big boy?' Gabe asked. 'Come on, mate, let's see you live.'

Gabe was fondling him behind the ears, speaking softly, and the dog responded. He gave Gabe another of those gut wrenching looks, another moan, then heaved. He managed to stand.

Standing up, he looked like a bag of bones with a worn rug stretched over him. Only his ears were still full fur. They hinted at a dog who'd once been handsome but that time was long past.

He swayed and Gabe stooped and held him, still fondling him, while the dog leaned heavily against him.

'So you decided to come and find some help?' he said softly. 'Great decision. You're safe here. You even seem to have found a friend. Mind, you need to beware of pokers.' But he wasn't glancing up to see how she took the wisecrack; he was totally focused on the dog. 'Let's get you warm. Miss Morrissy, could you fetch us some towels, please? A lot of towels. Put some in the tumble dryer to warm them.'

'It's Nikki,' she said numbly.

'Nikki,' he repeated, but he still didn't look up.

The dog took a staggering step forward and then stopped. Enough. Gabe lifted him into his arms as if he were a featherweight, and the dog made no objection. Maybe he knew he was headed for Gabe's fireside.

Nikki headed for towels.

But, as she went, she carried the image of Gabe, a big man with his armful of dog.

He was making her heart twist.

It was the dog, she told herself fiercely. Of course it was the dog.

Only the dog. Anything else was ridiculous.

She did not need hormones.

Horse was freezing. It hadn't been raining, yet he was soaked—had he been standing in the water all night?

Nikki fetched her hairdryer. Gabe sponged the worst of the salt crust from his coat, then towelled him dry as she ran warm air over his tangled fur. The big dog lay passive, hopeless, and Nikki felt an overwhelming urge to pick him up and hug him.

He was so big… She'd have to hug him one end at a time.

She also wanted to kill whoever had abandoned him. To do something so callous…

'Your cop friend said he was thrown from a boat.'

'He'll still feel loyal to the low-life who did it to him,' Gabe said grimly. 'I'd guess that's why he's been standing in the shallows howling.'

She sniffed. She sniffed more than once while she wielded her hairdryer, and she had to abandon her work for a bit to fetch tissues. She couldn't help herself. The emotions of the night, the emotions of the past two months, or maybe simply the emotions of now, were enough to overwhelm her. This gentle giant being betrayed in such a way…

She'd set towels by the fire for Gabe to lay him on. With her hairdryer and Gabe's toweling, they dried one side of him. Then Gabe lifted him. She replaced the sodden towels with warm ones and they dried his other side.

Gabe spoke to him all the time. Slow, gentle words of comfort. While Nikki sniffed.

Gabe's words were washing over her, reassuring her almost as much as the dog. His kindness was palpable. How could she ever have thought he'd ignore a dog in trouble on the beach? His hands stroking the dog's coat…his soft words…

He was a gruff, weathered fisherman but he cared about this dog.

He'd been rude and cold to her the day they'd met. Where was that coldness now?

She tried to imagine Jonathan doing what Gabe was doing now, and couldn't. And then she thought…what was she thinking? Comparing Gabe and Jon? Don't even think of going there.

Um…she was going there. Gabe's body was just a bit too close.

Gabe's body was making her body feel…

No. Stupid, stupid, stupid.

Focus on dog.

The big dog's body had been shuddering, great waves of cold and despair. As the warmth started to permeate, the shaking grew less. Gabe was half towelling, half stroking, all caring.

'It's okay, mate. We'll get you warm on the inside as well.'

'Do you think he got the steak?'

'I'm guessing not,' he said. 'Not in the state he's in—the food would have warmed him and he wouldn't be so hopeless. There's all sorts of predators on the beach at night—owls, rats, the odd feral cat. I'm guessing that's why he's here. He came back round the headland looking for the steak, then when we were gone he followed our scent. There was nowhere else to go.'

'Oh, Horse.'

Grown women didn't cry. Much. She concentrated fiercely on blow-drying—and realised Gabe was watching her.

'Horse?' he said.

'I've been thinking of him all night,' she said. 'In between worrying that I killed you. A dog that looks like a horse. A landlord who might have been dead.'

'Happy endings all round,' Gabe said wryly and she cast him a scared look. She knew what he was going to say. She was way in front of him.

The vet.

'Do you have any more steak?' She couldn't quite get her voice to work. She couldn't quite get her heart to work. But she wasn't going to say the vet word.

'No. You?'

'I have dinners for one. Calorie controlled.'

'Right, like Horse needs a diet.'

'I'll bring four.'

They worked on. Gabe hauled on a T-shirt and jeans and so did she, but the attention of both was on the dog. Hostilities were suspended.

The dog was so close to the edge that the sheer effort of eating seemed too much. By the look of his muzzle, he'd been sick. 'Sea water,' Gabe said grimly as he cleaned him. 'There's little fresh water round here. If he's been wandering since the van crashed he's had almost a week of nothing.'

That was a lot of speech for Gabe. They should take him to the vet, Nikki thought, but with the vet came a decision that neither of them seemed able to face. Not yet.

Save him and then decide. Dumb? Maybe, but it was what her gut was dictating, and Gabe seemed to be following the same path.

Gabe was encouraging the dog to drink, little by little. He found some sort of syringe and gently oozed water into the big dog's mouth. Once they were sure he could swallow, Nikki shredded chicken, popping tiny pieces into Horse's slack mouth and watching with satisfaction as he managed to get it down.

Slowly.

'If we feed him fast he'll be sick and we'll undo everything,' Gabe said. He sounded as if he knew what he was doing. How come he had a syringe on hand? Had he coped with injured animals before?

He was an enigma. Craggy and grim. A professional fisherman. Broad, but with muscles, there was not an inch of spare flesh on him.

He flashed from silence and anger, to caring, to tender, just like that. His hands as he cared for the big dog were gentle as could be; rough, weathered fisherman's hands fondling the dog's ears, holding the syringe, waiting with all the patience in the world for Horse to open his mouth.

Horse.

Why name a stray dog?

Why look at her landlord's hand and think…and think…?

Nothing.

She should be back on her side of the house right now, enmeshed in plans for the air conditioning system for a huge metropolitan shopping centre. The centre had been the focus of an outbreak of legionnaires' disease. Their air conditioning system needed to be revamped, and the plans needed to be finalised. Now.

Her plans were urgent—even if they bored her witless.

And Gabe should be fishing. He obviously thought that was urgent.

But nothing seemed more important than sitting by the fireside with Gabe and with Horse, gradually bringing the big dog back to life.

They were succeeding. The shuddering ceased. The dog was still limp, but he was warm and dry, and there was enough food and water going in to make them think the worst was past.

So now what?

The dog was drifting into sleep. Nikki glanced briefly at Gabe and caught a flash of pain, quickly suppressed. His head? Of course it was his head, she thought. That bruise looked horrible. What was she doing, letting him work on the dog?

'You need to sleep, too,' she told him.

'We should make a decision about this guy. Take him…'

'Let him sleep,' she said, cutting him off. 'For a bit. Then…maybe we could clean him up a bit more.

If we take him back to the shelter looking lovely, then he has a better chance…'

'He's never going to look lovely,' Gabe said. 'Not even close.'

Maybe he wouldn't. The dog was carrying scars. Patches of fur had been torn away, wounds had healed but the fur hadn't grown back. An ugly scar ran the length of his left front leg. And what was he? Wolf-hound? Plus the rest.

'It's drawing it out,' Gabe said and Nikki flinched. She looked down at the dog and felt ill—and then she looked at Gabe and felt her own pain reflected in his eyes.

'Not yet,' she said, suddenly fierce. 'Not until he's slept. And not until you've slept. You have the day off work. I know you're angry, and you can be as angry as you like with me, but what's done's done. Your head's hurting. Go back to bed and sleep it off, and let Horse sleep.'

'While you play Florence Nightingale to us both?'

'There's no need to be sarcastic,' she said, struggling to keep her voice even. 'A nurse is the last thing I could ever be, but it doesn't take Florence to see what you need. You and Horse both. I need to do some work…'

'You and *me* both.'

'Get over it,' she snapped. 'You're wounded, I'm not. So what I'm suggesting is that I bring my paper-work in here and do it at your dining table so I can keep an eye on Horse. I'll keep checking the fire, I'll keep offering Horse food and drink, and you go back to bed and wake up when your body lets you.'

'You'll check on me, too?'

'Every two hours,' she said firmly. 'Like a good Florence. Though I'd prefer you to leave your door open so I can make sure you're not dead all the time.'

'This is nonsense. I need to mend cray-pots.'

'You've got the day off,' she snapped. 'I told Hattie you were ill. Don't make a liar of me.'

'You really will look after the dog?'

'I'll look after both of you, until you wake up. Then…' She glanced down at Horse and looked away. 'Then we'll do what comes next.'

He rang Raff from the privacy of his bedroom. The Banksia Bay cop answered on the first ring. 'Why aren't you at sea?' Raff demanded. 'Hattie says you hit your head. I thought you sounded bad last night. You want some help?'

This town, Gabe thought grimly. Banksia Bay was a great place to live unless you hankered for privacy. He did hanker for privacy, but he loved the place and intrusion was the price he paid.

'And Hattie says your tenant's looking after you. Mate…' Raff drew the word out—*maaate*. It was a question all by itself.

'She hit me,' he said before he could help himself.

'Did she now.' Raff thought about that for a bit. 'She had her reasons?'

Nip that one in the bud. 'She thought I was a bunyip. She was searching for the dog. I was searching for the dog. We collided. She was carrying a poker. And that goes no further than you,' he said sharply, as he heard a choke of laughter on the end of the line.

'Scout's honour,' Raff said.

'We never made Scouts.' Raff had been one of the town's bad boys. Like him.

'That's what I mean. You need any help?'

'No. We found the dog. That's why I'm ringing.'

'*We* found the dog? You and Miss Morrissy?'

'Nikki,' he said before he could help himself and he heard the interest sharpen.

'Curiouser and curiouser. So you and Nikki...'

'The dog's here,' he snapped. 'Fed and watered and asleep by my fire. I'll bring him down to Fred when I've had a sleep.'

'You're having a sleep?'

'Nikki's orders,' he said and suddenly he had an urge to smile. Quickly suppressed. 'She's bossy.'

'Well, well.'

'And you can just put that right out of your head,' he snapped. 'I don't want a dog, and I don't want a woman even more. Tell Henrietta the dog's found and we'll take him to Fred tonight.'

'We?'

'Go find some villains to chase,' he growled. 'My head hurts. I'm going to sleep.'

'On Nikki's orders?'

He told Raff where to put his interest, and he hung up. Stripped to his boxers again. Climbed into bed. Following orders.

His head really did hurt.

She was going to check on him every two hours. The thought was...

Nope. He didn't know what the thought was.

He didn't want her checking him every two hours.

'I'd prefer you to leave your door open so I can make sure you're not dead...'

He sighed and opened his door. Glanced across at Nikki, who glanced back. Waved. He glowered and dived under the covers.

He didn't want a woman in his living room.

Nor did he want a dog.

What was he doing, in bed in the middle of the morning?

He put his head on the pillow and the aching eased. Maybe she had a point. A man had to be sensible.

He fell asleep thinking of the dog.

Trying not to think of Nikki.

It was so domestic it was almost claustrophobic. The fire, the dog, Gabe asleep right through the door.

The work she was doing was tidying up plans she'd already drawn—nothing complex, which was just as well the way she was feeling. Her head was all over the place.

Biggest thought? Gabe.

No. Um, no, it wasn't. Or it shouldn't be. Her biggest thought had to be—could she keep a dog?

As a kid she'd thought she might like a dog. That was never going to happen, though. Her parents were high-flyers, both lawyers with an international clientele. They loved her to bits in the time they could spare for her, but that time was limited. She was an only child, taken from country to country, from boarding school to international hotel to luxury resort.

And after childhood? University, followed by a top paying job, a gorgeous apartment. Then Jonathan.

Maybe she could get a small white fluff ball, she'd thought occasionally, when she was missing Jon. When he was supposedly working elsewhere. But where would a dog fit into a lifestyle similar to her parents'?

And now…

Her job still took her away.

Her job didn't have to take her away. Or not for long. She could glean enough information from a site visit to keep her working for months. Most queries could be sorted online—there was never a lot of use stomping round construction sites.

She quite liked stomping round construction sites. It was the part of her job she enjoyed most.

It was the only part…

Salary? Prestige?

Both were less and less satisfying. Her parents thought her career was wonderful. Jonathan thought it was wonderful. But now…

Now was hardly the time to be thinking of a career change. She was good at what she did. She was paid almost embarrassingly well. She could afford to pay others to do the menial stuff.

So maybe a little white fluff ball?

Or Horse.

Horse was hardly a fluff ball. Ten times as big, and a lot more needy.

Maybe she could share parenting with Gabe, she thought. When she was needed on site, he could stay home from sea.

Shared parenting? Of a dog who looked like a mangy horse, with a grumpy landlord fisherman?

With a body to die for. And with the gentlest of hands. And a voice that said he cared.

She glanced across the passage. The deal was she wouldn't check on him every two hours as long as he kept his door open.

If he dropped dead, she was on the wrong side of the passage.

There wasn't a lot she could do if he dropped dead.

At least the dog was breathing. She watched his chest rise and fall, rise and fall. He was flopped as close to the fire as he could be without being burned. Gabe had set the screen so no ember could fly out, but she suspected he wouldn't wake even if it did.

He looked like a dog used to being hurt.

Maybe he'd be vicious when he recovered.

Maybe her landlord wouldn't let her keep a dog.

Was she really thinking about keeping him?

It was just…

The last few weeks had been desolate. It was all very well saying she wanted a sea change, but there wasn't enough work to fill the day and the night, and the nights were long and silent. She'd left Sydney in rage and in grief, and at night it came back to haunt her.

She also found the nights, the country noises… creepy.

'Because of guys like you howling on beaches,' she said out loud, and Horse raised his head and looked at her. Then sighed and set his head down again, as if it was too heavy to hold up.

How could someone throw him off a boat?

A great wounded mutt.

Her new best friend?

She glanced across the passage again. Gabe was deeply asleep, his bedding barely covering his hips.

He was wounded too, she thought, and with a flash of insight she thought it wasn't just the hit over the head with the poker. He was living in a house built for a dozen, a mile out of town, on his own. Not even a dog.

'He needs a dog, too,' she told Horse.

Shared parenting was an excellent solution.

'Yes, but that's complicated.' She set down her pen and crossed to Gabe's bedroom door to make sure his chest was rising and falling. It was, but the sight of his chest did things to her own chest…

There went those hormones again. She had to figure a way of reining them in.

Return to dog. Immediately.

She knelt and fondled the big dog's ears. He stirred and moaned, a long, low doggy moan containing all the pathos in the world.

She put her head down close to his. Almost nose to nose. 'It's okay,' she said. 'I've given up on White and Fluffy. And I think I do like dogs. You're not going to the vet.'

A great shaggy paw came up and touched her shoulder.

Absurdly moved, she found herself hugging him. Her arms were full of dog. His great brown eyes were enormous.

Could she keep him?

'My parents would have kittens,' she told him.

Her mother was in Helsinki doing something important.

Her father was in New York.

'Yes, and I'm here,' she told Horse, giving in to the weirdly comforting sensation of holding a dog close, feeling the warmth of him. 'I'm here by the fire with you, and our landlord's just over the passage. He's grumpy, but underneath I reckon he's a pussycat. I reckon he might let you stay.'

The fire was magnificently warm. She hadn't had enough sleep last night.

She hesitated and then hauled some cushions down from the settee. She settled beside Horse. He sighed, but it was a different sigh. As if things might be looking up.

'Perfect,' said Nikkita Morrissy, specialist air conditioning engineer, sea-changer, tenant. She snuggled on the cushions and Horse stirred a bit and heaved himself a couple of inches so she was closer. 'Let's settle in for the long haul. You and me—and Gabe if he wants to join us. If my hit on the head hasn't killed him. Welcome to our new life.'

Chapter 4

Gabe woke and it was still daylight. It took time to figure exactly why he was in bed, why the clock was telling him it was two in the afternoon, and why a woman and a dog were curled up on cushions on his living room floor.

Horse.

Nikki.

Nikki was asleep beside Horse?

The dog didn't fit with the image of the woman. Actually, nothing fitted. He was having trouble getting his thoughts in order.

He should be a hundred miles offshore. Every day the boat was in harbour cost money.

Um…he had enough money. He needed to forget fishing, at least for a day.

He was incredibly, lazily comfortable. How long

since he'd lain in bed and just…lain? Not slept, just stared at the ceiling, thought how great the sheets felt on his naked skin, how great it was that the warm sea breeze wafted straight in through his bedroom window and made him feel that the sea was right here.

Lots of fishermen—lots of his crew—took themselves as far from the sea as possible when they weren't working. Not Gabe. The sea was a part of him.

He'd always been a loner. As a kid, the beach was an escape from the unhappiness in the house. His parents' marriage was bitter and often violent. His father was passionately possessive of his much younger wife, sharing her with no one. If Gabe spent time with his mother, his father reacted with a resentment that Gabe soon learned to fear. His survival technique was loneliness.

As he got older, the boat became his escape as well.

And then there was his brief marriage. Yeah, well, that had taught him the sea was his only real constant. People hurt. Solitude was the only way to go.

Even dogs broke your heart.

Sixteen years…

'Get another one fast.' Fred, the Banksia Bay vet, had been brusque. 'The measure of a life well lived is how many good dogs you can fit into it. I'm seventy years old and I'm up to sixteen and counting. It's torn a hole in my gut every time I've lost one, and the only way I can fill it is finding another. And you know what? Every single one of them stays with me. They're all part of who I am. The gut gets bigger.' He'd patted his ample stomach. 'Get another.'

Or not. Did Fred know just how big a hole Jem had left?

Don't think about it.

Watch Nikki instead.

He lay and watched woman and dog sleeping, just across the passage. Strangers seldom entered his house. Not even friends. And no one slept by his fire but him.

Until now.

She looked…okay.

She'd wake soon, and she'd be gone. This moment would be past, but for now… For now it felt strangely okay that she was here. For now he let the comfort of her presence slide into his bones, easing parts of him he didn't know were hurting. A dog and a woman asleep before his fire…

He closed his eyes and sleep reclaimed him.

She woke and it was three o'clock and Horse was squatting on his haunches rather than sprawled on his side. His head was cocked to one side, as if he was trying to figure her out. Sitting up! That had to be good.

She hugged him. She fed him. He ate a little, drank a little. She opened the French windows and asked him if he needed to go outside but he politely declined, by putting his head back on his paws and dozing again.

She thought about going back to work.

The plans on the table were supremely uninteresting. Engineering had sounded cool when she enrolled at university. Doing stuff.

Not sitting drawing endless plans of endless air conditioning systems, no matter how complex.

Gabe's living room, however, was lined with bookshelves, and the bookshelves were crammed with books.

And photograph albums. Her secret vice.

Other people's families.

Nikki had been sent to boarding school at seven. If friends invited her home for the holidays her parents were relieved, so she'd spent much of her childhood looking at families from the outside in.

Brothers, sisters, grandmas, uncles and aunts. You didn't get a lot of those the way she was raised.

Her friends could never understand her love of photograph albums, but she hadn't grown out of it, and here were half a dozen, right within reach.

A girl had to read something. Or draw plans.

No choice.

The first four albums were thosc of a child, an adolescent, a young woman. School friends, beach, hiking, normal stuff. Nikki had albums like this herself, photographs taken with her first camera.

The albums must belong to Gabe's mother, she decided. The girl and then the woman looked a bit like Gabe. She was much smaller, compact, neat. But she looked nice. She had the same dark hair as Gabe, the same thoughtful eyes. She saw freckles and a shy smile in the girl, and then the woman.

After school, her albums differed markedly from Nikki's. This woman hadn't spent her adolescence at university. The first post-school pictures were of her beside stone walls, wearing dungarees, heavy boots, thick gloves. The smile became cheeky, a woman gaining confidence.

There were photos of stone walls.

Lots of stone walls.

Nikki glanced outside to the property boundary, where a stone wall ran along the road, partly built, as if it had stopped mid-construction. Wires ran along the unfinished part to make it a serviceable fence.

She turned back to the next album. Saw the beginnings of romance. A man, considerably older than the girl, thickset, a bit like Gabe as well, looking as if he was struggling to find a smile for the camera. Holding the girl possessively.

An album of a wedding. Then a baby.

Gabe.

Really cute, she thought, and glanced across the passage and thought…you really could see the man in the baby.

Gabe before life had weathered him.

The photos were all of Gabe now—Gabe until he was about seven, sturdy, cheeky, laughing.

Then nothing. The final album had five pages of pictures and the rest lay empty.

What had happened? Divorce? Surely a young mum would keep on taking pictures. Surely she'd take these albums with her.

She set the albums back in place, and her attention was caught by a set of books just above. *The Art of Stone Walling. The Stone Walls of Yorkshire*. More.

She flicked through, fascinated, caught in intricacies of stone walling.

Gabe slept on.

She was learning how to build stone walls. In theory.

She'd kind of like to try.

She reached the end of the first book as Horse struggled to his feet and crossed to the French windows. Pawed.

Bathroom.

But… Escape?

Visions of Horse standing up to his haunches in the shallows sprang to mind. She daren't risk letting him go. The faded curtains were looped back with tasseled cords, perfect for fashioning a lead.

'Okay, let's go but don't pull,' she told him. At full strength this dog could tow two of her, but he was wobbly.

She cast a backward glance at Gabe. Still sleeping. Quick check. Chest rising and falling.

She and Horse were free to do as they pleased.

When Gabe woke again the sun was sinking low behind Black Mountain. He'd slept the whole day?

His head felt great. He felt great all over. He was relaxed and warm and filled with a sense of well-being he hadn't felt since…who knew?

He rolled lazily onto his side and gazed out of the window.

And froze.

For a moment he thought he was dreaming. There was a woman in the garden, her back to him, crouched over a pile of stones. Sorting.

A dog lay by her side, big and shaggy.

Nikki and Horse.

Nikki held up a stone, inspected it, said something to Horse, then shifted so she could place it into the unfinished stretch of stone wall.

He felt as if the oxygen was being sucked from the room.

A memory blasting back…

His mother, crouched over the stones, the wall so close to finished. Thin, drawn, exhausted. Setting down her last stone. Weeping. Hugging him.

'I can't…'

'Mum, what's wrong?'

'I'm so tired. Gabe, very soon I'll need to go to sleep.' But using a voice that said this wasn't a normal sleep she was talking about.

Then…desolation.

His father afterwards, kicking stones, kicking everything. His mother's old dog, yelping, running for the cover Gabe could never find.

'Dad, could we finish the wall?' It had taken a month to find the courage to ask.

'It's finished.' A sharp blow across his head. 'Don't you understand, boy, it's finished.'

He understood it now. Nikki had to understand it, too.

People hurt. You didn't try and interfere. Unless there was trouble you let people be and they let you be. You didn't try and change things.

He should have put it in the tenancy agreement.

Stone wall building was weirdly satisfying on all sorts of levels.

She'd always loved puzzles, as she'd loved building things. To transform a pile of stones into a wall as magnificent as this…

Wide stones had been set into the earth to form the

base, then irregular stones piled higher and higher, two outer levels with small stones between. Wider stones were layed crosswise over both sides every foot or so, binding both sides together. No stone was the same. Each position was carefully assessed, each stone considered from all angles. Tried. Tried again. As she was doing now.

She'd set eight stones in an hour and was feeling as if she'd achieved something amazing.

This could be a whole new hobby, she thought. She could finish the wall.

Horse lay by her side, dozy but watchful, warm in the afternoon sunshine. Every now and then he cast a doubtful glance towards the beach but she'd fashioned a tie from the curtain cords, she had him tethered and she talked to him as she worked.

'I know. You loved him but he rejected you. You and me both. Jonathan and your scum-bag owner. Broken hearts club, that's us. We need a plan to get over it. I'm not sure what our plan should be, but while we're waiting for something to occur this isn't bad.' She held up a stone. 'You think this'll fit?'

The dog cocked his head; seemed to consider.

The pain that had clenched in her chest for months eased a little. Unknotted in the sharing, and in the work.

She would have liked to be a builder.

She thought suddenly of a long ago careers exhibition. At sixteen she'd been unsure of what she wanted to do. She'd gone to the career exhibition with school and almost the first display was a carpenter, working on a delicate coffee table. While other students moved from one display to the next, she stopped, entranced.

After half an hour he'd invited her to help, and she'd stayed with him until her teachers came to find her.

'I'll need to get an apprenticeship to be a carpenter,' she'd told her father the next time she'd seen him, breathless with certainty that she'd found her calling.

But her father was due to catch the dawn flight to New York. He'd scheduled two hours' quality time with his daughter and he didn't intend wasting it on nonsense.

'Of course society needs builders, but for you, my girl, with your brains, the sky's the limit. We'll get you into Law—Oxford? Cambridge?'

Even her chosen engineering degree had met with combined parental disapproval, even though it was specialist engineering leading to a massive salary. But here, now… She remembered that long ago urge to build things, to create.

Air conditioning systems didn't compare. Endless plans.

Another stone… This was so difficult. It had to be perfect.

'What do you think you're doing?'

She managed to suppress a yelp, but only just. Gabe was dressed again, in jeans and T-shirt. He'd come up behind her. His face was like thunder, his voice was dripping ice.

He was blocking her sun. Even Horse backed and whimpered.

The sheer power of the man…the anger…

It was as much as she could do not to back and run.

Not her style, she thought grimly. This man had her totally disconcerted but whimpering was never an option. 'I thought I'd try and do some…' she faltered.

'Don't.'

'Don't you want it finished? I thought… I've been reading the books from your living room.'

'You've been reading my mother's books?'

Uh-oh. She'd desecrated a shrine?

'I'm sorry. I…'

'You had no right.'

'No.' She lifted the book she'd been referring to. Caught her breath. Decided she'd hardly committed murder. 'I'll put this back,' she said placatingly. 'No damage done. I don't think I've done anything appalling.'

But then…he'd scared her. Again.

Shock was turning to indignation.

He was angry?

She met his gaze full on. Tilted her chin.

Horse nosed her ankle. She let her hand drop to his rough coat and the feel of him was absurdly comforting.

What was with this guy? Why did he make her feel—how he made her feel? She couldn't describe it. She only knew that she was totally confused.

'I've only fitted eight stones,' she said, forcing her tone down a notch. Even attempting a smile. 'You want me to take them out again?'

'Leave it.' His voice was still rough, but the edges of anger were blunted. He took the book from her. Glanced at it. Glanced away. 'How's the dog?'

'He's fine.' She was still indignant. He sounded… cold.

The normal Gabe?

A man she should back away from.

'We need to make a decision,' he said.

'I have,' she said and tilted her chin still further.

'Hi!'

The new voice made them both swivel. A woman was at the gate. She was middle-aged and sensibly dressed, in moleskin trousers and a battered fleecy jacket. She swung the gate open and Horse whined and backed away.

Even from twenty yards away Nikki saw the woman flinch.

'It's okay,' the woman said, gentling her voice as she approached. 'I hate it that I lock these guys up and they react accordingly. I can't help that I'm associated with their life's low point.'

Horse whined again. Nikki felt him tug against the cord. She wasn't all that sure of it holding.

Gabe was suddenly helping. His hand was on the big dog's neck, helping her hold on to her curtain-fashioned collar. Touching hers. His hand was large and firm—and once more caring?

Where had that thought come from? But she felt Horse relax and she knew the dog felt the same. Even if this guy did get inexplicably angry, there was something at his core…

'Raff told me you'd found him,' the woman was saying. 'Hi, Gabe.' She came forward, her hand extended to Nikki, a blunt gesture of greeting. 'We haven't met. I'm Henrietta. I run the local dog shelter. This guy's one of mine.'

Horse whimpered and tried to go behind Nikki's legs. Nikki's hand tightened on his collar—and so did Gabe's.

Hands touching. Warmth. Strength. Nikki didn't pull away, even though Henrietta's hand was still extended, even though she knew Gabe could hold him.

'You want me to take him?' Henrietta asked.

No.

Her decision had already been made but she needed Gabe's consent. He was, after all, her landlord.

'I'd like to keep him,' she said, more loudly than she intended, and there was a moment's silence.

Henrietta's grim expression relaxed, then did more than relax. It curved into a wide grin that practically spilt her face. But then she caught herself, her smile was firmly repressed and her expression became businesslike.

'Are you in a position to offer him a good home?'

'Am I?' she asked Gabe. 'I think I am,' she said diffidently. 'But Gabe's my landlord. I'll need his permission.'

'You're asking me to keep him?' Gabe's demand was incredulous.

'No,' she said flatly. Some time during this afternoon her world had shifted. She wasn't exactly sure where it had shifted; she only knew that things were changing and Horse was an important part of that change. 'I want to keep him myself. Just me.' Her life was her own, she thought, suddenly resolute. No men need apply.

No man—not even her landlord—was needed to share her dog.

'I need to do a bit of reorganisation,' she said, speaking now to Henrietta. 'At the moment I'm working away...'

'I can't look after him,' Gabe said bluntly. 'Not when I'm at sea.'

'I'm not asking you to,' she flashed back at him. There were things going on with Gabe she didn't understand. He had her disconcerted, but for now she needed to focus only on Horse. And her future. Gabe had to be put third.

'I'm reorganising my career,' she told Henrietta. 'At the end of this month and maybe next, I'll need to go away for a few days. After that I won't need to.' That was simple enough. She'd hand her international clients over to her colleagues.

Her colleagues would think she was nuts.

Her colleagues as in Jonathan?

Don't go there.

Could she keep working for him?

'I might even be rethinking my career altogether,' she said, a bit more brusquely than she intended. She glanced down at the stones and then glanced away again, astounded where her thoughts were taking her. How absurd to think she could ever do something so… so wonderful.

Was she crazy? This surely could only ever be a hobby.

Concentrate on Horse. The rest was nonsense. Fanciful thinking after an upset night. 'Whatever I do, I've decided I can keep Horse,' she managed. 'If I can get some help for the first two months.'

But Gabe was looking at her as if she was something that had just crawled out of the cheese.

'You've decided this all since last night?' he demanded. 'Do you know how much of a commitment a dog is? He's not a handbag, picked up and discarded on a whim. Sixteen years…'

'We're not talking Jem here,' Henrietta said sharply.

'Jem?'

'Gabe's dog,' Henrietta told her. 'Gabe found Jem on the beach sixteen years ago. She died three months back.'

'I'm sorry,' Nikki said, disconcerted, but her apologies weren't required or wanted. Gabe's face was rigid with anger.

'We're not talking Jem. We're talking you. What do you know about dogs?'

'I'll learn.'

'You mean you know nothing.'

'You're trying to talk me out of keeping him?'

'I'm talking sense.'

'I can keep him for the days you're away,' Henrietta interjected, but she was watching Gabe. 'I run a boarding kennel alongside the shelter, so if you really are going to reorganise…'

'You'd let her keep him?' Gabe's voice was incredulous.

'It's that or put him down,' Henrietta snapped. 'Nikki's offering.'

'And if I say no?'

There was a general intake of breath. If he said no… What would she do?

Take Horse and live elsewhere? Somewhere that wasn't here? There were so few rental options.

Go back to Sydney.

No! Here was scary, but Sydney was scarier.

Move on. Who knew where? With dog?

This was dumb. To move towns because of a dog…

But this afternoon she'd felt his heartbeat as he slept. The thought of ending that heartbeat…

Horse was as lost as she was, she thought, and she glanced at Gabe and thought there were three of them. She could see pain behind Gabe's anger; behind his blank refusal to help.

She couldn't think of Gabe's pain now. She'd do this alone.

No. She'd do it with Horse.

'He's my dog,' she said, making her voice firm.

Henrietta turned to Gabe. 'So. Let's get this straight. Are you planning on evicting Nikki because she has a dog?'

'She doesn't know what she's letting herself in for.'

'You work at home, right?' Henrietta asked her, obviously deciding to abandon Gabe's arguments as superfluous.

'Yes.'

'Fantastic. When do you need to go away again?'

She did a frantic mental reshuffle. 'I can put it off for a while. Three weeks…'

'Then you have three weeks to learn all about dogs,' Henrietta decreed. 'If at the end of that time you decide you can't keep him then we'll rethink things. So Gabe… I have a happy ending in view. What about you? You'll seriously evict her if she keeps him?'

They were all looking at him. Nikki and Henrietta… Even Horse seemed to understand his future hung on what Gabe said right now.

'Fine,' he said explosively.

'That's not what I want to hear,' Henrietta said. 'How about a bit of enthusiasm?'

'You expect me to be enthusiastic that there's a dog about to live here? With a totally untrained owner?'

'You're trained,' Henrietta said. 'I'd feel happier if you were offering, but I have a feeling this guy will settle for what he can get. If the heart's in the right place, the rest can follow, eh, Nikki?'

'I…yes,' she said weakly, wondering where exactly her heart was.

'That's great,' Henrietta said and patted Horse. who was still looking nervous. 'What will you call him?'

'Horse,' Nikki said. 'I'll need stuff. I don't know what. Can you tell me?'

'Gabe might give you a…' Henrietta started and then glanced again at Gabe. Winced. 'Okay, maybe not. Let's take your new dog inside and I'll make you a list myself. Unless you want to evict her first, Gabe?'

'I'm going to the boat,' he snapped. 'Be it on your head.'

He headed for the boat, away from women, away from dog. Away from stuff he didn't want to deal with.

He needed to sort cray-pots, mend some. He started but it didn't keep his head from wandering. He kept seeing Nikki, sorting through her pile of rocks. *His mother's pile of rocks.*

He kept seeing Nikki curled in front of the fire, sleeping beside Horse.

Horse. It was a stupid name for a dog.

What was also stupid was his reaction, he told himself. What was the big deal? His tenant had found herself a dog. It was nothing to do with him. As for the stone walling…

She wouldn't touch it again.

Why not let her finish it?

Stupid or not, he felt as if he was right on the edge of a whirlpool, and he was being pulled inexorably inside.

He'd been there before.

There was nothing inside but pain.

The cray-pots weren't hard enough.

He'd check the *Lady Nell*'s propeller, he decided. It had fouled last time out. They'd got it clear but maybe it'd be wise to give it a thorough check.

Ten minutes later he had a scuba tank on, lowering himself over the side.

He should do this with someone on board keeping watch. If there was an accident…

If there was an accident no one gave a toss; it was his business what he did with his life.

He had scores of employees, dependent on him for their livelihood.

He also had one tenant. Dependent?

If Horse decided to head for the beach again, he was bigger than she could possibly hold.

It was none of his business. She didn't need him. The dog didn't need him. No one did. Even if something happened to him, the legal stuff was set up so this town's fishing fleet would survive.

How morbid was that? He was about to check a propeller. He'd done it a hundred times.

He needed to see things in perspective.

He dived underwater. Right now underwater seemed safer than the surface—and a whole lot clearer.

* * *

Henrietta left and came back with supplies, and Nikki was set. Dog food, dog bed, dog bowls. Collar, lead, treats, ball times six… Practically a car full.

'You'll need a kennel, but they don't come prefabricated in Horse's size,' Henrietta told her. 'I've brought you a trampoline bed instead. You'll need to get a kennel built by winter. Oh, and there's no need to spread it round town that I've brought this. Normally my new owners need to show me their preparations before I'll agree to let them have the dog.'

'So why the special treatment?' Nikki had made tea. Henrietta was sipping Earl Grey from one of Nikki's dainty cups, looking a bit uncomfortable. Maybe she ought to buy some mugs.

Maybc hcr lifc was going to change in a few other ways, she thought. Her apartment was furnished with thc clcgant posscssions shc'd acquircd for the Sydney apartment. Some her parents had given her. Some she and Jon had chosen together. This teaset was antique, given to her by Jon for her last birthday.

The owner of a dog like Horse wouldn't serve tea in cups like this. She hadn't thought it through until now, but maybe she should shop…

'I hate putting dogs down,' Henrietta was saying. 'Sometimes, though, I don't have a choice. I can't keep them all. And if potential owners don't care enough to commit to buying or scrounging dog gear, then they don't care enough to be entrusted to a dog. These dogs have been through enough. I'd rather put them down than sentence them to more misery.'

'But me…'

'You live with Gabe,' Henrietta said simply. 'You mistreat Horse, you'll have him to answer to. Even if he says it's nothing to do with him, he'll be watching. And that's the second thing. This place without a dog is wrong. Gabe needs a dog. If he gets it via you, that's fine by me.'

'He's not getting him via me. This is my call. My dog.'

'Yes, but you live with Gabe,' Henrietta repeated, and finished her tea in one noisy gulp. 'Living so close, you're almost family, and now you have a dog. Welcome to Banksia Bay, and welcome to your new role as dog owner. Any more questions, ask Gabe. He's grumpy and dour and always a loner but he has reason to be. Underneath he's a good man, and he'll never let a dog suffer. He treated Jem like gold.' Then she hesitated. Made to say something. Hesitated again.

Nikki watched her face. Wondered what she'd been about to say. Then asked what she'd like to know. 'Could you tell me about him?' she ventured. 'What happened to his mother?'

Henrietta considered for a long moment and then shrugged.

'I shouldn't say, but why not? If you don't hear it from me you'll hear it from a hundred other people in this town. Okay, potted history. Gabe's mother died of cancer when he was eight. His dad was an oaf and a bully. He was also a miser. He forced Gabe to leave school at fourteen, used him as an unpaid deck hand. Maybe Gabe would have left but luckily—and I will say luckily—he died when Gabe was eighteen. He left a fortune. He left no will, so Gabe inherited. Gabe was a kid, floundering, desperately unhappy—and suddenly rich. So along came Lisbette, a selfish cow, all surface glitter, taking advantage of little more than a boy. She married him and she fleeced him, just like that.'

'Oh, no...'

'I'd have horsewhipped her if I'd had my way,' Henrietta said grimly. 'But she was gone. And Gabe took it hard. He still had his dad's boat and this house, but little else. So he took Jem and headed off to the West, to the oil rigs. A good seaman can make a lot if he's prepared to take risks and, from what I can gather, Gabe took more than a few. Then the fishing here started to falter and suddenly Gabe returned. He's good with figures, good with fishing, good with people. He almost single-handedly pulled the fleet back together. But he's shut himself off for years and so far the only one to touch that is Jem.' She touched the big dog's soft ears. 'So maybe...maybe this guy can do the same. Or maybe even his owner can.'

'Sorry?' Nikki said, startled.

'Just thinking,' Henrietta said hastily, and rose to leave. 'Dreaming families for my dogs is what I do. Good luck to the three of you.'

She looked at the teacup. Grinned. 'Amazing,' she said. 'They say owners end up looking like their dogs. These cups fit poodles, not wolfhounds.' She grinned down at Horse, asleep draped over Nikki's feet, and then looked back to Nikki. 'Poodle,' she said. 'Maybe now, but not for much longer. I'm looking forward to big changes around here. For everyone.'

Gabe slipped underwater, checked the propeller and inspected the hull. Minutely. It was the best checked hull in the fleet. Then he went back to mending craypots. By nine he was the only person in the harbour.

The rest of his boats were out, and he was stuck on dry land. Because of Nikki.

What was she about, removing his alarm? Telling Hattie to go without him?

He'd needed to sleep, he conceded. His head still ached.

Because she'd hit him.

It was an accident. She meant no harm.

She meant to keep the dog. Horse.

It was a stupid name for a dog. A dog needed a bit of dignity.

Dignity.

She'd have to get that fur unmatted, he thought, and getting the tangles out of that neglected coat was a huge job. Did she know what she was letting herself in for?

It was nothing to do with him. Nothing! He wasn't going near.

She was living right next door to him. With her dog who needed detangling.

He'd yelled at her. Because she'd picked up a few rocks.

He'd behaved appallingly.

Why?

He knew why. And it wasn't the memory of his mother. It wasn't the dog. It was more.

It couldn't be more. He didn't want more, and more wasn't going to happen.

It was dark. Time to head home.

Maybe he could take Jem's old brushes across to her. A peace offering.

That wasn't more. It was sensible. It felt…okay.

But when he got home there wasn't a light on, apart from the security light he kept on in the shared porch.

Were she and the dog asleep?

She'd slept this afternoon. He'd seen her, curled on the hearth with the dog.

With Horse.

They were nothing to do with him.

He glanced at the gap in the stone wall. Sensed the faint echo of Nikki. And Horse.

By his side… Shades of Jem.

He was going nuts. Thc hit on his head had obviously been harder than he thought. Ghosts were everywhere, even to the feel of Jem beside him. Jem had always been with him, on the boat, under his bed, by the fire, a heartbeat by his side.

Whoa, he was maudlin. Get over it.

Disoriented, he found himself heading for the beach. A man could stare at the sea in the moonlight. Find some answers?

But the only answers he found on the beach were Nikki and Horse.

Chapter 5

They were sitting just above the high water mark, right near the spot where Horse had stood and howled last night. Gabe saw them straight away, unmistakable, the silhouette of the slight woman and the huge, rangy dog framed against a rising moon.

Maybe he'd better call out. Warn her of his approach. Who knew what she was carrying tonight?

'Nikki!'

She turned. So did Horse, uttering a low threatening growl that suddenly turned into an unsure whine. Maybe the dog was as confused as he was.

'Gabe?' She couldn't see him—he was still in shadows. She sounded scared.

'It's Gabe.' He said it quickly, before she fired the poker.

'Are you still angry?'

Deep breath. Get this sorted. Stop being an oaf. 'I need to apologise,' he said, walking across the beach to them. 'I was out of line. Whether you keep Horse is none of my business. And snapping about the stones was nuts. Can we blame it on the hit on the head and move on?'

'Sure,' she said, but she sounded wary. 'I did hit you. I guess I can afford to cut you some slack.'

'Thank you,' he said gravely. 'Are you two moon watching?'

'Horse refuses to settle.' She shifted along the log she was perched on so there was room for him as well. 'He whined and whined, so finally I figured we might as well come down here and see that no one's coming. So he can finally settle into our new life.'

'Your new life?' he said cautiously, sorting wheat from chaff. 'You really intend changing your life?'

'My life is changed anyway,' she said. 'That's what comes of falling for a king-sized rat. It's messed with my serenity no end.'

Don't ask. It was none of his business.

But she wasn't expecting him to ask. She was staring out to sea, talking almost to herself, and her self containment touched him as neediness never could.

Since when had he ever wanted to be involved?

Horse nuzzled his hand. He patted the dog and said, 'You fell for a king-sized rat?'

Had he intended to ask? Surely not.

'My boss.'

He had no choice now.

'You want to tell me about it?'

* * *

She had no intention of telling him. She hadn't told anyone. The guy she'd thought she loved was married.

Her parents knew she'd split with Jonathan but both her parents were on their third or fourth partner; splits were no big deal. And in the office, to her friends, she'd hung onto her pride. Her pride seemed like all she had left.

But here, now, sitting on the beach with Horse between them, pride and privacy no longer seemed important.

So she told him. Bluntly. Dispassionately, as if it had happened to someone else, not to her.

'Jonathan Ostler of Ostler Engineering,' she said, her voice cool and hard. 'International engineering designer. Smooth, rich, efficient. Hates mixing business with pleasure. My boss. He asked me out four years ago. Six months later we were sharing an apartment but no one in the office was to know. Jonathan thought it'd mess with company morale. So... In the office we were so businesslike you wouldn't believe. If we were coming to work at the same time we'd split up a block away so we'd never arrive together. He addressed me as Nikki but I addressed him as Mr Ostler. Strictly formal.'

'Sounds weird.'

'Yes, but I could see his point,' she said. 'Sleeping with the boss is hardly the way to endear yourself to the rest of the staff, and Jon was overseas so much it wasn't an effort. A few people knew we were together but not many. So there I was, dream job, dream guy, dream apartment, four years. Dreaming weddings, if you must know. Starting to be anxious he didn't want to settle, but too stupidly in love to push it. Then two months ago there was an explosion in a factory where we'd been overseeing changes. The call came in the middle of the night—hysterical—our firm could be sued for millions. Jon caught the dawn plane to Düsseldorf with minutes to spare, and in the rush he left his mobile phone sitting on his—on *our*—bedside table. The next day our office was crazy. The Düsseldorf situation was frightening and the phone was going nuts. Jonathan's phone. Finally, I answered it. It was Jonathan's wife. In London. Their eight-year-old had been in a car accident. Please could I tell her where Jon was.'

'Ouch.'

'I coped,' she said, a tinge of pride warming her voice as she remembered that ghastly moment. 'I made sympathetic noises. I made sure Jonathan Junior wasn't in mortal danger, I got the details. Then I left a message with the manager of the Düsseldorf factory, asking Jon to phone his wife. I told him to say the message was from Nikki. Then I moved out of our apartment. Jonathan returned a week later, and I'd already arranged to move here, to do my work via the Internet.'

'But you still work for him?'

'Personal and business don't mix.'

'Like hell they don't,' he snapped. 'I've had relationships go sour between the crew. It messes with staff morale no end, and there's no way they can work together afterwards.'

'I'm good at my work.' But her uncertainty was

growing and she couldn't put passion into her voice. 'The pay's great.'

'Can you work for yourself?'

'It's a specialist industry,' she said. 'I couldn't set up in competition to Jon. I could work for someone else, but it would have to be overseas.'

'So why not go overseas?'

'I don't want to.' But she'd been thinking. Thinking and thinking. She'd been totally, hopelessly in love with Jonathan for years and to change her life so dramatically…

Why not change it more?

Tomorrow. Think of it tomorrow.

'And now I have a dog,' she said, hauling herself back to the here and now with something akin to desperation. 'So here I am.' Deep breath. Tomorrow? Why not say now? 'But I have been thinking of changing jobs. Changing completely.'

'To what?'

How to say it? It was ridiculous. And to say stone walling, when she knew how he felt…

But the germ of an idea that had started today wouldn't go away.

Putting one stone after another into a wall.

Crazy. To turn her back on specialist training…

Oh, but how satisfying.

It was a whim, she reminded herself sharply. A whim of today. Tomorrow it'd be gone and she'd be back to sensible.

Don't talk about it. Don't push this man further than you already have.

'I don't know,' she managed. 'All I know is that I

need something. Woman needs change.' She hugged Horse, who was still gazing out to sea. 'Woman needs dog.'

'No one needs a dog.'

'Says you who just lost one. I wonder if Horse's owner misses him like you miss Jem.'

'Nikki…'

'Don't stick my nose into what's not my business? You've been telling me that all day. But now… I've told you about my non existent love life. You want to tell me why I can't finish your stone wall?'

'It's my mother's wall.'

'And she disapproves of completion?'

'She died when I was a child. She didn't get to finish it.'

'So the hole's like a shrine,' she said cautiously, like one might approach an unexploded grenade. 'I can see that. But you know, if it was me I'd want the wall finished. Are you sure your mum's not up there fretting? You know, I'm a neat freak. If I die with my floor half-hoovered, feel welcome to finish it. In fact I'll haunt you if you don't.'

'You don't like an unhoovered floor?' They were veering away from his mother—which seemed fine by both of them.

'Hoovering's good for the soul.'

His mouth twitched. Just a little. The beginning of a smile. 'Do you know how much hair a dog like Horse will shed?'

'He has to grow some hair back first,' she said warmly. 'He grows, I'll hoover. We've made a deal.'

'While you've been sitting on the beach, staring at the moon.'

'It's filling time. How long do you reckon it'll take him to figure whoever he wants isn't coming?'

'Dogs have been faithful to absent masters for years.'

'Years?'

'Years.'

'I was hoping maybe another half an hour.'

'Years.'

'Uh-oh.'

'And years.'

'I don't know what else to do,' she whispered.

Her problem. This was her problem, he thought, and it was only what she deserved, taking on a damaged dog…

As he'd taken on a damaged dog sixteen years ago and not regretted it once. Until it was over.

He'd had his turn. Yes, this was Nikki's dog, Nikki's problem, but he could help.

'I don't think you're doing anyone any favours by letting him stare at where a boat isn't,' he said.

'I'm doing my best.'

'Yes,' he said. 'I know that.'

She cast him a look that was suspicious to say the least. 'I didn't mean to mess with your mother's memory,' she told him.

'Yeah.' He deserved that, he conceded. Like he'd deserved the hit over the head? But she had her reasons for that. Her heart was in the right place even if it was messing with…his heart?

That was a dumb thing to think, but think it he did.

Since Lisbette left…well, maybe even before, a long time before, he'd closed down. Lisbette had whirled into his life, stunned him, ripped him off for all he was worth and whirled out again. He'd been a kid, lonely, naïve and a sitting duck.

He wasn't a sitting duck any longer. He'd closed up. Jem had wriggled her way into his life, he'd loved her and he'd lost her. She'd been the last chink in his armour, and there was no way he was opening more.

But this woman…

She wasn't looking to rip him off as Lisbette had—he knew that. Lisbette, getting up every two hours because she was worried about him? Ha!

Nor was she trying to edge into the cracks around his heart like Jem had. She might be needy but it was a different type of needy.

It was Nikki and Horse against the world—when she didn't know a blind thing about dogs.

She was blundering. She was a walking disaster but she was a disaster who meant well.

'I overreacted with the wall,' he conceded. 'I looked out and saw you and the dog and that's what I remember most about my mother. Her sitting for hour after hour, sorting stones. She did it everywhere. She and Billy.'

'Billy?'

'She had a collie. He seemed old as long as I can remember. He pined when she died, and my dad shot him.'

'He shot him?' She sounded appalled.

'He was never going to get over Mum's death.'

'You were how old?'

'Eight.'

'You lost your mum, and your dad shot her dog?'

How to say it? The day of the funeral, coming home, Billy whining, his father saying, 'Get to your room, boy.' A single shot.

He didn't have to tell her. She touched his hand and the horror of that day was in her touch.

'And I hit you over the head,' she whispered. 'And Henrietta said your wife left you. And your own dog died. If I were you I'd have crawled into a nice comfy psychiatric ward and thought up a diagnosis that'd keep me there for the rest of my life. Instead…'

'How did we get here?' He had no idea. One minute this woman was irritating the heck out of him, the next she was putting together stuff he didn't think about; didn't want to think about. This was his place, his beach. He'd come down here for a quiet think, and here he was being psychoanalysed.

He felt exposed.

It was a weird thing to think. She hadn't said anything that wasn't common knowledge but it was as if she could see things differently.

She had her arm round Horse's neck and she was tugging him close, and all of a sudden he felt a jolt, like what would it feel to be in the dog's place?

The dog whined. Stupid dog.

'You want dog lessons,' he said, more roughly than he intended.

'Horse doesn't need lessons. He's smart.'

'He's staring at an empty sea,' he said.

'He's devoted. He'll get over it. Needs must.'

'Says you who's still pining for your creepy boss.'

'I'm trying to get over it,' she said with dignity. 'I'm not sitting on the beach wailing. I'm doing my best. Don't we all?'

She rose and brushed sand from the back of her trousers. With his collar released, Horse took a tentative step towards the sea. Nikki's hand hit the collar at the same time as his did. Their fingers touched. Flinched a little but didn't let go. Settled beside each other, a tiny touch but unnerving.

Settling.

Things were settling for him. He wasn't sure why.

Maybe it was watching her reaction to what he'd told her tonight, added to what he knew local gossip would have told her. His mother's death, his father, Lisbette, his mother's dog and Jem… Her reaction seemed to validate stuff he tried not to think about.

Permission to feel sorry for himself?

Permission to move on.

Towards Nikki? Towards yet another disaster?

Not in a million years. He'd spent all his life being taught that solitary was safe. He wasn't about to change that now.

But he could help her. It was the least he could do.

'Horse needs a master,' he told her.

'He's only got me,' she said defensively. 'Why are we being sexist? A master?'

'I mean,' he said patiently, 'a pack leader. He's lost his. He's looking for him; if he can't find him he needs a new one.'

'Right,' she said. 'Pack leader. Can I buy one at the Banksia Bay Co-op?'

He grinned. His hand was still touching hers. He

should pull it away but he didn't. Things were changing—had changed. There was something about the night, the moonlight on the water, the big needy dog between them…

There was something about her expression. She was sounding defiant, braving it out, but things were rotten in this woman's world as well. Nikki and Horse, both needy to the point of desperation.

That need had nothing to do with him. He should pull away—but he didn't.

'Attitude,' he said, deciding he'd be decisive, and she blinked.

'Pack leader attitude?'

'That's it. So who decided to come down the beach, you or Horse?'

'He was miserable.' She sounded defensive.

'So you followed.'

'I held onto him. He would have run.'

'But he walked in front, yes? Team leaders walk in front. The pack's at the back.'

'You're saying I need to growl at him? Make him subservient? He's already miserable.'

'He'll be miserable until you order him not to be, and he decides you're worth swapping loyalty.'

'I shouldn't have let him come down to the beach?'

'There's not a lot of point being down here, is there?' he said, gentler as he watched her face. And Horse's face. He could swear the dog was listening, his great eyes pools of despair. 'He's been dumped by a low-life. How's it going to make him feel better to stare at an empty sea? It's up to you to take his place.'

'The low-life's place?'

'That's the one.'

'I haven't had much practice at being the low-life,' she said. 'I'm a follower. Dumb and dumber, that's me.'

'We're not talking about your love life.'

'We're not?'

'That's shrink territory, not mine.'

'Like your stone wall.'

'Do you mind?'

'Butt out?' She sighed and tried for a smile. 'Fine. Consider me butted. What do I need to be a pack leader? A whip? Leathers?'

'Discipline.'

She grinned. 'Really? Don't tell me, stockings and garters as well.'

He stared at her in the moonlight and he couldn't believe it. She was laughing. Laughing!

The tension of the night dissipated, just like that. Except…a sudden vision of Nikki in stockings and garters…

He almost blushed.

'I mean,' he said, trying to stop the corners of his mouth twitching, 'you tell Horse what you expect and you follow through. He's hungry? Use it. Call him, reward him when he comes. Teach him to sit, stay, the usual dog things. But mostly teach him no. He's galloping towards you with a road in between; you need to hold your hand up, yell no and have him stop in his tracks. The same with coming down here. You can bring him down here on your terms, with a ball, something to do to keep him occupied. The minute he stares out to sea like he's considering the low-life, then that's a no. Hard, fast and mean it.'

'You're good at training dogs?'

'I had a great dog. Smart as Einstein. She trained me.'

'I'm sure Horse is smart.'

'Prove it.'

'I'm not sure…'

'Henrietta's daughter takes personal dog coaching. I'm amazed Henrietta hasn't introduced you already.'

'Henrietta left a card,' she conceded.

'There you go.'

'You're not interested in helping yourself?

'No.' Hard. Definite. He watched her face close and regretted it, but couldn't pull it back.

'I'm not scary,' she said, almost defiantly, and he thought what a wuss—was he so obvious?

'I'm busy,' he said. 'This is the first full day I haven't worked since…'

'Since Jem died?'

'Nikki…'

'I know.' She tugged Horse towards her a little, which forced his hand to let go of the collar. Which meant they were no longer touching. 'You want me to butt out. Respect your boundaries. I've been respecting boundaries for years. You'd think I'd be good at it.'

'I didn't mean…'

'You know, I'm very sure you did,' she told him. 'Tell me what to do.'

'What do you mean?'

'With Horse,' she said patiently. 'Training. What should I do first?'

'Take his collar and say "Come".' This was solid ground. Dog training. He could handle this.

'Come,' she said and tugged and Horse didn't move. Stared rigidly out to sea.

'Come!' Another tug.

Gabe sighed. 'Okay, you're on the head end. We're going to roll him.'

'What?'

'He has to learn to submit, otherwise he'll spend the rest of his life waiting for his low-life. Say "Down".'

'Down.'

'Like you mean it!'

'Down!'

'You sound like a feather duster.'

'I do not.'

'Pretend the boat's sinking. The kid at the other end is standing there with a tin can and a stupid expression. He bails or you drown. Are you going to say "Bail" in that same voice?'

'He's an abandoned dog. He nearly died. He's hurt and confused. You want me to yell at him?'

'He's hurt and confused and he needs to relax. The only way he can relax is if he thinks someone else is in charge. You.'

'You do it.'

'I'm not his pack leader. Do it, Nikki, or you'll have him howling at the door for weeks, killing himself with exhaustion. You say "Down" like you mean it and we bring him down.'

'I don't…'

'Just do it.'

'Down,' she snapped in a voice so full of authority that both Gabe and the dog started. But he had the dog's back legs and Nikki had his collar. Gabe hauled his legs from under him and rolled him before Horse knew what had hit him.

The big dog was on his back. Shocked into submission.

'Tell him he's a good dog but keep him down,' Gabe said.

'This is cruel. He's not fit…'

'He's going to pine until we do it. Do it.'

'G… Good dog.'

'Now let him up again.'

The dog lumbered to his feet.

'Now down again.'

'Down!'

Once again Gabe pushed his legs from under him. The dog folded.

'Good dog,' Nikki said, holding him down and the dog's tail gave a tentative, subjugated wag.

'Once more.'

'Down!' And this time Gabe didn't have to push. The dog crouched and rolled with only a slight push and pull from Nikki.

'Good dog. Great,' Nikki said and her voice wobbled.

The dog stood again, unsure, but this time he moved imperceptibly to Nikki's side. He looked up at her instead of out to sea.

'Now tell him to come and tug,' Gabe said, and Nikki did and the big dog moved docilely up the beach by her side.

'Good dog,' Nikki said and sniffed.

'Why are you crying?'

'I'm not.'

'You're allergic to command?'

'I'm not built to be a sergeant major.'

'Horse needs a sergeant major,' he said as he fell in beside her. 'You are what you have to be. Like me being owner of half a dozen boats, employing crews.'

'You don't like that?'

They were walking up the track, Nikki with Horse beside her, Gabe with his hand hovering, just in case Horse made a break for it. But Horse was totally submissive. He was probably relieved. He'd spent too long as it was waiting for his scumbag owner. He needed a new one.

There were parallels. Caring for Horse…

Taking on this town's fishing fleet.

Nikki was waiting for an answer. Not pushing. Just walking steadily up the track with her dog.

She was a peaceful woman, he thought. Self contained. Maybe she'd had to be.

Why the sniff? Tears?

Ignore them.

'I never saw myself as head of a fleet,' he told her. 'But when the fishing industry round here started to falter I was single with no responsibilities. I'd been away, working on the rigs, making myself some serious money. I could afford to take a few risks. But in the end I didn't need to. Fishing's in my blood and I knew what'd work.'

'But now… You enjoy it?'

'Fishing's my life.'

'It sounds boring.'

'So you do what in your spare time?' he demanded. 'Macramé?

'Dog training,' she said steadily. 'I now have a career and a hobby and a pet. What more could a girl want? What do you have, Gabe Carver?'

'Everything I want.'

They reached the house in silence. Reached the porch. Nikki opened the door and ushered Horse inside. Hesitated.

'He'll stand at the door and howl,' she said, and he looked at her face and saw the tracks of tears. What had he said to upset her?

'Only if you let him.'

'How do I not let him?'

He sighed. 'Where's he sleeping?'

'In my bedroom.'

'Not on your bed. You're pack leader.'

'I know that much. Besides, the bed's not big enough.'

'So show me.'

She swung open the bedroom door. A bed, single, small. He looked at her in surprise. He hadn't been here when her furniture was delivered so he was seeing this for the first time. It was practically a child's bed.

'You don't like stretching?'

'Not if there's no one to stretch to.'

Silence. There were a million things to say, but suddenly nothing.

The bedroom was chintzy. Pretty pink. Dainty. It made a man nervous just to look at it.

Horse whined and he thought *I'm with you, mate.* To sleep in a bedroom like this…

But at least Horse had a sensible bed. Henrietta

knew dogs, and she'd provided a trampoline bed that was almost as big as Nikki's.

'Say "Bed",' he told Nikki.

'Bed.' Horse didn't move an inch.

Gabe sighed. 'Bail the dratted boat.'

'Bed!' That was better. Sergeant major stuff.

Gabe shoved Horse from behind. Horse lumbered up onto the trampoline.

'Say "Down."'

'Down,' Nikki said and the dog rolled.

'Stay,' Nikki said and stepped back and grinned as Horse did just that.

Horse looked up at her and put a tentative paw down onto the floor.

'Stay!' Her best 'bail the boat' voice.

The paw retreated.

'How about that?' Nikki said, her smile widening. 'I'm a pack leader.'

'You'll make a great one.'

'I will,' she said and turned to him. Fast.

She was suddenly a bit too close.

She was suddenly very close.

'Make sure the dog stays there,' he said, a bit too gruffly. They were by the dog's bed, so close they were almost touching. They were by Nikki's bed as well. It was just as well it wasn't his bed, he thought, the wide, firm, king-sized bed he'd bought for himself when he'd come back here to live.

He had a sudden flash of recall. Last night. Nikki tiptoeing in to check he wasn't dead, leaning over him…

He could have…

No.

But she was so close. He turned to go—a man had to make a move—but suddenly she'd taken his hands in hers, tugging him back to face her.

'Thank you,' she said. 'For coming down to the beach to find me.'

'You're welcome.' He hadn't gone down to find her, he thought, but he wasn't thinking clearly and it seemed way too much trouble to explain.

'And I can see why you don't want to get involved. I won't ask you to. I've been a nuisance. But I meant well. I mean well.'

'You do.' Big of him to concede that much.

'And your head really is better?'

'Not hurting at all.' Almost the truth.

She smiled. It was a really cute smile, he thought. He could see the tracks of those unexplained tears and it made her seem cuter. All in all…

All in all, Nikki Morrissy was really cute all over.

'Goodnight,' she said and then, inexplicably, unaccountably, she stood on tiptoe and she kissed him. Lightly, a feather-touch. Maybe she'd even meant it to be an air-kiss but he moved. Maybe he tugged her a bit closer and her lips brushed his.

Burned.

She pulled back, startled. Which was how he felt. Startled.

To say the least.

'Just…thank you,' she said. Struggled for words. Struggled to find something to talk about other than the kiss. 'And…and I'm so sorry your dog died. Jem must have been amazing.'

'She was.'

'You want to tell me about her?' she said but there were limits, even if she was looking at him with eyes that'd melt an iceberg.

She was his tenant. *His tenant.*

He'd helped her as much as he could.

'Goodnight,' he said and backed to the door.

'I didn't mean to kiss you,' she murmured, but he hardly heard her.

A man had to take a stand some time. A man had to know when to retreat.

He retreated.

Chapter 6

There was no reason to get up. The sensation was so novel it had Gabe lying in bed at five in the morning thinking the world was off balance.

All but one of his boats were out. They'd left in a group yesterday morning and weren't due back until tomorrow. The one stuck in harbour through lack of crew—the *Lady Nell*—was the one needing least attention. The propeller was checked. The cray-pots were mended.

Even his dratted bookwork was up to date.

He could sleep until midday if he wanted.

He didn't want. His world was out of kilter.

Because of lack of work?

Because of Nikki.

Because she'd kissed him?

Because she'd touched him with her crazy floundering from assertive career woman to a woman who was exposed on all sides.

She'd taken in a dog as big as she was. She'd given her heart and in doing so... She'd pierced a part of him he'd protected with care for years.

And he didn't want it pierced. He had to close it off again fast, but the fact that she was living right through the wall was enough to do his head in.

He could evict her. Because of the dog?

He was turning into his father.

His window was wide open. From where he lay he could see the gap in the stone fence. He thought of Nikki's face as he'd yelled.

He'd hurt her.

Last night she'd cried and he didn't know why.

The wall was there, looking at him, as it had looked at Nikki.

He climbed out of bed and went to get his mother's books. Went back to bed. He read for an hour.

Looked at the wall.

The thought of picking up those stones, taking up where his mother had left off...

How could he do that?

How could he start again?

His mother. Lisbette. Jem. Pain at every turn.

He thought of the appalling time after Lisbette left. Realising that all she'd said had been lies. Realising the extent of what she'd stolen from him.

After Lisbette, he'd taken Jem and headed west, where his experience landed him a job on a rig supply boat. Jem was included—he was a package deal, employ me, my dog comes too. But it was no problem. Jem loved their life at sea and Gabe was good. Within a year he was captaining his own boat. He could get stuff to the rigs in weather no one else would face.

He worked hard. Crew came and went. Jem was his only constant.

The protective layer he'd built around himself grew thicker. He was okay.

Moving back here… That'd been a risk, but he'd heard stories of the trouble with the fleet. Maybe the loneliness had got to him. It wouldn't hurt to help the people who'd once been good to him; who'd tried in their way to stand between him and his father.

And that was okay, too. By the time he came home the house had lost the worst of its memories. Only the shades of his mother remained.

He'd been able to step in and maintain his distance. He and Jem.

Now, just him.

And Nikki and Horse.

Who made him think of finishing the wall…

He did not need them interfering with his solitary lifestyle.

He tossed the books aside. Pulled on his fishing gear. He'd head to the harbour.

He had to get out of here.

He had to get away from Nikki?

Away from the thought of letting down some of his carefully built defences. How could a man ever do that? And why would he want to?

Nikki and Horse sat on the wharf, watched the seagulls and watched the early morning sun glinting over the distant sea.

The harbour was deserted. Most of the boats were out. The only ones left were pleasure craft and the tenders used to take owners out to bigger boats at swing moorings.

Swing moorings. Tenders. She smiled to herself. She'd only been here three weeks and already she was learning the local lingo.

'Do you know it already?' she asked Horse. 'Were you a fishing dog?'

Horse was subdued but pliant. He'd woken at first light and whined. Nikki had taken him outside. He'd done what he needed to do and then looked longingly towards the beach.

'No,' Nikki told him in her best Leader-Of-The-Pack voice and hauled him back inside. She cooked bacon and eggs for breakfast and shared. She was fed up with Dinners For One and it was fun to cook for an appreciative appetite. Horse wolfed the bacon and nuzzled her hand in what seemed like gratitude, but then he whined and looked at the door again.

He was torn between two loyalties. Lady with the bacon or the sod who'd abandoned him.

'Choose me,' Nikki said but Horse still whined.

She needed displacement activity.

So here they were, sitting on the jetty, trying not to stare at the only decent boat in port.

Gabe's boat. The *Lady Nell*.

Big and powerful and workmanlike. Like Gabe himself.

He'd made her cry.

Not...not him, she thought. It was the mixture of all sorts of stuff.

For the last two months she'd been caught up in her own drama, her own betrayal. But so much more had happened to Gabe.

He didn't want sympathy. There was no way he'd take it, but the touch of his mouth on hers…

It made her want to take him and hold, tell him the world wasn't such a bad place; there were decent people, people who could love…

He didn't want to hear it. Neither did she.

Was she still in love with Jon?

If Jon appeared in front of her right now, told her his marriage was over, had been over for years, it had all been a misunderstanding, would she go back to him?

It was doing her head in.

She was sitting on the wharf letting her head implode.

It was still really early. Six-thirty. Uncivilised. What was she doing here?

Horse whined and turned and jerked on his lead and Nikki swivelled to see. Gabe was striding along the jetty.

Dressed for work. Fisherman's overalls with braces. Rubber boots. His shirt sleeves were once more rolled to above the elbow.

Striding purposely towards his boat, seeing her, stopping dead.

'Nikki,' he said in a tone that said she was the last person he wanted here. She flinched but Horse surged forward and was too strong for her to hold. Henrietta had provided her with a choke chain—to be used 'just for the first week or so because he's so big and there's nothing of you'—but there was no way she was using it. So Horse hauled and she followed.

Feeling foolish.

His expression said she ought to hike out of here fast, taking her dog with her.

'H… Hi,' she managed as Horse reached him and attempted to jump. Gabe caught the dog's legs, placed him firmly down.

'Sit,' he growled and Horse sat. 'Hey,' Gabe said, unable to hide pleasure. 'He must have had some training.'

'I'm worried someone's looking for him,' she ventured. It seemed as good a way as any to start a conversation with someone who obviously wanted her somewhere else.

'Henrietta kept him for ten days. Raff, our local cop, broadcast his details to every cop, to every marine outfit, to every fisherman within two hundred miles up and down the coast. He was found with no collar and evidence of severe neglect. There's no suggestion there of a happy ending.'

'Well, he has one with me,' she snapped, because he was looking at her as if…she was stupid. Dumb for offering this dog a home?

'You can't hold him,' he said mildly and she flushed. Maybe she was reading more into his words than he intended but she was keeping this dog, regardless of what her tough-guy landlord thought.

'Henrietta gave me a choke chain. I tried it on myself. That's exactly what it does—choke. There's no way I'm putting it on Horse.'

'You tried it on yourself…?'

'It's awful. You tug on it, you think you're choking.'

'You only use it while you're training.'

'Did you use one on Jem?'

'I got Jem as a pup. And I'm bigger than you.'

'I do weights,' she said, glaring. 'If I want to stop Horse, I can.'

He nodded. Grinned. Walked the few steps to his boat and leaped aboard. Disappeared into the wheelhouse and came out holding…what?

A chunk of salami.

He walked back to Horse, showed him the sausage, let him sniff, backed off and called. Waving the salami.

'Here, boy. Nice sausage. Come and get it.'

Horse lunged forward.

Nikki held with all the power she possessed and yelled with all the power in her lungs. 'No!'

She wrenched Horse back, then dived in front of him so she was a barrier between dog and sausage. She planted her feet.

'Sit,' she said in a voice she didn't know she had.

Horse sat.

Wow.

She looked down at the dog, at his great goofy desperate-to-please expression, and once again she wanted to cry.

She glanced back at Gabe and caught an expression on his face that was almost similar. 'Wow!' His echo of her thought was so pat she found herself grinning.

'We've been practising all night,' she lied smugly, bending down and hugging Horse. 'Good dog. Great dog.'

She straightened, still grinning—and Horse surged forward to Gabe and grabbed the sausage.

She burst out laughing. Horse wolfed the sausage in two gulps, returned to her side and sat like a benign angel. Obedience personified.

'I think I'm in love,' Nikki said and knew she was.

'You've made a good start,' Gabe conceded.

'I…are you going fishing?' Stupid question. He was dressed for fishing.

'Just checking pots.'

'Pots?'

'I have cray-pots laid along the coast. I don't have a crew but I can do that myself.'

'You're taking your boat out by yourself?'

'Yes.' He swung himself on board and unlocked the wheelhouse. 'I'll be back this afternoon.'

'What about your head?'

'It's fine.'

'I read on the Internet. Forty-eight hours after concussion…'

'You're not still expecting me to drop dead?'

'I keep feeling that crunch,' she said miserably. 'And the side of your face looks awful.'

It did, he conceded. He'd looked in the mirror to shave and pretty near died of fright.

'I'm fine,' he said.

'Please don't go fishing alone.'

What else was he expected to do? 'There's no one else to go fishing with,' he said explosively. 'Since you sent the rest of my crew out without me.'

'I meant it for the best. You can't go out.'

'You're going to stop me how?'

She took a deep breath. She collared Horse and she tugged him forward.

Horse reacted almost too well. He leapt the gap between wharf and boat, and Nikki was hauled after.

She caught her foot on the safety line and sprawled. Gabe reached her before she slid into the water. Tugged her up so she was standing on the deck beside him.

Held her.

'What sort of crazy stunt…? You could drown yourself.'

'I'm an excellent swimmer,' she managed, gasping, hauling herself back from him. She felt winded and stupid, and the feel of those arms… They had a girl thoroughly discombobulated. 'And if I hadn't fallen over Horse…'

'Anyone would fall over Horse,' he said grimly, and turned to see Horse heading along to the bow, standing there like a figurehead on a bowsprit. Any minute now he'd raise one paw and lean into the wind.

'He's used to boats,' he said.

'He needs to be used to boats,' she said. 'We're staying on board until you see sense. Your crew will be back tomorrow. It won't kill you to stay on land.'

'I want to check my cray-pots.'

'Then take someone with you.'

He glared. She crossed her arms and jutted her jaw. Tree-hugger chaining herself to a mighty oak. Or ship.

He sighed. He slipped into the wheelhouse and started the engine. Strode aft and released the rear stay. Strode forward—and their connection to the wharf was gone.

She gasped. 'What…?'

'You want me to have company?' Gabe snapped. 'Fine. Make yourself at home and stay out of my way.'

* * *

When tree-huggers chained themselves to trees they didn't expect their trees to get up and walk. Or get up and sail out of the harbour.

Uh-oh. Uh-oh, uh-oh, uh-oh.

There was a twenty-yard gap between wharf and boat. Should she jump off and swim for it?

Dragging Horse behind her?

Horse was still doing his merman impersonation at the bow. His nose was pointing into the wind, every sense quivering.

Yesterday he'd looked half dead. Now…he almost looked beautiful. If you looked past the mangy coat.

Coat.

She was wearing a light pullover. Cotton. She glanced at Gabe, who was intent behind the wheel, ignoring her. He was in his weatherproofs, dressed for work.

Her pullover was pale pink. Her jeans were a soft blue.

She was wearing her Gucci loafers.

Hardly fishing gear.

'There's a jetty at the harbour mouth,' Gabe growled, seemingly intent on keeping the wheel steady. 'I'll put you off there.'

'You've done this to frighten me.'

'I've done this because I have work to do,' he snapped. 'You're in the way.'

'I'm not in the way,' she muttered. 'It's a big boat.'

'You don't seriously want to come to sea with me?'

Deep breath. Resolution. 'If you're stupid enough to want to take the boat out by yourself, then yes, I do,' she said. 'It was me who hit you. I feel responsible. If someone else hit you, you'd be welcome to be as stupid as you want. I wouldn't care.'

'You don't have to care.'

'I told you. I hit you, I don't have a choice.'

'Get off at the jetty.'

'No.' Back to tree-hugging. She was not, however, sounding as sure as she might have been.

'You'll get seasick.'

There was a thought. Hmm.

She'd been on a couple of cruises with her parents. One with Jon. 'I don't get seasick.' Or sometimes, just a little.

'We're going around reefs, checking pots in rough water. Have you ever been on a small boat in rough water?'

'I don't care,' she burst out. 'It's you who's being stubborn and ridiculous and a totally dumb, masochistic male. Your call. If you go out, you take me with you, seasick or not.'

'Fine,' he said and shifted the wheel so instead of pointing to the jetty at the harbour mouth they were pointing to the open sea.

Um...what had she done?

She kept her arms crossed and felt stupid.

The sea breeze wasn't all that warm.

They hit cross waves at the harbour entrance and she had to uncross her arms to hold on. Whoa, cruise liners never rocked like this.

'Nikki?'

'What?' She was glowering. Trying to stay righteous and purposeful.

'Put these on.' They were clear of the harbour mouth and he'd left the wheel for a moment. He took the couple of steps to where she stood and handed her a coat even more disgusting than his.

'I'm not sure…'

'Put it on,' he growled. 'And the life jacket with it. There's a packet of seasick pills on the bench below. Take one. Then tie a safety line to Horse. Then you can watch for signs of concussion all you want, as long as you stay out of my way.'

It took half an hour to reach the reef where he'd set the cray-pots. For all that time Nikki sat in the bow, holding onto Horse.

She was right in his line of vision, a slight figure in a battered coat way too big for her, with Horse draped over her knees. Both of them were gazing into the wind. Horse's ears flopped about in the breeze.

Nikki's hair practically had a life of its own.

She had a pert bob, cut to sculptural perfection. It was smooth and glossy and lovely—or it had been until the first burst of spray flew over the bow.

Her hair sort of forgot about being smooth. It kinked a bit.

He watched, fascinated, as the spray and the wind did their worst. By the time they were halfway to their destination her hair was a mass of curls. She no longer looked like a smooth, professional city woman. She was enveloped in a coat liberally embellished with fish scales, her hair was a riot and she was draped in a huge dog.

She hadn't succumbed to seasickness. On the

contrary, once she'd settled, once she'd forgotten to glower, she almost looked as if she was enjoying herself. When she was hit by spray she turned her face into it, even laughed. She hugged her dog, and Horse looked pretty happy, too.

She'd forgotten she was checking him for concussion, or maybe she figured as long as the boat was on course she didn't need to. She was simply enjoying the ride and Gabe, who'd practically kidnapped her, felt a pang of…

Of something he didn't know how to handle. He'd brought her with him because he was frustrated and angry and he'd wanted to teach her a lesson. *Stay out of my life.*

Now she was in his life even more, and it was making him feel…

He didn't know how it was making him feel. As if he wanted to turn the boat round and head back for harbour, dump her and run?

Yeah, as if that was a sensible thing to do.

Her hair was amazing.

'Gabe!'

She was on her feet, yelling to him. 'Gabe!'

He pulled back the throttle, alarmed, and swung out of the wheelhouse to see.

Seals.

He'd been too busy watching her, watching her crazy hair, to notice, and he didn't look for seals anyway. It wasn't that he didn't like seeing them—he did, apart from when they were after his fish—but there was a massive seal colony on a rocky island a couple of miles south of Banksia Bay, and seals were simply part and parcel of his life.

They weren't part and parcel of Nikki's life. She was gazing down at them in awe.

They were riding his bow wave.

They truly were wonderful, he conceded, trying to see them as Nikki must be seeing them. These were pups, half grown, still mostly fed by their parents so they were here to have fun. The bow wave and the wake made by the *Lady Nell* were just right for them to surf. There were dozens of them, streaming in and out of the waves, riding alongside the boat, surging ahead and slipping behind. Leaping up, leaping over each other, simply having fun. Nikki was holding the rail and gasping with pleasure.

An old bull seal pulled out of the wave, reared back, surged on ahead.

Gabe grinned. He knew this guy. Mostly the bull seals held themselves apart, but this old guy had lost his harem long since. Instead of moping alone, he'd decided to relive his youth.

He slipped back into the wheelhouse, pushed the throttle back to full power and went out again. The seals practically whooped with joy at the bigger bow wave.

'They're tame,' Nikki whispered, awed.

'Not them. They're wild and free. They know what they want from me, though. Decent surf.'

'They're magnificent. Oh…' One of the young ones, smaller than the rest, surged up, leaped right out of the water ahead of the wave, then sank out of sight. If she'd reached out she could have touched him.

She was clutching Gabe's arm, gazing down with pure delight. 'Oh…'

'They eat my fish,' Gabe growled but his heart wasn't in it. He was watching her. Where was his sleek, perfectly groomed tenant now? She was in a battered, fishing sou'wester. Her hair was a mass of tangled curls, getting more and more wild as the spray soaked her. A sliver of mascara had smudged down her cheek.

He had this really strong urge…

A wave hit them broadside, not so big to worry him—he'd never have left the wheelhouse if there was a possibility of a big sea—but it was big enough to make Nikki stagger and clutch.

He let her clutch. His arm came round her waist and held—and she didn't appear to notice.

She was totally absorbed in the seals, in the antics of the pups. They were born clowns. It was as if they were putting on their own personal show, with the old bull seal trying valiantly to keep up.

The pups were jumping the bull seal, darting round his massive body as if he was a rock and they were playing tag around him.

'He's huge,' Nikki whispered.

'Cecil. He's a local legend. He's the only seal in the known world who runs his own playgroup. Most bull seals when they're past their prime head for a lone rock and live out the rest of their lives sulking. Cecil thinks this is a great alternative.'

She chuckled, a lovely throaty chuckle that made something kick inside Gabe's gut. Something he wasn't sure how to handle.

His arm was still around her. She was nestled

against him, watching the seals. Her eyes were alight with laughter, her body curved against him as if this was the most natural position in the world.

He wanted, quite badly, to kiss her.

Very badly.

Defences? Why would a man want defences?

'Nikki…'

But right at that moment one of the pups leapt up and twisted right next to where they stood, so close it almost brushed Horse's nose.

Horse had been staring over the side with bemusement, not sure what he should do in this situation.

This, however, called for action. There were some things which a mature dog should not put up with, and cheeky pups taunting him was obviously one of them.

He crouched under the side rail so he was leaning right over the side and he barked, a massive, throaty bark that said, *Oi, enough—this is my territory; you guys know your place.*

Nikki chuckled and stooped to hug him, and Gabe felt her leave his side with a wrench of loss.

Given the choice, he wouldn't have let her go.

'Hey, it's okay, they're having fun,' Nikki told Horse, and Horse wagged his tail, practically beaming, and crouched again and went back to barking.

The seals backed away a little, darted out, darted back, started leaping again.

It seemed Horse was no threat.

Horse barked on, fit to wake the dead.

'Tell him "No" or he'll deafen us,' Gabe said, half laughing himself, but still with that wrenching feeling of loss.

'No!' Nikki said and then raised her voice. 'No!'

Horse subsided.

Nikki looked smug.

He wanted to kiss her so badly…

Another wave hit them broadside and the boat rolled. He reached to steady Nikki but she'd already clutched the rail. She was fine.

They were nearing the reef; the waves were building. He needed to head back into the wheelhouse and leave Nikki to Horse and to her seals.

He did, but it was a wrench.

The desire to kiss her went with him.

He pulled up twenty cray-pots and felt as if he'd done a decent morning's work. The hold was now full of live crays. Good, big ones.

Maybe he'd cook one for dinner, invite Nikki over.

Was he out of his mind?

But a man could think about it. Resolutions were made to be broken. How long since he'd invited a woman out?

She was his tenant. It was asking for trouble.

She was adorable.

That was asking for more trouble.

She'd insisted on helping and, to his astonishment, she really could help. He explained the winch system once, and she got it straight away. It was hard winching in cray-pots by himself. The pots were set in shallow water at the back of a low-lying reef. The boat had to be held steady or they'd end up on the rocks. If he'd been working by himself it was a matter of watching the sea, then heading in during a glimmer of calm, hooking the pot and winching it up from back in the wheelhouse while he could watch the sea as it came up. Then get back to safe water before he could swing the pot over the side.

But Nikki got it. She watched him do one, she demanded to try, she hooked the second on the third run—not bad for an amateur—and she hauled the pot in by herself.

Horse objected to the weird crustaceans in the traps but he only barked once. 'No,' Nikki said and the big dog subsided and watched.

He had a crew, he thought. A woman and a dog.

He thought of the morning he'd have had if she hadn't come, and he thought why had he not wanted to take her? She lit his day.

There was a dangerous thought.

Why was it dangerous?

With the last pot was lifted he headed back from the dangerous waters of the reef,

The water out here was calm. Nikki had untied Horse—they'd needed Horse's spot to stack the pots while they worked and he seemed settled. With the pots all emptied, woman and dog were back to watching the seal pups. Nikki was hugging Horse. She was smiling at Horse. She was smiling at the pups.

She was smiling at him.

It felt…

Dangerous.

Insidious in its sweetness.

Why was he so nervous?

Because his gut said this was a woman who had the power to mess with his equanimity.

Was equanimity such a big deal anyway?

All his life he'd been a loner, except…

Yeah, except for his mother. She'd loved him. She'd held him, cuddled him, stood between him and his brute of a father.

Left him. Not her fault, though. There was no word bad enough to describe cancer.

Lisbette. Held him, loved him, ripped him off for everything he was worth.

He'd thought he was in love. How did a man recover trust in his judgement after that?

He didn't. Why should he? Was it worth the risk?

Jem. Dogs.

Back in the wheelhouse, he glanced out at Horse and Nikki, and he thought big dogs and short lifespans. Nikki was giving her heart to a dog, and in a few short years she'd have the heart ripped out of her.

She was laughing now, watching Horse watch a couple of gulls swooping overhead. Horse was trying to figure whether they were a threat. Putting his paws over his head in case they were.

When she lost Horse she'd stop laughing.

He could be there…

Where was he going with this?

Back to port. He gunned the motor, pushing the revs, deciding he needed to be back on dry land fast. Thinking he needed to get his head together fast. Then he noticed a boat on the horizon, coming fast. Much faster than his boat.

It was a pleasure craft, he saw, as the distance between them grew smaller. A couple of yahoo guys were speeding for the sake of it, gunning their flimsy fibreglass craft to the limit. Using gas for the sake of it. Thrill-seeking. They wouldn't even see the seals, he thought, or anything else. They were only intent on speed.

They veered nearer, stupidly close, probably trying to catch his bow wave to give them a more exciting ride. They yelled and waved and veered in and out of his wake. They did a three-sixty degree turn—and then they were gone, speeding into the distance.

And before he realised what was happening…

Horse gave a long, low howl, he lurched out of Nikki's arms, out of her hold and he headed over the side of the boat and after them.

Chapter 7

No.

'Horse!' Nikki screamed, hauled off her sou'wester, kicked off her shoes and, before Gabe could react, she was over the side and after him.

No!

They were in seal territory. Pup's playground.

Shark country.

His heart hit his boots as he hauled the boat around, headed out on deck, threw lifebuoys. His gut reaction was to jump straight in after them but a fat lot of use that would be. Three of them in the water while the boat drifted to the reef… He needed to manoeuvre his way to them fast.

He headed back to the wheel. Tried to see.

Horse was a hundred yards from the boat already.

Nikki was half the distance but she was heading after him, swimming strongly.

At least she could swim.

She had a life vest on, two bars across her shoulders to be inflated with the pull of a cord. He should be grateful she hadn't pulled it off with her jacket.

She hadn't pulled the cord. She was intent on reaching the dog—who was intent on reaching the speedboat.

Which was now practically out of sight.

'Nikki, head for the lifebuoy,' he yelled, his voice hoarse with panic, but she was still heading for the dog.

Stupid, stupid, stupid.

Panic would achieve nothing. Stay cool. Think.

He gunned the boat, heading after her. He cut her off from the dog and hit neutral.

'I can reach him,' she yelled, changing direction to go round the boat.

'*We* can reach him,' he yelled back. 'Get back in the boat. Now!' He hauled one of the buoys back into the boat and threw it again so it was just in front of her. 'Hold on and I'll pull.'

'Let me go. I can…'

'Get back in the boat or I'll cosh you with the gaff and drag you in.' And he meant it.

They were in seal pup territory. Great White Sharks fed round here, cruising the waters for easy pickings. Pickings like injured seals. The locals knew never to dive near the seal colony. A human in the water, creating a splash, looked just like an injured seal.

He knew the dangers. She didn't. She had to get out of there.

'Horse…' she yelled, sounding desperate. Not as desperate as him.

'We'll get him.' He couldn't manoeuvre the boat closer. It was too big; he risked her being sucked under the propeller. 'Grab the buoy. Now! I mean it, Nikki. Get back on the boat.'

She cast him a look that was half fearful, half angry—and grabbed the buoy.

He hauled her to the side in seconds. Reached down and pulled.

Tugging a grown woman from the sea was no easy task—he'd had guys go overboard before and he'd had to use a harness. Not Nikki. They said women could lift the weight of a car if their child was trapped underneath—that was what this felt like. He lifted her straight up, clinging to the lifebuoy, and he didn't even feel her weight.

He felt nothing until she was on the deck, all of her, whole, fine, safe.

'Horse…' For a nanosecond she clung but she was already pulling away, swivelling to search. 'Horse…'

She was in love already, he thought. She loved the great mangy mutt who was swimming steadily to the horizon.

How…?

'We use the lifeboat,' he snapped. 'There's no way he'll cling to a lifebuoy and we won't be able to grab and lift him from this height. I'm gunning the boat to cut him off. Get up on top of the wheelhouse, haul the ties off and slide the lifeboat down to the foredeck. Go!'

He was back at the wheel, hauling the boat round so he was heading out past Horse. Veering round him in a wide arc. Heading to a spot between the dog and where the speedboat had headed.

So Horse would be forced to swim past.

The sick feeling in his gut was growing with every moment. He knew the odds. He'd seen sharks here before. Often. Please…

At least Nikki was safe.

She wouldn't thank him if he didn't get the stupid dog.

Only the dog wasn't stupid, he conceded, as he manoeuvred the boat into position and hit the winch controlling the anchor. The dog was crazily devoted, still loyal to the low-life who'd abandoned him. He was somehow associating the speedboat, the thrill-riding idiots, with his previous owner. He was desperate to find those he'd given his heart to.

Giving your heart… It was the way to destroy yourself.

The lifeboat slipped down over the glass in front of him onto the deck. Nikki clambered down after, water streaming from her soaked clothes, her dripping hair. She seemed almost calm, carefully, sensibly, avoiding blocking his view as she clambered down. She steadied the life-raft on the deck and started unhooking the cleats of the metal stays that formed the side rails.

Woman with sense. Woman who'd just jumped into the midst of a seal colony. Where White Pointers fed…

Any minute…any minute…

He had the boat in position. The dog was swimming towards them now, starting to veer because the *Lady Nell* was in his path.

Drop the anchor.

The anchor struck and held. But it wasn't deep enough for safety; the waves were short and sharp and threatening to break.

'Nikki,' he yelled. 'Come here!'

She cast him a fearful glance, not wanting to let go of the life-raft.

'Here!' he yelled in a voice that matched her dog training voice, and she abandoned the life-raft and headed to the wheel.

'Anchor chain,' he snapped, pointing to the lever that attached to the control. 'Gears. Throttle. Watch the sea.'

'I'm going after…'

'You don't know how to manage the motor on the life-raft and you don't have the strength to haul a dog up. You watch the sea. Every moment. Not me. Not the dog. The sea. I mean it, Nikki, all our lives depend on it. Watch from the east. You see any big sea coming, anything at all, you haul the chain up, wait five seconds, no longer, just so the anchor's clear, then shove her into first gear like this, and turn her nose into the wave. You take action before you need to. Any suspicion of a decent wave, you turn her. Ride the wave, then drop back into neutral, drop the anchor again.'

'Should I just keep her in first gear?'

'No.' Because she couldn't watch the depth sounder, watch the dog, watch the sea all at once, and he didn't want to end up on the rocks. Lowering and raising the anchor was the best way to keep her in position. But he didn't have time to say it. He was already out on deck, lowering the life-raft and slipping down into it.

* * *

She saw him slip over the side and then she turned to watch the sea. The waves were coming from the far side of the *Lady Nell* to where Gabe was steering the little boat towards Horse.

Watch the sea. Do not watch Gabe.

She could just glance. Tiny glances in between fierce concentration. A wave was building; she saw the swell further out.

Up with the anchor, into first gear, nose into the wave.

Up and over.

The sea calmed again. Neutral. Drop the anchor.

Another glance.

He was almost there, almost to Horse. The swells were pushing Horse inshore; he was almost to the reef. Gabe was manoeuvring at the back of waves that were threatening to flip his tiny craft.

Watch the sea.

Gabe. Horse.

She'd forgotten to breathe.

The seals had disappeared. Dear God, the seals were gone.

He knew what that meant.

He was closing in on Horse but the dog was veering away, sensing that Gabe was intent on stopping him.

'Horse!' He cut the motor so it hardly purred, keeping just enough revs to hold the little craft on course. He was calling in a voice he was struggling to keep calm. 'Come on, boy.'

The dog veered sharply away.

A wave hit broadside. Gabe did a one-eighty, the wave almost tipped—and boat and dog collided.

He had his hand under the dog's collar before they were down the other side of the wave; before Horse could realise what was happening.

Now pull.

The life-raft was soft sided, industrial strength rubber. If Horse fought… He could tear the craft apart.

Where were the seals? What was happening under the surface?

Don't think. Just do.

He grabbed the collar with both hands, leaned backward so that if the dog came he'd end up full length on the floor rather than lurching out of the other side.

Pulled with all his strength.

The dog hauled back. Fought him.

Where were the seals?

He flicked a glance sideways. Nothing. Calm water. Not a seal.

'Come,' he yelled, and he roared the word, a deep, harsh yell that sounded out over the reef to the land beyond. It startled the dog into stillness.

He had an instant only. He hauled as he'd never hauled before.

And the dog came, lurching up and sliding in, toppling over the top of him so he was lying full length in the back of the life-raft with a mass of quivering, sodden dog on top of him.

He had him. He was in the boat!

Look back to the sea, Nikki told herself. Concentrate on the sea.

She sniffed.

Stupid salt water. How did it get to be streaming down her face when she was in the wheelhouse?

It wasn't over yet.

Luckily, once Gabe had him, Horse ceased to struggle. Maybe it was because the speedboat was out of sight and he knew it wasn't worth it. Or maybe it was because Gabe's hand on his collar was implacable.

'You want to be shark meat? You want me to have to explain that to Nikki?'

Maybe the dog understood. Maybe he didn't. Either way, he submitted as Gabe reached the *Lady Nell*, roped the dinghy to the side, tried to figure how to get him up.

Figured he couldn't. Not here.

Nikki was still watching the sea. He'd half expected her to emerge from the wheelhouse as he approached but she had the sense to stay where she was.

She was, it seemed, calm in a crisis. Apart from jumping into shark-infested water.

'Anchor up, into first gear, nose her out into deep water. Head straight into the waves rather than broadside,' he yelled. 'Slow and steady, because we're tied to the side.'

And she did it, amazingly well for a landlubber, nosing the big boat carefully out, heading into the swells, changing course so no waves caught her broadside, which might have risked jerking the lifeboat, tossing him and Horse into the sea.

Still he saw no seals. He knew what that meant.

There was no use telling Nikki that, though. She had enough to think about.

And finally they were out past the sharp inshore swells, to where the sea flattened into long, low rolls.

'Enough?' she yelled.

'Great. Anchor and help me.' He couldn't climb aboard to get what he needed, because he didn't trust Horse not to lurch over the side again and head for the horizon.

But Nikki was there, following instructions. He roped Horse, looping stays under his midriff, rear and aft, tying his collar, using rope work to fashion a sling.

Once secured, he swung himself up on board the *Lady Nell*, hooked the sling to the cray-pot winch, put the gears into motion.

Instead of a cray-pot being hauled up, a dog.

Nikki caught Horse's head as he reached the top, he looped his arms around the dog's back legs and they hauled him over the side, kneeling, tugging backwards, ending up a tangle of man, woman, dog and sea water.

And laughter. Nikki was laughing. Crying a little too, but hugging her dog as if he was the most wonderful thing she'd ever seen.

And then, because they were lying flat on the deck, side by side, under the dog, she was suddenly hugging him. Tight.

'Oh, Gabe…thank you. You were wonderful. Just wonderful.'

She turned, just a little so she could see him, but he moved at the same time, not intentionally, he'd swear, but it didn't matter because they were nose to nose.

She was holding him, her eyes were inches from his, her mouth was just…there…

He kissed her. Of course he kissed her; a man would have to be inhuman not to.

She was streaming sea water. Her curls were dripping and wild. She looked like a drowned rat, only of course it was a ridiculous analogy because her eyes were huge and glowing, and her mouth was soft and full, and…and…

His mouth met hers and the world stilled.

She was cold and shivery and shocked.

She was warm and yielding and wonderful.

She'd been laughing, and for a moment the kiss was an extension of that laughter. An extension of the joy. He felt it blaze between them—shared triumph, awe of what they'd achieved, an extension of drama, shock, fear.

But only for a moment because, as his mouth met hers, things changed. Dissolved. Turned to something else entirely in the power of the link between them.

Heat.

It was like an electric current jolting between them, forging a link, surging with a power so great it threatened to overwhelm him. Her lips were full and tender and yielding, and they felt as if they were melting to him, fire to fire, merging to be part of him, a part he hadn't known was missing until this moment. A part of his whole.

She'd turned to hug him and her arms were around him, holding him close. They were lying almost full length on the deck. Horse was draped over their legs, soaking them. The boat was riding up and down at anchor and all he could feel, all he could sense, all he could focus on, was her lips.

Her mouth.

Nikki.

His arms came around her, tugging her to him as naturally as joining two pieces of a puzzle, setting two pieces where they belonged and feeling the rightness of it.

She was wearing a light sweater. The fabric seemed to have almost disappeared in the wet; he could feel the wonder of her body underneath, the soft, luscious contours of her breasts, the way her body yielded, melted, crushed against him.

Against his sou'wester. Against his fishing gear. He was holding a woman who wore almost nothing and he was dressed for wet weather. He hardly noticed except he wanted her closer, closer and his clothes were getting in the way.

Her mouth…

Nikki.

He'd never felt like this. He'd never known he could feel like this. He had everything he wanted in his life right here, right now.

Stupid? Maybe it was, but there was no way he was going to think that; there was no way he was thinking anything while she was kissing him.

Her hands were in his hair, tugging him closer, deepening the kiss. She wanted this as much as he did. It was as if a key deep within had been turned, releasing emotion he hardly knew he'd locked away. He let himself kiss, he let himself be kissed, and a well of bitterness was unleashed, flowed outward, away and disappeared into the warm salt spray over the ocean.

Nikki…

And then Horse barked.

The dog had been lying limp over their legs, a dead weight neither of them noticed, but when a dog Horse's size barked from your knees and stood and headed for the side again it was time to stop kissing and pay attention.

No matter how much it hurt. No matter that it was a wrench that almost tore him apart.

But he moved. He caught Horse's collar and held. Horse was still attached to the harness but he wasn't taking any chances. Nikki tried to help. She looked as if she was struggling back from somewhere she hadn't known existed. Her eyes held wonder.

Wonder for both of them?

Horse barked again and hauled to the side. Then whined. Gabe tugged him back and looked to see what Horse was barking at.

Something floated to the surface in a pool of crimson.

A seal. Sliced neatly, horribly, in half.

There was a flash of streamlined silver and the thing was gone, hauled down, out of sight, with only the pool of blood remaining.

Nikki's face lost all its colour. He grabbed her as well as Horse, scared she'd faint. He hadn't put the side lines back up; there was no way he was risking her falling.

He had the dog in one hand. His other arm was

holding Nikki while she stared in appalled fascination at the disappearing streaks of blood.

'What...what...?' She choked on the words as if she was having trouble breathing. 'It was a seal. What...?'

'A White Pointer,' he said grimly, holding her fast. Trying not to think how close they'd come.

'A White...'

'Sharks,' he said. 'This is seal territory and sharks eat seals.'

'I could have... Horse...'

'That's why I was yelling,' he told her. It was no use lying. She lived here now. If she told anyone about Horse's escapade she'd be told about the sharks. 'Any injured seal is fair game. Sharks sense them by thrashing. Seals are sleek in the water. You guys were asking for trouble.' He motioned to the bloodstained water. 'The shark will be here because of you. He'll have circled for a bit, watched, and then I hauled his supper out of reach. So the seal was the alternative.'

'Oh...' she gasped, and choked back a sob of pure terror, then tugged away from him and stared at him in horror. 'You let me jump over the side.'

'I hardly...'

'You could have yelled "Shark".' *She* was yelling.

'You might have drowned with fright.'

'You could have...'

'What? Yell *Shark*, but nice harmless shark with no teeth? Pat-a-shark territory. Oh, but get out anyway because you might be allergic.'

She choked on something that was half laughter, half shock, then stared again down to where the streaks of blood were now dissipating, leaving a faint crimson tinge to the sea. She shuddered.

Horse whined again and she held him close, and Gabe thought, *Why not me? If you want comfort, why not me?*

It was a dumb thought. *Back away*, he told himself. *You've kissed her, do you want to take this further?*

Yes.

That was another dumb thought, but it was there and it wasn't going away.

Clothes. Practical stuff. Any minute she'd figure she was freezing and, as if the thought was relayed, she shuddered again.

'There's dry stuff in the locker below,' he said, and his voice came out gruffer than he intended. 'It might not be what you're used to...'

She rose. Wiped her wet hands on her tight wet jeans. Made a visible effort to pull herself together. 'Dry?'

'There's towels, overalls, sweaters, boots. We're used to wet. One size fits most. Or actually one size doesn't fit anyone—spares are huge; you roll 'em up, tuck 'em in, do what you can. Best I can do, I'm afraid.'

'The best you can do is awesome,' she whispered. 'I'm sorry I yelled.'

'You had a fright.'

'So did we all. And I'm still sorry I yelled. I never meant... I would never mean...'

She ran out of things to say. Instead, she reached for him, took his hands in hers, kissed him again, lightly on the lips, a feather-touch. And then she was gone, slipping below, leaving him with one sodden dog who was looking as confused as he felt.

Chapter 8

The trip home was made in near silence. Too much had happened. Too much was happening.

Nikki towelled Horse and cuddled him while Gabe stayed in the wheelhouse. He needed to stay in the wheelhouse. The fact that he wanted to be on the deck with them was irrelevant. More than irrelevant. There were things going on that needed careful thought.

When your foundations shifted, you didn't race to build again. You waited to see if your foundations shifted some more.

That was how he felt, he decided, as he headed back to harbour. As if the solid ground had been pulled from under him.

He didn't know where to take this. He didn't know… anything.

Horse, at least, had settled. He draped himself over

Nikki, he whined occasionally but he'd stopped looking at the horizon.

By the time they reached port he was dry and starting to scratch.

Gabe steered the *Lady Nell* back into her berth. Crew members usually stepped onto the jetty, attached stays to bollards, helped.

Nikki didn't know what crew members were supposed to do. She stayed where she was, under Horse.

Gabe could manage. He'd taken the boat out by himself a thousand times. He'd taken his boat out with crew a lot more.

Taking it out, even with a crew, seemed lonely compared with what he'd had today.

Woman and dog.

Remember Lisbette, he told himself harshly. The one time he'd let himself believe, he'd come close to losing his livelihood.

He'd been lucky. Then it had just been Gabe who'd been affected. If it happened again...if he got into financial trouble now, the fishing industry of this town could well go under.

A man needed to keep his head.

Steer clear of women.

How could he do that now? Where were resolutions when you needed them?

He roped the last stay, tightened cleats, collected Nikki's wet gear from below.

Nikki struggled to rise from under Horse. He couldn't help himself. He gave her a hand and tugged her to her feet.

Mistake. She was too close.

His hand didn't release hers.

Horse scratched. Distraction. Good.

He managed to get his hand back.

'He's spent too much time in salt water,' he said, deciding he had to concentrate on the practical. 'All that sponging I did last night has been undone. He'll scratch himself sore with the salt. There's shampoo you can buy at the Co-op. Ask Marcia. She'll tell you. Tell her I sent you or she'll sell you the expensive stuff.'

'Thank you,' she said. 'Gabe...'

'Yes?' He turned away, tugged up the hatch, showing by his actions that he was moving on.

He was thinking he should go home and help her bathe the dog.

He had crays to deal with. A man had to be sensible.

Dog. Shampoo. Bath. His thoughts were no longer sensible in the least.

Nikki.

He had to give himself time to get his head in order.

Stay clear.

Nikki was a smart woman, he told himself harshly, and Horse was docile. She could bathe the dog.

Her bath was big enough. But the thoughts wouldn't be vanquished. Dog. Shampoo. Bath. He had a clear vision of them in her bathroom, in the vast old tub, soap everywhere...

Um...no.

'You were wonderful,' she said.

'And you weren't shark meat,' he retorted, not turning back. Determined on being sensible. 'Excellent.'

'It is excellent,' she said. 'For all sorts of reasons. Come on Horse, we're going home.'

And Nikki and Horse stepped from the boat onto the wharf without him even helping. They walked away.

He concentrated on the crays.

He didn't watch their going, but it took real effort.

Nikki and Horse walked slowly home around the headland, following the cliff path so they wouldn't necessarily see anyone. She had some pride, and the oversized overalls and huge fisherman's Guernsey weren't exactly elegant.

Nor was her dog.

'We match,' she told him. Horse was plodding wearily beside her. She should never have taken him on the boat. He should have slept today.

He should be sleeping now.

He looked desolate, big and ragged and defeated. It wasn't his health, she thought. It was his heart. He'd leaped into the water to follow what he thought was someone who loved him.

They were on the dirt track in the middle of bushland leading back to the house. No one was around. She squatted and hugged him.

'It's okay,' she told him, burying her face in his salt-encrusted coat. 'You can move on. It's possible.'

Like she was moving on? By kissing Gabe instead of kissing Jonathan?

'I didn't actually do it to distract me from feeling bad about Jonathan,' she told Horse, who didn't understand at all. 'But it did distract me.'

It certainly had. She sat and hugged her dog, the sun shone on her face and she thought…she thought…

Life was full of possibilities. Exciting possibilities.

Possibilities that looked pretty much like Gabe Carver.

She'd thought she was alone, but she wasn't quite. A couple of elderly walkers strode round the bend and she had to shift so they could pass. They were stocky, sensible women with hiking poles, walking with intent.

They reached her and stopped.

Two days ago she might have cringed. Woman pulled from sea, dressed in fisherman's clothes, hugging a scraggy dog. This was pretty much as far from her life in Sydney as she could get.

'Are you all right?' one of the women asked, and she even managed a smile.

'My dog's a bit subdued,' she said. 'We're having a wee rest.'

'That's not one of Henrietta's dogs?' the woman demanded, staring down at Horse. 'I remember him. I saw the accident when the dogs escaped. This one just bolted. Terrified. And you'll be the lady living with Gabe Carver. I saw Hen at the post office this morning and she said you're keeping him. Oh, my dear…'

'I'm not looking after him very well,' Nikki admitted. The sun was warm on her face. Horse was settling. She was prepared to be expansive.

The world felt expansive, she decided. Plus the way the lady had said it… *You'll be the lady living with Gabe Carver.* It gave her a local identity, something she hadn't had until now. She wasn't sure why, but she liked it. Maybe it was sexist. Maybe it was stupid. Whatever, but she still liked it. 'Gabe took us out on his boat this morning and we fell in.'

'You fell in?'

'Gabe took you out on his boat?'

Both women looked at her, then looked back at each other. Stunned.

'I went to help with the cray-pots,' Nikki said, the odd happy feeling not fading. 'But we were worse than useless. We caught some crays. Then Horse dived in and it was all downhill from there.'

'Horse?'

'My dog.'

My dog. That sounded good, too. It sounded great. There were things happening inside her that felt delicious.

She hadn't planned on staying out today. She should be rushing home now to finish her engineering plans. But instead she was sitting in the middle of a walking trail discussing her very exciting morning with a couple of strangers.

Discussing Gabe?

'That's his sweater,' one lady said and Nikki glanced down at the oversized Guernsey and giggled. Being caught in Gabe's sweater felt good, too.

'He had spare clothes,' she said and grinned. 'I didn't pinch his.'

'Oh, my dear…'

'Where's Gabe now?' the first lady asked.

'Unloading his crays. I'm going home to bathe Horse. He's itchy.' She hesitated. 'Though I'm not sure how. I could use my bath but I don't trust the plumbing. And how would I lift him in?'

'Gabe might help,' the first lady ventured.

'Gabe?' the other said incredulously and they both made wry faces.

'Gabe might do it,' the lady explained as Nikki looked a question. 'But he'd do it at midnight when no one was looking. He's a very private person, our Gabe. He helps. But he helps when no one's looking.'

'That's not a lot of use to me,' Nikki said. Waiting for Gabe to bathe Horse at midnight? Maybe not. 'Don't worry. I'll manage.' She had to. This was her dog. She needed to be independent.

But he was so big!

'I'll tell you what,' the first lady said. 'You take the doggy home and let him have a sleep. He looks exhausted. Maudie and I will finish our walk, we'll fetch the right shampoo for an itchy coat and we'll drive my truck around and help. I have a big plastic tub; I'll bring that. I'm Hilda, by the way, and you must be Nikki. While we bathe your dog you can tell us all about yourself.'

Nikki considered. She should bathe Horse herself.

Or wait for Gabe?

The first might be impossible.

The second?

A girl had some pride. She'd kissed him. That didn't mean she depended on him.

She'd been dependent on a man for the last four years, she told herself. If she was to be independent, the time to start was now.

But Horse was enormous. Be sensible. She needed to accept help when it was offered.

If she was going to be a part of this community she might as well start now.

'Thank you,' she said. 'That would be lovely.'

She could be a little bit dependent, she decided. She just couldn't be dependent on Gabe.

A working bee was therefore following her home.

Horse headed for his trampoline, flopped and was asleep in seconds. Nikki showered, then tried to figure what to wear for dog bathing. Her one pair of jeans was sodden, everything else was classy and she didn't want to scare Maudie and Hilda with her city clothes. Finally she simply put Gabe's clothes back on. She felt ridiculous, but oooh, she was comfortable.

She stared at herself in the mirror. Fisherman Nikki.

Her hand reached automatically to the can of product designed to smooth her crazy curls. She flicked the power switch on her straightener—and then flicked it off.

She ran the hairdryer through her curls and they flew every which way. She looked at her reflection and she hardly recognised herself.

She grinned.

What next? She needed to stoke up for dog-washing.

She headed for the kitchen. Made herself a cheese sandwich. Considered. Made another. Sat on the doorstep in the sun and ate them. Thought about the sushi and black coffee she'd have eaten at her desk back in Sydney.

Hilda and Maudie were taking ages. While she waited, Horse slept.

She looked at the gap in the stone wall and it looked back at her.

It was Gabe's hole in the wall. Do not touch.

Find her own?

She had work to do. Air conditioning plans.

In Gabe's study, his books on dry stone walling…

Find your own.

She headed down to the pile of stones by the hole in the wall. Picked up stones, considered them, matched them, put them back on the pile. Gabe's hole in the fence remained just that.

Just practising. Just learning. Keeping an ear out for Gabe's truck so she could disappear fast.

There must be somewhere round here where she could get her own pile of stones.

Maybe there was someone to teach her.

Plans. Engineering. Her career.

The sun was too warm to think about plans.

She'd finish this set of plans, she told herself, and the next contracted job. But then…

She had enough money to be independent for quite a while. Her pay for the last few jobs had been enormous, and living in Jon's apartment had cost very little.

She'd been living Jon's life.

'This could be *my* life,' she said out loud.

Then she heard a 'Halloo' from along the road. Maudie and Hilda had arrived, bearing dog stuff.

'We're here to help,' Hilda called. 'I have the world's biggest ice-bucket as a bath. We have shampoo and conditioner and scissors and brushes and two hairdryers and six old towels. Do you think that should do it?'

'I hope so,' Nikki said and grinned. She felt as if she was stepping into a new life. Or maybe she'd stepped into it the moment she'd met Horse.

Or the moment she'd hit Gabe over the head?

There were people in his front yard. Lots of people. Seven? Eight? Ten?

They'd lit the barbecue.

When he'd asked Dorothy in the rental agency about setting this place up, she'd included a barbecue on her list.

'Put in a barbecue where your tenant can cook and see the sea. It'll almost double the rent.'

Up until now it hadn't been lit.

It was lit now. He climbed out of the truck and the smell of sausages and onions hit him like a siren song.

'Gabe!' It was Henrietta from the Animal Shelter, waving a bread-wrapped sausage. Henrietta's son was on barbecue duty. He recognised Hilda and Maudie, founding members of the town's stalwart walking group, deep in conversation with Joe, his own personal handyman.

Joe's springer spaniels were checking out Horse. Horse was snoozing on his trampoline which had obviously been brought outside so he could catch some late afternoon sun.

Nikki was deep in conversation with a lady older than Methuselah.

Aggie, Henrietta's mother. What the…?

'Nikki needed help bathing Horse,' Henrietta called, her voice filled with reproach. 'Where have you been?'

'I took a load of crays to Whale Cove.'

'Nikki needed help.'

'He's Nikki's dog,' he said shortly. *What was Aggie doing here?*

'It doesn't matter. We got on fine without you.' Nikki smiled and waved and he was hit by a blast of...difference.

She was still in his clothes. They were way too big for her. He'd thought until today that her hair was straight. Her hair was currently a riot. Curls everywhere.

She was sitting on the grass beside Horse. The springer spaniels were at her feet, nosing Horse, who was interested but he wasn't getting off his trampoline.

Someone had carried a chair outside for Aggie. She was about a hundred. Best guess. She'd been about a hundred ever since he could remember.

What was she doing here?

'Tell us what you think of Horse,' Henrietta demanded. 'Horse, show Uncle Gabe what you look like.'

Uncle Gabe? He had people in his backyard. He was starting to feel...

Horse stood up. It was a bit of a struggle but he managed it. His great tail wagged and something inside Gabe...

No. Don't go there. That ended with Jem.

He tried to look—dispassionately.

Horse had been worked on. Bathed. Combed. Anointed. The remnants of his coat were gleaming, knots cut or teased out, then brushed until it shone.

He wobbled a little on his long legs but his crazy tail wagged, the feathering underneath waving wildly. He looked almost beautiful. He looked…almost happy.

He flopped back down on his belly. He gazed up at Gabe and his tail still waved.

So much for dispassionate. He was a sucker for dogs.

And after all, he told himself, this was Nikki's dog. Gabe could bend and scratch him behind the ears without committing himself to anyone. To anything.

But what was Aggie doing here? And all these people…

No one messed with his privacy.

Renting out part of his house had been a bad idea.

'You approve?' Nikki asked and he could tell she was anxious. She was kneeling beside Horse. Because he'd stooped to pat Horse, he was close.

Really close.

'He looks great.'

'Doesn't he?' She beamed. 'I know it looks like we've done a lot to a dog who needs to rest, but he just lay in the sun and we worked on him slowly.'

'We?'

'Hilda and Maudie.'

'And Henrietta and Joe and…and Aggie?'

'They came later, didn't you, guys?' She beamed round at all of them. 'Hilda met Joe at the Co-op and told him what we were doing. She suggested a barbecue so Joe got it working. There were spiders. Big ones. Even Hilda and Maudie suggested we needed Joe. And look at Horse.'

He was looking at Horse. It was safer, he decided, to look at Horse rather than Nikki.

'What do you think?'

Horse had draped himself back over his trampoline, three quarters on but a quarter out, as if he'd like to join in but he still needed the security of his own place.

The trampoline Henrietta had supplied was plain canvas, what a sensible dog needed, but someone—*someones* by the look of the people around him—had decreed plain wasn't enough. A soft green velveteen throw had been added. Also a couple of pillows that looked as if they were down-filled, soft and squishy. Two stuffed toys, a rabbit and a giraffe.

There was a sausage resting by Horse's nose, and a new red water bowl.

Horse looked bemused. As if he didn't have a clue what was happening to his life.

Like Gabe.

These people were barbecuing in his backyard.

Or… Nikki's backyard.

He'd strung a couple of wires on fencing posts when he'd first let the place, delineating boundaries, but until now no one had needed delineation. No one had been in the backyard.

He should have planted a hedge. Fast growing.

He still could.

Nikki was smiling up at him, standing, offering him a sausage, glowing, and he thought yep, hedge. Or back away fast. But…

'Why is Aggie here?' he asked.

Maudie handed him a beer. Aggie passed him a bowl of pretzels.

'Aggie's teaching me to make stone walls,' Nikki said and he almost dropped both.

Maybe his face froze. How did you control your face? He didn't know what he was showing but, whatever it was, it made Nikki's smile slip.

'What is it?'

'What are you playing at?'

'Sorry?' She didn't have a clue what he was talking about. Or did she? She'd seen the books. She knew about his mother.

'I taught his mother to make stone fences,' Aggie said sedately from her chair. The little old lady was wrinkled and gnarled and unfussed, unmoving. Watching Gabe thoughtfully. Watching Nikki. 'Best student I ever had. Last, too. After her, no one. No one wants to spend their days piecing little bits of stone together. Why would they?' Her voice grew sad, distant. 'They're all falling down, my walls. The walls Gabe's mama helped me build. They're built to last for generations but people knock holes in them. They use the capping stones for wedging gates open, that sort of thing. They break 'em and don't know how to repair them. Can't believe you want to learn.'

'You don't want to learn,' Gabe said flatly.

'Why not?' Nikki demanded. 'Why don't I?'

The question hung. They'd all turned to listen now, every one of them caught by the flat anger in Gabe's voice. He couldn't help it. Anger was just…there.

'I don't want my wall finished,' he growled, knowing as he said it that it made no sense at all.

'I know that,' Nikki said. 'I even understand it. Sort of. But this is nothing to do with you, or your mum, or your wall. I'm sorry I borrowed your books without asking, but you have them back now and that's as far as my interference with you goes. I told Henrietta I was bored with what I was doing, that I needed a break while I thought about what I wanted to do. I told her I'd been playing…' She hesitated and then decided to be truthful. 'I'd been playing with your stones. It feels good. I'd like to try it, as a hobby at least. I told Hen and she went to get Aggie, and Aggie says she'll teach me.'

'I don't want you to.'

The flat denial didn't even sound like him. The words were from some gut level he couldn't begin to understand. And, of course, Nikki couldn't understand either.

'It has nothing to do with you,' she retorted, sounding astounded. 'I'm your tenant, Gabe. If I go out in the morning and learn how to make stone walls instead of sitting inside drawing plans, how can that be interfering with you? Or don't you want anyone to learn stone walling ever again because of your mother?'

There was no answer to that. No answer at all. She was right; he was being stupid.

He'd seen stone wallers working since his mother died; of course he had. There were none working locally, but occasionally he'd see them by the roadside outside this area. He liked their quiet craft, was glad that stone walls were still being built.

It was just… Nikki. It was how she made him feel.

He should never have let her kiss him. He should never have kissed her.

He thought of Nikki, in the water where he knew sharks fed. Nikki, on the night she'd hit him, staring down at him with her eyes full of terror. Nikki, hugging this bedraggled, unloved dog, jumping into the water to save him, bringing this motley collection of people back to his house. To his home.

'I have things to do,' he said curtly, knowing he was being a bore, not knowing what to do about it. Setting his beer and plate aside.

Horse whined.

'You're going to cook your own dinner on your side of the wire?' Nikki demanded with a flash of anger.

He'd hurt her. He'd hurt them all.

But what Nikki did on her side of the fence was her business. He should have climbed straight out of the truck and gone inside, closing the door behind him. Instead…they were all looking at him. Judging him.

'Our Gabe's a loner,' Hen said placatingly to Nikki, as if she was explaining the behaviour of a difficult dog. 'This is his space.'

'He's renting it to me,' Nikki said dangerously. 'I pay for this side of the boundary wire. If he'd wanted me to stay inside with the door shut, he should have written a different tenancy agreement. Gabe, these people helped me this afternoon. They're my friends. They're Horse's friends. So we will keep on with our barbecue. As I'll continue with learning how to make stone walls. This isn't about you, Gabe. This is my back lawn—my barbecue. You can accept my invitation to join us, in which case you'll be pleasant and not treat us as intruders, or you can head inside and keep your own company. Your choice.'

His choice. He made it.

He turned, stepped over the dividing fence and went inside.

* * *

She was shaking. Of all the boorish, rude, arrogant…

'Don't mind him, dear,' Aggie said comfortably. 'His dad brought him up hard and a leopard can't change his spots. Till his dad died, any kid who came here risked being horse-whipped and Gabe too, for inviting them. There's ghosts in that man's head and, like it or not, you've brought 'em out. Now, are you going to eat that sausage or not? Dry stone walling's not for sissies. If you're starting tomorrow you need to get your strength up. Don't mind Gabe; he's a good man at heart, even if he never let us close. You just stay on your side of the fence and let him be.'

Midnight. She'd gone to sleep and dreamed of sharks. And Gabe.

Horse was snoring under her bed. He grunted in his sleep and suddenly she was wide awake, staring at the ceiling.

Thinking of sharks—and Gabe.

She put her hand down and Horse nuzzled her palm. She liked it. Something warm and solid in the night.

Go back to sleep.

The sharks were still there. And Gabe.

She padded out to the kitchen, made a pot of tea, hesitated, made a cheese sandwich.

Horse padded after her. She grinned and made two.

She thought about going back to bed. Went out on the veranda instead.

The stars were hanging low over the night sky. The moonlight was glinting over the ocean.

Horse whined and nuzzled her underarm. They ate sandwiches together and watched the distant sea.

Horse settled his great head under her arm, on her knee. He sighed a great dog sigh, and she agreed entirely.

Too hard. Everything.

Gabe?

She should still be thinking about Jonathan, she thought. Was she doomed to forget one appalling man, only to focus on another?

Then Horse stiffened, whined and pulled away. Her hand instinctively grabbed his collar but Horse was swivelling back towards the house. The door opened—the porch door leading to Gabe's side.

Gabe.

He could have guessed she'd be out here. He'd heard the wuffling and thought maybe she'd let Horse outside without her. He was worried about fences. How high could Horse jump?

She had him safe. The big dog was straining towards him but she had him by the collar and she wasn't letting go.

She was wearing pyjamas. Cute pyjamas. Ivory silk with pink embroidery.

Her hair was a mass of tumbled curls. She looked…

Like a man should back into the house and close the door.

'I'm out here,' she said. 'You should back into the house and close the door. Or make me another entrance so you don't need to see me.'

'Nikki…'

'I'm sorry about your mother,' she said before he

could get a word in. 'I'm sorry she died and left you alone. And about your dad, who sounds like he was a bully and a pig. But you rented this place to me. If I'm going to feel like it's home, I can't spend my time figuring whether you're likely to come through the door so you can avoid me. And,' she said, taking a breath, obviously gearing up to say something that took courage, 'you were rude to my friends. You need to apologise. Joe's sausages and onions were great.'

'Joe's not your friend,' he snapped before he could think about it. 'He works for me.'

'The two are mutually exclusive?'

'I don't want you in my life.'

Why had he said that? He had no right. He had no need. It was harsh, hurtful, unnecessary. He saw her flinch, then stand and back away. To her door.

'Gabe, what you're saying…it's nonsense.' She was starting to shake. 'You've never asked me to be in your life. I've never suggested…'

'You don't have to,' he said explosively. 'You just are. You stand there, looking at me… You make me feel…'

'How do I make you feel?'

'I don't want it. I don't do relationships. I don't want to feel—anything.'

'Then don't.'

'You're saying you don't sense it, too? This thing between us?'

'If I am, I'm keeping it under control a whole lot more than you are,' she said bluntly. 'You think I'm about to launch myself at you and dig in my claws? Of all the insulting…'

'I didn't say that.' He raked his hair. 'It doesn't make sense. What I'm feeling.'

'It doesn't,' she said, and somehow she managed to sound calm. 'I'm not Lisbette, Gabe.'

'I know that.'

'And I'm not interested in another relationship,' she added and she thought… Was that a lie? Because the way she felt…

She didn't understand the way she felt. Gabe was voicing his confusion. Hers…she'd managed to keep it internal. Anger was a great help.

But… *This thing between us...*

Gabe was right. It was there, tangible, real. It had to be ignored.

This big man was wounded, needy, wonderful. She wanted to reach out and touch him. Heal him. Heal herself in the process.

He didn't want it. She couldn't.

'You want me to find somewhere else to live?'

What was wrong with him? Was he nuts?

The town thought he was nuts.

No. They thought he was a loner.

There was a fine line between loner and nuts, he decided, and the way Nikki was looking at him… He'd just stepped over it.

'I'm sorry,' he said heavily. 'I'm behaving like an oaf.'

'You are.'

'There's no need to agree!' He wasn't making sense, even to himself.

'Yes, there is.' She sounded wary. But also…amazingly, she sounded amused. 'You kissed me, but so what? The way you're acting… Why? There's no need to think I'm planning weddings, kids, holes from your side of the house to my side, mortgages, puppies and old age homes with rockers side by side.'

'Old age homes?' he said faintly.

'That's how you're looking. Like a man faced with the whole domestic catastrophe. It was a barbecue. Eight people, including you, plus three dogs. On my side of the dividing line. You want to go out tomorrow and buy some twelve foot high screening?'

'I said I was sorry.'

'You still look like you expect me to jump you.'

'I don't.'

'It was just a kiss. I was scared. People do stupid things when they're scared. I won't go swimming with sharks again and I won't go out on your boat.'

'I won't ask you to.'

'Aren't you the gentleman?' She hauled open the door to her side of the house. 'I'm going back to bed. Do you have anything else to say? If so, say it now. I paid three months in advance. You want to give me notice to vacate? That'll be nine weeks where we need to coordinate using this porch so you won't have to look at me. And,' she said savagely, as if this was the final straw, 'I won't even demand that you fix the pipes.'

'The pipes?'

'They still make noises.'

'Talk to...'

Joe. I know. I have. Because there's no way I'd ask my landlord to take a personal interest. There's no way he would.'

'There's no need...'

'There's not, is there? Tell me in the morning whether

you want me to vacate. Meanwhile, I'm going to bed. I'm taking my dog with me. I'll lock my door after me and stay on my side of the wall… Oh, and Gabe…'

He was way out of line. He was being an oaf and there didn't seem to be a thing he could do about it. Even Horse was clinging to Nikki's side, as if he knew who his friend was.

'Yes?' He couldn't even find the words to apologise again. He was appalled at his own behaviour.

'I *am* learning to make stone walls,' she said. 'Aggie's teaching me, starting tomorrow. We're working on restoring a wall out the back of Black Mountain, so if the idea offends you you'd better steer clear.'

'I'll be at sea tomorrow.'

'Hooray,' she said. 'You can head for the horizon and never think about us again. Come on, Horse, it looks like our peace in the moonlight is over.'

She walked inside with as much dignity as she could muster. Horse sidled in with her.

She stood with her back to the door and she shook.

Horse was shaking, too.

She was scaring the baby.

With something between a sob and a laugh, she knelt and hugged the big dog. He licked her face.

Ugh. It was as close as a girl could come to having a shower. A warm shower.

The urge to sob subsided. She sank so she was sitting on the floor with Horse draped over her.

They both stopped shaking.

She'd managed to make her escape with dignity, but it had been a near thing.

'He's just a bore,' she told Horse. 'He's a guy who's been brought up with no manners. A woman-hating, dog-fearing hermit.'

His crew liked him. Joe liked him. The town made excuses for him and they wouldn't do that if he wasn't a good man at heart.

Was it just her?

Was he reacting that way because she'd kissed him?

'I can't take it back,' she told Horse. 'I don't even want to.'

Drat him—he had her thoroughly confused. And Nikki was a girl who didn't like being confused.

'I'm straightening my hair again tomorrow,' she told Horse, but he didn't seem impressed. She wasn't sure if she was either.

'But I *am* going to learn dry stone walling. It'll be a great job for a dog to come along and help. You want to do that?'

She got another lick for her pains. Grinned. Pushed herself to her feet and headed back to bed.

'Coming?'

Horse looked at her. Looked at the door. Whined.

Was he wanting the beach? Or Gabe?

Gabe or beach?

'Neither,' she said, tugging Horse to her bedroom with her. 'If it's your low-life owner, get over it, your future's with me. And if it's Gabe...exactly the same.'

He felt about two inches high. Justifiably. What had she done to deserve the lambasting he'd given her?

She'd borrowed his books? She was trying to learn how to make a stone wall?

She'd twisted his heart.

There was the problem. Heart-twisting. It made him feel as if he was wide open, vulnerable to a woman. Vulnerable to Nikki.

He'd been nuts to ever rent the apartment out.

But if he'd met Nikki any other way he'd have felt the same, he thought. It wasn't that she was living next door. It wasn't that she was dragging him into her life. It was just that she was… Nikki.

A man'd be mad not to want her.

He wanted her.

It was a hunger so fierce it made him feel his world was no longer stable.

He'd get it stable again, he thought. Maybe he already had. Even if he was to let weakness prevail, after tonight he'd burned his bridges. The way she'd looked at him…

He deserved nothing less.

Maybe it was just as well.

The fleet would be in at dawn. He'd help sort the catch and he'd be out again. Deep sea fishing, he decided. Out for four or five days.

He could rotate the crews so he could be out for weeks.

Great.

Or not great.

Nikki was just through the door. He'd hurt her.

So knock and apologise?

He'd already done that. Not one of his finest moments.

He had to do something. He couldn't just leave.

That was exactly what he intended.

* * *

She heard his alarm through the wall. Five a.m.

Horse whined and hauled himself up beside her. Her bed was ridiculously small. What sort of masochistic streak had made her buy a single bed? No matter, she wasn't pushing her new pet off.

'Gabe's going fishing,' she told him. 'It's just as well. He's…unsettling.'

Unsettling or not, when she heard his truck disappear she felt…she felt…

Like she had when Jonathan left—but worse.

She hadn't needed Jonathan.

She didn't need Gabe.

Liar.

How can you need him? she demanded of herself. You don't know him.

But she did. It was like…meeting a part of her that had been missing.

They were alike, she thought. Hers had been a barren childhood. Gabe's had been worse but something in him resonated with her, touched her at a level she couldn't begin to explain.

Nonsense. Sentimental garbage.

But then she heard his truck return. Footsteps. A heavy thump on the porch. Her heart twisted.

Nonsense or not, if he knocked…

He didn't. Receding footsteps. The truck's engine restarting. He was gone again.

Horse headed for the door, barking, sounding excited. She hopped out of bed and opened the door with caution.

An ice tub was on her back step.

Crayfish, prawns, mud-crabs, oysters, mussels were arranged to perfection on a massive tub of ice. A bottle of champagne was wedged on the side.

She recognised the champagne label and gasped. Even Jonathan would have been impressed.

A note:

> Apologies. I'm not used to being social. Make yourself at home. I don't even mind if you go onto my side of the fence. Take care of Horse. Give him an oyster or six.

The ice tub was lavish. She should be touched by such a gift. She should at least smile at his note.

Instead? Desolation.

Expensive food. Champagne. Things.

Jonathan used to give her gifts when he left her.

She wouldn't waste this. She'd share, and not just with Horse. She had friends now.

But she wouldn't share with Gabe. Gabe, who couldn't apologise in person.

Did she care?

'I'm a woman of independent means,' she said out loud to the world in general, but she didn't know what she meant.

Independence…

Horse nuzzled her leg.

She wasn't independent at all. Luckily, she had Horse, and he was a dog she could lean on.

'Want an oyster?' she asked. 'Because I don't.'

Chapter 9

A girl had to have a passion. If it couldn't be Gabe—and it couldn't—then the next best thing was stone walling, and at least there her passion was uncomplicated.

Quite simply, walling felt as if a lost piece of her had been reinstated. Sitting on the edge of a paddock, dirty, sometimes damp—Aggie paused for rain but not for showers—watching her wall grow, stone by stone, Nikki felt as if she'd found her home.

Aggie was a fine teacher, happy with nothing less than perfection. Her walls were built to withstand livestock, age and weather. Knowing she had a teacher who could give her those skills was a source of satisfaction Nikki couldn't begin to explain.

Aggie was content as well. 'If you knew how much it hurts to see walls I've built be damaged and no longer be fit enough to fix 'em… If you really love this, girl, it'd be my pleasure to teach you. And don't fret about an income. Farmers love these walls. They get the stones out of their paddocks, they get walls that'll last for a hundred years and they look great. It's win win. They even get grants for repair—they're heritage, you know. We can charge almost what we want to fix 'em and build more. If you're serious…'

There was no doubting she was serious. She worked and worked, and every minute she loved it more. Horse lay beside her as she worked. Dog paradise. Two weeks into lessons a rabbit stuck its nose from behind the fence. She'd tied Horse to Aggie's chair—even though they weren't in sight of the sea, she was taking no chances. But, 'Let him off,' Aggie said as Horse nearly went crazy on the end of his lead.

'Really?'

'Really.'

So she did and Horse spent the afternoon chasing rabbits, more rabbits and more rabbits still. He never came close to catching one, but every time one escaped he zoomed back to her, almost as if he needed to tell her about it. His big body practically vibrated with exhilaration.

She took him home that night as filthy and as happy as she was. She had a rabbit-chasing dog. She wanted to tell Gabe.

Gabe wasn't home. Again.

She'd barely seen him. He came home only to replenish supplies and leave again. Solitude was his life since his father had died; since the woman called Lisbette had screwed him for everything he had. She understood—but it still felt bad when she turned into the driveway and Gabe's truck wasn't there; when she flicked open the curtains before she went to bed and there was no light in his window.

She was being dumb. Needy. Adolescent, even. She shouldn't be twitching the curtain to see if he was at home. She shouldn't care.

She didn't.

What a lie.

He'd spent so long at sea he was starting to see fish in his dreams.

He loved his work. He took pride in his fleet, in the men and women who worked for him, in their skills and endurance. He also loved Banksia Bay. After Lisbette he'd left, swearing never to return, but he'd left his house, his boat, the two things he'd salvaged from Lisbette's financial raid. So maybe he'd never intended to let it go completely, and when the fleet was in trouble he'd been glad to come home.

The sea was the same.

But, in truth, the last few years had even seen him tire of the endless sea. As Jem had aged he'd spent more time on land, reading in front of the fire, taking the old dog for gentle walks around the cliffs, cooking. Settling.

When Jem had died he'd headed back to sea. It was the only place he knew how to…be.

A man knew where he was at sea. Especially if the work was hard.

So now he moved from crew to crew, ostensibly to spend time with each of his skippers, to work through problems with each of the boats, but in reality it was because when he was on board the crew worked harder, and he could work to match.

If he worked, then he slept. Mostly.

He couldn't stay at sea for ever.

How long until she grew tired of playing with stones and took herself back to Sydney?

How long before a man could put her out of his head?

She finished the tail ends of her contracted work—the last part of her life as an engineer. She needed to make one last trip to Sydney and that part of her life would be over. She could make it a day trip.

She didn't want to leave Horse with Henrietta. Even though Hen was lovely and her boarding kennels were great, Horse still shook when he saw her.

She'd like to leave him with Gabe.

Fat chance. Gabe was never at home.

'Leave him with me,' Aggie said diffidently. 'My cat won't like it but it's time he had a spot of excitement. And you needn't worry. The walls around my place would keep a herd of elephants in.'

So she left Horse with Aggie and drove to Sydney. She'd checked Jonathan wouldn't be in the office. She left her final work on his desk—and her letter of resignation.

She walked out feeling not one shred of regret.

She wanted to ring Gabe and tell him.

How dumb was that?

Instead, she headed to a specialist work-wear firm. She bought heavy duty overalls, leather gloves, sturdy boots, goggles and a bright yellow jacket so she could be seen if she was working by the roadside.

Bright yellow, like Gabe's sou'wester used to be before he wore it in.

Gabe.

Her thoughts shouldn't always turn to Gabe.

They just did.

There was nothing left to do in Sydney. She'd left at dawn, thinking she might need to spend time in the office, but her former colleagues were cool. She'd dumped more work on them. There was no suggestion of socialising. The work gear had taken all of half an hour to buy so she was back in Banksia Bay by three. At Aggie's, Horse greeted her with joy.

'He's been sitting by the door all day, pining for you,' Aggie said. 'I've been fearful to let him out. I had to let him chase the cat to cheer him up. Mind, that might be the last time I can take care of him—if you bring him back, my poor old cat might leave home for ever.'

Nikki grinned. She hugged her dog and loaded him back into her car, resolving to buy Aggie's cat some gourmet cat food. Thinking she wouldn't need to leave Horse again anyway. Who needed Sydney? What more could a woman want than what she had right now?

Gabe.

Stupid or not, she wanted Gabe.

And he was at home.

Aggie's normal working day was nine to five. It was barely four when Nikki turned into the drive and Gabe was on the veranda. She could tell by his face that he hadn't been expecting her.

Her heart…quivered?

This was nuts. She was behaving like a moonstruck adolescent. The tension between them was a construct that could and should be eliminated. Now.

'Hi,' she said, pretending cheeriness. Horse, however, didn't need to pretend. He headed up to the veranda, leaped to place his huge paws on Gabe's shoulders and Gabe only just managed not to fall.

Adolescent or not, she wouldn't mind putting her arms there either. Holding.

Stupid. She was a mature woman approaching her landlord. Her rude, hermit-of-a-landlord who wanted nothing to do with her. Or her dog.

He was hugging her dog.

She turned her back on the pair of them and started hauling stuff from the car. Carrier bags labelled 'Grey's Industrial Work Gear'. Cool stuff.

She lugged her bags up the porch steps. Gabe—and Horse—stood aside to let her pass.

'Work gear?' Gabe queried, and she flashed him a suspicious look. The way he'd said it…

'Get over it,' she said. 'You don't have a monopoly on wearing overalls.'

'You've bought overalls?'

'Four pairs. Serious stuff.'

'Aggie's still teaching you, then?'

'I imagine you've heard. Five days a week. I went back to Sydney today to drop final plans off and to resign. Then I went and bought overalls.'

'You've resigned?'

She sighed. 'Yes.'

'You can't be serious.'

'What on earth does it have to do with you?' she demanded. 'Just because your mother made stone walls, is that a reason no one else can?'

'Only you.'

Only you. The two words hung. She didn't know what they meant, but she did know they were important.

'What is it about me,' she said at last, 'that makes you think I can't be a stone waller?' *That makes you think I'm threatening?*

'Nothing.'

Horse had sunk to all fours and was nosing Nikki's packages. They were interesting. They were tools for her new life.

She was not going to let this man interfere with it.

Get it onto a normal plane, she told himself. Forget about…*this thing between us.* Move on.

'Come and see what we're doing,' she heard herself say, surprising herself by the dispassionate tone she managed. 'We're working behind Black Mountain on Eaglehawk Road. We'll be there tomorrow from about nine.'

'I'll be back at sea tomorrow.'

'Only if you want to be. You're the owner of the fleet. You can decide.'

'I can't make money unless I go to sea.'

'Maybe you have enough money,' she said gently. 'That's what I've decided. I've been doing a job that fills my head and my bank account, but not my heart. Horse and I are moving on.'

'I give you three months tops before you're bored.'

'How long did your mother build for?' she asked—and then regretted it. The look on his face…

He had demons, this man, and she didn't want to make them worse.

'You don't need to answer,' she said, softening. 'I had no right to ask. Don't come and see what Aggie and I are doing—I'm sure you're not interested and if it reminds you of things you'd rather forget then it's not worth the pain. Let me pass now, Gabe. I'll see you next time you're on shore.'

He stared at her for a long moment. His face was blank and still.

He wanted to say something, she thought, but he didn't know what. Or he didn't know how.

He was a big, silent man with demons. She wanted, quite suddenly, quite desperately, to hold him. Just hold him until the demons disappeared.

This wasn't an adolescent crush, she thought. There really was some intangible link…

'Gabe…'

'I'm holding you up,' he said and moved aside so there was no danger of her brushing against him. 'You have things to do.'

'Unpacking,' she managed, trying to sound cheerful. Trying to sound unconcerned. 'I've been shoe shopping. I have steel capped boots. They'll be eating their hearts out on the Paris catwalks.'

He smiled but only just, and the smile didn't reach his eyes. 'Sensible,' he said gruffly.

'That's me. Sensible.'

'Can you get your job back when you…?'

'I don't want my job back!' Enough of cheerful.

Enough of sympathy. She practically yelled the words. Glared.

'Happy stone walling, then,' he said grimly.

'Thank you.'

There was nothing else to say. She walked straight by him. Horse cast him a doubtful glance and then followed his new mistress home.

Why couldn't she get Gabe out of her head? Why was he messing with her equilibrium? Why?

He was damaged goods. He made no effort to be friendly. He didn't want anyone close.

She was forging her own life. She was making friends. She could live happily ever after.

She could buy her own little house, she decided, with a big backyard for Horse. Then she wouldn't have to see Gabe except in occasional passing, one resident of Banksia Bay to another.

She had enough money for a decent deposit. She could start searching straight away—before she annoyed Gabe so much he evicted her.

She should be proactive in her dealings with men.

In her dealings with Gabe.

That was sensible.

But there was a part of her that was refusing to be sensible. Even if Gabe didn't make her feel…like she did…she kind of liked living next door to him.

'It's safety. It's because he's the size of an oak,' she muttered to Horse, but she knew it was much, much more.

She stalked into the kitchen, put on the kettle, picked up one of her pretty china cups.

Looked at it with care.

'That's what Gabe thinks I am,' she told Horse. 'Tomorrow I'm buying mugs. Can you buy industrial strength mugs as well? And I'm changing into my new stone walling gear now.'

She'd invited him to see what she and Aggie were working on. Wanting to go was irrational, but he couldn't stop thinking of it.

It was as if there were chisels wedging themselves under the armour he'd spent thirty years building.

Why?

She was his tenant. She was learning to do dry stone walling with Aggie. Both of those things were unthreatening; neither should pierce his armour.

They did.

He had to get used to it. The new normality was that Nikki was his neighbour, his tenant, the local stone wall builder.

He would go and see one of her walls, he decided. He could behave rationally, it was simply that he hadn't until now.

The forecast for the next few days was for bad weather. He knew the crew would prefer to stay in—he'd been working them all too hard. The grass around the house needed mowing. He'd do that tomorrow—and then in the afternoon he'd casually drive around the back of Black Mountain and see where Aggie was working.

Both Aggie and Nikki.

The day was warm and blustery. 'We'll be in for a storm tonight,' Aggie said, settling down with her folding chair and her Thermos. The old lady was supremely content. Her body was failing her, she could no longer handle the stones, but she could watch Nikki with a gimlet eye, ordering Nikki's hands to do what Aggie's longed to.

In Aggie, Nikki had found a world-class stone waller, and a world-class teacher. She realised that as she worked, as Aggie's eyes found the perfect stone in seconds while Nikki would have searched an hour, as Aggie decreed a fit Nikki thought perfect was appalling— 'It'll blow a gale through the cracks; take it out and start again.'

The work was physically demanding but satisfying on a level Nikki had never guessed she needed. The farmer whose property they were working on came often to inspect, and his pride and pleasure added to hers.

'I never thought I'd get this fence fixed,' he told them. 'It's been here since my great-great-granddad's day. I've been filling the gaps with wire but now Aggie has a student… Lass, you'll have your life's work cut out for you.'

It felt great.

Horse agreed. When Nikki moved, so did he. He was becoming hers, Nikki thought with even more satisfaction.

This was her perfect life. Except for the small niggle of Gabe.

Who turned up mid-afternoon.

She was having trouble fitting a stone. Aggie assured her it'd fit; she just needed to rotate the stones above and behind. She was figuring whether she'd have to chip a bit off the stone—a process Aggie regarded with scorn as there was always the 'right' stone—when suddenly Horse was on his feet, wagging his shaggy tail and barking with delight.

'Look who the cat dragged in,' Aggie said, her voice full of pleasure as Gabe climbed from his truck.

He was wearing jeans and T-shirt, not as rough as usual. He'd shaved.

He still looked big and dark and dangerous.

He still made her heart flip.

'To what do we owe this honour?' Aggie demanded, and Nikki thought thank heaven for Aggie because there was no way she could think of anything sensible to say.

'I decided I'd come and see if she's as good as my mum,' Gabe said and smiled at her, and her heart did a backward somersault. *As good as my mum...* What sort of statement was that?

A statement without anger. A statement of a man accepting things as they were.

'She's got a long way to go but she's going to be better,' Aggie said roundly. 'Your mum had distractions. Husband. Baby. A working girl needs to focus.'

'So Nikki's focusing?'

'Yes, she is. Don't you distract her.'

'I wouldn't dream of it.' He hesitated while Nikki found another stone and tried to fit it. It was nowhere near the right size. Funny, maybe her mind was somewhere else.

'You coped with distractions,' Gabe told Aggie mildly. 'I seem to remember a husband, kids, a farm and a fishing boat. And world-class stone walling medals.'

'My Bert supported me,' Aggie growled. 'He was one in a million. He'd spend the night fishing, sleep for a couple of hours, then if I was on a rush job he'd come out and sort stones for me. They don't make 'em like Bert any more.'

'What did you do with the kids?' Nikki asked, fascinated.

'Playpens,' Aggie said. 'They don't hold with 'em any more, do they? But I had 'em corralled while I worked, then, as soon as they were big enough, they sorted stones. Can't figure why none of them wanted to stone wall for a career.'

'I can't imagine,' Nikki said faintly. She caught Gabe's eye and laughter met laughter.

He made her toes curl.

'Can I help?' he asked and there was a statement to take her breath away.

She didn't need to answer. Aggie was way before her.

'Sure you can,' she said, beaming. 'Nikki's got a way to go to get those muscles strong enough to set the base stones. There's a good twenty yards where they've been moved out of alignment. Some moron decided to drive cattle through here, can you believe that? They pushed a bulldozer through the lot of it. Twenty yards when two would have done. How fat's a cow? At least Frank wants it fixed now, so we just need you to dig along the line, flattening a trench and I'll tell you what stones to put in. Spade's in the back of my truck. What are you waiting for?'

The laughter was still there, Nikki thought. It was suppressed—there was no way Aggie would concede anything she said was funny—but it flashed between Nikki and Gabe and it warmed something she hadn't known was cold. It made her feel…

'If you stare at that stone for any longer it'll grow teeth and bite you,' Aggie snapped. 'We're wasting time. With Gabe to help us, I reckon we can get a couple of yards done by dusk. Get to work.'

'Yes, ma'am,' Nikki said and Gabe saluted and grinned and went to get the spade.

It felt weird.

It felt excellent.

Hard physical work—and it was hard, as hard as hauling in nets, as heaving crates of fish.

Digging along the trench. Setting the lines so he could pack straight. Then heaving rock after rock into the trench, following Aggie's orders, moving, shifting, discarding, trying again, until he had the perfect line.

Normally an afternoon like this he'd be frustrated, stuck at home, itching to get to sea again.

He was having fun. Being bossed by one tyrannical old lady.

Listening to Nikki being bossed.

Watching Nikki take pleasure in her stones.

He remembered his mother. 'There's nothing like it, Gabe, when you find the perfect stone and it fits like it's meant to be there. When you know that's its place.'

She'd never locked him in a playpen or ordered him to help, but he had helped, and the pleasure of it returned to him now.

He'd never remembered his mother without pain, but this afternoon…watching Nikki…

His mother seemed to be there. And Jem.

Horse was lazily watching, and it seemed the ghost of Jem was with him as well. There was a peace here he hadn't known was missing.

The armour was peeling back.

He worked on. Little was said, but when Aggie got vocal, chastising them for fools, idiots, anyone could see that stone was way out of line, he flicked a glance at Nikki and their shared laughter grew.

And something else.

Something that had nothing to do with his mother. Or Jem. Or anyone or anything else.

It was something about the way Nikki knelt, intent, her crazy curls—how long since she'd abandoned that sophisticated straight cut?—flying in all directions. It was watching her sorting, fitting, rejecting, choosing another, listening to Aggie's criticism, sitting back, surveying what she'd done and finally, finally accepting that she'd found the right stone and the right place.

She'd give a tiny sigh of happiness as the stone slotted in and, as each stone fitted, she'd turn and hug Horse and tell him how clever he was for helping.

Horse wagged his tail, accepting praise with decorum.

Dog and woman looked totally, gloriously happy.

She was a city girl. A highly trained specialist engineer. This wasn't her world.

It looked as if it was her world.

He thought back to the woman he'd met the day she'd moved in. She'd worn a sophisticated outer skin. Now it seemed she'd shed it and she was who she truly wanted to be.

She was beautiful. Dirty, bedraggled, windblown, totally absorbed, she was the most beautiful woman he'd ever seen.

He turned a little and found Aggie was watching him. Bemused.

'A worthwhile project,' she said and grinned, and Gabe figured he'd never blushed in his life and he wasn't about to now.

'It'll be good when it's finished,' he said.

'She's beautiful now,' Aggie said and she wasn't looking at the wall. Her grin broadened but then a sudden gust of wind slapped around the slight shelter their partially made wall was giving them, and Aggie's hat sailed off her head, a woollen beanie. Gabe retrieved it, Aggie sighed, shoved it on her head and pushed herself out of her folding chair.

'That's it. The hat barometer says it's time to call it a day.' She shoved her chair into the back of her disreputable truck. 'I drove Nikki here, but you can take her home. Can you fit that dog in as well?'

'Sure,' Gabe said and glanced at Nikki—and the laughter was gone.

Replaced by uncertainty? Fear, even? Just because he'd agreed to drive her home?

He'd been an oaf.

He had a lot of ground to make up.

They drove in silence. He wasn't sure where to start, and maybe she thought the same. But it was up to him, he decided as he pulled up at his house. At *their* house.

'I need to apologise,' he said, and she twisted in her seat and looked at him. Horse was at her feet, his great head on her lap. She'd been stroking him. Her hand stilled.

'I thought you already had.'

'Not properly.' He hesitated. 'I've been a git,' he said at last. 'My dog died four months ago. It threw me. I know it's dumb to get emotional about a dog, but I didn't want to have another around the place.' He raked his hair. Tried to figure where to go from here. 'Horse is your first dog?'

'Yes,' she said, brisk and cool. 'And I hope he lives for ever. But the way you reacted to me… It's not all about Jem, is it?'

'No.' He shook his head, trying to figure it out. 'You remind me of my mother.' It was trite. It was barely true. There was so much more, but he couldn't begin to put it into words.

'That's so what every girl wants to hear,' she retorted but, amazingly, she grinned. 'Woohoo. But I'll take it as a compliment. After a day with Aggie, I'll take any compliment I can get.'

'You're serious enough to cope with Aggie's criticism?'

'I've never been more serious. If I can make a go of it…'

'You will.'

'I intend to try.' She reached for the door handle but Gabe reached over, caught her hand and held.

'I haven't finished apologising.'

'You've said you were a git. And you gave me crayfish.' She looked down at his hand holding hers and she couldn't quite stop a tremor entering her voice. 'That'll do nicely. Plus you've dug my trench, which

I would have had to do tomorrow. It would have taken me all day and it took you two hours. So apology accepted, thank you very much.'

'Can I cook you dinner?'

She stilled. Looked down at their linked hands. 'You don't want me on your side of the wall.'

'I might have changed my mind,' he said. No. That wasn't enough. He had to say it properly. 'I was nuts. I do want you on my side of the wall. There's nothing I'd like better than to cook you dinner.'

'Can I bring Horse?'

A woman and a dog on his side of the wall. In his sitting room.

Nikki and Horse.

Suddenly Jem was right by him, egging him on.

The measure of a life well lived is how many good dogs you can fit into it.

Did that go for love, too?

He'd never truly loved. He didn't know how.

He could try.

He stir-fried prawns, Thai style, with chilli, coriander, snap peas, lime juice. He served them over rice noodles that melted in her mouth.

They ate on the veranda looking over the sea. Looking out over the hole in the stone wall. Looking out at the world.

'Where did you learn to cook?' she asked. She'd eaten at some wonderful restaurants in her time. What she'd eaten tonight was right up there.

'I've cooked since my mum got sick. It's fun.'

Fun. The word hung between them.

Fun, she thought.

Fun wasn't a concept that sat easily with this man.

'Do you cook on the boat?'

'Life's too short for a bad meal,' he said simply. 'I'll take you to sea one night and cook you calamari straight from the line. There's nothing in the world to beat it.'

I'll take you to sea one night... It was a promise.

She felt as if she were standing on the edge of a precipice.

He brought out panacotta then, so creamy it was to die for, with brandied segments of mandarin and slivers of chocolate on the side.

'When did you do this?' she demanded.

'This morning. Before I came to find you. When I decided the fleet would stay in port, I had the whole day to kill.'

So he'd planned dinner, and then he'd come to find her.

She wasn't sure what was happening. All she knew was that Gabe's grim face had disappeared. He was shedding something. Opening himself.

Horse was between them, stretched under Gabe's chair. Gabe was rubbing his belly with his boot. Horse was practically purring.

Horse, too, had eaten prawns for dinner. Life was looking good from Horse's angle.

From Nikki's as well.

Every night she came home from work with aching muscles. Tonight she wasn't feeling an ache.

'Can I ask if you and Aggie can schedule in finishing my wall?' Gabe asked and the night stood still.

'Do you really want that?' she asked, breathless.

'I do.'

'Gabe…'

'Mmm.'

'You're not just doing it to be nice?'

'I'm not,' he said, and his tone was suddenly back to being grim. 'I'm doing it because I've lived with ghosts all my life. They've controlled what I do, and now I've decided it's time I was doing the controlling. The ghosts can come along if they want—and maybe they will—but they can watch what I do rather than dictate.' He rose. 'Come and tell me what needs doing.'

He held out his hand, imperious, and she looked at it for a moment, considering.

But there was nothing to consider. This was Gabe. Gabe, whose outside armour held a man she was… wanting to love?

The concept was frightening, but not as frightening as ignoring the hand, turning away from the need.

She laid her hand in his and let him tug her up. She came, a little too fast. Ended up a little too close.

He smiled and kissed the tip of her nose. It was a gesture of laughter and friendship, surely nothing more, but it brought back the memory of that first kiss.

Of her need.

She tugged back a little—but she didn't let go of his hand. He smiled ruefully.

'Slow,' he said. 'I have the sense to be slow. The way I'm feeling…'

There was enough in that statement to take her breath away all over again.

But she kept breathing. A girl had to do something

as he led her off the veranda and down to the pile of stones and the gap in the fence. Breathing was all she could manage.

Horse followed. They stood on the dew-wet grass and gazed at the pile of stones. The moon was just starting to rise over the sea. The wind was from behind them. The long, low house provided them with shelter. The night was…perfect.

'Where do we start?' Gabe asked.

'Where your mother left off. Did your father never want it finished?'

'My father loved my mother in his fashion,' he said simply. 'He didn't show it. She loved me and she loved her walls. After she died…he hated us both.'

'That's appalling.'

'Yes, but it's past time I made my peace.'

'By finishing the wall?'

'By more than that.' He hesitated. She could feel things breaking inside him, two sides warring. One side winning? The side she was starting to ache for.

'By letting go of my ghosts,' he said softly, his voice almost a whisper. Intimate and wonderful. 'By moving into a future where life isn't grim and harsh. By seeing what's in front of my eyes.'

And his eyes were all on her.

She thought about that for a bit, standing in silence, her hands in his. It felt momentous. But also… It felt simple.

As simple as falling in love?

That was what it felt like. Right now, she was giving her heart.

She thought of the convolutions of falling in love

with Jonathan, the sophistry of his courtship, the elegant dinners, opera, amazing weekends in exotic places, horizon pools, butlers, champagne breakfasts.

The lies, deceit, heartache.

For years she'd thought she loved. And yet, here it was, hands linked, nothing more. Nothing to be said while something grew.

He'd made no promises. But this was a start, she thought. And if he was prepared to start…

Her heart wanted to leap into the breach, declare what she was feeling, move forward right now. But there was still wariness in his eyes, as if he expected things to implode.

He was hoping it wouldn't. Hope was wonderful.

She turned into him and tugged him to her. Wanting him close. Just…close.

Nothing more. She held him, her breasts against his chest, feeling her heartbeat merge to his.

The feeling grew. Something huge.

'I don't know how to do this,' Gabe said simply, holding her close. 'I've never learned to…let go.'

'You've been married.'

'Not married. Joined by a contract to someone I didn't know. And you?'

'I felt like I was. It was a lie.'

'Same with me. Nikki…'

'Mmm?' She tugged away a little, looked up at him in the moonlight. Saw trouble.

'I don't want to hurt you.'

'I don't think you can.'

'If I don't know that myself…' Hesitated. 'My

dad… He did love my mother. He wanted all of her. I'm afraid…'

'That you're like your father?'

'Yes.'

'You're not,' she said simply. 'I know.'

The wind was rising, swirling around either end of the house, closing in again in the trees beyond. They had this one triangle of peace.

One fleeting moment.

She suddenly shivered, a premonition. He felt it, held her close, tugged her harder against him.

'There's so much I need to learn,' he said.

'Me, too. But if I can learn about stone walls, I can learn about you.'

She tilted her chin and pushed herself up on her toes. He caught her face in both hands and kissed her.

Wonderfully.

She felt loved.

That was what his kiss told her. She felt the heat, the aching need, the longing, the sheer want.

The tenderness and the passion, leashed, held under control but only just.

The smell of him…the taste…the feel…

Gabe.

The kiss lingered, stretched out, filled her. She was falling…falling…and it was so easy.

So easy to fall in love.

It was done. Just like that. If he wanted to take her…

No. Not right now. Indignant for lack of notice, Horse whimpered and pushed his great head between them. Gabe released her and Nikki thought…was there a touch of relief in the way he put her aside?

He'd committed, but only so far. There was still reserve.

Ghosts.

'No further,' Gabe said and she could have wept with frustration but he was right. If he wasn't sure…

She was sure.

'Of course not,' she said with as much dignity as she could muster. 'I… I need to go to bed. I have stone walls to build in the morning. It's all very well for lay-about fishermen, taking every tiny excuse of a wee bit of wind to stay in port…'

'We've a gale predicted by morning.'

'Pussycat,' she teased and stepped back.

Go slow.

She didn't want to go slow.

And suddenly the muscles she'd forgotten about… ached.

'You know what I want to do?' she asked.

'What?' He still sounded wary.

'Have a bath,' she said. 'I haven't been brave enough. My pipes gurgle.'

'Your pipes…'

'Joe tried to fix them,' she said with patience. 'He hit them with a spanner. But they still make the most horrific gurgle. You want to come and hear?'

And she saw him withdraw, right there.

Okay, it had been a ruse. She didn't want to go inside and calmly close the door on him. Come inside and see my etchings? Come inside and listen to my pipes?

Corny.

Unwise.

'I don't think that's wise,' he said, and she shrivelled a bit. Felt…stupid.

She'd kissed him. He'd kissed her back and it was wonderful, but the next step was up to him. His face said it.

This relationship would be on his terms.

Like her relationship with Jonathan. He called the tune.

She felt…a little bit ill.

'Sorry,' she managed. 'That was dumb.'

'Nikki…'

'No, you're right, standing in my bathroom listening to pipes there's every chance I could jump you. That'd be dreadful.'

'I didn't mean…'

'Of course you didn't,' she managed but she thought, bleakly, Gabe had his demons, but so did she. Standing back and waiting for him to decide…

Like she'd stood back and let Jonathan decide for years.

Pushing would get her nowhere. Do damage. Crush a bud that'd had no chance to unfurl.

The problem was that her bud had unfurled and was wide open. She wanted this man in her arms. In her heart.

In her bed?

He'd just said no.

He'd said no to her pipes. Not to bed.

They both knew it was more.

'I can manage without a bath,' she said with as much dignity as she could muster.

'I'll check them in the morning.'

'That's big of you.'

'Nikki…'

'No, that was uncalled for. I'm sorry.' She lifted her hand and ran her fingers down his jaw, a feather-touch. 'I didn't mean to snap. You're being wise for both of us, and that's good. Tomorrow you can call the plumber. Not Joe but not you. You can come to my bathroom when you're ready but not before.'

There was still doubt. She saw it in his eyes.

He wanted her—she could see it, she could feel it, she could almost touch it. But he was…afraid?

'You're not like your father,' she said as evenly as she could. 'But I'm not Lisbette, either.'

'I know that.'

'You don't,' she said. 'Otherwise you'd check my pipes for me, right here, right now. Trust me, Gabe.'

'I do.'

'No, you don't. And whether you can learn… You can't open yourself a little and protect the rest. That's what Jonathan did. That's what I'm used to and I've moved on. I think… I think I love you, Gabe, but I'm not going to love a man who spends his life protecting his boundaries.'

She stepped back. Hoping he'd stop her.

He didn't and she felt sick.

Feeling bad was dumb. She should give him space.

She had to give him space.

Like she'd given space to Jonathan?

'Goodnight, Gabe,' she said as firmly as she could.

'Thank you for a wonderful dinner. Horse and I loved it. See you…see you tomorrow. Come on, Horse, bed.'

Why hadn't he taken the next logical step? No, the next instinctive step. The step every part of him except one tiny last shred of pathetic armour was screaming at him to take.

He was every kind of fool.

He'd wanted to pick her up and take her to his bed. As simple as that.

She'd have come. She'd yielded, every sweet part of her pressed against him, wanting him as much as he wanted her. But that scrap of residual armour was screaming that it was way too fast.

He was a loner. A man didn't give away a lifestyle in a heartbeat.

He headed out to the edge of the garden, staring into the dark where the sea was starting to rise in the wind. He was staring into an abyss.

He remembered how he'd felt when his mother died. When he'd realised why Lisbette had married him. When Jem had ceased breathing.

How many times could a man expose himself to that sort of pain?

He wouldn't be exposing himself. This was Nikki he was wanting. Nikki he was falling in love with?

He'd been a loner for most of his life. Why stop now?

Because of Nikki.

But to let that sort of hurt in…

He could be sensible. One step at a time, he told

himself. Take it as it comes, don't rush it, leave it so you can back out any time you want.

He had backed out. He'd refused to enter her house, to check her pipes, to do something so simple.

But he knew if he'd walked into her side of the house he'd have stayed there.

In her crazy bed?

A woman like Nikki needed a king-sized bed.

He needed a woman like Nikki.

Not tonight.

Yes, tonight.

No.

She'd walked away and closed her door. She was giving him space and he appreciated it.

He didn't. A man was a fool.

She was probably already running the bath. The thought of her…

He closed his eyes. He was falling…

Step away from the edge.

Tomorrow, he thought. Tomorrow.

How could he learn to trust—to shed that last vestige of protection from pain and gather her against his heart?

If he was wrong… If he hurt her… If they self destructed as his parents had…

It was one step forward and he didn't have the courage to take it.

'I don't want another Jonathan,' she told Horse, sinking onto the hall floor to give him a hug. 'Oh, but it's hard. How to make him trust me?'

If he didn't trust her there was nothing she could do.

Trust. It was throwing your heart into the ring. He worried that he was like his father. She'd told him he wasn't. She was sure of it.

Because she trusted him.

Maybe she was a fool. Maybe she was heading down the Jonathan path all over again.

Her whole body felt as if it was sensitised, every nerve tingling.

She knew what she wanted.

Not happening.

What to do?

She glared at the wall dividing her place from his. He was so close—and so far.

'Toerag,' she muttered but she didn't believe it.

But why couldn't he trust her? It hurt.

She felt exposed and vulnerable and a tiny bit stupid.

Okay, a lot stupid.

What to do? Go calmly to bed? Look forward to a nice polite good morning in the porch tomorrow?

Great.

She wanted, quite suddenly, to throw something. Hard.

How immature was that?

'Forget the pipes,' she told Horse. 'I'm having a bath. It's the only thing I can think of. A nice hot soak and see if I can get my body to behave.'

And her mind.

Bath. Instead of Gabe.

What a substitute.

'No matter,' she told Horse and climbed resolutely to her feet and marched into the bathroom.

Don't think of Gabe.

The bath ran beautifully, despite the gurgle. See, who needed a man?

And then…it didn't run beautifully at all.

He walked slowly back to the house, hands thrust in his pockets, deep in his thoughts. Glanced up at the house…

Nikki burst out of her door with Horse behind her and headed across the porch to his door. She thumped on his door as if she wanted to break it down.

She was wet to the skin. Soaking.

She was wearing a dripping bathrobe. She was carrying her purse.

She was carrying her car keys.

Horse was wet as well.

'What the…? What's happened?'

She swivelled and faced the darkness, trying to see him. Her glare made him take a step back.

'Ask Joe,' she snapped as she focused. *Snapped?* Maybe that was the wrong word. Yelled might be a better description. 'Don't you ever come onto my side of the house,' she mimicked. 'Because I might jump you. Instead, you send Joe and he comes and thumps my pipes with his spanner. Sooo useful. Not!'

'Nikki…'

But she'd barely got started. 'I ran a bath,' she said, spitting fire. 'It ran beautifully, even if it did make weird noises. So I hopped in and tried to relax even though I was smouldering. Smouldering, Gabe, and why would I be smouldering? Because someone round here doesn't trust me enough to check my pipes. And the water wasn't hot enough so I wiggled the tap with my big toe and suddenly the whole wall burst. I'm guessing the pipe behind the wall disintegrated.'

'Uh-oh,' he said. He couldn't think of anything more…wise.

'Uh-oh is right,' she snapped and he decided saying anything at all had been stupid. Really stupid. 'Or maybe you can think of something worse to say. I surely can. Because there's water shooting out all over the bathroom, but that's not all. The bath backs onto my bedroom and that wall burst, too. So my bed's soaked. And my wardrobe, and my dresser. Everything. So I've rung Aggie and I'm going there. You'll have to care for Horse tonight. Aggie's cat doesn't like him. Take his keep out of the amount I intend to sue you for. So it's over to you, landlord. Walk over my threshold and do something about it or phone Joe. Tell him to bring a bigger spanner, and my nine weeks' notice starts now.'

'Nikki, come in and we'll dry you,' he said, struggling not to laugh. She was a flaming virago, soaked to the skin.

But she wasn't seeing the humour.

'You'll dry me?' she demanded, barely getting the words out. 'What, with towels? Close? How do you know I won't jump you? You don't even trust me enough to check my pipes. What would happen with a naked woman and a towel? Get out of my way, Gabe Carver. I'm going to Aggie's. All by myself.'

He needed to gather her up, carry her soggy person into his side of the house, take charge. But he was… gobsmacked.

She stalked across the yard and flung the gate open, all flaming temper and outraged beauty. He was stunned to immobility.

By his side, Horse whimpered and Gabe agreed. He needed to fight the desire to laugh. He needed to…

But she was already in her car, moving fast.

Maybe she'd sensed the laughter.

'Nikki…' he yelled but it was too late.

Her car wheels spun on the gravel. She turned out of the gate and disappeared into the night.

And Horse lunged after her.

'Horse!'

He was too late there as well.

Nikki was gone and Horse had followed.

Chapter 10

Anyone but Aggie might have been surprised. Aggie, however, had a husband who'd fished and her sons still did. Wet didn't shock her, and when she opened the door to a dripping, seething Nikki she merely stepped aside and said, 'Bathroom's that-a-way—use the yellow towel. Yell at Gabe in the morning—get dry first.'

'How did you know it was Gabe's fault?'

'Has to be someone's,' Aggie said. 'You're looking hopping-mad. Gabe's closest. Male. Why look further? You want pyjamas, or something to sit up in and seethe a while longer?' Then the phone rang and Nikki was left to dry herself while Aggie went to answer it.

A minute later Aggie was back and an armload of clothes was handed round the bathroom door. Oversized trousers, a fisherman's sweater, thick socks, boots.

And Aggie's voice had changed. 'They're too big, but it don't matter. Get dressed fast.'

'Why?'

'Word is Horse chased after you. The road to Gabe's place hits the cove at the bottom of the hill, then rounds the bend. Horse didn't reach there before you disappeared so he must've figured you went the way of the last scumbag who owned him. He's headed out to sea. Phil Hamer noticed your car turn into here. You know you can't do anything round here without being noticed—he was on his way home from stocking the supermarket and wondered about me getting visitors late at night. Then he met Gabe further on, heading for the cove. He stopped to help but there was nothing he could do. Horse's already out past the breakers. Gabe's headed for the harbour to get the boat. Phil figured you'd want to know. If you head straight for the jetty at the entrance you might catch him. Otherwise, he'll be heading out alone. Filthy weather—he'll need all the help he can get. You're wasting time, girl. I'd come with you but I'd only hold you back. Go.'

He'd run, but Horse was on a mission and wasn't to be stopped. By the time Gabe reached the cove Horse was already in the surf.

He yelled, desperate. 'Horse!' No response. Of course not. Horse wanted Nikki.

'She's in the car, not out to sea,' he yelled and that was dumb as well because Horse wasn't listening. He'd seen Nikki disappear and he knew where people who disappeared went. He gave one long, low, despairing howl and swam for the horizon.

Gabe swore and swore again. Headed into the surf after him. Hoping he'd be washed in.

Maybe he would. Maybe he'd have the sense to realise he couldn't swim against the current—but the undertow was fierce. Gabe stood chest-deep in water, fighting the undertow, hoping the dog would turn.

Nothing.

The tide was going out. It'd be impossible to fight.

There was no sense trying to swim after him. Gabe knew he didn't have the strength to fight that sea.

He stood thigh-deep as the waves battered him, as he forced himself to think.

Outgoing tide. Northbound current. Big sea.

What hope of finding him?

Zero.

He felt sick to the stomach.

He was vaguely aware of Phil Hamer, the fussy little supermarket manager, uttering sounds of distress at the water's edge. Trying to give comfort.

There was no comfort to be had if he lost Horse.

He waited for as long as he dared, hoping against hope Horse could fight his way back. But even if he'd wanted to return… Once he was out the back of the surf the current would take him further.

He'd take the boat out. Try to find him.

He was a stray.

He was Nikki's dog.

He was Horse. He had to try.

But on a night like this… To take the boat out alone… It would be worse than useless.

He couldn't ask for help. To ask his crew to put to sea in the face of an oncoming storm for a stray dog…

'What can I do?' Phil bleated, immeasurably distressed.

'Nothing, mate,' he said bleakly. 'I'll head out and do what I can, but I need a miracle.'

She left the lights on in her car, shining straight out over the entrance. She stood out on the jetty at the harbour entrance, putting herself deliberately in the path of her car light, so whoever was in a boat heading out to sea could see her.

So Gabe could see her.

The wind was fierce and there was no moon. Water was washing up over the ancient timbers.

For an awful moment she thought she'd missed him. She stood in the rising wind on the tiny jetty and felt sick.

But then the *Lady Nell* emerged from the darkness and she started yelling. 'Gabe! Gabe!'

He couldn't miss her. Hysterical woman screaming at harbour mouth. Waving as if she were drowning.

He didn't veer in.

'Gabe!' She put everything she possessed into that scream and the boat turned. Came alongside.

'It's rough. You can't…' he yelled but he'd come close enough for her to jump and she jumped.

Possibly a distance an Olympian would be proud of.

She staggered, grabbed the handrail, lurched sideways.

But Gabe had her before she could fall, grabbing her, hauling her roughly against him and half dragging her back into the wheelhouse.

'What the…? You could have been killed. Of all the stupid…'

'Why didn't you come closer?'

'You weren't meant to jump. You weren't meant to be here. There's a storm coming.'

'You were going out without me? *To find my dog?*' Hysterical didn't cut it. She was screaming.

'I lost him.'

'He's my dog.'

'It's dangerous.'

'He's my dog!' She couldn't get any louder if she tried. But with that last yell… The adrenalin of dressing, driving way too fast to reach the entrance, thinking she'd missed him, jumping. Knowing she'd lost Horse… Something gave.

She folded and he caught her and held her hard against him.

She let herself crumple against him, taking mute comfort in the size of him, the strength. The boat was heading out to sea. He wasn't taking her back.

'I can't let you risk…' he muttered.

She thought about that. Got incensed. Anger helped. She hauled back and thumped him hard on the chest. Started yelling again. 'What gives you the right to say who risks?'

'I lost…'

'You didn't. Horse lost himself. He's a crazy mutt who hasn't figured out for himself where his heart is. It's my fault. I shouldn't have left him. I shouldn't have lost my temper.' She thumped him again and it was like striking oak. 'So don't you dare say we can't share. We're finding him together.'

He folded her against him again, her thumps totally useless.

'We won't find him,' he said. Facing facts. Bleak as death.

'We can try. But we do this together.'

'It'd be better if you let me do it alone.'

'Better for who? Are you out of your mind? We love him to bits. We both love him and we both do this. Both or no one.'

Aggie watched Nikki leave and turned to the phone. No one could expect an old lady to calmly go back to bed when Horse was at risk.

Banksia Bay was a tight-knit community. Gabe employed half the fishing fleet, and their families and friends encompassed the town.

The dog community was big, too.

All she had to do was rally the troops.

She rang Henrietta first. 'Ring round, let people know. Skippers of the other boats. Crews.' She hung up as she heard Hen yelling at her son to get off the Internet, to come and help.

Then she rang Raff. The local cop and Gabe were mates. She had Raff onside in a heartbeat.

'I'll ring Whale Cove,' Raff said curtly. 'Harry at North Coast Flight Aid owes me a favour or six. If the chopper's free…'

But… 'It's a filthy night. Raff, this is for a dog,' Aggie faltered, thinking she should just remind him.

'This is for *Gabe's* dog,' Raff said. 'This town's been wanting to help Gabe for years and he doesn't let 'em close. You think we'll miss a chance now?'

'It's Nikki's dog.'

'Same thing,' Raff said curtly. 'He mightn't think so but the rest of us do.'

He knew the currents. Gabe knew the vague direction where Horse might be swept, but in the darkness in a storm-tossed sea…

The thing was hopeless.

He had to try.

He had, he thought, two hours maximum before the storm closed in and he had to take Nikki home. He hated that she was out here. He hated having to share this risk.

To risk Nikki…

She was out on the deck, watching desperately as his floodlights lit the sea.

His heart twisted in pain for her. And for him.

Horse was out here somewhere because he thought Nikki had headed to the sea. Three weeks of Nikki, and Horse knew where his heart lay.

Whereas he…

Tonight he'd backed off. He'd sent her to her side of the house alone. Then, when she'd appeared at her door, a drowned rat, a flaming virago, he'd stood like a great idiot while she yelled and handed over her dog and headed away.

Away from him.

He wanted to hold her, right now, desperately, but he had to stay in the wheelhouse and she had to search.

They needed more eyes.

Call for help?

Sure. Call the town, say, *Come out guys, risk the storm sweeping in early, to save a dog.*

This was his pain.

No. It was Nikki's pain. Shared.

This was what he didn't want to happen. This awfulness. Grief was to be faced alone. To make others share it was appalling. Worse than suffering it yourself.

He watched Nikki's rigid frame at the rail and he felt ill.

Her eyes didn't leave the sea. He was making parallel runs from behind the breakers to out where Horse could conceivably be swept.

So much sea.

Hopeless.

But then…

A helicopter came, sweeping in fast and low from the south. Searchlights flooded the ocean.

The radio. Raff…

'Gabe, that's Harry up there. Signal him that he's focused on the right boat. He'll pick up your frequency from this conversation.'

Harry—North Coast Flight Aid. What the…?

He signalled upward and Harry banked the chopper, heading into the cliff. Starting parallel runs of his own.

There'd be a crew in the chopper. More eyes.

'There's more boats coming out,' Nikki yelled, her voice cracking, and Gabe turned to glance at the harbour entrance.

This wasn't one or two boats. It was a flotilla, heading out into the storm.

What did they think they were doing? It was only just safe now. In another hour or two…

'We're thinking we have a two-hour window,' Raff yelled through the radio. 'Keith's back at base working out currents, search paths. He's allocating runs. You're furthest out, you do the north most run. Straight from where you are now into the back of the breakers and back again. You've only got one pair of eyes, so Nikki does the north lookout. *Mary Lou*'s got you covered; Tom has four aboard so he'll search your south side and his north, then the next boat takes over where his limit is. The chopper goes closer to the reef. Any questions?'

'I can't ask…'

'Who said anything about asking?' Raff snapped. 'Let's find this dog and get home.'

They were one of a pack.

Searchlights were playing over the water. Boats were everywhere—the flotilla was making parallel runs, heading into the cliffs, as close as they dared, then along, then out to the maximum distance the current could take a dog.

The helicopter was above, sweeping as well, so the whole surface of the sea was lit. They needed the moon, but with the approaching storm they had nothing.

They needed luck.

Nikki hadn't moved since they'd left the harbour. She'd hardly registered the approaching armada. She watched and watched.

Maybe she prayed as well. Gabe hadn't prayed since he was a kid. He prayed now.

One dog in a huge sea.

He might well already be drowned. He'd been near death three weeks ago. Three weeks wasn't enough to get his strength back.

He watched the sea and in between he watched Nikki.

What had he been thinking?

He'd tried to keep his distance.

He glanced around at the flotilla who'd set out in filthy weather to save one dog.

No one was keeping their distance this night.

And with that knowledge…something was breaking within him. The armour he'd built with such care…

He'd told himself he needed no one. He depended on no one.

Not true. It had been an illusion. It had taken one crazy dog and one loving woman to make him see the truth.

Plus an army of Banksia Bay dog-searchers.

Where was his illusion now? Gabe Carver, who walked alone, had ceased to exist.

For Gabe Carver was breaking his heart for a dog, breaking his heart for a woman, and there wasn't a thing he could do about it.

And the town, his crew, his friends… They were breaking their hearts for him.

A tiny flotilla in an approaching storm, searching the sea for one stray dog.

Where was the use of armour here? He tossed it aside and he knew it was gone for ever.

Horse.

Nikki.

The people surrounding him.

His heart was wide open.

Please…

There was no fast find here.

Back and forth. Back and forth.

Twelve-thirty. One.

The wind was rising, the sea steadily growing. Soon the helicopter would have to call it quits, and also the smaller boats.

Back and forth…

The chopper was making parallel runs ahead of the fleet, moving further out, making sure of the boundaries.

Slow, methodical sweeps.

Then, suddenly, as one of the smallest boats notified Gabe reluctantly that it was time to turn back, the helicopter banked and turned and hovered.

The down-draught flattened the sea close to the cliff.

The boats hadn't gone so far in. It was too close to the cliffs, too shallow, dangerous.

The chopper was hovering over a reef—Satan's Lookout. A shard of granite reached from the sea, further out than the bulk of the reef. A trap for unwary shipping.

The radio crackled to life. Harry from the chopper, yelling into his headset. 'He's down there. We can see him. He's clinging to the lee side of the reef. If it was a person we'd drop a harness but there's no way we can pick up a dog of that size. I'm not sure even you guys can get him off there.'

* * *

The good news? Horse was alive.

But Horse didn't do things in halves, Gabe thought. Swimming with sharks. Satan's Lookout. How many lives did one dog have?

Nikki was beside him, clinging. She must have seen his face change as he listened to Harry. 'What's happening?' she asked and if her face lost any more colour she'd disappear entirely. She was probably seasick, Gabe thought, and she hugged her stomach and he knew he was right.

What to do? Rough seas and shallow water. There was no way they could take the big boats close. They'd have to take a lifeboat.

But to steer close to the rock and lift Horse... They'd need two people to pull it off, Gabe thought, feeling sick himself. Usually he had Frank and Hattie as crew, both experienced. Tonight he had Nikki.

Nikki would never be competent enough to cope in the life-raft. Could he leave her at the wheel? Could he do it on his own?

No.

But to ask it of others...

The radio crackled into life again. 'Boss?' It was Bert, skipper of the *Mariette*. 'We're all lowering lifeboats. Mick and Mike'll go in ours. Sara and Paula are doing the same from *Bertha*, and Tom and Angie are coming off *Mary Lou*. That's three boats to look after each other. *Mary Lou*'s lifeboat's the most solid, so Angie and Tom'll try and get him off. There's backup to pick up the pieces if needed, and we'll use harnesses and link to each other. This dog doesn't bite, does he?'

'No, but…' His crew had obviously talked on another frequency. This was being taken out of his hands. What he couldn't ask was being offered.

'So he's a pussycat?' Bert demanded.

'A great hulking, sodden pussycat.' But his mind was racing. For others to risk their lives to save his dog… Nikki's dog… 'But I can't ask…'

'You're not asking, we're telling,' Bert said and there was even a note of humour in his voice. 'Takes a bit of getting used to, don't it? Accepting help. You just keep your nose into the wind and keep our Nikki from jumping over the side. We'll get her dog back to her in a trice. Or maybe in more than a trice but we'll get him back. Right, guys.' He was linked to the communal radio—obviously they'd changed frequency to hatch their plan but they were back on common frequency now. 'Let's go fish ourselves a dog.'

So Gabe was forced to wait, to stay idle, to depend on others, while men and women put themselves in danger over a dog he'd been stupid enough to let go.

He should have crew with him so he could do this himself. He should at least help. But there was no way he could ask Nikki, a seasick landlubber, to take over the *Lady Nell*. She had no skills.

But she did have skills, he conceded as he watched the lifeboats be launched. Different skills.

Changing direction and following her dream? Turning her back on her past?

Giving her heart?

She'd gone back to the rail. She was sick and cold and frightened.

He wanted to hold her.

He had to stay at the wheel. This sea was rough and getting rougher. It took experience and skill to keep the *Lady Nell* steady.

He had to depend on others.

He needed others.

He needed Nikki.

His armour was gone. He was no longer bothering to cling to remnants, no longer thinking about what he still needed to protect.

There was nothing to protect. What he needed was outside the armour.

Nikki. Horse. And these peoplc—his crew, his town.

He felt terrified. Totally exposed. If one of those boats capsized…

They didn't.

There were three small boats with three magnificent seamen in charge. The chopper stayed overhead, flattening the water, lighting the scene like day. They all wore lifelines. If someone fell in, Harry would have someone down with a harness in seconds.

The biggest fear was right at the rock.

Horse was clinging to the lee side—sensible dog. But still, for a boat to get in there…

Angie was in the bow of the biggest lifeboat. Like him, Angie was born of a fisher-family. She was older and more experienced than he was, but she had three teenagers at home. What was she thinking?

She was going whether he permitted it or not. He was no longer in charge.

The focus of the community was saving a dog.

Please… It was a muddle of a prayer.

He should be where Angie was.

He had to stay at the wheel. He had to depend on others.

They were at the rock, Angie and Tom. Angie was wearing a headset. Harry was watching the sea from above, giving her instructions. Watching the sea from on high.

Nikki was clinging to the rail, watching every move as if she could guide them by sight.

He wanted to hold Nikki.

His job was to hold the wheel and wait. And to depend on others.

And feel his foundations shift under him. He'd never felt such fear.

Depending on others.

They were twenty feet out from where Horse clung now. They were watching, waiting, waiting.

A lull. *Go.*

Did he yell it? His ears rang, maybe every skipper had yelled it in unison over the radio.

They were already there, surging into the rock. Angie stood to reach…

Horse had to let go.

'Let go of the bloody rock.' It was Angie, yelling into the radio headset like she boomed to the other boats over the water. It was a voice to wake the dead, to shock the unshockable, to make Horse release his grip.

And Angie had Horse around the midriff, dragging him back.

They were in the boat but they were still in danger. The next wave…

Tom had the tiller, the boat swung, hit the wave head on, rode through it—and they were safe.

The lifeboat headed for the *Lady Nell* rather than back to the *Mary Lou*. They figured Horse needed Nikki.

Still Gabe couldn't help. It nearly killed him, but he had to hold the *Lady Nell* steady so there was a modicum of shelter on the side they were boarding.

They made two runs before they got a patch of clear water. Angie heaved the big dog up as Nikki reached down.

Then Horse, almost flaccid until now, looked up and saw Nikki. His great paws found purchase on the side and Angie no longer had to heave. Horse launched himself at Nikki as if it were she who'd been drowning. Nikki and Horse subsided onto the deck, one sodden tangle of woman and dog. Together.

Tom and Angie hauled themselves up onto the *Lady Nell* as well. Tom tied the lifeboat behind. They'd try and tow it back to harbour but even if they had to let it go it was safer than risking the run back to the *Mary Lou*; another boarding.

The chopper was still overhead. The rest of the boats surrounded them.

The chopper's floodlights lit the scene—woman and dog reunited.

A happy ending.

No, Gabe thought, looking out at the sea of people surrounding him. The sea of people who cared. It was a happy beginning.

These were his people. He belonged.

He and Nikki and Horse…they'd come home.

'Tom,' he called, because he was the head of this fleet and a man had to take a stand some time.

'Yeah?' Tom was watching Nikki hugging Horse, grinning and grinning.

'Come and take this wheel,' Gabe growled. 'There's a woman and a dog I need to hug.'

'I didn't think you did hugging,' Tom said, grinning even more, and Gabe managed a grin back.

'I do now.'

Chapter 11

The problem with depending on others was sharing. Every single person wanted a piece of happiness.

The boats streamed into the harbour and it seemed half the town was there to greet them—the half who hadn't been out on boats.

Women were fussing over Nikki, hugging her, saying, *Oh, it's a sign that the dog's been saved—you're meant to stay here, dear.*

Henrietta and her troop of dog-lovers were fussing over Horse. Drying him, warming him, giving him warmed feed to settle his stomach. Maybe Nikki needed some of that.

Aggie was there, beaming and beaming.

And the men were fussing over Gabe. Okay, not exactly fussing—Banksia Bay's fishermen didn't do that. They gripped his hand, one after the other, grinning, exultant at their shared triumph. 'Pleasure, mate,' they said almost universally as he tried to thank them, and he knew it was.

This *was* a shared triumph. Sharing. It was a concept he needed to embrace.

But… How soon could he get Nikki alone?

'You want us to whisk you back to Whale Cove?' Harry asked. He'd set the chopper down in the unloading dock and come to share the happy ending. He and his crew were delighted. Without the chopper, they'd never have succeeded.

Without any of these people…

'I hear there's a great honeymoon suite in the Sun Spa resort at Whale Cove,' Harry said reflectively. 'We could whisk you there right now. I'm not sure if they take dogs, though.'

Maybe he'd been looking at Nikki a bit too long, Gabe thought. Maybe what he needed was plain for all to see, for Harry gripped his shoulder and grinned. 'Another one bites the dust. I thought you were a confirmed bachelor, like me. Oh, well, can't win them all. Good luck, mate, welcome to the other side.'

He left, still chuckling.

Others were going, too. Reluctantly. It was after two in the morning.

'You want me to take Horse back to my place and take care of him for the night?' Henrietta asked, and Nikki, a whole six inches from Horse, tugged him closer.

'No. Thank you but…no.'

'Just thought,' Hen said airily. 'Just saying. If you guys need space…'

'We don't need space,' Gabe said and Nikki glanced up at him and he thought…uh-oh.

A man needed to tread warily. He was, after all, the guy who'd refused to fix her pipes—the guy who'd lost her dog.

'I'm hoping we don't need space,' he said.

'You still want to stay the night at my place?' Aggie asked Nikki, and Nikki looked at him—really looked at him. And something changed in her eyes. Something…

'Thank you,' she said. 'But no. Thank you all. You've been absolutely wonderful, but Horse and I need to go home.'

He took her home.

Her side of the house was still sodden. Water was running down her walls. It had been running since they'd left.

There'd be one nightmare of a mess to clear up later, but now…they turned off the water to Nikki's side of the house and let it be.

Who needed two sides to a house anyway?

Nikki was shivering. She hadn't stopped shivering. He whisked her into the bathroom. His bathroom. Ran the bath, good and hot, propelled her in.

'H… Horse…' she muttered.

'I'll take care of Horse,' he said, and it nearly killed him to leave her but he needed to warm the house.

He stoked up the fire. Made it blaze. Dried Horse with warm towels and more warm towels.

Horse looked devotedly up at him from the fireside. Like: *I'm sorry I caused you trouble but I needed Nikki.*

He and Horse both.

They sat by the fire. Waited.

Nikki came out, wrapped in a towel.

He stood and she walked straight into his arms. He held her close and he knew… This was his woman, his heart, his life.

'I need you,' she whispered and it was an echo of his own heart.

'I've gone about this all the wrong way,' he said into her hair.

'What do you mean?' Their breathing was synchronised. Their heartbeats were synchronised.

'I should have welcomed you with pleasure, cut down the dividing fence, shared Horse, helped with the barbecue, loaned you my mother's books, been proud of you.'

'Nah,' she said. 'I probably would have thought you were wet.' She hesitated. 'Come to think of it, you are wet. I'm warm and dry. You need dry clothes.' But she was still against his heart.

'Not yet. I'm still apologising.'

'There's time to make amends,' she said. 'You can hug me with pleasure, cut down the dividing fence, share Horse, help with any future barbecues—and I think we should have one soon to thank everyone for tonight—lend me your mother's books, be proud of me. Do you think my apartment's underwater?'

'What's a little water? Nikki, I love you.'

She stilled.

She didn't speak. She just…melted.

He was holding her tight, feeling the warmth of her. Accepting the reality that he was holding the woman of his dreams, right here in his arms.

'I don't suppose you'd consider marriage,' he said and he hadn't known he intended to say it; it was just there.

It shocked them both. She almost dropped the towel. She grabbed it just in time. Made a recovery. Sort of. Took a step back.

'Marriage,' she whispered.

'Just a thought.' He tried to figure how to say all the things that were in his heart and couldn't. Made a bad joke instead. 'It'd make Horse legitimate. You'd be Mum and I'd be Dad.'

She choked. 'You'd marry me—for a dog?'

'I'd marry you for you.'

'You're grumpy.' She was eyeing him with caution now, as if he had the poker.

'Only when hit on the head. I'll try not to be grumpy for anything less.'

'I still want to learn stone walling.'

'I love that you still want to learn stone walling.'

'You go to sea thirteen nights out of fourteen.' She took a deep breath. 'I've learned tonight… I do get seasick.'

'I won't go to sea in rough weather.'

'Promise?'

'Not very rough.'

'Thirteen nights out of fourteen?'

'I'm the fleet owner. I can decide. How about only when I must? And if you were home in my bed… there'd hardly be a must.'

'Of course there would. First hint of a barracuda and out you'd go.'

'Not if you were in my bed.'

'You have a bed on the boat.'

'So I do. But…'

'Then I guess I could take pills and come with you,' she ventured. 'If you'll dig my trenches.'

'Is this business we're talking?'

'I like things to be clear.'

'You want me to find pen and paper and we'll sign stuff before I kiss you?'

'You want to kiss me?'

'More than anything on earth.'

She sighed, a long, drawn-out sigh where things seemed to be let go.

'If I kissed you back I might drop my towel,' she said, smiling and smiling.

'You want to risk it?'

'Horse would be shocked.'

'I believe,' he said softly, in a low, husky growl because that seemed all he was capable of right now, 'I believe our Horse is asleep. Dead to the world.'

'Don't say dead.'

'Alive,' he said, smiling down at her. Smiling and smiling. 'Like I am. I feel more alive right here, right now, than I've ever been in my life. You want to risk the odd towel?'

'I'd risk more than that,' she said, stepping forward, stepping into his arms. 'I'd risk my heart. Or wait… maybe I can't. Maybe my heart's no longer mine to risk.'

It took a while to plan a wedding, mostly because the tiny church on the headland on the far side of

Banksia Bay was surrounded by a crumbling stone wall. No one was marrying in that church, Aggie decreed, until the wall was mended, so instead of planning wedding dress, bridesmaids, flowers, Nikki sat on the headland overlooking the sea and fitted stones into a wall that would last for another hundred years.

She loved it—and there was no problem that her attention was focused on the wall, for she had others to do the 'tizzy bits' for her wedding. Aggie and Henrietta and Angie and Hattie and Hilda and Maudie… So many friends.

Her day would be splendid, they decreed, and so it was.

In the end the church was too small. In the end the day was perfect so Gabe stood under frangipani, with the sea as his backdrop, while all the town clustered close by to wait for his bride.

Nikki's parents were here, astounded, bemused, and in the end even confusedly proud that their daughter knew so definitely where she was going, what she was doing.

'She can charge a lot more than she's doing,' her father decreed of his daughter. 'With a skill like this…'

'I can't believe he didn't go to university,' her mother said of Gabe, but they were here, they were smiling, and they'd accepted her new life.

They had no choice, for this *was* Nikki's life. This place. Banksia Bay. Gabe.

A bagpipe sounded, a blast of triumph, and Aggie squeaked in triumph herself. This was her wedding gift, her son the bagpiper, whether Nikki willed it or not.

Nikki did will it. She'd grinned when Aggie had told them. 'Bagpipes,' Gabe had said faintly.

She'd tucked her arm into his and said, 'I won't have it any other way.'

Nikki. His bride.

The bagpipes meant she was here.

Horse was lying beside him, groomed, gleaming, almost handsome. The big dog understood it now, that Gabe and Nikki were one—equals. He'd stay with Gabe or he'd stay with Nikki, but he was only truly content when they were together.

Which was great because that was exactly where Gabe and Nikki intended to be.

Bagpipes. Nikki.

Horse lumbered to his feet and Gabe held his collar. Someone had put a garland of frangipani round Horse's neck. How corny was that?

He loved it.

Then Raff was elbowing him aside, taking Horse's collar firmly in his.

'Priorities, mate,' he said. 'Bride first, dog second.'

He didn't need to be told, for Nikki was here, and he only had eyes for Nikki.

His bride.

Her gown was gorgeous, white silk with an exquisitely beaded bodice and a deceptively simple skirt that draped and flared as if she were floating. She looked as if she was tied to her father's arm to stop her rising. Her hair was beautiful. She'd never again tried to straighten it. Angie had tucked frangipani into her curls.

But Gabe wasn't looking at her hair. He wasn't looking at her gown. He looked only at Nikki. Her smile.

Her lovely, lovely smile as she met his gaze, at the shared laughter that was always there. Laughter and love.

He was truly loved.

There was momentary drama. Horse tugged away from Raff and Raff was dumb enough to let him go. But Horse didn't go far. He trod sedately down the carpet they'd laid for the bridal approach, and he greeted his mistress with quiet dignity. Then he turned and walked calmly back to Gabe, preceding the bride.

He glanced around at the congregation as if to say, *See, I know what a real dog should do.* Then he sat beside Gabe to watch.

And watch he did, as his Nikki married her Gabe.

As his mistress found her home.

As life truly began for them all.

* * * * *

MISTY AND THE SINGLE DAD

With grateful thanks to Anne Gracie and her Chloe,
a matched pair of great friends; to Trish Morey,
whose skill with words is awesome;
and to the Maytoners, because we rock.

To Buster Keaton,
who loved our family with all his small heart.

Chapter 1

How many drop-dead gorgeous guys visited Banksia Bay's First Grade classroom? None. Ever. Now, when the heavens finally decreed it was time to right this long-term injustice—it would have to be a *Friday.*

Misty took her class of six-year-olds for swimming lessons before lunch every Friday. Even though swimming had finished an hour ago, her braid of damp chestnut curls still hung limply down her back. She smelled of chlorine. Her nose was shining.

Regardless, a Greek God was standing at her classroom door.

She looked and looked again.

Adonis. God of Desire and Manly Good Looks. Definitely.

Her visitor looked close to his mid-thirties. Nicely mature, she thought. Gorgeously mature. His long, rangy body matched a strongly boned face and almost sculpted good looks. He wore faded jeans and an open-necked shirt with rolled up sleeves. Looking closer—and she *was* looking closer—Misty could see muscles, beautifully delineated.

But…did Adonis have a six-year-old son?

For the man in her doorway was linked by hand to a child, and they matched. They both wore jeans and white shirts. Their black hair waved identically. Their coppery skin was the colour that no amount of fake tan could ever produce, and their identical green eyes looked capable of producing a smile to die for.

But only Adonis was smiling. He was squatting and saying to the child, 'This looks the right place. They're painting. Doesn't this look fun?'

Son-of-Adonis didn't look as if he agreed. He looked terrified.

And, with that, Misty gave herself a mental slap, hauled herself back from thinking about drop-dead gorgeous males and back to where she should be thinking—which was in schoolmarm mode.

'Can I help you?'

Frank, Banksia Bay School Principal, should have intercepted this pair, she thought. If this was a new student she'd have liked some warning. There should be an empty place with the child's name on it, paints with paper waiting to be drawn on, the rest of the class primed to be kind.

'Are you Miss Lawrence?' Adonis asked. 'There's no one in the Principal's office and the woman down the hall said this is Grade One.'

She smiled her agreement, but directed her smile

to Son-of-Adonis. 'Yes, it is, and yes, I am. I'm Misty Lawrence, the Grade One teacher.'

The child's hand tightened convulsively in his father's. This definitely wasn't a social visit, then; this was deathly important.

'I'm sorry we're messy, but we're in the middle of painting cows,' she told the little boy, keeping her smile on high beam. She was standing next to Natalie Scotter's table. Natalie was the most motherly six-year-old in Banksia Bay. 'Natalie, can you shift across so our visitors can see the cow you're painting?'

Natalie beamed and slid sideways. Misty could see what she was thinking. Hooray, excitement. And the way this guy was smiling… Misty felt exactly the same.

Um…focus. Get rid of this little boy's fear.

'Yesterday we went to see Strawberry the cow,' she told him. 'Strawberry belongs to Natalie's dad. She's really fat because she's about to have calves. See what Natalie's done.'

The little boy's terror lessened, just a little. He gazed nervously at Natalie's picture—at Natalie's awesomely pregnant cow.

'Is she really that fat?' he whispered.

'Fatter,' Natalie said, rising to the occasion with aplomb. 'My dad says it's twins and that means he'll have to stay up all night 'cos it's always a b…' She caught herself and gave Misty a guilty grin. 'I mean, sometimes he needs to call the vet and then he swears.' She beamed, proud of how she'd handled herself.

'Here's her picture,' Misty said, delving into the pocket of her overalls for a photograph. She glanced at Adonis, asking a silent question, and got a nod in response. This, then, was the way to go. 'Would you like to sit by Natalie and see if you can paint as well?' she asked. 'If it's okay with your dad.'

'Of course it is,' Adonis said.

'You can share my paints,' Natalie declared expansively, and Misty gave a tiny prayer of thankfulness that Natalie's current best friend was at home with a head cold.

'Thank you,' Son-of-Adonis whispered and Misty warmed to him. He was polite as well as cute. If he *was* a new student…

'We're here to enrol Bailey for school,' Adonis said, and she smiled her pleasure, but she was also thinking, *Where is Frank?* And why did this pair have to arrive now when she felt like a chlorinated wet sheep?

'I know I should have made an appointment,' Adonis said, answering her unspoken question. 'But we only arrived in town an hour ago. The closer we got, the more nervous Bailey was, so we thought the sensible thing would be to show him that school's not a scary place. Otherwise, Bailey might get more nervous over the weekend.'

'What a good idea. It's not scary at all,' she said, warming to the man as well as to the son. 'We like new friends, don't we, girls and boys?'

'Yes.' It was a shout, and it made Misty smile. In this sequestered town, any newcomer was welcomed with open arms.

'Are you here for long?' she asked. 'You and your… family?' Was Mrs Adonis introducing another child to another class?

'There's only Bailey and me, and we're intending to live here,' he said, stooping to load Bailey's paintbrush with brown paint. Being helpful. But Bailey checked Strawberry's photograph again, then looked at his father as if he'd missed the point. He dipped his brush in the water jar and went for red.

His father grinned and straightened, and held out his hand. 'I'm Nicholas Holt,' he said, and Misty found her hand enveloped in one much larger, much stronger. It was a truly excellent handshake. And his smile…

Manly Good Looks didn't begin to cut it, she thought. Wow! Forget Greek Gods. Adonis was promptly replaced with Nicholas.

She was absurdly aware of her braid, still dripping down her back. She wanted, quite suddenly, to kill Frank. It was his job to give warning of new parents. Why wasn't he in his office when he should be?

She didn't have so much as powder on her nose. It was freckled and it glowed; she knew it did. Her nose was one of the glowingest in the district. And five feet four inches was too short. Where were six inches when she needed them? If Frank had warned her, she might have worn heels.

Or maybe not.

'Miss…' a child called.

'I'm sorry; we shouldn't be disturbing your class,' Nicholas said and she managed to retrieve her hand and force herself to think schoolteacherly thoughts. Or mostly schoolteacherly thoughts.

'If Bailey's to be my student, then you're not interrupting at all,' she said and turned to the child who'd called. 'Yes, Laurie, what do you need?'

'There's a dog, miss,' Laurie said from across the room, sounding agitated. 'He's bleeding.'

'A dog…' She turned to the window.

'He's under my table, miss, in the corner,' Laurie said, standing up and pointing. 'He came in with the man. He's bleeding everywhere.'

Help.

There were twenty-four children looking towards Laurie's table. Plus Nicholas Holt.

A bleeding dog…

There were kids here who'd make this up but Laurie wasn't one of them. He wasn't a child with imagination.

Laurie's table was in the far back corner, and the row of shelving behind it made for a small, dark recess. If a dog was under there…it couldn't be a very big dog.

'Then we need to investigate,' she said, as brightly as she could. 'Laurie, can you go and sit in my teacher's chair, please, while I see what's happening?'

Laurie was there like a shot—the best treat in the world was to be allowed to sit in his teacher's big rotating chair. With the way clear, Misty would be able to see…

Or not. She stooped, then knelt. It was dark under the table. Her hands met something wet on the floor—something warm.

Blood.

Her eyes grew accustomed to the gloom. Yes, there was a dog, cowering right back into the unused shelves.

She could see him clearly now, cringing as far back as he could get.

An injured dog could snap. She couldn't just pull him out.

'Can I help?'

He was Adonis. Hero material. Of course he'd help.

'We have an injured dog,' she said, telling the children as well as Ad…as well as Nicholas. 'He seems frightened. We all need to stay very quiet so we don't frighten him even more. Daisy, can you fetch me two towels from the swimming cupboard?'

'Do you know the dog?' Nicholas asked as Daisy importantly fetched towels. He was standing right over her, and then he was kneeling. His body was disconcertingly solid. Disconcertingly male.

He was peering underneath Laurie's table as if he had no idea in the world what his presence was doing to her.

What, exactly, was his presence doing to her?

Well, helping. That was a rarity all by itself. Misty was the fixer, the one who coped, the practical one. She did things by herself, from necessity rather than choice.

She didn't often have a large attractive male kneeling to help.

Often? Um…never.

'Do you know the dog?' he asked again and she got a grip on the situation. Sort of.

'No.'

'But he's injured?'

'There's blood on the floor. Once I have the towels, I can reach in…'

'It'll be safer if I lift the table so we can see what we're dealing with. Tell you what. If we move the kids back, it'll give him a clear run to the entrance. If he wants to bolt, then he can.'

'I need to see what's wrong.'

'But you don't want a child getting in the way of an injured animal.'

'No,' she said. Of course not.

'I left the outside door open from the porch,' he said. 'I'm sorry; that's how he must have come in. I can shut it now. That means if I lift the table and he bolts we have a neat little space to hold him.

She thought that through and approved. Yes. If the dog was scared he'd run the way he'd come. They could close the classroom door into the porch and they'd have him safe.

But to trap an injured dog…

This was NYP. Not Your Problem. That was what Frank would say. The School Principal was big on what was or wasn't his problem. He'd let the dog go, close the door after it and forget it.

But this wasn't Frank. It was Nicholas Holt and she just knew Nicholas wasn't a NYP sort of guy.

And in the end there wasn't a choice—the dog didn't give her one. She knelt, towels at the ready. Nicholas lifted the desk, but the dog didn't rush anywhere. The little creature simply shook and shook. He backed harder into the corner, as if trying to melt into the wall, and Misty's heart twisted.

'Oh, hush. Oh, sweetheart, it's okay, no one's going to hurt you.'

This little one wasn't thinking of snapping—he was well past it. She slipped the towels around him carefully, not covering his head, simply wrapping him so she could propel him forward without doing more damage.

He was a cocker spaniel, or mostly cocker spaniel. Maybe a bit smaller? He was black and white, with black floppy ears. He had huge black eyes. He was ragged, bloodstained and matted and there was the smell of tyre rubber around him. Had he been hit?

He had a blue collar around his neck, plastic, with a number engraved in black. She knew that collar.

A couple of years back, Gran's ancient beagle-cross had slipped his collar and headed off after a scent. Two days later, he'd turned up at the Animal Welfare Centre, with one of these tags around his neck.

This was an impounded dog. A stray.

No matter. All that mattered now was that the dog was in her arms, quivering with fear. There was a mass of fur missing from his hind quarters, as if he'd been dragged along the road, and his left hind leg looked… appalling. He was bleeding, sluggishly but steadily, and his frame was almost skeletal.

He needed help, urgently. She wanted to head out to her car right now and take him to the vet.

She had twenty-four first graders looking at her—and Nicholas was looking at her as well. NYP? She had problems in all directions.

'He's hurt.' It was a quavering query from Bailey. The little boy had sidled back to his father's side and slipped his hand in his. His voice was full of horror. 'Has he been shot?'

Shot? What sort of question was that?

'He looks like he's been hit by a car,' she said, to the class as well as to Bailey. Every first grader was riveted to the little animal's plight now. 'He's hurt his leg.' Anything else? She didn't know.

She looked down at him and he looked up at her, his eyes huge and pain-filled and hopeless. His shivering body pressed against hers, as if desperate for warmth.

She'd owned dogs since childhood. She loved dogs. She'd made a conscious decision not to have another one.

But this one… He was an injured stray and he was looking at her.

Uh oh.

'Do you want me to call someone to deal with him for you?' That was from Nicholas—with that question he surely wasn't Adonis. This wasn't a hero type of question. This the sort of response she'd expect from Frank.

Find someone to deal with him. Who?

Frank himself? If the Principal wasn't in his office, she had no one to turn to. Every other teacher had their own class.

She could make a fast call to Animal Welfare. This was their dog. Their problem. They'd collect him.

That was the sensible solution.

But the dog quivered against her, huddling tight, as if he was desperate for the poor amount of warmth she could provide. His eyes were pools of limpid despair.

He looked at her.

NYP. NYP.

Since when had anything ever been Not Her Problem? There was no way this dog was going back to one of the Welfare cages.

She did not need a dog. She did not!

But in her arms the dog quivered and huddled

closer. She felt the silkiness of his ears. She could feel his heart, beating so fast… He was so afraid. He was totally at the mercy of the decision she made right now.

And, with that thought, her vow to leave dogs behind disintegrated to nothing.

What were dreams, anyway?

'Mr Holt, I need your help,' she said, attempting to sound like a teacher in control of the situation.

'Yes,' he said, sounding cautious. As well he might.

'I can't leave the children,' she said. 'This dog needs to go to the vet. That's what happens with sick dogs, doesn't it, boys and girls. You remember Dr Cray? We visited his surgery last month. I'm going to ask Bailey's father if he'll take him to Dr Cray for us. Will you do that for us, sir?'

Then she looked straight at Nicholas, meeting those deep green eyes head on. Not His Problem? Ha. He was asking her to teach his child. Payback happened early in Banksia Bay.

'I don't know about dogs,' he said, sounding stunned.

'That's okay,' she said, wrapping the little dog more tightly in his towels. Before he could demur, she handed him over, simply pressing the dog against his chest and letting her hands fall. She wasn't about to drop him, but he wasn't to know that. He was forced to release Bailey to take the dog.

'Dr Cray does a midday surgery, so he should be there,' she said. Then, as he still looked flabbergasted, she thought maybe a little more explanation might be required. Explanation but no choice. She couldn't afford to give him a choice.

She so wanted to take this dog herself, but some things weren't possible. Nicholas would have to do.

'I'm not sure where our Principal is,' she said. 'These children are mostly country kids. We know about injured animals. We know the vet can help, only first we need to get him there. We ask our parents to help all the time—four of our mums and dads helped with swimming lessons this morning. I know Bailey's only just joined the class but we know you'll want to help as well. So please, can you take this dog to the vet? Tell Dr Cray I'll be there after work and I'll take care of the expenses.'

And she mustn't forget Bailey, she told herself. She was asking a lot here—of both father and son.

She looked down at Bailey and something in his expression caught her. Made her remember…

Her mother, walking into her classroom on one of her fleeting visits. Misty might have been as old as Bailey, or maybe a little younger.

Her mother staying for all of two minutes—'just to see my kid'. Speaking gaily to her teacher as she walked out. 'You look after my Misty; she's such a good girl.' Then leaving. As she always left. Sending postcards from a life that didn't include Misty.

Whoa. In the midst of this drama, where had that thought come from? But the memory of it was there, in Bailey's eyes. She knew instinctively that his world wasn't certain, and she was asking more of him.

But, unfair or not, she had no choice. She couldn't leave the classroom and she could hardly toss the dog outside untended. What to do?

Give him the choice, as she'd never been given the choice.

She stooped. 'Bailey, we need your father's help to take this dog to where he can get bandages on his cut leg. Will you go with your dad to the vet's, or will you stay here with us and paint cows? Your dad will come back after he's left the dog with the vet. Won't you, sir? Is that okay with you, Bailey?'

Big breath. She was asking so much. And if she was right in what she sensed…if this little boy had been left in the past…

But it seemed Bailey trusted his father far more than she'd trusted her mother. He thought about it for a moment, looked up at the little dog wrapped in towels and then he gave a solemn nod, answering for both of them.

'My dad can take the dog to the vet.'

'That's wonderful.' It was indeed wonderful. 'Aren't dads great? Will you stay with us or will you go with him?'

'Stay with us,' Natalie said urgently, and Misty blessed Natalie's bossy little boots. 'I have heaps of paint.'

'I'll stay,' Bailey said, giving a cautious smile to Natalie.

'That's excellent.' She straightened and the look she gave Bailey's father was pure pleading. This was outrageous. If Frank could hear what she was doing he'd sack her on the spot. But what choice did she have?

'So will you do it for us?' she asked, and the dog looked hopelessly out at her from where it was cradled against his chest and she knew she was pleading for all of them. For the kids in her classroom, too. Every single one of them wanted a happy outcome for this dog.

'Please?'

Chapter 2

What had just happened?

One minute he had been a father intent on enrolling his son in his new school. He'd been ready to fill in forms, reassure Bailey, do all the things a responsible dad did.

The next he was standing in the sunshine, his arms full of bleeding dog, with a worried schoolteacher watching his rear. Making sure he followed directions.

An army commander couldn't have done it better.

Bailey would be safe with her.

That was a dumb thing to think at such a time—after all, what risk was there in leaving his son in a country primary school, in Australia, in a tiny seaside town where the most exciting thing to happen was…was…

Well, a dog being run over, for a start. Even that was more excitement than Nick wanted.

And it was a whole lot more excitement than this dog wanted. As Nick felt the dog tremble he put the *me* angle aside and focused on the creature he was carrying.

There'd been no time to examine him in the classroom. Miss Lawrence had wanted him out of there.

That was unfair. Her first responsibility must be to the children in her class and she'd put them first. If she'd taken the time to see exactly what was wrong, then the children, too, would have seen. Maybe that would have been distressing.

So he did what he was told. He turned his back on the school and headed for the car.

To the vet?

That, at least, was easy. Banksia Bay's commercial centre consisted of the one High Street running down to the harbour. Right on the town's edge was a brick building set back from the road. There was a big tree out front, a large blue sign saying 'Vet' and a picture of a dog with a cocked leg, pointing to the tree.

He and Bailey had smiled at it when they'd arrived in town. It was barely a block and a half from the house he'd rented.

'We could get a dog,' Bailey had said, but tentatively because maybe he'd already known the answer.

The answer would be no. Nick wanted nothing else that would tear their hearts. He was totally responsible for Bailey now, and for Bailey to have any more tragedy…

Look at this dog, for instance—running away, being hit by a car. He didn't know how badly it was injured. In all probability, there was still a tragedy here.

If there was then he'd lie to Bailey, he decided. This dog obviously belonged to a nice farmer who lived a long way out of town. The farmer would come and collect him. No, it'd be too far to visit…

The dog in question quivered again in his arms—the trembling was coming in waves—and he stopped thinking of difficulties. The sensible thing would be to set the dog on the car seat beside him but when he went to put him down he shook so much he thought okay, if it's body warmth he needs, then why not give it to him?

If Miss Lawrence was here she'd hold him. She'd expect him to hold him too.

She was one bossy woman.

Strong? Independent? Like Isabelle?

Not like Isabelle. She was a country schoolteacher. She wasn't a risk-taker.

She was…cute?

Now there was a dumb thing to think. He'd come here to set himself and Bailey up as safe and immune from any more risk—from any more tragedy.

From any more complications.

Isabelle had been dead for little more than a year. Even though their marriage had been on the rocks well before that, it hadn't made her death less shocking. Less gut-wrenching. It was far too soon to think that anyone, much less Bailey's new schoolteacher, was cute.

Hard not to think it, though. And maybe it was okay. Normal, even. She was a country schoolteacher and her ability to intrude on his life would be limited to teaching his son.

And asking him to take a dog to the vet.

It took two minutes to drive the short distance to the vet's. When he carried the dog in, an elderly guy with heavy spectacles and a grizzled beard emerged from the swing doors behind Reception. His glance at Nick was only fleeting; he focused straight away on the blood-stained towel.

'What's happened?'

A man after my own heart, Nick thought. Straight to the core of the problem.

'Miss Lawrence from the local school asked me to bring this dog in,' he said as the vet folded back an edge of the towel so he could see what he was dealing with.

'Misty?' The vet was touching the dog's face, running his fingers down his neck. Feeling for his pulse. 'Misty doesn't have a dog.'

'No, he ran into the schoolroom while...'

But the vet had found the collar. He fingered the nylon—checked the number, winced.

'It's the second.'

'Sorry?'

'From our local Animal Welfare Centre.' The vet took the dog from him, holding him with practised ease. 'Henrietta gives dogs every chance, only there are never enough homes. When the dogs have stayed there for...well, it's supposed to be ten days but she stretches it as long as she has room...she brings them to me. Three months after Christmas, cute pups turn into unwanted dogs. Yesterday morning she had a van full and some driver ran into the back of her. Dogs went everywhere. This is one of them.'

'So…' Nick said, and paused.

'So,' the vet said heavily. 'Thank you for bringing him in.' He paused and then craggy eyebrows raised. 'It's okay,' he said gently. 'I promise it'll be painless.' And then, as Nick still hesitated, 'Unless you want a dog?'

'I…no.'

'You're not a local.' It was a statement.

'My son and I have just moved here.'

'Have you just? Got a house with a yard?'

'Yes, but…'

'Every kid needs a dog.' It was said neutrally, probing a possible reprieve.

'No.' Yet still he hesitated.

'No pressure,' the vet said. 'The last thing this guy needs is another place that doesn't want him.'

'Miss Lawrence says she'll pay,' Nick said. 'For you to treat him.'

'Misty said that?'

'Yes.'

'She wants to keep him?'

'I'm not sure.'

The vet seemed confused. 'Misty's dog died last year. She's sworn she won't get another.'

'I'm sorry. I don't know any more than you do.'

'She won't have realised he's due to be put down. Or maybe she has.' The vet sighed. 'Trust Misty. Talk about a soft touch…' He glanced at his watch. Grimaced. 'I need to talk to her, but I won't be able to catch her until after school. That's almost three hours.' He looked at the dog again and Nick could see what he was thinking—

that three hours was too long to make a dog suffer if the end was inevitable.

This wasn't Nick's problem. He should walk away. But…

But he had to face Misty, the bossy little schoolteacher with the pleading eyes. Did she see this as her dog?

She'd said she'd cover the expenses. He had to give her the choice.

'I'm going back to the school anyway,' he said diffidently. 'I was enrolling my son when we found the dog. I could talk to her and phone you back.'

The vet's face cleared. 'Excellent. Let's do a fast assessment of this guy's condition so Misty knows what we're dealing with. She's not a girl to mess me around—it'll be yes or no. Can you give me a hand? I'll give him some pain relief and we'll tell her exactly what she is or isn't letting herself in for.'

Bailey drew a great cow. Misty gazed down at the child's drawing with something akin to awe. He was six years old, and his cow even looked like a cow.

'Wow,' she said as she stamped his picture with her gold elephant stamp—gold for Effort, elephant for Enormous. 'You must really like drawing, Bailey.'

'My dad can draw,' Bailey said. 'People pay him to draw pictures of boats.'

His father was an artist?

'Then you've come to the right place,' she said, glancing out of the window towards the distant harbour.

Nicholas Holt didn't look like an artist, she thought,

but then, what did she know of artists? What did she know of anything beyond the confines of this town?

Don't think it. There was no point going down that road. For now, Banksia Bay was her life.

And for how much longer? She'd just offered to pay for a dog.

How long did dogs live?

'Story time,' she said determinedly. 'Tell you what, Bailey, as you're the new boy today, you can choose the story. Any book from the rack. Take a look.'

Bailey looked at her dubiously but he'd obviously decided this was an okay environment—this was somewhere to be trusted. And chubby little Natalie was right beside him, his new Friend For Life.

'Choose *Poky Little Puppy*,' Natalie whispered as only a six-year-old could whisper. "Cos it's all about a puppy getting into trouble, like your new dog.'

Like your new dog...

Uh oh.

'He's not Bailey's new dog,' Misty said as she settled on the reading stool with the kids around her.

'Then whose is he, miss?' Natalie asked, and she knew the answer. She'd known it as soon as she'd seen the plastic collar.

She sighed. She was stuck here anyway. Why keep fighting the odds? Her dreams had already stretched a lifetime and it seemed they needed to be stretched a while longer.

'I guess he's mine.'

And ten minutes later when Nick walked back into the classroom the thing was settled. He entered the room, Natalie's hand shot up and she asked before Misty could give permission.

'Please, sir, how's Miss Lawrence's dog?'

Miss Lawrence's dog. He flashed a look at Misty and she met his gaze with every evidence of serenity. As if she picked up stray dogs all the time.

Why? Dogs must give her heartache upon heartache, he thought. The lifespan for a dog was what? Sixteen years? The mutt in question was around ten years old already and battered, which meant he was sliding towards grief for all concerned. He had six years, at most—if he made it through the next twenty-four hours.

'He has a broken leg,' he said, aware of a classroom of eyes, but aware most acutely of Bailey. Bailey, who'd seen far too much horror already. Because of his father's stupidity…

'Is Dr Cray fixing him?' Misty asked from the front of the room, and his gaze locked on hers. He could reply without speaking; he knew this woman was intelligent enough to get it.

'It's an extremely expensive operation to fix his leg,' he said, trying for a neutral tone. 'He's already an elderly dog, so there may be complications. Apparently he's from the Animal Welfare Centre—a stray—but Dr Cray says he's willing to take care of him for us. All he needs is your permission. I can phone him now and let him know it's okay.'

She got the message. He saw her wince.

The vet was letting her off the hook. All she had to do was nod and go back to reading to the children.

Nicholas would relay her decision and the problem would be solved.

But this woman didn't work like that. He sensed it already and her response was no surprise.

'How expensive?'

So she couldn't save the dog at any cost. She was a schoolteacher, after all.

What to say? He ran over the options fast.

Could they talk outside? Could he say, *Let's talk without the children hearing.* Let's give you the cold facts—that this dog's going to cost a mint; he's a stray with a limited lifespan. No one wants him; the kindest thing is to let Dr Cray do what he thinks best, which is to put him down.

He'd come to Banksia Bay to be sensible. He had to be sensible.

But then… Bailey was looking up at him with huge eyes. Bailey would want details about what happened to the dog. Could he tell him the story about the distant farmer?

Could he lie?

All the children were looking at him. And their teacher?

Their teacher was looking trapped.

She had a dog.

The dog had trembled and cringed against her. He'd looked up at her, and she'd disappeared into those limpid eyes. His despair had twisted her heart.

But reality had now raised its ugly head and was staring her down.

How much was *extremely expensive*?

Becky, her best friend from school days, had just spent twelve thousand dollars on her Labrador's hip. But then, Becky had a property developer husband. Money was no problem. How badly was this dog's leg damaged?

Was she being totally stupid?

She thought of her wish list—twelve lovely things for her to dream about. To replace her list with a dog…

'I might not be able to aff…' But she faltered, knowing already that she would afford—how could she not? The moment she'd seen those eyes she knew she was hooked.

But then, amazingly, Nick stopped her before she could say the unsayable.

'He's a stray,' he said gently. 'But if you're offering to keep him, then Bailey and I will pay for his operation. We left the school door open. It may even have been our fault that he was run over—maybe he saw the open door from across the street and ran here for shelter. You tell me that in Banksia Bay parents are asked to volunteer for jobs? This, then, is our job. If he's your dog, then we'll pay.'

Misty stared up at him, astounded. Her thoughts were whirling.

Extremely expensive was suddenly no cost at all.

No cost except putting her dreams on hold yet again.

How could she not?

Nicholas was looking at her. Her whole class was looking at her.

'Fine,' she said weakly. 'I do need a dog.'

Dreams were just that—dreams.

* * *

Frank arrived then, blustering away his absence, playing the School Principal to Nicholas and to Bailey. Misty used the time to excuse herself and phone Dr Cray to say she was accepting Nicholas's very kind offer.

'Misty, love, are you out of your mind?' the vet demanded. 'You need this dog like a hole in the head. He's old, neglected and he'll need ongoing treatment for the rest of his life.'

'He's got lovely eyes. His ears… He's a sweetheart, I know he is.'

'You can't save them all. You swore you didn't want another dog. What about your list?'

'You know that's just a dream.'

Of course he did. This was Banksia Bay. The whole town knew everyone else's brand of toothpaste. So the town knew about her list, and they'd know her chances of achieving it had just taken another nosedive.

She cringed, but she couldn't back down now. It'd be like tearing away a part of herself—the part that said, *Good old Misty; you can always depend on her.* The part where her heart was. 'I've fallen for him,' she said, softly but determinedly. 'Now that Mr Holt's paying…'

'And that's something else I don't understand. Who is this guy?'

'I don't know. A painter. New to the town.'

A pause. Then… 'A painter. I wonder how he'd go painting props.'

Fred Cray was head of Banksia Bay Repertory Society. There was a lot more to moving to Banksia Bay than just emptying a moving van. Did Nicholas realise it?

Maybe he already had.

'Give him a day or so before you ask,' she pleaded. 'Just save my dog.'

'You're sure?'

'Yes.'

So she had a dog again. At one time she'd been responsible for Gran, for Grandpa and for four dogs. Her heart had been stretched six ways. Now she was down to just Gran.

But who was wishing Gran away? She never would, and maybe taking this dog was simply accepting life as it was.

Banksia Bay. What more could a girl want?

New blood, at least, she thought, moving her thoughts determinedly to a future. With a dog.

And, with that, she decided she wouldn't mind a chance to get to know Nicholas Holt. She at least needed to thank him properly. But when she returned to the classroom Frank ushered Nicholas straight out to his office, and that was the last she saw of him for the day.

Bailey stayed happily until the end of school—any hint of early terror had dissipated in the face of Natalie's maternal care—and then Frank declared himself on gate duty, probably so he'd be seen by this new parent to be doing the right thing.

For there was something about Nicholas…

See, that was the problem. There was something about Nicholas Holt that made Frank think maybe he ought to stick around, be seen, just in case Nicholas turned out to be someone important.

He had the air of someone important.

A painter?

It didn't seem…right, Misty thought. He had an air of quiet authority, of strength. And he also had money. She knew now what the little dog's operation would cost and he hadn't hesitated. This was no struggling single dad.

She cleared up the classroom and headed out to find a deserted playground. What did she expect? That he'd stick around and wait for her?

He'd made one generous gesture and he'd moved on. He had a house to move into. A future to organise.

Boats to paint?

She headed for the car and then to where she always went after school, every day without fail. Banksia Bay's nursing home.

Gran was in the same bed, in practically the same position she'd been in for years. One stroke had robbed her of movement. The last stroke had robbed her of almost everything else. Misty greeted her with a kiss and settled back and told her about her day.

Was it her imagination or could she sense approval? Gran would have rescued the little dog. She'd probably even have accepted money from a stranger to do it.

'It's not like I'm accepting welfare,' she told Gran. 'I mean, he's saving the dog—not paying me or anything. It's me who has to pay for the dog's ongoing care.'

Silence.

'So what shall we call him?'

More silence. Nothing new there. There'd been nothing but silence from Gran for years.

'What about Nicholas?' she asked. 'After the guy who saved him.'

But it didn't seem right. Nicholas seemed suddenly...singular. Taken.

'How about Ketchup, then?' she asked. 'On account of his broken leg. He'll spend the next few months ketching up.'

That was better. They both approved of that. She just knew Gran was smiling inside.

'Then I'd best go see how Ketchup's getting on,' she told her grandmother. 'He's with Dr Cray. I'm sorry it's a short visit tonight, but I'm a bit worried...'

She gave her grandmother's hand a squeeze. No response. There never was.

But dogs had been her grandmother's life. She'd like Ketchup, she thought, imagining herself bringing a recuperating Ketchup in to see her. Who knew what Gran could feel or sense or see, but maybe a dog on her bed would be good.

It had to be good for someone, Misty thought. Another dog...

Another love?

Who needed freedom, after all?

Nick and Bailey had the house sorted in remarkably short time, probably because they owned little more than the contents of their car. The house was only just suitable, Nick thought as they worked. Maybe it hadn't been such a good idea to rent via the Internet. The photographs he'd seen appeared to have been doctored.

The doors and windows didn't quite seal. The advertised view to the sea was a view *towards* the sea—there'd been a failure to mention a fishermen's co-op in between. There were no curtains, bare light bulbs, sparse floor coverings.

But at least it was a base to start with. They could make it better, and if the town worked out they'd buy something of their own. 'It's like camping,' he told Bailey. 'We'll pretend we're explorers, living rough. All we need is a campfire in the backyard.'

Bailey gave him a polite smile. Right. But the school experience had made them both more optimistic about the future. They set up two camp beds in the front room, organised the rudiments of a kitchen so they could make breakfast, then meandered down to the harbour to buy fish and chips for tea.

They walked for a little afterwards, past the boats, through the main street, then somehow they ended up walking past the vet's.

Misty had just pulled up. She was about to go in.

He should stay clear, he thought. Paying for the dog was one thing, but he had no intention of getting personally involved.

But Bailey had already seen her. 'Miss Lawrence,' he called, and Misty waved. She smiled.

She smiled at Bailey, Nick told himself sharply, because a man had to do something to defend himself in the face of a smile like that.

He didn't have any intention of smiling back. Distance, he told himself harshly. He'd made that resolution. Stay clear of any complication at all. The only thing—the only one—who mattered was his son.

He'd messed things up so badly already. How many chances did a man have to make things right?

But Misty was still smiling. 'Hi,' she said. 'Are you here to see how Ketchup is?'

'Ketchup?' Bailey was beaming, and Nick thought back to the scared little boy of this morning and thought, *What a difference a day makes*. 'Is that what his name is?'

'Absolutely.'

'Why?'

'He's a hopalong. He'll spend his life ketching up.'

Bailey frowned, his serious little brow furrowing as he considered this from all angles. Then his face changed, lit from within as he got it. 'Ketchup,' he said and he giggled.

Nick had no intention of smiling, but somehow... This felt good, he thought. More. It felt great that Bailey giggled. Maybe he could afford to unbend a little.

'Great name,' he told her.

'He'll be a great dog,' Misty said.

'How is he?'

'He was still under anaesthesia last time I rang. Did you know his leg was broken in three places?'

'That's bad,' Bailey said, his giggle disappearing. 'When I got shot my arm was only broken in one place.'

Misty stilled. 'You were shot?'

'I'm better now,' Bailey said and tugged up his sleeve, revealing a long angry scar running from his wrist to his shoulder. 'I had plaster and bandages on for ages and it hurt a lot. Dad and I stayed at the hospital for ages and ages while the doctors made my fingers wiggle again but now I'm better. So we came here. Can we see Ketchup?'

'Of course,' she said, but her voice had changed. He could well imagine why. She'd have visions of drug deals, underworld stuff, gangsters… For a small boy to calmly say he'd been shot…

So maybe that was okay, he thought. Maybe it'd make her step back and it suddenly seemed important that she did step back.

Why did he think this woman might want to get close?

What was he thinking? *He wanted her to think he was a gangster?* What sort of future was he building for his son? Maybe he needed to loosen up.

'Now?' Bailey was asking.

Misty glanced at Nick. Okay, he didn't want to be a gangster, and he had to allow Bailey to form a relationship with his teacher. He nodded. Reluctantly.

And, even if she was thinking he might be carrying a sawn-off shotgun under his jacket, despite his curt, not particularly friendly nod, Misty smiled down at his son and her face showed nothing but pleasure.

'Wow, wait until we tell Ketchup you've had a broken arm,' she said. 'You'll be able to compare wounds.' She took Bailey's hand and tugged open the screen door. 'Let's see how he's doing.'

And she didn't even care if he was a gangster, Nick thought, feeling ashamed. All she cared about was his son.

Ketchup had looked bad this morning but he looked a lot worse now. He lay on towels in an open cage. His hind quarters were shaved, splinted and bandaged. He had a soft collar around his neck, presumably to stop him chewing his bandages, but he wasn't about to chew any time soon. He looked deeply asleep. The tubes attached to his foreleg looked scary.

'I have him heavily sedated,' Dr Cray said. 'Pain relief as well as something to calm him down. He's been deeply traumatised.'

'Do we know anything about him?' Misty looked down at the wretched little dog and she felt the same heart twist she'd felt this morning. Yes, it was stupid, taking him on, but there was no way she could help herself. This dog had come through so much... He had to have a second chance.

'He was at the Shelter for two weeks,' Fred Cray said, glancing at his card. 'No one's enquired about him. Rolf Enwhistle found him and another dog prowling round his poultry pen but they weren't exactly a threat to the hens. This one rolled over and whimpered when Rolf went near. They were both starving—no collars. They looked like they'd been dumped in the bush and been doing it tough for weeks.'

'Oh, Ketchup,' Misty breathed. She looked back to Nick then, and she smiled at him. Doubts about the wisdom of keeping this dog had flown. How could she consider anything else? 'And you've saved him for me.'

'It's okay,' Nicholas said, sounding uncomfortable.

'Will he be your dog now?' Bailey asked.

'He certainly will,' she said, still smiling, though her eyes were misting. 'I have the world's biggest couch. Ketchup and I can watch television together every night. I wonder if he likes popcorn.'

'He's a lucky dog to have found you lot,' Fred said—but Bailey was suddenly distracted.

'We don't have a couch,' he said urgently to his father. 'We need one.'

'We'll buy a couch,' Nicholas said. 'On Monday.'

'Can we buy a couch big enough for dogs?'

'We'll buy a couch big enough for you and me.'

'Can Miss Lawrence and Ketchup come over and sit on our couch?'

'There won't be room.'

'Then we need to buy a bigger couch,' Bailey said firmly. 'For visitors.'

'I suspect Ketchup might want to stick around home for a while,' Misty said, seeing conflicting emotions on Nicholas's face and deciding he'd paid for Ketchup's vet's fees—the least she could do was take the pressure off. 'Ketchup needs to get used to having a home.'

'That's what Dad says we need to do,' Bailey said.

'I hear you're moving into Don Samuelson's old place,' Fred said neutrally. 'That's a bit of a barn. You could fit a fair few couches in there.'

'We don't have anything except two camp beds and a kitchen table,' Bailey said, suddenly desolate, using the same voice he used when he said he really, really needed a hamburger. 'Our new house is empty. It's horrid. We don't have pictures or anything.'

'Hey, then Misty's your girl,' the vet said, nudging Misty. 'Give 'em your spiel, Mist.'

'No, I…'

'She wanted to be an interior designer, our Misty,' the vet said before she could stop him. 'Sat the exams, got great marks, she was off and flying. Only then her gran had the first of her strokes. Misty stayed home, did teaching by correspondence and here she is, ten years later. But we all know she does a little interior decorating on the side. Part-time, of course. There's not enough interior decorating in Banksia Bay to keep a girl fed, eh, Mist? But if you're in Don Samuelson's place… There's a challenge. A man'd need a good interior designer there.'

'I'm a schoolteacher,' Misty said stiffly.

'But the man needs a couch.' Fred could be insistent when he wanted to be, and something had got into him now. 'New to town, money to spend and an empty house. It's not exactly appealing, that place, but Misty knows how to make a home.'

'You could come and see and tell us what to buy,' Bailey said, excited.

'Excellent idea. Why don't you do it straight away?' the vet said. He glanced down at the little dog and his eyes softened. Like Misty, Fred fell in love with them all. That Nick had appeared from nowhere with the wherewithal to pay…and that Misty had offered the dog a home…

Uh oh. Misty saw his train of thought and decided she needed to back off, fast. Fred Cray had been a friend of her Grandpa's. He was a lovely vet but he was also an interfering old busybody.

'I need to go home,' she said.

'You've visited your gran and you ate a hamburger at Eddie's half an hour ago,' Fred said, and she groaned inside. There was nothing the whole town didn't know in Banksia Bay. 'The little guy and his dad had fish and chips on the wharf, so they've eaten, too. So why don't you go by his place now and give him a few hints?'

'There's no rush,' Nicholas said, sounding trapped.

'Yes, there is. We need a couch.' Bailey was definite.

'See,' Fred said. 'There is a rush. Misty, I'm keeping this little guy overnight. Come back in the morning and we'll see how he is. Nine tomorrow?'

'Yes,' she said, feeling helpless. She turned to Nicholas. 'But there's no need… I'm not really an interior decorator.'

'Bailey and I could do with some advice,' he admitted, looking as bulldozed as she felt. 'Not just on what couch to buy but where to buy it. Plus a fridge and beds and a proper kitchen table. Oh, and curtains. We need curtains.'

'And a television,' Bailey said.

'You really have nothing?' Misty asked, astonished.

'I really have nothing. But I don't want to intrude…'

'You're not intruding. You're the answer to her dreams,' the vet said, chortling. 'A man with a blank canvas. Go with him, Misty, fast, before some other woman snaffles him.'

'I don't…' She could feel herself blush.

'To give him advice, I mean,' Fred said, grinning. 'You'll get that round here,' he told Nicholas. 'Advice, whether you ask for it or not. Like me advising you to use Misty. But that's good advice, sir. Take it or leave it, but our Misty's good, in more ways than one.'

Chapter 3

Pick a quiet town in rural Australia, the safest place you can imagine to raise a child. Rent a neat house on a small block without any trees to climb and with fences all around. Organise your work so you can be a stay-at-home dad, so you can take care of your son from dawn to dusk. Hunker down and block out the world.

His plan did not include inviting a strange woman home on day one.

The vet had obviously embarrassed her half to death. She emerged from the clinic, laughing but half horrified.

'Fred's the world's worst busybody,' she said. 'You go home and choose your own couch.'

That was good advice—only Bailey's face fell.

If she was old and plain it'd be fine, he told himself, but her blush was incredibly cute and when she laughed she had this kind of dimple… Danger signs for someone who wished to stay strictly isolated.

But maybe he was being dumb. Paranoid, even. Yes, she was as cute as a button, but in a girl-next-door way. She was Bailey's schoolteacher.

Maybe they needed a couch, he told himself, and found himself reassuring her that, yes, he would like some advice. There were so many decisions to be made and he didn't know where to start.

All of which was true, so he ushered her in the front door of their new home and watched her eyes light up with interest. Challenge. It was the way he felt when he had a blank sheet of paper and a yacht to design.

For Fred was right. This place was one giant canvas. They'd set up camp beds in the front room and slung a sheet over the windows for privacy. They had a camp table and a couple of stools in the kitchen. They'd picked up basic kitchen essentials.

They had not a lot else.

'You travel light,' she said, awed.

'Not any more, we don't.'

'We're staying here,' Bailey said, sounding scared again. The minute they'd walked in the door he'd grabbed his teddy from his camp bed and he was clutching it to him as if it were a lifeline. The house was big and echoey and empty. This was a huge deal for both of them.

Bailey had spent most of his short life on boats of one description or another, either on his father's classic clinker-built yacht or on his grandparents' more ostentatious cruiser. The last year or so had been spent in and out of hospital, then in a hospital apartment provided so Bailey could get the rehabilitation he needed. He had two points of stability—his father and his teddy. He needed more.

But where to start? To have a home…to own furniture… Nick needed help, so it was entirely sensible to ask advice of Bailey's schoolteacher.

He wasn't crossing personal boundaries at all.

'You really have nothing?' she asked.

'We've been living on boats.'

'Is that where Bailey was hurt?'

'Yes. It's also where Bailey's mother was killed,' he said briefly. She had to know that—as Bailey's teacher, there was no way he could keep it from her.

'I'm so sorry,' she said, sounding appalled.

'Yeah, well, we've come to a safer part of the world now,' he said. 'All we need to make us happy is a couch.'

'And a dog?'

'No!'

'No?' she said, and she smiled.

She smiled ten seconds after he'd told her his wife had died. This wasn't the normal reaction. But then he realised Bailey was still within hearing. She'd put the appalled face away.

Bailey had had enough appalled women weeping on him to last a lifetime. This woman was smart enough not to join their ranks.

'A girl can always try,' she said, moving right on. 'Do you want all new stuff?'

'I don't mind.'

'Old stuff's more comfortable,' she said, standing in the doorway of the empty living room and considering.

'It'd look better, too. This isn't exactly a new house.' She stared around her, considering. 'You know, there are better houses to rent. This place is a bit draughty.'

'It'll do for now.' He didn't have the energy to go house-hunting yet. 'Do you have any old stuff in mind?'

She hesitated. 'You might not stay here for long.'

'We need to stay here until we're certain Banksia Bay works out.'

'Banksia Bay's a great place to live,' she said, but she was still looking at the house. 'You know, if you just wanted to borrow stuff until you've made up your mind, I have a homestead full of furniture. I could lend you what you need, which would give you space to gradually buy your own later. If you like, we could make this place homelike this weekend.'

'You have a homestead full of old stuff?'

'My place is practically two houses joined together. My grandparents threw nothing out. I have dust covers over two living rooms and five bedrooms. If you want, you can come out tomorrow morning to take a look.'

'Your grandparents are no longer there?'

'Grandpa died years ago and Gran's in a nursing home. There's only me and I'm trying to downsize. You're settling as I'm trying to get myself unsettled.'

He shouldn't ask. He shouldn't be interested. It wasn't in his new mantra—*focus only on Bailey*. But, despite his vow, she had him intrigued. 'By getting a new dog? That doesn't sound unsettled.'

'There is that,' she said, brightness fading a little. 'I can't help myself. But it'll sort itself out. Who knows? Ketchup might not like living with me. He might prefer a younger owner. If I could talk you into a really big couch…'

'No,' Nick said, seeing where she was heading.

'Worth a try,' she said and grinned and stooped to talk to Bailey. Bailey had been watching them with some anxiety, clutching his teddy like a talisman. 'Bailey, tomorrow I'm coming into town to pick up Ketchup. If I spend the morning settling him into his new home, would you and your dad like to come to my house in the afternoon to see if you can use some of my furniture?'

'Yes,' Bailey said. No hesitation. 'Teddy will come, too.'

'Excellent,' Misty said and rose. 'Teddy will be very welcome.' She smiled at Nick then. It was a truly excellent smile. It was a smile that could…

That couldn't. No.

'Straight through the town, three miles along the coast, the big white place with the huge veranda,' she was saying. 'You can't miss it. Any time after noon.'

'I'm not sure…'

'Oh, sorry.' Her face fell. 'You probably want all new furniture straight away. I got carried away. I'm very bossy.'

And at the look on her face—appalled at her assertiveness but still…hopeful?—he was lost.

Independence at all costs. He'd had enough emotion, enough commitment and drama to last a lifetime. There were reasons for his vows.

But this was his son's schoolteacher. She was someone who'd be a stalwart in their lives. He could be friendly without getting close, he told himself, and the idea of getting furniture fast, getting this place looking like home for Bailey, was hugely appealing.

And visiting Misty tomorrow afternoon? Seeing her smile again?

He could bear it, he thought. Just.

'We'll be extremely grateful,' he said, and Bailey smiled and then yawned, as big a yawn as he'd ever seen his son give.

'Bedtime,' he said, and Bailey looked through to the little camp bed and then looked at Misty and produced another of the smiles that had been far too rare in the last year.

'Can Miss Lawrence read me a bedtime story? She reads really good stories.'

'I'd love to,' Misty said, smiling back at him. 'If it's okay with your dad.'

It was okay, he conceded, but…

Uh oh.

There were all sorts of gaps in their lives right now, and this was only a small one, but suddenly it seemed important—and he didn't like to admit it. Not in front of a schoolteacher. In front of *this* schoolteacher.

'We don't have any story books,' he conceded.

What sort of an admission was that? He'd be hauled away to be disciplined by…who knew? Was there a Bad Parents Board in Banksia Bay? He felt about six inches tall.

They did own books, but they'd been put in storage in England until he was sure he was settled. Containers took months to arrive. Meanwhile… 'We'll buy some tomorrow,' he'd told Bailey.

'I have story books,' Misty said, seemingly unaware of his embarrassment.

'We've been living in a hospital apartment. Story books were provided.'

'You don't need to explain,' she said, cutting through his discomfort. 'My car's loaded with school work—there'll be all sorts to choose from. If you would like me to read to Bailey…'

They both would.

Forget vows, he told himself. He watched Bailey's face and he felt the tension that he hadn't known he had ease from his shoulders.

For the last twelve months the responsibility for the care of his little son had been like a giant clamp around his heart. He'd failed him so dramatically… How could Bailey depend on him again?

Over the last year he'd been attempting to patch their lives back together and for most of that time he'd had professional help. But today they'd left behind the hospital and all it represented. This was day one of their new life together.

To admit that he needed help…to have Bailey want help and to have it offered… It should feel bad, but instead it made his world suddenly lighter; it made what lay ahead more bearable.

'We'd love you to read to Bailey,' he admitted, and it didn't even feel wrong.

'Then that's settled,' she said, beaming down at Bailey. 'I'm so glad you started school today. All weekend I'll know I have a new friend. Right, you get into your pyjamas and clean your teeth and I'll fetch a story book. I have my favourite in the car. It's about bears who live in a house just like this one, but every night they have adventures.'

'Ooh, yes, please,' Bailey said and the thing was settled.

So Nick sat on the front step, watched the sunset and listened to Misty telling his son a story about bears and adventures—and he found himself smiling. Unlike the bears, they'd come to the end of their adventures. The house was terrible but they could do something about it. This place was safe. This place could work.

He'd chosen Banksia Bay because it was a couple of hours drive to Sydney. It had a good harbour, a great boat building industry and it was quiet. He should have come and checked the house before he'd signed the lease but to leave Bailey for the four hours it'd take to get here and back, or explain what he was doing… He'd have had to come during office hours, and those hours he spent with his son.

Choosing this house was the price he'd paid, but even this wasn't so bad.

He couldn't see the sea from here but he could hear it. That was good. To be totally out of touch with the ocean would be unthinkable.

He'd set up his office over the weekend. On Monday Bailey would start regular school hours. He'd be able to get back to work.

Work the new way.

The bear story was drawing to its dramatic conclusion. He glanced in the open window and Bailey's eyes were almost shut.

He'd sleep well in his new home—because of this woman.

She was so not his type of woman, he thought. She was a country mouse.

No. That was unjust and uncalled for. He accepted she was intelligent and she was kind. But her jeans were faded and her clothes were unpretentious. Her braid was now a ponytail. She'd changed since she'd cradled the dog this morning. She'd lost the bloodstains, but she must have changed at school because this shirt had paint on it already.

She was stooping now to give his son a kiss goodnight, and her ponytail looked sort of…perky? Actually, it was more sexy than perky, he thought, and he was aware of a stab of something as unexpected as it was unwanted.

The thought of those curls… He'd like to run his fingers through…

Whoa. How to complicate a life, he thought—have an affair with the local schoolteacher. He had no intention of having an affair with anyone. Let's just keep the hormones out of this, he told himself savagely, so when Misty came outside he thanked her with just a touch too much formality.

And he saw her stiffen. Withdraw. She'd got his unspoken message, and more.

'I'm sorry. I should have given you the book and left. I didn't mean to intrude.'

She was smart. She'd picked up on signals when he'd hardly sent them.

'You didn't intrude,' he said, and this time he went the other way—he put more warmth into his tone than he intended. He gripped her hand, and that was a mistake. The warmth…

How long since he'd touched a woman?

And there was another dumb thought. He'd been shaking hands with nurses, doctors, therapists every day. Why was Misty different?

He couldn't permit her to be different.

'You want to tell me about Bailey?' she asked and he did the withdrawal thing again. Released her hand, fast.

'It's on his medical form at school.'

'Of course it is,' she said, backing off again. 'I left school in a hurry because I wanted to get to the vet's, so I haven't caught up with the forms yet. I'll read them on Monday.' She turned away, heading out of his life.

She'd see the forms on Monday…

Of course she would, he thought, and he'd been frank in what he'd written. He'd had no choice. There were a thousand ways that keeping what happened to Bailey from his classroom teacher could cause problems. *Okay, boys and girls, let's pretend to be pirates…*

She had to know, and to force her to read the forms on Monday rather than telling her now… What was he trying to prove?

'I can tell you now,' he said.

He was all over the place.

He felt all over the place.

'There's no need…'

'There is a need.'

Why did it feel as if he were stepping on eggshells? This was Bailey's teacher. Treat her as such, he told himself harshly. Treat her professionally, with cool acceptance and with an admission that she needed to know things he'd rather not talk about.

'I'm not handling this well,' he admitted. 'Today's been stressful. In truth, the last year's been stressful. Or maybe that's an understatement. The last year's been appalling.' He paused then, wanting to retreat, but he had to say it.

'I don't want to interrupt your evening any more than I already have, but if you have the time… You're Bailey's teacher. You need to know what he's been through.'

'I guess I do,' she said equably. 'We both want what's best for Bailey.'

That was good. It took the personal out of it. He was telling her—for Bailey.

He paused then and looked at her. She was a woman without guile, his kid's teacher. She was standing on the veranda of the home he was preparing for his son. She was a warm, comforting presence. Sensible. Solid. *Safe.*

His parents would approve of her, he thought, and the idea sent a wave of emotion running through him so strongly that he felt ill. If he'd chosen a woman like this rather than Isabelle…

Someone safe.

Someone he could trust if he let his guard down.

When had he last let his guard down?

'So tell me, then,' she said—and he did.

There was no reason not to.

It took a while to start. Nick fetched lemonade. He said he'd rather be drinking beer but he hadn't yet made it further than the supermarket. He apologised for there being no food but cornflakes. She said she didn't need beer and she wasn't hungry. She waited.

It was as if he had to find his mindset, as well as his place on the veranda.

Nick didn't look like a man who spent a lot of time in an easy chair, Misty thought, and when he finally leaned his rangy frame on the veranda rail she wasn't surprised. She was sitting on the veranda steps. The width of Bailey's window was between them. Maybe that was deliberate.

For a while he didn't say anything, but she was content to wait. She'd been teaching kids for years. Parents often needed to tell her things about their children; about their families. A lot of it wasn't easy. But what Nick had to say…

'Bailey's mother was shot off the coast of Africa,' he said at last, and the words were such a shock she almost dropped her lemonade.

No one ever got shot in Banksia Bay. And…*off the coast of Africa?*

If this was one of her students, she'd give them a sheet of art paper and say, 'Paint it for me.' Dreams needed expression.

But one look at this man's face told her this was no dream. It might not happen in her world, but it did happen.

'She was killed instantly,' he said, and he was no longer looking at her. He was staring out at the blank wall of the fisherman's co-op, but she knew he was seeing somewhere far off. Somewhere dreadful. 'Bailey was shot as well,' he told her. 'It's taken almost a year to get him this far. To see him safe.'

What to say after a statement like that? She tried not to blurt out a hundred questions, but she couldn't think of the first one.

'It's a grim story,' he said at last. 'Stupidity at its finest. I've needed to tell so many people over the last year, but telling never gets easier.'

'You're not compelled to tell me.'

'You're Bailey's teacher. You need to know.'

'There is that,' she said cautiously. If she didn't know a child's history, it was like walking through a minefield. 'Oh, Nicholas...'

'Nick,' he said savagely, as if the name was important.

'Nick,' she said—and waited. 'It's okay,' she said gently. 'Just tell me as much as I need to know.'

He shrugged at that, a derisory gesture, half mocking. 'Right. As much as you need to know. I was working on a contract in South Africa, Bailey and Isabelle were with Isabelle's parents. They were on a boat coming to meet me, they were robbed and Isabelle and Bailey were shot.'

'Oh, Nick...'

His face stopped her going any further. There was such emptiness.

'What's not obvious in that version is my stupidity,' he said, and she sensed that she was about to get a story that he hadn't told over and over. He no longer seemed to be talking to her. He seemed somewhere in his head, hating himself, feeding his hatred.

The hatred made her feel ill. She wanted to stop him, but there was no way she could.

If this man needed to talk, ugly or not, maybe she had to listen.

'As a kid I was…overprotected,' he said at last into the silence, and the impression that he wasn't talking to her grew stronger. 'Only child. Protected at every turn. So I rebelled. I did the modern day equivalent of running away to sea. I studied marine architecture. I designed boats, won prizes, made serious money. I built a series of experimental boats, and I took risks.'

'Good for you,' she murmured. Then she added, before she could help herself, 'Half your luck.'

'No,' he said flatly. 'Risks are stupid.'

'It depends on the risks,' she said, and thought of how many risks she'd ever encountered. Approximately none.

But then…this wasn't about her, she reminded herself sharply. Listen.

'My kind of risks were definitely the stupid kind,' he said and, despite her interjection, she still had the impression he was talking to himself. 'Black run skiing, ocean racing in boats built for speed rather than safety, scuba-diving, underwater caving… Fantastic stuff, but the more dangerous the better. And then I met Isabelle. She was like me but more so. Risks were like breathing to her. The stuff we did… Her parents were wealthy so she could indulge any whim, and Isabelle surely had whims. In time, I learned she was a little bit crazy. If I skied the hardest runs, she didn't ski runs at all. She skied into the unknown. Together, we did crazy stuff.'

'But you had fun?' She was trying to keep the wistfulness from her voice, not sure if she was succeeding. Nick glanced at her as if he'd forgotten she was there, but he managed a wry nod.

'We did. We built *Mahelkee*, our gorgeous yacht, and we sailed everywhere. I designed as I went. We had an amazing life. And then we had Bailey, and that was the most amazing thing of all. Our son.'

He hesitated then, and she saw where memories of good times ended and the pain began. 'But when I held him…' he said softly, 'for the first time I could see where my parents were coming from. Not as much, of course, but a bit.'

'So no black ski runs for Bailey?'

He was back staring at the side of the co-op. No longer talking to her. 'There were no ski runs where we lived but there was no way Isabelle was living in a house. We kept living on the boat. It caused conflict between us but we kept travelling. We kept doing stuff we loved. Only…when I saw the risky stuff I thought of Bailey. We started being careful.'

'Sensible.'

'Isabelle didn't see it like that.'

Silence.

This wasn't her business, she thought; she also wasn't sure whether he'd continue. She wasn't sure she wanted him to continue.

'You want to finish this another day?' she ventured, and he shook his head, still not looking at her.

'Not much more to tell, really. I'd married a risk-taker, and Isabelle was never going to change. Bailey and I just held her back. We were in England when

I got a contract to design a new yacht. She was to be built in South Africa. I needed to consult with the builders.'

'So you went.'

'We were docked at a pretty English port. Isabelle's parents own the world's most ostentatious cruiser and they were docked nearby. Isabelle was taking flying lessons and they were keeping her happy. Everyone seemed settled; we were even talking about enrolling Bailey in kindergarten. So I flew across to South Africa. But Isabelle was never settled for long. She got bored with her flying lessons and persuaded her parents to bring their boat out to surprise me.'

'To Africa?'

'In a boat that screamed money.' There was no mistaking the bitterness in his voice now. The pain. 'To one of the poorest places on the planet. When I found out they were on their way I was appalled. I knew the risks. I had security people give them advice. I sent people out to meet them, only they were hit before they arrived.'

'Hit?'

He shrugged. 'What do you expect? Poverty everywhere, then along comes a boat with a swimming pool, crew in uniform, dollar signs practically painted on the sides. But they'd had good advice. If you're robbed, once you're boarded, just hand over everything. Isabelle's father carried so much cash it'd make your head swim. He thought he could buy himself out of any trouble. Maybe he could, but Isabelle…she decided to defend,' he said savagely.

Misty knew she didn't exist for him right now.

There was no disguising the loathing in his voice and it was directed only at himself. 'I knew she owned a gun before we were married, but she told me she'd got rid of it. And I believed her. Of all the stupid…' He shook his head as if trying to clear a nightmare but there was no way he could clear what he was going through. 'So, as her father tried to negotiate, she came up from below deck, firing. At men who made their living from piracy. Two shots—that's all it took. Two shots and she was dead and Bailey was close to it.'

She closed her eyes, appalled. 'So that's why you're here,' she whispered.

'That's why we're here. Bailey's spent a year in and out of hospital while I've researched the safest place in the world to be. I can design boats from here. Most of my designs are built internationally. I've hired an off-sider who can do the travelling for me. I can be a stay-at-home dad. I can keep Bailey safe.'

'You'll wrap him in cotton wool?' She felt suddenly, dreadfully anxious. 'Small risks can be exciting,' she ventured. 'I can make my bike stand on its front wheel. That's meant the odd bruise and graze. There's risks and risks.'

'I will not take risks with my son's life.'

The pain behind that statement… It was almost over-whelming.

What to do?

Nothing.

'No one's asking you to,' she said, deciding brisk and practical was the way to go. 'You have a house to organise, a child to care for and boats to design. Our vet, Fred, has plans for your painting, and I might even persuade you to get a dog. You can settle down and live happily ever after. But if you'd never had those adventures…'

What was she talking about? Don't go there, she told herself, confused at where her mind was taking her. If he'd never had those adventures…like she hadn't?

This was not about her.

She made herself step down from the veranda. This man's life, his past, was nothing to do with her. She needed to return to the nursing home to make sure Gran was settled for the night. She needed to go home.

Home… The home she'd never left.

Nick didn't stop her. He'd withdrawn again, into his isolation, where risks weren't allowed. He seemed as if he was hardly seeing her. 'Thank you for listening,' he said formally.

'You're welcome,' she said, just as formally, and she turned and left before she could ask him—totally inappropriately—to tell her about Africa.

What was he about, telling a total stranger the story of his life? It was so out of character he felt he'd shed a skin—and not in a good way. He felt stupid and naive and exposed.

He'd never done personal. Even with Isabelle… He'd hardly talked to her about his closeted childhood.

So why let it all out tonight? *To his son's schoolteacher?*

Maybe it was because that was all she was, he decided. Bailey's teacher. Someone whose focus was purely on his son. Someone prepared to listen when he needed to let it all out.

Why let it out tonight?

Justification?

He stared around at the shabby house, the empty walls, the lack of anything as basic as a storybook, and he thought that was where it had come from. A need to justify himself in the eyes of Misty Lawrence.

Why did he need to justify himself?

He didn't want her to judge him.

That was stupid, all by itself. She was a country hick schoolteacher. Her opinion didn't matter at all.

If it did… If it did, then it'd come under the category of taking risks, and Nicholas Holt no longer took risks.

Ever.

She went home, to her big house, where there was only herself and the sound of the sea.

Africa.

She'd just got herself a dog.

Africa.

Nick's story should have appalled her. It did.

But Africa…

Since Gran's stroke, she'd started keeping her scrapbooks in the kitchen where recipes were supposed to be. Dreams instead of recipes? It worked for her. She tugged the books down now and set them on the kitchen table.

She had almost half a book on Africa. Pictures of safaris. Lying at dawn in a hide, watching a pride of lions. The markets of Marrakesh.

Africa was number eight on her list.

She had a new dog. How long would Ketchup live?

She picked up a second scrapbook and it fell open

at the Scottish Highlands. She'd pasted in a picture of a girl in a floaty white dress lying in a field of purple heather. Behind her was a mass of purple mountains.

She'd pasted this page when she was twelve. She'd put a bagpiper in the background, and a castle. Later, she'd moved to finer details. Somewhere she'd seen a documentary on snow buntings and they had her entranced—small birds with their snow-white chests and rippling whistle. Tiny travellers. Exquisite.

Birds who travelled where she never could. She had pictures of snow buntings now, superimposed on her castle.

She flicked on, through her childhood dreams. Another scrapbook. The Greek islands. Whitewashed houses clinging to cliff faces, sapphire seas, caiques, fishermen at dawn…

These scrapbooks represented a lifetime of dreaming. The older she was, the more organised she'd become, going through and through, figuring what she might be able to afford, what was feasible.

She'd divided the books, the cuttings, into months. She now had a list of twelve.

Exploring the north of England, the Yorkshire Dales, a train journey up through Scotland, Skara Brae, the Orkneys… Bagpipers in the mist. Snow buntings. Number ten.

Greece. Number two.

Africa.

Risks.

Bailey.

She closed the book with a snap. Nicholas was right. You didn't take risks. You stayed safe.

She'd just agreed to keep another dog. She had no choice.

Her computer was on the bench. On impulse, she typed in *Nicholas Holt, Marine Architect* and waited for it to load.

And then gasped.

The man had his own Online Encyclopaedia entry. His website was amazing. There were boats and boats, each more wonderful than the last. Each designed by Nicholas Holt.

This man was seriously famous.

And seriously rich? You didn't get to design boats like these without having money.

That a man like this could decide Banksia Bay was the right place to be…a safe place to be…

'It makes sense,' she told herself, and she flicked off the Internet before she could do what she wanted to do—which was to research a little more about Africa.

'I have a dog now,' she told herself. 'Black runs are probably cold and wet. Doesn't Scotland have fog and midges? Who knows what risks are out there? So gird your loins, accept that dreams belong in childhood and do what Nick Holt has done. Decide Banksia Bay is the best place in the world.'

But dreams didn't disintegrate on demand.

Dogs don't live for ever, she told herself. Her list money was still intact. She could hold onto her dream a while longer.

One day she'd complete her list. In her retirement? Maybe.

Just not one day soon.

Chapter 4

Ketchup decided to live.

At nine the next morning Misty was gazing down at the little dog with something akin to awe. He was still hooked up to drips. His back leg was splinted and bandaged. He had cuts and grazes everywhere, made more gruesome by the truly horrid-coloured antiseptic wash, but he was looking up at her with his huge black eyes and…his tail was wagging.

It had lost half its fur and it had probably been a pretty scrappy tail to start with, but it was definitely wagging. The eyes that looked at her were huge with hope, and she fell in love all over again.

'How can he have been at the shelter for two weeks and no one claimed him?' she demanded of Fred, and the old vet smiled, took out the drips, bundled the little dog up and handed him over.

'Not everyone has a heart as big as yours, Misty. Not everyone accepts responsibilities like you do.'

'What's one more responsibility?' she said and, yes, she felt a little bitter but, as she carried Ketchup out to her car, she wondered how she could feel bad about giving this dog a home.

There was no way she could leave Banksia Bay with Gran like she was. Ketchup would make life better—not worse.

She settled him onto the passenger seat and she talked to him the whole way home.

'You're going to like it with me. I have a great house. It's old and comfy and close to the beach, where you'll be able to run and run as soon as your leg's better. And there's so many interesting smells…' Then she couldn't stop herself adding a bit more exciting stuff because, for some reason, it was front and centre. 'And this afternoon we have two friends coming out to visit. Bailey and Nick. Nick's the one who saved you.'

He really had saved him. Fred had given her the facts.

'He's left his credit card imprint. Every cost associated with this dog, long-term, goes to Mr Holt. There's nothing for you to take care of. Yeah, he'll need ongoing care, but it's sorted.'

'He's a real hero,' she said, thinking of the website, of Nick's image, and of Nicholas last night. His care of his little son. His willingness to pay for Ketchup. The fact that he was haunted by his perceived failure to protect Bailey.

He was in such pain…

Ketchup wriggled forward and put his nose on her

knee. Yes, he should be in a crate in the back but she figured this guy had had enough of crates to last a lifetime.

She was still thinking of Nick.

'He's our hero,' she told him. 'He's come to Banksia Bay to be safe, not heroic, but he's saved you. So maybe there's a little bit of hero left in him.'

A little bit of Adonis?

No. He was done with adventure. He was done with risk-taking.

He wanted to settle in Banksia Bay and live happily ever after.

Maybe even marry the local schoolteacher?

Where had that idea come from? A guy like that… She felt herself blush from the toes up.

But you need to settle as well, she told herself as she took her dog home. You have a great life here. A comfortable existence. All you need is a hero to settle with.

And put another rocker on the front porch so you can rock into old age together? I don't think so.

So what is it you want? she asked herself, and she knew the answer.

Life.

'Life's here,' she told herself out loud. 'Life's Banksia Bay and a new dog and a new pupil in my class. Woohoo.'

Ketchup pawed her knee and she felt the familiar stab of guilt.

'Sorry,' she told him. 'I love it here. Of course I do. I'd never do anything to upset you or Gran or anyone else in this place. You can come home and be safe with me.'

Safe with Misty.

A flash of remembered pain shafted through her thoughts. Her grandfather's first heart attack. Her grandmother, crippled with arthritis, terrified. Misty had been thirteen, already starting to understand how much lay on her shoulders.

And then her hippy mother had turned up, as unexpectedly and as briefly as she'd turned up less than half a dozen times in Misty's life. Misty remembered standing beside her grandfather's bedside, watching her grandmother's face drawn in fear. She remembered the mother she barely recognised hugging her grandmother, then backing out, to friends who never introduced themselves, to a psychedelic combi-van waiting to take her to who knew where? To one of the places the postcards came from.

'You'll be fine,' her mother had said to her grandmother, and she'd waved inappropriately gaily. 'I'm glad I could fit this visit in. I know Dadda will be okay. He's strong as a horse, and I know you'll both be safe with Misty.'

'See,' she told the little dog. 'My mother was right all along.'

There was no way he could miss Misty's house. It was three miles out of town, set well back from the road. There were paddocks all round it, undulating pastures with cattle grazing peacefully in the midday sun. The sea was its glittering backdrop, and Nick, who'd been to some of the most beautiful places on the earth, felt that this was one of them.

Here was a sanctuary, he thought. A place for a man to come home to.

Misty was on the veranda, easy to spot as they pulled up. She was curled up on a vast cane rocker surrounded by faded cushions. There was a rug over her knee.

Ketchup was somewhere under that rug. As they climbed from the car, Nick could see his nose.

Once again, that pang. Of what? Want? Of the thought that here was home? This place…

This woman.

He'd bared his soul to this woman last night. It should feel bad. Somehow, though, it didn't feel threatening.

'I can't get up,' she called, her voice lilting in a way he was coming to recognize, beginning to like. 'We've just gone to sleep.'

As if in denial, a tail emerged and gave a sleepy wag.

Bailey scooted up the steps to meet her, but Nick took his time, watching his son check the dog, smile at Misty, then clamber up onto the rocker to join them.

Something was happening in his chest.

This was like a scene out of *Little House on the Prairie*, he told himself, at the same time telling the lump in his throat to go down and stay down. The way he was feeling was kitsch. Corny.

Any minute now, Misty would invite them inside for home-baked cookies and lemonade. Or maybe she'd have a picnic to take down to the beach. She'd have prepared it lovingly beforehand, with freshly baked cakes, fragrant pies, home-made preserves.

They'd be packed in a cute wicker basket with a red gingham cover…

'It's about time you got here,' she called, interrupting his domestic vision. 'I'm stuck.'

'Stuck?'

'I've been aching for lunch but Ketchup gets shivery every time I put him down. So I'm hoping I can stay here while you make me a sandwich.' She peeped up at him—cheeky. 'Cheese and tomato?'

'I could do that,' he said, waving goodbye to schmaltz and deciding cheeky was better. Much better.

'The bread's on the kitchen table. Cheese is in the fridge and tomatoes are out the back in the veggie garden. I like my cheese thick.'

Mama in *Little House on the Prairie* would never demand her man make a sandwich, Nick thought, and he grinned. Misty saw it.

'What?'

'I was expecting the table to be laid, Dresden china and all.'

'I have Dresden china,' she said, waving an airy hand. 'It's in the sideboard in the dining room. You're right, Ketchup and I would like our sandwich on Dresden china.'

'You're kidding.'

'Why would we kid about sandwiches on Dresden china?' She was helping Bailey snuggle down beside her. 'Important things, sandwiches. Would you like a sandwich, Bailey?'

'We've had lunch,' Bailey said shyly.

'Since when did that make a difference?' she asked, astonished. 'It's not a school day. We can eat sandwiches all afternoon if we want. Will we ask your daddy to make you a sandwich as well? Is he a good cook?'

'He cooks good spaghetti.'

'Not sandwiches?'

'I can make sandwiches,' Nick said, offended.

'Wonderful.' She beamed. 'Bailey, what sort of sandwich would you like?'

'Honey.' That was definite.

'We have honey. Can I add that to our order?' Misty asked and smiled happily up at Nick. 'Please?'

So he made sandwiches in Misty's farmhouse kitchen overlooking the sea, while Bailey and Misty chatted just outside the window.

He felt as if he'd been transported into another universe. He was making sandwiches while Bailey and Misty admired Ketchup's progress and compared Ketchup's bandaged leg to Bailey's ex-bandaged arm.

'My dad drew pictures on my plaster cast. Of boats.'

'Ketchup's more into bones. We'll ask him to draw bones on Ketchup's bandages.'

Bailey was giggling. *Giggling.*

This was too good to be true. His son was giggling on the veranda of a woman who was a part of his future.

His future?

Surely he meant Bailey's future. Misty was Bailey's teacher.

But his treacherous mind said *his* future.

He stabbed the butter and lifted a chunk on his knife, considering it with care. Where to take this?

This did not fit in with his plans.

He'd come to this place with a clear path in view. A steady future. Nothing to rock the boat.

Misty wouldn't mess with that.

So maybe he could just…see. He could let his barriers down a little. He'd let them down last night and there was no issue.

There were no risks down this road.

'Are you planning to hoist that butter on a flagpole or put it on our bread?' Misty called through the window and he saw what he'd been doing and chuckled—and that in itself was amazing. When was the last time he'd felt like chuckling?

He made his sandwiches. He carried them outside, plus a bottle of not home-made lemonade, and he watched as Misty and Bailey munched and Ketchup woke a little and accepted a quarter of a sandwich and retired again.

'This is the best place for a dog,' Nick said. He'd settled himself on the veranda steps, not bothering so much about distance now but thinking more of view. If he leaned back at the top of the stairs he got a full view—of Misty.

And of Bailey and Ketchup, he reminded himself, but he was forgetting to remind himself so often,

'It's the best place for anyone,' Bailey declared. He'd eaten two more sandwiches on top of his lunch. For a child who'd needed to be coaxed to eat for a year, this was another thing to be amazed at.

Teddy, Nick noticed, had been set aside.

'It's pretty nice,' Misty said, but suddenly her voice sounded strained.

'Don't you like it?' Bailey asked.

'Yes.' But she didn't sound sure.

'Where else would you like to live?' Nick asked.

'In a yurt.'

He and Bailey both stared. 'A yurt?'

'Yep.'

'What's a yurt?' Bailey asked.

'My mother sent me a postcard of one once. It's a portable house. It's round and cosy and it packs up so I can put it on the back of my camel. Or my yak.'

Bailey was intrigued. 'What's a yak?'

'It's a sort of horse. Or maybe it's more like a sheep but it carries things. The yurt on my postcard had a camel in the foreground but I've been reading that camels bite. And yaks seem to be more common in Kazakhstan,' she said. 'That's where yurts are found. Probably in lots of other places, too, but I've never been there to find out. Yaks seem pretty friendly, or at least I think they are. I've never met one, but some day I will. That's my dream. Me and my yak will take our yurt and head into the unknown.'

'In term vacations?' Nick asked before he could help himself. Bailey did not need his new-found teacher to be heading off into the unknown.

'I'd need more than term vacation,' she retorted. 'To follow the dreams I have…' The lightness in her voice faded a little and she gave a wry smile. 'But of course you're right. Term vacations aren't long enough. It's only a dream.'

'And you have a really nice house,' Bailey said placatingly. 'It's big and comfy.' Then he looked at Misty's face and maybe he could see something there that Nick was sensing—something that was messing with his domestic harmony as well. 'Could you buy a little yurt and put it in the backyard?' he asked. 'Like a tent?'

'Maybe I could.' The lightness returned but it was determined lightness. 'Maybe I could buy a yurt on the Internet—or maybe we could build one as a school project.'

Bailey's eyes widened with interest. 'My dad could help you build one. He's good at building.'

'Could he?' Misty smiled, but Nick saw a wash of emotions put aside and thought there were things here he didn't understand. But then… Why should he want to understand this woman?

He did. There was something about her… Something…

'Can you, Dad?' Bailey asked.

'I'm not sure…' he started.

'Well, I am,' Misty declared. She tossed off her blankets in decision. 'I think Ketchup needs to stand on the grass for a bit and then we need to remember why you came. We need to look at spare beds—I counted them last night and we have ten. Then I'm going to make a list of everything else you need in your house while you and your dad draw me a picture of a little yurt we could build in the school yard.' She rose and hugged her little dog tight against her. 'A little yurt would be fun and we can do without yaks. We don't need anything but what's in Banksia Bay, and why would a woman want anything but what's right here?'

They searched the Internet and learned about yurts. They drew more and more extravagant plans and then

Nick got serious and sat down and designed one they really might be able to construct in the school yard. Then they explored the muddle of furniture in the largely unused house.

Misty was right—the place was huge. It had been a big house to start with, and she told him her great-grandparents had built an extension when her grand-parents married. She had two kitchens and three living rooms. She owned enough furniture to cater for a small army, and she was offering him whatever he liked.

With Bailey's approval, Nick chose two beds, two couches, a table and chairs. He chose wardrobes, side-boards, armchairs. So much…

'Why don't you want it?' Bailey asked, intrigued.

'There's only me,' Misty said. 'And Ketchup,' she added. She was carrying the dog along with her. He seemed content in her arms, snuggled against her, snoozing as he chose, but taking comfort from her body heat. 'I've tried to rent out the other half but no one wants to live this far out of town. So now I'm clos-ing rooms so I won't need to dust.'

'Won't it feel creepy when it's empty?' Bailey asked. 'Like our place does?'

'Ah, but you've forgotten, I have a watchdog now. Ketchup's messed with my plans but now he's here I can make use of him.'

'Were you thinking of moving somewhere smaller?' Nick asked, and she gave him a look that said he didn't get it.

'I told you. I want a yurt. But I'm amenable. Is this all you want? If we're done, then how about tea?'

'You can't be hungry again.'

'How can you doubt it? It's four hours since my sandwich.'

Four hours! Where had the time gone? In drawing yurts. In exploring. In just…talking.

'I'd like a picnic on the beach,' she said and visions of gingham baskets rose again—to be squashed before they hit knee height.

'There's a great pizza place in town,' she said. 'I bribe them to deliver all the way out here.'

'Pizza,' Bailey said with joy, and Ketchup's ears attempted to rise.

'We've hit a nerve.' She grinned. 'Picnic pizza it is. If that's okay with you, Mr Holt?'

'Nick,' he said and it was almost savage.

She made him take three trips to her favourite spot on the sand dunes, carrying cushions, rugs and food, because she was carrying Ketchup.

They ate pizza until it was coming out of their ears. Ketchup ate pizza, too.

'I have a feeling Ketchup's met pizza in a former life,' Misty said, watching in satisfaction as he nibbled round the edges of a Capriccioso.

'He looks like he might be a nice dog,' Nick said—cautiously. He was feeling cautious.

He was feeling strange.

Ketchup and Bailey were lying full length on the rug. They were playing a gentle boy-dog game that had them touching noses, touching finger to paw, touching paw to finger, then nose to nose again. They were totally absorbed in each other. Bailey was giggling and Ketchup seemed at peace.

The evening was warm and still. The sun was sinking low behind the sand hills and the outgoing tide sent a soft hush-hush of surf over the wet sand. Sandpipers were sweeping up the beach as the water washed in, then scuttling out after the waves to see what had been washed bare.

Misty's house looked out over paradise.

How could a man want adventure when he had this?

And this woman… She was watching Bailey with contentment. She seemed secure in herself, a woman at peace.

She was so different from Isabelle. A woman like this would never need adrenalin rush, danger.

A woman like this…

'Why don't you have a dog already?' he asked and Misty stopped squashing pizza boxes, glanced at Ketchup and looked rueful.

'We had a surfeit of dogs.'

'Who's we?'

'My grandparents and me.'

He thought about that. It seemed safer than the other direction his thoughts were taking. Actually, he wasn't sure where his thoughts were taking him, only that it seemed wise to deflect them. 'Not your parents?'

'My mother didn't live here.'

'Never?'

'Not since she was eighteen. She left to see the world, then turned up only for brief visits, bringing things home. Weird people, artwork, dream-catchers. One day she brought me home. She didn't stay any longer than the time she brought the dream-catchers, but she left me for good. Gran and Grandpa kept the dream-catchers and they kept me.'

'That sounds dreadful.'

'Does it?' She smiled and ran her fingers the length of Ketchup's spine, causing the little dog to roll his eyes in pleasure. 'It never seemed dreadful. Sad, yes, but not dreadful. We saw her world through postcards, and that gave me a presence to cling to. An identity. And, as for needing her… I wasn't deserted. Gran and Grandpa did everything they could for their daughter, and they did everything they could for me.'

'But you stayed, while your mother left.'

'I loved my grandparents, and they loved me,' she said, sounding suddenly uncompromising. 'That's something I don't think my mother's capable of. It took me a while to figure it out but I know it now.' Her smile faded. 'It's her loss. Loving's fine. Like I fell in love with Ketchup yesterday. I'm a soft touch.'

'You've never fallen in love before?'

'With other dogs?' That wasn't what he'd meant but maybe she'd purposely misunderstood. 'Of course I have. Five years ago we had four. The last one died six months ago. He's buried under Gran's Peace rose in the back garden. And now Gran herself…'

But something there gave her pause. She gave herself a shake, regrouped, obviously changed direction. 'No. Gran's okay. She's had a couple of strokes. She's in a nursing home but she's only seventy-three. I thought… When she had the second stroke and our last dog died I thought…'

Pause. Another shake.

'Well, it doesn't matter what I thought,' she said,

almost to herself. 'It's right to get another dog. When you fall in love, what choice do you have?'

'There's always a choice.'

'Like you could walk away from Bailey?' Bailey looked up at that, and she grinned. 'See? I defy you not to love that look.'

'My son's look?'

'Your son.'

'How can you compare a dog…?'

'Love's love,' she said simply. 'You take it where you find it.'

Where he found it? He'd thought he had it with Isabelle. He'd been out of his mind.

Bailey stretched out and yawned. The sun was sinking low in the evening sky.

Misty sat and watched the sandpipers, and he thought she was such a peaceful woman. She was also beautiful. And the more he looked… She was quite astonishingly beautiful.

He wanted, quite badly, to kiss her.

And that was a really bad idea. This was his son's schoolteacher. His son was two feet away.

But not to touch her seemed impossible.

Her hand was on the rug, only inches from his. How could he not? He reached out and ran his fingers gently over the back of her hand and she didn't flinch.

Her skin wasn't silk-smooth like Isabelle's had been. There were tiny scars. Life lines.

The world was still. Maybe…

'No,' she told him and tugged her hand away.

'No?' The contact had been a feather touch, no more. But she'd said no, and even now he knew her well enough to realise that she meant it. And for him? No was sensible. What was he thinking of?

'Parent-teacher relationships are disasters,' she said.

'Always?' The word was out before he could stop it.

'Always.'

'You've tried a few?'

'That's my business.'

He smiled but it was an effort, and that was a puzzle on its own. What was happening here? He had to get this back on a lighter note.

'I've told you about Isabelle,' he said, in a dare you tone.

'You want me to tell you about Roger Proudy kissing me behind the shelter sheds when I was eight?'

'Did he?'

'Yes, and it was sloppy.' She was also striving to make this light, he thought. That was good. She had a handle on things, which was more than he did.

'When Grandma kisses me it's sloppy,' Bailey said dreamily from where he was snoozing against Ketchup, and the conversation suddenly lost its intensity. They were back on a plane where he could keep his balance.

'Do you have one grandma or two?' Misty asked Bailey.

'Two, but Grandma Holt cries, and she gets lipstick all over me.'

'That sounds yuck,' Misty said. 'Do you see your grandmas often?'

'Gran Rose and Papa Bill live on a boat like we used to,' Bailey said. 'They came to see me in hospital lots of times. They gave me computer games and stuff. But Grandma and Grandpa Holt only came once. Grandma said computer games are the work of the devil, and Grandpa yelled at Dad when he said we weren't going back to Pen… Pennsylvania. Then Grandma Holt cried, and kissed me too hard, and it was really, really sloppy.'

'Double yuck.' Misty smiled, then turned to Nick, her eyes lighting with laughter. 'Would Grandma Holt be the no risk grandma? Someone should tell her you can share germs with sloppy kisses.'

And suddenly Nick found himself grinning.

The decision to bring Bailey to Australia had been made under all sorts of constraints. If he'd returned to the States, his parents would have given him a hard time. They'd give Bailey a hard time. But if he'd stayed in England…

Isabelle's parents were based in England. They loved Bailey desperately, but loving had its own challenges. They'd smother Bailey, he thought, and maybe Bailey would react as Isabelle had reacted.

Since Isabelle's death, he'd been in a haze of grief and self-blame. Banksia Bay offered a new start. Here, they were away from Isabelle's parents, with their indulgence. They were away from his own parents saying the things they'd always said, only this time with the rider: 'I told you so.'

Moving to Banksia Bay meant Bailey was spared sloppy kisses.

He looked at Misty and he thought…kisses equal germs?

His grin faded.

'We need to go home,' he said, and he knew he

sounded harsh but he couldn't help himself. What he was feeling was suddenly pushing him right out of his comfort zone. This was his kid's schoolteacher. He'd touched her. He shouldn't have touched her.

He shouldn't want to touch her.

But she was right beside him, and she was warm, open and loving in a way he could only sense. She was smiling a question at him now, wondering at the sudden change in his tone.

She wouldn't react with anger, he thought, flashing back to Isabelle's moments of fury, of unreasonable temper. Here was a woman who saw everything on an equable plane. Who moved through life with serenity and peace.

And beauty. She really was beautiful, he thought. Those eyes…those curls…

No. He had to leave.

'We need to get moving,' he told his son, rising too fast. 'Let's get this gear up to the house and go.'

'I don't want to go home.' Bailey's voice was slurred by sleep. He was nestled against Ketchup, peaceful now as he hadn't been peaceful for a year. Or more. Maybe never? 'Why can't we stay here?'

'We can't sleep on the beach.'

'I mean in Miss Lawrence's house.' It was as if Bailey was dreaming, drifting into fantasy. 'I could sleep in one of her big, big beds. Me and Ketchup. I could see Ketchup every morning.'

What the…? The idea took his breath away. 'Miss Lawrence doesn't want us here.'

'Ketchup wants us here.'

'No,' Misty said, sounding strange. She also rose,

and she looked just as taken aback as he was. 'That's not a good idea, Bailey. You have a house.'

But suddenly Bailey was fully awake, sitting up, considering his suggestion with care. 'Our house is horrid. And we could help look after Ketchup.'

'I can look after Ketchup on my own.'

'He likes me.'

'I know he does,' she said. She stooped and hugged Bailey, then lifted Ketchup into her arms. 'But Ketchup's my dog. Your dad's paid his bills and that's all the help I'll ask. I look after Gran and I look after Ketchup. I can't look after anyone else. I'm sorry, but you and your dad are on your own.'

Chapter 5

She needed to visit Gran. She needed to find her balance.

Once Nick and Bailey were out of sight she settled Ketchup back into her car. He'd be best off sleeping in his basket at home, but every time she walked away he started shaking.

She could worry about Ketchup. She couldn't worry about Bailey and his father.

She couldn't think about Bailey's father.

Was it only yesterday she'd been celebrating Adonis arriving in her classroom? One touch and her equilibrium was shattered.

Think about the dog. Much, much safer.

'You've sucked me in,' she murmured. 'Where did you come from, and how exposed have you made me? Oh, Ketchup.'

But he hadn't made her exposed—he'd simply shown her what life was. Yurts were fantasy. Ketchup was real.

Bailey was real.

She was a total sucker.

'I'm sorry, but you and your dad are on your own.' She'd watched Bailey's face as she'd said it and she'd seen him become…stoical.

She'd been stoical at six. For all her bravado about not needing her mother…surviving on postcards had hardly been survival at all.

She'd ached to go with her. Other kids had mothers. She'd got postcards in the mail.

Bailey got nothing.

He had his dad. It was more than she'd ever had.

No, she told herself sharply. She'd had grandparents who loved her. But grandparents never, ever made up for what a mother was supposed to be. She had a clear idea of what was right, even at six.

'So you're thinking you can possibly turn yourself into a substitute mother for Bailey? Take them in and coddle them?

'Of course I can't.' She was talking to herself, out loud, the habit of a woman who lived alone.

'Why not? The place they're in is awful. You've been looking for tenants for months. Bailey would love living with Ketchup. Why reject them out of hand?

'Because Nicholas scares me.'

Think about it.

She did think.

She couldn't stop thinking.

She was out of her mind.

* * *

'Why can't we live with Miss Lawrence?'

There were a million reasons. He couldn't tell his son any of them.

Except one.

'You heard her. She said no. I think Miss Lawrence likes living alone.'

'She doesn't. She said she tried to rent part of her house. And we wouldn't have to move furniture.'

Why was he blessed with a smart kid with big ears?

'Maybe she wants a single person. Maybe another lady.'

'We're better than a lady.' Bailey wriggled down into his seat and thought about it. 'It'd be good. I really like Ketchup.'

Nick thought Ketchup was okay, too. Ketchup and Bailey touching noses. Bailey truly happy for the first time since his mother died. Ketchup had made him smile.

'Maybe we could get our own dog,' he said and then he heard what he'd said and couldn't believe it.

Here was a perfect example of mouth operating before head. Was he out of his mind? Where were his resolutions?

But he'd said it, and it was too late to haul it back. Bailey's face lit like a Christmas tree. 'We can get a dog?' he breathed.

'Maybe we can,' he said, feeling winded. 'Seeing as we can't live with Miss Lawrence.'

But Bailey had moved past Miss Lawrence. He was only seeing four legs and a tail. 'I can have a dog of my own?'

Miss Lawrence had a lot to answer for, he decided. His plans had *not* included a dog. 'A young dog,' he said. That, at least, was sensible. A young healthy dog wouldn't cause grief. A young dog *probably* wouldn't cause grief.

He'd have to reinforce fences, he thought. He'd have to keep the dog safe, too.

'He'll be able to play with Ketchup,' Bailey said, not hearing his reservations. He was almost rigid with excitement. 'Do you think we can find a dog who'll touch noses? Me and Ketchup touch noses. Like you and Miss Lawrence touch hands.'

'That's got nothing to do…'

But Bailey wasn't listening. The touching hands thing was simply a passing fact. 'Dogs are great,' he said, breathless and wondering. This was turning into a very good day in the World According to Bailey, and he was starting to plan. 'We'll be able to take our dog to visit Ketchup. We'll all have picnics on the beach. We'll all still be able to touch.'

What was a man to say to that?

'Can we build a kennel?'

'I…yes.'

'I can't wait to tell Miss Lawrence,' Bailey said.

'We may not see Miss Lawrence until Monday.'

'We need to get our furniture,' Bailey said happily. 'We'll see her tomorrow. Can we get a dog tomorrow?'

'Do you think having Nicholas Holt and his son as tenants is a bad idea?'

It *was* a bad idea. There were complications on

every side. She shouldn't even think it but Bailey's expression wouldn't go away. Bailey's need.

What was it in him that had touched such a chord within?

Other kids lost mothers.

It was the way he'd touched noses with Ketchup, she thought. She'd watched him find huge pleasure in that simple contact, and she remembered how important dogs had been to her as a child. Bailey couldn't go his whole life without a mother—and without a dog.

If they became her tenants he'd share Ketchup. Ketchup would be on Bailey's bed in no time. Kid and dog. Perfect fit.

Their house was truly appalling. Bailey's suggestion was even sensible.

If only she could ignore Nicholas.

She was a grown woman. Could a grown woman get her hormones under control enough to consider a sensible plan?

Surely she could.

Misty set the whole thing in front of Gran, and Gran considered it. Misty knew she did. Gran did a lot of considering these days.

Gran's eyes were closed tonight but, when Misty settled Ketchup on her bedclothes, against Gran's hand, she saw Gran's fingers move against his furry coat. Just a little, convulsively, as if she was remembering something she'd forgotten.

Gran loved dogs.

Love was a dangerous concept, Misty thought. She'd fallen for Ketchup, she was falling for Bailey, and where were her plans now? In a muddle, that was where.

'I shouldn't have agreed to keep Ketchup.'

Gran's fingers moved again.

'You're a soft touch, too. We both are.' She lifted Gran's spare hand to her cheek. 'Oh, Gran, this is dumb. I have fallen for Ketchup, and I would like someone living in the other side of my house. Bailey needs a good place to live and it's sensible. It's just… Nick touched me. I'm scared I'll get involved and I want to be free. But free's not an option. I'm being dumb.'

She had to let her plans go.

She already had, she thought, or she almost had, the moment she'd fallen for Ketchup. And maybe letting her plans go was her only option.

Six months ago, the doctors had told her Gran had weeks to live. But Gran was still here, and there was no thought of her dying. And in the end… How could Misty possibly dream of a future with Gran not here?

Ketchup was deeply asleep now. He'd had a huge day for an injured dog. She should have him at home, right now.

'It's okay to live alone,' she told her grandmother. 'I don't need anyone to help me care for Ketchup, and I don't need complications.'

Gran's hand slid sideways. The tiny moment of awareness was gone.

Misty's thoughts telescoped, out of frame. To a future without Gran?

She'd thought of what she'd do when Gran was

gone, but now… Gran was here but not here, and she could well be like this for years.

The future looked terrifying. Living in that great house alone. Never leaving this town.

What to do?

Since Gran's first stroke she'd been trying to plan, trying to figure her future. But in truth she'd been planning since before she could remember. Making lists.

Maybe she should stop planning and just…be.

She wouldn't mind Nicholas and his little son living next door. It wasn't exactly a bleak thought.

She wouldn't need to rush home to feed Ketchup on nights when she had to stay back at school.

That was a sensible thought.

And then… Another sensible thought. The resurgence of the dream.

'You know, if anything happened to Gran,' she told Ketchup as she settled him back into her car. 'Just saying… If it did, and if Nicholas and Bailey were living in my house… They could look after you while I tried out a yurt. Just for a while.'

Yes. Her dream re-emerged, dusted itself off, settled back into the corner of her mind, where it had been a comfort for years.

'You're making me realign my existence,' she told Ketchup. 'Two days ago, I was alone. What are you doing with my life?'

Ketchup looked at her and shifted his tail, just a little, but enough to make her smile. She did want this dog.

'Maybe you're my nemesis,' she told him. 'I thought Gran's death would be the thing that changed my life. Maybe it's you.'

She bent over to hug him and got a lick for her pains.

'Enough.' She chuckled. 'I'm not used to kisses.'

A kiss. A touch? She was thinking again of Nick's hand on hers. The strength of his fingers. The warmth of skin against skin.

Ketchup wasn't her only nemesis. There was something about Nicholas that was messing with her plans in a far bigger way. In a way that was much more threatening.

She had to be sensible, she told herself. She had a dog and a grandmother and a house that was too big for her. And if there was something about Nicholas that scared her…

Yep, she just had to be sensible.

He'd agreed to get a dog.

Bailey had gone to sleep planning dog kennels. Tomorrow they'd build a kennel and they'd start to make this place habitable. They were settled. Here.

He'd leased this place for three months. He'd find somewhere else after that, maybe near the school. It'd be okay.

He and Bailey and dog—a young healthy dog—could live happily ever after.

So what was there in that to make him stare up at the ceiling and think…and think…?

And think of Misty.

She tossed the concept around all night and in the morning there was only one answer.

So ask him. Now, before she chickened out.

She didn't have Nick's cellphone number. She could go into school and fetch his parent file, only she'd have to drive past his house to get it. Which was stupid. Cowardly, even.

Ketchup was deeply asleep. She'd had him in a basket beside her bed all night. At dawn he'd stirred. She'd taken him outside and he'd smelled the sea and sniffed the grass. He looked a hundred per cent on yesterday. She'd cuddled him and cooked them both breakfast. He'd eaten two bacon rashers and half a cup of dog food and returned to his basket.

He was now fast asleep on Gran's old woollen cardigan and he didn't look as if he'd stir any time soon.

Unlike Misty, who was stirring so much she felt as if she was going nuts.

It was eight o'clock. The world must surely be awake.

So ask him *now.*

He heard the knock as he stood under the shower. Which was cold. The hot water service gave exactly thirty seconds of tepid water. 'Bailey…'

'I heard,' Bailey yelled, sounding excited, which was pretty much how he'd sounded since Nick had said the D word last night.

'Don't answer it.' He groped for his towel, swearing under his breath. It could be anyone out there. *Do not take risks.*

'Bailey, don't…' he yelled again but it was too late. There was a whoop of pleasure from the hall.

'It's Miss Lawrence. Dad, it's Miss Lawrence. She's come to visit.'

* * *

Bailey was still in his pyjamas, clutching his teddy, rumpled from sleep. He was beaming with pleasure to see her. He looked adorable.

He also looked big with news. He was jiggling up and down, stammering with excitement.

'I'm getting a dog,' he told her before she could say a word, and she blinked in astonishment.

'A what?'

'A dog.' He did another jig. 'We've talked about it. I think we should look at the lost dogs' home 'cos Dad says Ketchup was from the dogs' home and he's good. But I want a dog who can run. Dad says I can choose but he can't be old. And he can't be sick. We're going to build a dog kennel, only Dad says he doesn't know if we can buy wood and stuff on Sunday.'

His joy was enough to make the hardest heart melt, and Misty's wasn't all that hard to start with. A dog of his own…

This little boy had lost his mother in dreadful circumstances. His only friend was his father. But now… To have his own dog…

'That's…' But she never got to answer.

Nick strode from the bathroom, snapping orders. 'Bailey, don't answer the door to strangers…'

He was wearing nothing but boxers.

Misty was a woman with sound feminist principles. She didn't gasp. She didn't even let her knees buckle, which she discovered they were more than willing to do. Women with feminist principles did not gasp at the sight of near naked men. Nor did they allow their knees to buckle, even if they wanted to.

Nick had towelled in a hurry and he wasn't quite dry. His bare tanned chest was still wet. More, it sort of glistened under the hall light. This was a male body which belonged…which belonged somewhere else but in her universe.

'H…hi,' she managed, and was inordinately proud she'd made her voice work.

'It's Miss Lawrence,' Bailey told Nick unnecessarily. He was still jiggling. 'I told her we're getting a dog.'

'Why are you here?' There was a pause, and Nick seemed to collect himself. It was possible he hadn't intended to sound as if she might be a child-snatcher. He took a deep breath, started again. 'Sorry. Obviously I need to get used to country hours. So…' He hesitated and tried a smile. 'You've already milked the cows, churned the butter…'

'Swilled the pigs and chewed the buttercups,' she agreed, managing to smile back. She might be disconcerted, but Nick looked even more disconcerted. Which was kind of…nice. To have such a body disconcerted because of her…

Get serious, she told herself, but it was really hard to be serious in the face of those pecs.

'It's me who should be sorry,' she managed. 'Ketchup woke me at dawn and I've been thinking. Actually, I was even thinking last night.'

'Thinking?'

'That maybe I was wrong to knock Bailey back so fast. 'That maybe it's not a bad idea at all. That maybe it might suit us all if you share my house.'

Silence.

More silence.

Whatever reaction she'd expected, it wasn't this. Nick was staring at her as if he wasn't quite sure who—or what—she was.

As well he might. He'd only met her yesterday. What sort of offer was this?

But they didn't need to be friends to be a landlady and tenant, she reminded herself. They hardly needed to know each other. This was business.

Still there was silence. She wasn't quite sure how to break it, and finally Bailey did it for her. 'We can live with you?' he breathed, and his question hauled her straight down to earth.

Uh oh. Stupid, stupid, stupid. This was not strictly business. Here was the first complication. A basic principle of teaching: don't make children excited before plans are definite. She and Nick should have had this conversation out of Bailey's hearing.

What had she been thinking, just to blurt it out?

She knew what she'd been thinking about. This was all about Nicholas Holt's wet, glistening body. It had knocked the sense right out of her. Understandably, she decided. There was something about Nicholas Holt that was enough to throw any right-minded woman off balance.

'If your father thinks it's a good idea,' she managed, struggling to make it good. She allowed herself to glance again at that glistening body and she thought maybe she'd made a king-sized fool of herself.

He was still looking at her as if she'd grown two heads. That was what she felt like, she decided. As if there was the one-headed Miss Lawrence, the woman who made sense. And the two-headed one who was making all sorts of mistakes.

No matter. She'd made her offer.

If he wanted to live with a two-headed twit then she'd left herself open for it to happen.

She was asking him to live with her?

No. She was asking if he'd like to rent the spare side of her gorgeous house.

Nick was cold. This house was cold.

He'd tried to make toast and the fuse had blown. Half the house was now without electricity. He'd checked the fuse box and what he saw there made him wince. This house wasn't just bad, it was teetering on unsafe.

There were possums—or rats—in the roof. He'd lain awake all night trying to decide which.

A breeze was coming up through the floorboards.

This was not a suitable house for Bailey. He'd made that decision at about four o'clock this morning in between muttering invective at possums. He needed to go find the letting agent, throw back his keys, threaten to sue him for false advertising, find somewhere else…

Before tonight?

But here was Misty, warm and smiling and friendly, saying come and live in her house, with her squishy old furniture, with a veranda that looked over the sea, with Misty herself…

Um…take Misty out of the equation fast, he told himself. This was a business proposition. A good one?

Maybe it was. It'd get him out of immediate trouble. To have his son warm and comfortable and safe…

He wouldn't need to get a dog.

He looked down at Bailey. Bailey looked up at him with eyes that were pure pleading.

A comfortable house by the sea. No dog. Misty.

This was a very sensible plan.

'We accept.'

He accepted? Just like that? The two words seemed to make Misty's insides jolt. What had she just done?

But Nick was sounding cautious, as well he might. *She* was feeling cautious. What sort of crazy impulse had led her here?

For, as soon as he accepted, complications crowded in. Or maybe as soon as she'd seen his wet body complications had crowded in, but she'd been so overwhelmed she'd made the offer before she thought.

And now…

Now he'd accepted. Warily. So where to take it from here?

This was still sensible, she told herself. Stick to business. She needed to avoid looking at his body and remember what she'd planned to say.

'You might need to think about it,' she managed. 'You…you'll need to agree to my rent. And we'd need to set up rules. We'd live on opposite sides of the house. You'd look after yourselves. No shared cooking or housework. Separate households. I'm not turning into your housekeeper.'

'I wouldn't expect you to.' He raked his fingers through his damp hair, looking flummoxed. 'You're serious?'

'I think I am.' Was she serious? She was probably seriously nuts—but how did a girl back out now?

She couldn't.

A sudden gust of wind hit the outside of the house and blew straight through the floorboards. This house was colder inside than out, she thought. Bailey shouldn't be here and Nick knew it.

'Would there be gossip?' he asked.

So he knew how small towns worked. He was right. In most small towns, gossip would be an issue.

But there was never gossip about *her*, Misty thought, feeling suddenly bitter. She was Banksia Bay's good girl. It'd take more than one man and his son to mess with the stereotype the locals had created for her.

'It'll be fine,' she told him. 'The town knows I'm respectable and they know I've been looking for a tenant for months. And people already know about Bailey. Believe it or not, I've had four phone calls already saying how can you—*you*, Nicholas Holt—take care of a recuperating child in this house, and why don't I take pity on you and ask you to move into my place?'

And every one of those calls had been engineered by Fred. The old vet was a Machiavellian busybody.

She loved him to bits.

'So all I need to do is tell the people who've suggested it how brilliant they are,' she added.

And keep this businesslike, she added to herself, because, respectable or not, any sniff of anything else would get around so fast…

But, in truth, Banksia Bay might decide *anything else* was a good thing, she thought, letting herself wallow in bitterness a bit longer. The locals knew of her dreams, but they flatly rejected the idea she could ever leave. They'd approve of anything that kept her here.

Despite that, she was still fighting to get herself free. And this could help. Having people share her house. Share Ketchup.

Businesslike was the way to go, she told herself again. Adonis or not, involvement messed with her dreams.

As did the sight of Nicholas Holt's bare chest.

But in her silence Nick had been thinking. 'It could work well,' he said slowly. 'We can share Ketchup.'

Here was an echo of her thoughts. 'Share?'

'I told Bailey if we didn't move into your house we'd get a dog.'

'Dad…' Bailey said, unsure.

'We don't need our own dog if we have Ketchup,' Nick said.

And all the colour went from Bailey's face, just like that. All the joy. He'd opened the door for Misty looking puffed up like a peacock, a six-year-old with all the pleasure in the world before him.

Right now, he looked as if he'd been slapped.

'But you said,' Bailey whispered. Nick had seen Bailey's colour fade. In two strides he was beside him, lifting him up into his arms. Holding him close. 'Don't you want to stay with Miss Lawrence and Ketchup?' he asked.

'Yes, but I want a dog of my very own,' Bailey whispered.

'We don't need…' Nick started but Misty shook her head. She'd looked at Bailey and thought yes, he does. He does need a dog of his own.

Sharing wouldn't cut it.

Misty had had a solitary childhood, living out of town with her elderly, invalid grandparents. Her dogs had meant everything to her.

Last night she'd seen an echo of that. Noses on the beach. Ketchup.

Bailey was a great kid. She knew him well enough to realise he'd take great care of a dog.

So say it.

'What if I give you Ketchup?' she said, and both guys looked at her as if she'd just declared she was selling her grandmother.

'But Ketchup's yours,' Bailey whispered, appalled. 'He knows he is. He told me.'

'I've only just got him,' Misty said gently. 'He doesn't really know me. You and Ketchup had a wonderful game on the beach last night.'

'I want my dog and Ketchup to be friends.'

And Nick obviously had qualms as well, but they were different qualms. 'The vet says Ketchup's close to ten years old,' he said.

Now it was Misty's turn to look at Nick as if he was selling *his* grandmother.

'So?'

'So he'll…'

'He'll what?' she said dangerously.

'If we must get a dog, we'll get a young one. Ketchup will cause you grief.'

'Everyone causes you grief,' she said. 'That's what loving's about. Like you. You love Bailey so you promised him a dog.'

'I didn't actually promise.'

'You did,' Bailey said and buried his face in his father's shoulder.

'I believe I said if we didn't live with Miss Lawrence.'

His explanation didn't help at all. Bailey's sob was truly heart-rending—and Nicholas looked at her as if she'd personally caused this.

Enough. This was crazy. She was starting to feel as if she was causing nothing but heartache.

The sight of Nick hugging Bailey was doing weird things to her. Nick with his gorgeous body. Nick with the way he loved his son.

And Bailey? Somehow this small boy had managed to twist his way right around her heart.

Bailey's pyjama sleeve was hitched up as he clung round his father's neck. She could see the savage mark of the bullet, and the scars from the surgery after.

She was messing with Bailey by being here, she decided. Nick had had this sorted, and now she'd come in with an offer that was messing with Bailey's dreams.

Nick would find somewhere else to live. She didn't actually need these two guys in her house. Not if it messed with dreams.

'I believe I need to rescind,' she said before she could think it through any further.

'Sorry?' Nick sounded stunned.

'My offer is withdrawn.' She took a deep breath and met his gaze square on. 'Bailey needs a dog.'

'Not if he gets to share yours.'

'He's not sharing mine. I no longer want you as tenants. Not if it means Bailey misses out on a dog of his own.'

Once again, that look as if she had two heads. 'This is ridiculous.'

'It is,' she said, but then she thought that it wasn't. She thought of the white-faced little boy on Friday night, grabbing his teddy as soon as he got home. She thought of him last night on the beach, touching noses with Ketchup.

A dog of his own would be perfect.

But Nick's face…

How had this happened? He was stuck if he did, and stuck if he didn't.

So help him out. Make his decision for him. She'd always fought for her students' needs. For Bailey, there was never going to be a better time to fight than right now.

'So you're saying…' Nicholas said slowly.

'That I'm no longer offering you my house. Unless,' she said softly, watching Bailey, 'Bailey has his own dog.'

Nick's face turned to thunder.

'Henrietta Farnsworth runs the Animal Welfare,' she said, briskly efficient now she saw her way. Or Nick's way. 'It's only open weekdays, but on Sundays she feeds and cleans at eleven. You could go choose a dog and then accept my very kind offer by midday.'

'This is blackmail.' Nick's growl was truly menacing, but Bailey had turned to look at her and his look strengthened her resolve. She grinned at Bailey and she winked.

'I agree with Bailey. He needs his own dog.'

'Dogs cause you grief. I don't want Bailey to face that kind of hurt.'

'You're saying you won't get a dog because eventually you might lose him? What sort of argument is that? You're living in the country now. Country kids know about birth and death. Natalie's dad's cow lost one of her twins yesterday. Natalie will tell everyone all the gory details on Monday morning. It's sad but it happens. You can't shield Bailey for ever. Choose a young dog and take your chances.'

Silence. She let the silence run.

Nick set Bailey down and Bailey had the sense to remain silent. Nick raked his fingers through his hair again. She'd first noticed him doing it yesterday, when he was drawing his plans for her yurt. His long strong fingers, running through thick wavy hair, had made her feel… Was making her feel…

Uh oh. Let's not go there.

But she was there. Maybe this man was going to live just through the wall from her.

She shivered, but not with cold.

But he was still coming at her with arguments. 'I didn't mean to promise Bailey a dog,' he started.

She was ready for him this time, growing firmer. 'Yes, you did or you wouldn't have said it.'

'It was a rash moment.'

'You'll love a dog. You saw Ketchup and Bailey together. You'll both love a dog.'

'But Ketchup's recuperating.' He was starting to sound helpless. Helpless and sexy. It seemed an incredibly appealing, incredibly masculine combination.

Stop it. She was a respectable schoolteacher, she told herself. She was a potential landlady. Listen to what he's saying.

'Ketchup doesn't need company.' His arguments were getting weaker.

'Ketchup doesn't need a rough companion,' she agreed. 'Or not at first. But we can keep them separate. Like you and I will be separate. I want tenants, not friends.'

'Really?'

She drew her breath in on that one. *Really?*

'We can meet on the veranda occasionally,' she conceded.

'And Bailey can play with Ketchup,' he said, fast. 'See, he doesn't need a dog of his own.'

'I do,' Bailey said.

'He does,' she said. 'But this is no longer my call. Talk to your son about it. I'm happy to welcome you, your son and your dog into my house, or I'm happy to continue living alone. I need to check on Ketchup. Let me know.'

Enough. She'd thrown her hat into the ring.

Now it was up to him.

'Up to you,' she said and she turned and walked back down the veranda steps and drove away.

What had she done?

Nicholas Holt had just backed himself into a very small corner.

Maybe he'd be angry. Maybe he'd decide that yes, he'd buy a dog, but they wouldn't move into her place. If he thought she was a blackmailer, they just might.

Maybe he'd tell Bailey that yes, he'd buy him a dog, but not till, say, Christmas. Or when he reached twenty-one.

Ketchup was awake and watching for her. He hopped stiffly out of his basket, balancing on three legs as he nudged her ankles. He had a world of worry in his eyes.

'That makes two of us worried. But I don't know why I am,' she told him. 'I don't want them to move here. It'd cause complications.'

But she was lying. She did want them to move here. She wanted complications.

'Only because I can't have my yurt for a while longer,' she muttered. 'I need to let it go.'

She had let it go. And maybe she'd just let prospective tenants go.

'I've pushed him too far,' she told Ketchup.

Maybe he wasn't as wealthy as the Internet suggested. She knew the guy who owned the house he was in. He'd have demanded rent in advance.

Nick was already paying an expensive veterinary bill. He hadn't asked her how much she intended charging. Maybe… Maybe…

Maybe she was a complete fool. And the way he made her feel… What was she doing, hoping the phone would ring?

The phone rang.

She let it ring five times. It wouldn't do to be eager.

On the sixth ring she lifted it. 'Yes?' She was gearing herself for a blunt refusal. Anger. Maybe he had the right to be angry.

'You need to help me,' Nick said, sounding goaded.

'How can I do that?'

'You need to help my son choose a dog,' he said. 'What time did you say this woman will be at the Shelter? And then you need to give me a key to your front door. I believe you have two new tenants. Three, if you count our new dog.'

Chapter 6

Nick drove towards the Animal Shelter and beside him Bailey's face glowed. He held his teddy, but he was looking forward, all eagerness, to what lay ahead.

'A dog of my own,' he whispered as if he couldn't believe what was happening. 'And living with Miss Lawrence...'

'*Next door* to Miss Lawrence.'

'I know,' he said. 'I'm getting a dog.'

Dogs had germs. Nick could still hear the echo of his mother's horrified response when he'd asked for a dog thirty years ago.

Germs. Heartbreak. Loss. This was a risk—but Misty was right. He couldn't protect his son from everything. He needed to loosen up.

And his son would be safe with Misty. The sensation that caused was wonderful. It was like going into freefall, but knowing the landing was assured. And maybe the landing was more wonderful than the fall itself.

For, dog or not, once he'd agreed to her conditions, he felt as if he was landing. He was finding a home for his son—with Misty.

He was finding a home *beside* Misty, he reminded himself, but that wasn't how his body was thinking.

She'd teased him this morning. She'd backed him into a corner and she'd enjoyed doing it.

He'd been angry, frustrated, baffled—but he'd loved her doing it.

He turned the corner and she was already parked outside the Shelter. She was standing in the dappled sunlight under a vast gum tree, in her faded jeans, a sleeveless gingham shirt and old trainers. Her hair was caught back with a red ribbon and the sunlight was making her chestnut curls shine.

'Isn't she pretty?' Bailey whispered and he could only agree.

Beautiful.

'She has Ketchup,' his son added, and Bailey was right. She had her dog in her arms. Why did she have him here?

'We need Ketchup's approval,' she explained. 'If these dogs are to live next door, we can't have them growling at each other.'

'I want a running dog,' Bailey said.

'Fast is good,' Misty agreed. She wasn't looking at Nick. Her attention was totally on Bailey and he was caught by the fact that he was sidelined.

From the time he'd won his first design prize, aged

all of nineteen, Nick had moved among some of the wealthiest women in the world. His boat owners had money to burn and the boats he designed meant he had money to match them.

Women reacted to him. Even when he'd been married, women had taken notice of him. But now it was clear he came a poor second to his son and he thought the better of her for it.

More than that, the sensation had him feeling… Feeling…

Now's hardly the time to think about how you're feeling, he told himself. Not when you're about to move next door to her. You're here to choose a dog for your son.

'Let's get this over with,' he muttered, and Misty looked at him in astonishment.

'Don't sound so severe. This isn't a trip to the dentist.'

'It might as well be.'

She'd started walking towards the Shelter but his words stopped her. She turned and met his gaze full on. Carefully, she set Ketchup down on the grass and she disengaged her hand from Bailey's.

'If you really don't want a dog, then stop right now,' she said, her voice suddenly steely. 'The dogs in the Shelter have had a tough time—they've been abandoned already. They don't want a half-hearted owner. Bailey, if your daddy doesn't really want a dog, then of course I won't insist. You can still share my house, and you and I can share Ketchup.'

She was angry?

She was definitely angry.

'I got it wrong,' she told him, still in that cold voice. 'I thought it was just your stupid qualms about germs and risks. But if it's more…say it now, Nicholas, and we'll all go home. Bailey, if your father doesn't really want a dog, honestly, could you be happy with Ketchup?'

Bailey stared up at her, surprised. He looked down at Ketchup, who looked back at him. Kid and dog.

'Dad says we can have a dog,' he whispered.

'He needs to prove it. Why don't we leave it for a bit so he can make up his mind? Owning your own dog is a big thing. I'm not sure your dad's ready for it.'

He was a bright kid, was Bailey, and he knew the odds. He looked up at Nick and he tilted his chin. And then, surprisingly, he tucked his hand into Misty's.

'It's okay,' he told his father. He swallowed manfully. 'Miss Lawrence and I can share looking after Ketchup.' He sounded as if he was placating someone the same age as he was—or younger. 'If you really, really, really don't want a dog just for us, then it's okay, Dad.' He gulped and clutched his teddy.

It only needed this. Nick closed his eyes. When he opened them, they were still looking at him. Misty and Bailey. And Ketchup. Even Teddy.

If you really, really, really don't want a dog just for us…

Misty's gaze had lost its cool. Now she looked totally non-judgmental. She'd backed right off. She'd given him a way out.

Behind them, a woman was emerging from the Shelter. Glancing across at them. Starting to lock up.

Was this Henrietta, finishing early? She was letting him off the hook as well.

He felt about six inches high.

What had he got himself into?

He glanced once more, at his son and his son's teacher, and suddenly he knew exactly what he was getting into.

'You want to go home?' Misty asked and he shook his head.

'I'm an idiot,' he told her. And then… 'Are you Henrietta?' he called before any more of his stupid scruples could get in the way of what was looking more and more…he didn't know what, but he surely intended to find out.

'Yes,' the woman called back, cautious.

'Can you wait a moment before you lock up?' he asked her. 'If it's okay with you… My son and I are here to see if we can choose a dog. We both want a dog and we're hoping we can find one, right now. A dog that's fast. A dog that's young and a dog who can belong just to Bailey.'

And in the end it was easy.

Misty and Nick left things to Henrietta and Bailey. 'Henrietta knows her dogs,' Misty told Nick. 'She won't introduce him to one that's unsuitable.'

Bailey walked along the pens, looking worried. He looked at each dog in turn. They barked, they whined or they ignored him, and Bailey looked increasingly unsure.

But then he came to a pen near the end, and he stopped.

'This one's a whippet,' Henrietta said. 'She's fast. She's hardly more than a pup and she's a sweetheart.'

'She's hurt her face,' Bailey whispered.

'Most dogs in here have scars,' Henrietta told him and she was talking to him as if he was an equal and not six years old.

Bailey looked back along the lines of pens—then, as if he'd made some sort of decision, he sat beside the pen with the whippet. The whippet was lying prone on the concrete floor, her nose against the bars, misery personified.

Bailey put his nose against the dog's nose. Testing?

Nick started forward, worried, but Misty put her hand on his arm.

'Trust Henrietta. If she thinks a dog's safe with kids, she'll be right. And did you know kids from farms have twenty per cent fewer allergies than city kids? What's a nose rub between friends?'

Bailey looked back to them, his little face serious. 'She's skinny,' he said cautiously. 'Can I pat her?'

'Sure you can,' Henrietta said, and Nick and Misty walked forward to see. They reached the cage—and something amazing happened. Ketchup stared down at the whippet from the safety of Misty's arms. He whined—and then suddenly he was a different dog. He was squirming, barking, desperate to get down.

The whippet was stick-thin, fawn with a soft white face, and she was carrying the scars of mistreatment or neglect. She'd been flattened on the floor of the pen, shivering, but as Misty knelt with Ketchup in her arms she lunged forward and hit the bars—and she went wild.

Both dogs did.

They were practically delirious in their excitement. Two dogs with cold bars between them… That these dogs had a shared history was obvious.

'Hey, I'd forgotten. You've brought her friend back.' Henrietta grinned and stooped to scratch Ketchup behind his ears, only Ketchup wasn't noticing. He was too intent on the whippet.

'These two were found together,' Henrietta told them. 'I reckon they were dumped together. We put 'em in pens side by side but they seemed inseparable so they ended up together. Your little guy…' She motioned to Ketchup. 'He's cute and normally we'd have had no problem rehousing him, but no one's wanted the skinny one. And somehow no one wanted to separate them.'

'He's ugly,' Nicholas said, looking at the whippet, appalled, and the Shelter worker looked at him as if she wasn't sure where to place him.

'I like whippets,' she said neutrally. 'They're great dogs, intelligent and gentle and fun. Whippets always look skinny, but you're right, this one's ribs practically cross over. She's a she, by the way. She'll feed up, given time, but, of course, they ran out of time. They were both in the van when it crashed on Thursday. Dotty Ludeman found this one in her yard last night and brought her in. So here they are, together again.'

She smiled then, the tentative smile of a true animal-lover who thought she scented a happy ending. 'So Misty's saved one—and your little boy wants the other?'

'I'm not sure.' Nick had visions of something cute. Surely Bailey had visions of something cute.

'Whippets can run,' Bailey breathed.

'How do you know?'

'There was a book about dogs at the hospital,' Bailey told him. *'Whippy the Whippet.* Faster'n a speeding bullet.'

'I know that book,' Misty said. 'Ooh, I bet she could run on our beach.'

Our beach. That sounded okay. Nick crouched to get a better view of the…whippet? He knew zip about dogs.

'She's really skinny,' Bailey said.

'Are you sure she's safe with kids?' Misty asked, and Henrietta chuckled and nodded and opened the cage. The skinny dog wriggled out and wormed ecstatically around Ketchup. Misty and Bailey were sitting on the concrete floor now and the whippet wound round them and back, round them and back. Ketchup whimpered but it was a whimper of delight.

'Uh oh,' Misty said.

'Uh oh?' Nick queried.

'I need to tell you.' She smiled and sighed, letting the whippet nose her way into her arms along with Ketchup. 'What are lists, anyway? If you don't want this little girl, then I do.'

'Do you want her to live on your side of the wall?' Bailey demanded, watching the skinny dog with fascination.

'If you and your dad don't want her,' she said. 'But if you do…these two are obviously meant to be together.'

'So could we cut a hole straight away?'

'I guess we could,' she said, glancing at Nick. Who was glancing at her. Only he was more than glancing.

She'd take on the world, he thought. She'd taken on Ketchup. She'd take on this skinny runt of a dog as well.

Would she take on…?

No. Or…way too soon.

Or way too stupid.

'You want her?' Henrietta was clearly delighted. She checked out Nick, clearly figuring if she could go for more. 'If Misty wants hers plus the whippet, and your little boy wants another, then we have plenty…'

'No,' Misty and Nick said as one, and then they grinned at each other. Grinning felt great, Nick thought. Even if it involved a whippet.

'Do you think she'll let me pick her up?' Bailey asked.

'Try her out, sweetheart,' Henrietta said and Bailey scooped her up and the whippet licked his face like Ketchup had licked Misty's.

'There's been kids in these dogs' background,' Henrietta said, surveying the scene in satisfaction.

'And pizza,' Misty said. 'I bet this little girl likes pizza.'

'That means we need to have pizza tonight,' Bailey said. 'On the beach again. Or on the veranda. We're going to live together,' he told Henrietta. 'Can we take her, Dad?'

'I guess…'

'Then she's Took.'

'Took?' Nick said, bemused.

'Yes,' Bailey said in satisfaction, cuddling one

scrawny dog and one battered teddy. But then he glanced along the row of dogs and looked momentarily subdued. 'But… Only one?'

'Only one.' That was Misty and Nick together again.

'Okay,' Bailey said, with a last regretful look at the rest of the inmates. He hugged his new dog closer, as if somehow loving this one could rub off on the rest. 'She's mine. I'm calling her Took 'cos that's what she is.' He smiled shyly up at Henrietta. 'Me and Dad and Ketchup and Took are going to live on both sides of Miss Lawrence's house and we're going to cut a hole in the wall.'

'Why not just open the door?' Henrietta said, and chuckled, and went to do the paperwork.

They took the two dogs back out to the farm and left them in the laundry while they shifted Nick and Bailey's gear.

That took less than an hour.

The laundry was shared by both sections of the house. In theory, they could put the dogs there to sleep. During the day Misty could take Ketchup to her side of the house and Bailey could take Took to his side. But it was never going to happen. Bailey was in and out of Misty's side about six times in the first fifteen minutes.

'I need to go see Gran,' Misty decreed at last, so both dogs settled in the sun on the veranda. Together. When Misty came home, both dogs and Nick and Bailey were on the veranda. Together.

Two days ago, this veranda had been all hers. Now…

Now she had emotions running every which way.

But why quibble? If she had to put her dreams on hold, maybe this was the next best thing.

They ate pizza again—'Just to show Took we can,' Bailey explained. Then Nick read his son a bedtime story on his side of the house and he came outside again as Misty was thinking she ought to go into her side of the house. But Took had left her now-sleeping owner and come back to join Ketchup. Both dogs were at her feet. Why disturb them?

Rockers on the veranda? Any minute now, Nick would offer to make her cocoa.

'Can I make you cocoa?' Nick asked and she choked.

'What?' he demanded.

'It needed only that.'

'It is…cosy,' he ventured and she grinned and shook her head.

'Ma and Pa and Kid and Dogs. It's not the image I want to take to bed with me.' She rose and picked up her dogs. Her *dog*, she reminded herself. And Bailey's dog. In time, they might teach Took to sleep on Bailey's bed. But she had a very clear idea of exactly what would happen. Ketchup and Took would both be on Bailey's bed. Two dogs on a child's bed…

It was the same as cocoa.

She'd settle them in the laundry and go do some schoolwork, she told herself and turned to the door. But Nick was before her, opening the door, and then, as she struggled to keep Took's long legs under control, he lifted Took from her and followed her.

They'd set up two dog beds. They put a dog in each, side by side. Ketchup whimpered and Took sidled from her basket into Ketchup's. She sort of sprawled her long legs around Ketchup so Ketchup was wrapped in a cocoon of whippet.

'These guys are great,' Nick said, smiling and rising, and Misty smiled and rose, too, only she rose too fast and Nick was just…there.

His face was right by hers. His hands were steadying her.

Back away fast.

She couldn't.

There was something between them she didn't recognise. There'd been no guy in Banksia Bay who made her feel…like she felt like she was feeling now.

She didn't want him to let her go.

They were standing in her grandmother's laundry. How romantic was that? The dogs were snuffling at their feet. That was hardly romantic, either.

She didn't feel romantic. She didn't feel…

She felt…

She was tying herself in knots. She had to step away, but his hold on her was tightening. He was looking down at her, his eyes questioning. If she tugged then he'd let her go. She knew it.

How could a girl tug?

She smiled up at him, a silly quavery smile that said she was being a fool. A sensible adult would step away and close the doors between them and treat this as just…as just him steadying her because she'd risen too fast.

But one of his hands had released her shoulder, and now his fingers were under her chin, tilting her face to meet his.

Yes.

No?

Um…yes. Yes, and yes and yes. Her face was definitely tilting and there was no need for his fingers to propel. She was propelling all by herself. Her bare toes were rising so she was on tiptoe, so he could hold her tighter, so she could meet…

His mouth.

Her whole world centred on his mouth.

Her lips parted involuntarily, and why wouldn't they? She was being kissed by a man who'd made her body melt practically the first time she'd seen him. *See a man across a crowded room and your world turns to fire…* She'd read that somewhere, in a romance novel or a short story or even a poem. She'd thought it was nuts.

Nicholas Holt had walked into her classroom and she'd thought he was Adonis. Only he wasn't. He was just… Nicholas.

He was pressuring her mouth to open, gently, wondrously, and her lips were responding. She seemed to be melting. Her mouth seemed to be merging with his. His hands were tugging her up to him. Her breasts were moulding to his chest. The world was dissolving into a mist of desire and wonder and white-hot heat.

He tasted of salt, of warmth, of wonder. He tasted of…

Nicholas.

Her body no longer belonged to her. It felt strange, different, as if she were flying.

She let her tongue explore his. Oh, the heat…

Oh, but he felt good.

'Misty…'

It was his voice, but she scarcely recognised it. He'd put her a little away from him and his voice was husky, with passion and with desire. He wanted her.

It felt powerful to be wanted by a man like this. It felt amazing.

'Mmm?' Their mouths were apart, but only just. She let her feet touch the floor again, grounding herself a little with bare toes on bare boards. Cooling off.

'It's too soon,' he whispered into her hair, but he didn't let her go.

'To take me to bed, you mean?' she whispered back and she surprised herself by managing a trace of laughter. 'Indeed it is. So if you think…'

'I'm not thinking.'

Only of course he was. They both knew what they were both thinking.

And why not? She was twenty-nine years old, Misty thought with sudden asperity. If they both wanted it…

Um…she'd known the guy for two days. He was right. It was too soon.

'So back on your side of the door, tenant,' she managed and he smiled and put her further away, but he was still holding her. They were a whole six inches apart but his hands were on her shoulders and if he tugged…

He wouldn't tug. They were both too sensible for that.

'Let's just see where this goes,' he said and she nodded.

'Yes.'

'But not tonight.'

'No.'

'So different doors?'

'Yes,' she said.

'And a small hole in the wall for dogs and Bailey. But not for us.'

'But rockers on the veranda?' she said, trying to smile.

'Not cocoa?' He was laughing at her.

'No!'

'Dangerous thing, cocoa.'

'It is,' she said with asperity. 'Even cocoa has risks.'

Risks. She thought suddenly, inexplicably, of her list. Her scrapbooks.

Her scrapbooks were dreams. Maybe fate had sent her Nicholas instead.

Chapter 7

How could a girl sleep soundly after that? She managed a little, but she slept thinking Nick was just through the wall and she woke up thinking the same.

Nick was her tenant, but their worlds were already intertwined.

Was that a good thing?

Monday. School. No matter how muddled her thoughts, she needed to get going.

She went to check the dogs and found them already on the back lawn, with Nick supervising. He was wearing his boxers again, and nothing else. *Get dressed before you leave your side of the house,* she wanted to say, but she didn't because that'd tell him she'd noticed. And she didn't want to make a big deal of it.

Besides...she was absurdly aware that she wasn't dressed either, or she was, but just in her nightie that was a bit too short and her pink fluffy slippers that were just a bit too silly.

'Cute,' Nick said, surveying her from the toes up, and her toes were where her blush started.

'Inappropriate,' she said, flustered. 'Go get your son ready for school.'

'Yes, ma'am.' He hesitated and she felt like fleeing and finding a bathrobe.

She didn't have a bathrobe.

She'd buy one in her lunch hour this very day.

'If you take Bailey to school I'll look after the dogs,' he said.

'Okay,' she said cautiously, wondering what she was getting herself into. Suddenly she was committed to a school run? 'You'll need to pick him up, though,' she warned. 'I visit Gran after school.'

'Of course,' he said. 'The dogs can come with me.'

'They'll be okay by themselves if you need to leave.'

'Mostly I'll stay,' he told her. 'I have my desk set up overlooking the sea. My son's safe. I'll have dogs at my feet. What more could a man want?'

'A pipe and slippers,' she said, and she caught herself sounding waspish. What was wrong with a pipe and slippers?

'You'll need to think about shopping,' she told him. 'You can't live on pizza for ever.'

'Would you like to eat together tonight?'

'No!' It was a response of pure panic.

'No?'

'I… I may need to stay longer with Gran. Sometimes I grab a takeaway burger and eat with her.'

'Is she very ill?'

'She's not aware…' she started and then her voice trailed off at the impossibility of explaining the unexplainable. 'Or maybe she is. I'm not sure.'

'I'm sorry.'

'No, but sometimes I think she is. And then I stay.' She hesitated. 'Maybe she'd like to meet Bailey. I'll tell her about him. If you think Bailey…'

'We could do that,' he said gravely. 'Tell me when.'

When I'm ready, she thought as he retreated to his side of the house and closed the door behind him. When I'm ready to admit that these doors might stay open.

'That was fast.'

Playtime. She was on yard duty. Frank hardly ever graced the grounds with his presence, but today the Principal of Banksia Bay Primary wandered out as she supervised play and nudged her, grinning with a leer she hated. 'I didn't think you had it in you.'

'What?' Frank could be obnoxious, and she suspected he was about to give a display.

'Nicholas Holt. Taking him home to bed already?'

Great. She might have known Frank would make it into a big deal. Most locals wouldn't think less of her for taking Nick and Bailey in as tenants, but the school Principal had a grubby mind.

'And you've got a dog,' Frank said. 'I thought you were clearing the decks.'

'What do you mean?'

'So you could get out of here after your grandmother dies.'

No one else would say it to her face, Misty thought. No one else was so horrible.

But she'd known Frank for a long time, and she was well past the stage where he could upset her. 'Leave it, Frank.'

'Don't do it, Mist.'

'Sorry?'

Suddenly Frank's voice was serious. Once upon a time she and Frank had been friends. He was the same age as she was. At fifteen…well, they hadn't dated but they'd hung out together and they'd shared dreams.

'I'm going to be a politician,' he'd said. 'I'll go to Canberra, do Political Science. I can make a difference, Mist.'

And then he'd fallen head over heels with Rebecca Steinway and Rebecca had eyes for only one thing—marriage and babies and not necessarily in that order. So, instead of going to Canberra, at eighteen Frank had become a father, struggling to do the same teacher's course Misty was doing.

Their qualifications were the same. Misty could have applied for the top teaching spot when it became vacant—she'd done a lot better in the course than Frank—but, by the time the old Principal had retired, Frank had three babies and was desperate for the extra money.

And now…

'You'll be stuck in this dump with a stepkid,' he said, almost roughly.

'I'm taking in tenants, not getting engaged. And it's not a dump. It's a great place…'

'To raise a family? Is that what you want?' Then

he laughed and turned away. 'But of course it is,' he said. 'The only one who ever really wanted to get out of here was me. So much for your list, Misty. One dose of hormones and it's shot to pieces.'

She watched him go, his shoulders slumped. She didn't feel sorry for him, or not very. He could change what he was. Rebecca was nice, bubbly, cuddly. They had good kids. But staying here…being trapped…

It had changed him, destroyed something in him that was fundamental to who he was, she conceded. Frank was no longer faithful to Rebecca. He was no longer committed to this school.

Your list is fundamental to who you are, a voice whispered. *It's why you've got up in the morning for years.*

She closed her eyes. Her list wasn't important. Was it?

When she opened her eyes, Bailey was being towed to the sandpit by Natalie, the two of them giggling.

Bailey looked like his dad. Nicholas was gorgeous. Nicholas made her feel…

As Rebecca had once made Frank feel?

Stop it, she told herself harshly. Don't even go there. One day at a time, Misty Lawrence, and don't you dare pull back because of Frank, or a stupid, unattainable list. If you do, then you risk ending up with nothing.

But, decision or not, she didn't eat with them that night. Deliberately. Gran was more deeply asleep than usual when she visited her after school but she decided she'd stay on anyway. She did her schoolwork by Gran's bedside and at eight she finally went home.

Nick was on the veranda, by himself.

Her heart did this queer little twist at the sight of him. Stupid.

He wasn't by himself, she saw as she got nearer. The two dogs were at his feet and for some reason that made her heart twist all over again.

They looked up and wagged their tails and settled again.

'Is your gran okay?' Nick asked, and smiled, and her stupid heart did its stupid back flip with pike. Stop it, stop it, stop it.

'She's okay,' she managed. 'The dogs?'

'They've been missing you.'

'Really?' They'd done their tail wagging. Their eyes closed again. 'They're ecstatic to see me?'

'I'm ecstatic to see you.'

'At least they wagged their tails,' she retorted, deciding to treat that remark very lightly indeed.

'I don't do a good wag.'

'Neither do I. Especially when I'm tired.'

Was she tired? No, but it seemed the sensible thing to say. It was a precursor to walking right by him, going inside, closing the door.

'There's wine in my refrigerator,' he said, motioning to the glass in his hand. 'I'm only one glass down. It's good wine. I was hoping you'd join me.'

'I…' She gathered herself, her books, her resolution. 'Thank you, no. I need to do some work.'

'Really?'

'Really.'

'Scared, Misty?'

Scared? Maybe she was, but she wasn't admitting

it. Last night's kiss had done things to her she didn't want to admit, even to herself. 'It's you who's scared of risks,' she managed.

'I'm not fearful here,' he told her. 'And I'm not fearful for me. I'll do whatever it takes to make my son safe, and he's safe here.'

She didn't like that. The tiny sizzle inside her faded, cooled.

Last night's kiss had started something in her heart that she wasn't sure what to do with. There was a warmth, the promise of fire, the promise of things to come.

My son's safe here.

That was the statement of a man who loved his child above all else. As a teacher, she should have warmed to him saying it. She did.

But had last night's kiss been more of the same? Part of a strategy to make his son safe?

'I do need to work,' she said, trying desperately to tighten things inside that needed to be tightened. To sit on the veranda and drink wine with this man…to plan on doing it again tomorrow and the night after…

No. She would not be part of his safety strategy, or no more than she already was.

'Are the dogs okay?' she asked, managing to make her voice brisk.

'They're great,' he said. 'We carried Ketchup down to the beach after school. Took ran about ten miles in wider and wider circles until we all felt dizzy. Ketchup lay on the rug and watched Took and quivered all over. He'll be running in no time.'

She bit her lip. If she'd come straight home she

could have joined them. Maybe Nick and Bailey had been expecting her to come home in time to join them.

It was just as well she hadn't. Be practical.

'They're fed?'

'They're both fed. Ketchup's had his painkillers and his antibiotics. Would you like to take him inside with you?'

She looked down at her dog. He was nestled at Nick's feet, warm against Took. Took was so thin; she needed Ketchup's body warmth. And Ketchup would still be hurting. With Took…

With Nicholas…

'They need each other,' she said. 'They're fine with you.'

'Ketchup's supposed to be your dog.'

'Yours, mine, this is just home.'

'My thoughts exactly,' Nick said and rose. 'Are you sure you don't want wine?'

'No.'

'Cocoa?'

'No!'

'That got a reaction,' he said, and grinned. 'You don't see yourself as a cocoa girl?'

'I have some living to do before then.'

'This is a great spot to do some living,' he said contentedly.

'No,' she said, and she remembered Frank's words. They weren't about her, she thought. It shouldn't matter that one man had been trapped and turned bitter.

But, oh, the bitterness…

'This might be a place for you to retreat to and live the rest of your life after danger,' she whispered, bending to give Ketchup a pat, a scratch behind his ears, before she made her escape. 'But for me it's a place to come home to between living.'

He frowned. 'What do you mean?'

'Meaning I've never had danger at all,' she told him. 'Not…not that I want it. Of course I don't. But I would have liked one little adventure before I retired to my rocker and cocoa.'

He was looking confused. As well he might, she thought. Her dreams were nothing to do with this man.

'Sorry, I'm being dumb,' she managed. 'But I do need to do some work. Enjoy your evening.' And she bolted through the screen door onto her side of the house before he could probe any more.

I've never had danger at all… What sort of stupid statement was that? But she knew what she meant.

'Your list is hopeless,' she whispered to herself as she closed the door on man and dogs. So stop rabbiting on about danger. About adventures.

Deep breath. 'Okay,' she told herself. 'Let's get this in perspective. Yes, I kissed him and yes, I liked it. Or more than liked it,' she conceded. 'But I won't be kissed because I'm a safe haven. Nicholas Holt and his son are gorgeous but I'm not stupid. At least—please don't let me be stupid. Please let me keep my head. Please don't let me turn into Frank.

'And please give me strength to stay on my side of the door.'

How could she live in the house and avoid him? She tried, but in the mornings when Bailey bounced through to be taken to school she couldn't miss him.

She dressed early now—there was no way he was catching her in her nightwear again—but even when she was ready for them…

Nick leaned his long body against the kitchen bench while she finished her coffee and Bailey gave her a full report on all that had happened since she'd last seen him.

Seeing that was only since school finished the night before, it was hardly momentous but there was still a lot to tell—how many seagulls Took had chased, or that Dad had cooked sausages for them the night before—she'd smelled them and it had almost killed her not to dump her pasta and head next door—and how Dad's sketches of his new boat were almost finished and it was going to be beeyootiful and it was going to be built in England but Dad said they couldn't go and see it.'

'Why not?' She couldn't help herself asking. She could be polite. She just couldn't be involved.

She was not a safe haven.

But it seemed she was, like it or not. 'This is where we live now,' Bailey said happily. He hesitated. 'Gran Rose and Papa Bill still live in England but Dad says they might come out and see us soon.'

'Isabelle's parents,' Nick explained.

'Dad's Mom and Papa don't like us very much,' Bailey confided. 'When I was in hospital they told Dad, "Reap as you sow". I don't exactly know what it means but Dad got angry and Gran Rose started to cry and then they went away. And they think Australia's dangerous.'

'Oh, dear,' Misty said and abandoned the rest of

her coffee and bundled Bailey to school. Feeling ill for Nick.

Ill or not, she could not afford sympathy. It was important not to get caught up in his shadows.

Yeah, and pigs might fly but she didn't have to hang round the kitchen one minute longer than she must.

She didn't need to hang round Nicholas Holt.

She was not safe.

She arrived home the next night and Nick was in the laundry, inside her washing machine. Bits were spread everywhere. He was wearing greasy overalls and she couldn't see his head.

'So how long's it been taking itself on tours all over the laundry?' he asked, muffled by washing machine. 'And ripping the odd shirt.'

'I had someone look at it last week.' Indeed she had, and last month as well. 'Buy a new one,' the mechanic had said. 'It's well past its use-by date.'

Nick inflicted a couple of satisfactory thumps and a final one for good measure before hauling himself out from underneath. 'I'm thinking she'll be right now,' he said. 'I just need to put her back together.'

There was a long line of grease running down the side of his nose. He had grease in his hair. He looked… he looked…

She didn't want to think how he looked.

He put the washing machine back together. It purred like a kitten. She and Bailey watched the first load in respectful awe.

Nick tried not to look smug. Misty thought she wouldn't need to use her list money to pay for a new washing machine. Misty thought there was a man in greasy overalls in her laundry.

She was having trouble not purring herself.

Which just went to show, she thought, as she retreated hastily to her side of the house.

She wasn't the least bit safe—and Nicholas Holt was starting to look downright dangerous.

'I don't want it to be the weekend.' Bailey announced to the world on Friday morning, and she wasn't surprised. Bailey had taken to school with joy, and the thought of no school tomorrow seemed more than Bailey could bear.

'You'll have the dogs to play with, and it'll do you good to sleep in,' Nick told his son, delivering him to Misty's kitchen for the ride to school. 'It'll do us all good. Miss Lawrence works too hard.'

Um...she didn't need to, Miss Lawrence admitted to herself. There wasn't a huge amount of correction to be done for Grade One, and she'd created so many lesson plans over the last few evenings she could rest on her laurels for a month.

But she wasn't about to admit that out loud. If only he wouldn't wear those jeans in her kitchen. If only he wouldn't lean against her bench. If only he'd stop fixing things. If only he'd stop smiling. If only he wasn't so long, so rangy. So... Nicholas

No.

'I work no harder than I must,' she said primly and bustled Bailey out to the car with speed, but she was aware of him watching her as she drove away.

He was amused?

He knew she was attracted to him, she thought. But did he know just how afraid she was? Of being kissed.

No. She wasn't the least afraid of being kissed.

She was afraid of being safe.

She was afraid, he thought, and he wasn't sure why. Had she been burned in the past? Roger Proudy and his sloppy kisses?

Why was it important to figure it out?

It wasn't important. It couldn't be important. He'd known Misty Lawrence for less than a week. He'd made an absolute commitment to his son, to do what he must to give him the stability he needed. That did not include getting involved with any woman.

Only this wasn't any woman. This was Misty and she made him feel…different.

Yeah, she was warm, funny, loving. She didn't threaten his plans for the future in any way—rather she augmented them.

But what he was feeling was more than that.

He was working on plans for a seriously large yacht. She was being built in England. He should be there now, but this new way—delegating responsibility to a partner—was working fine. He sat in the big front room with his plans spread out over two tables. He was consulting via Skype. He could see what was happening every step of the way.

He should be excited by this project. He *was* excited, but undercutting his excitement was… Misty.

The vision of Misty was always there, in front of him.

The dogs were sleeping on his feet as he worked.

Misty and Bailey were both at school. He should be knee-deep in boat plans.

He was, but…

'But tomorrow's Saturday,' he told the dogs. 'Tomorrow we get to take a day off. We'll all take a day off. Together?'

Separate houses. Separate lives.

He looked at the two dogs. Separate lives? Yeah, right. They'd figured it out.

Misty.

He needed to do a bit of figuring himself.

Saturday morning, and Misty had every intention in the world of keeping the door between the sides of the house firmly shut.

She could use some extra sleep, she told herself, so she didn't set her alarm, and when she heard a door slam and a child giggle on the other side of the house she closed her eyes again and wished she'd closed the curtains.

Only when had she ever? Her almost floor-length windows opened out to the veranda, to the sea. The breeze was making the net curtains flutter outward. It'd be a great day, Misty thought, and yawned and stretched—and a dog landed on her chest.

Any dog but Took might have winded her, but Took was a very slight dog and she barely packed a whumph.

'Yikes,' she said and Took quivered and licked. It was good to have dogs back here, she thought. It was great.

And more. Bailey's head poked though the window,

peering around the net curtains. 'Took! Dad said we're not allowed to wake up Miss Lawrence.'

Took, it seemed, wasn't following instructions. She stood on Misty's chest and continued quivering, but not with fear. This was excitement.

So much for separate. Misty chuckled and moved sideways in the bed so Bailey could join them. Then she realised Ketchup was at the window, whining at being left out. With one gammy leg, he couldn't manage the twelve-inch sill, so she had to climb out of bed, scoop Ketchup up and scoot back to bed before anyone…anyone in particular…came looking for his son.

She tugged the covers to her chin. She was covered in two dogs and Bailey. She was respectable.

'Where's your father?' she asked, trying to sound…uninterested.

'In the shower. He takes ages. What will we do today?'

'I'm not sure what you're doing,' Misty said cautiously. 'This morning I'll visit my gran, and this afternoon I'm sailing.'

'Sailing.' Bailey lit with excitement. 'I like sailing. Can Dad and I come?'

'Come where?' And it was Nick—of course it was Nick—speaking from right outside the window. So much for showers taking ages. He did have the decency not to stick his head in, though. 'What are you two planning?'

'Sailing,' Bailey said and flew to the window to tug the curtains wide. 'Miss Lawrence and I are going sailing.'

Nick was wearing jeans again and a T-shirt, a bit too tight. His hair was wet. He looked… He looked…

Like it was totally inappropriate for him to be looking through her bedroom window.

At first glance he'd been smiling—his killer smile—but Bailey's words had driven the smile away.

'You're not sailing,' he told his son.

Misty thought that was his prerogative, but his voice was so hard, so definite, so unexpectedly angry that, before she could help herself, she heard herself say, 'Why not?'

'We don't sail.'

'You design yachts,' she said in astonishment. 'You built a yacht.'

'I design yachts, yes, but that's all. Bailey doesn't sail.' It was a grim snap, and somehow it was impossible not to respond.

'Says your mother.'

His face froze. Uh oh, she thought grimly. That was out of line. She'd overstepped the boundaries—of what was wise, of what was kind. This was not her business.

But she'd said it. The words hung. It was the second time she'd goaded him about his paranoia, and his smile wasn't coming back.

'I beg your pardon?' he said, icy with anger.

Should she apologise? Part of her said yes. The other part wasn't having a bar of it.

'Ooh, who's cross?' she ventured, thinking there was no unsaying what she'd said. It might even be a good thing that she had said it, she decided. Someone had to fight for Bailey. Maybe they should have this out when Bailey wasn't around, but Bailey looked interested rather than worried.

'Dad fusses,' he said and she nodded.

'I guess if I had a little boy who'd just come out of hospital I might fuss, too.' She peeped Bailey a conspiratorial smile, a smile of mischief. 'But the sailing I do is pussycat. I have a Sharpie, a tiny yacht, I'd guess it's far smaller than anything you guys have ever sailed. The bay's safe as houses. Bailey, if your dad lets you try *Mudlark* out—that's the name of my boat, by the way, because the first time I tried her out I got stuck in mud—we could stay in shallow water. And of course we'd wear life vests.'

'You got stuck in mud?' Bailey said, entranced.

'It was very embarrassing,' she told him. 'Philip Dexter, the town's lawyer, had to tow me off. I'm a better sailor now.'

'Dad…' Bailey said.

'No,' Nick said, refusing to be deflected.

'I can swim,' Bailey said, jutting his jaw at his father. They really were amazingly alike.

'No.'

'I'll wear a life vest.'

'Life vests are great,' Misty said. 'They take all the worry out of tipping over.'

'You tip over?' Bailey said, casting a dubious glance at his father.

'Sometimes,' she admitted, being honest. In truth, there was nothing she loved more than setting her little boat into the wind, riding out conditions that had more experienced yachtsmen retire to the clubhouse. Tipping was part of the fun. 'But today's really calm—

not a tipping day at all. If your dad did decide to let you come I'd be very careful.'

She ventured a cautious peek at Nick then and thought, *Uh oh.* She wasn't making headway. Nick looked close to explosion. But if he was about to explode… Why not take it all the way?

'You know, if your father was on board, too…' she ventured. 'I'm thinking your dad knows yachts better than I do. I bet he'd never let it tip over.'

'No!' Nick said, and it was a blast of pure icy rage.

Should she leave it? She glanced at Bailey and she thought Nick had brought him here, to this house, because he thought it was safe. Because he thought she was safe.

And something inside her matched his fury. She was *not* going to stick to his rules.

'So what else do you intend to forbid?' she demanded. 'Every kid in Banksia Bay plays in a boat of some sort. Canoes, dinghies, sailboards, surf-kites, water-skis. This is a harbour town.'

'Will you butt out?'

'No,' she said. 'Not when you're being ridiculous.'

'Ridiculous,' Bailey said and finally—and probably too late—Misty decided she'd gone too far. Nick's face was almost rigid. His own child calling him ridiculous…

A woman might just have to back off.

'Maybe your dad's right,' she told Bailey, and she hugged him against her. She was still in bed, with Bailey and dogs crowded in with her. Nick seemed suddenly an outsider.

She looked at his face and she saw pain behind his

anger. Worse, she saw fear. He'd been to hell and back over the last year, she thought. What was she doing, adding to it because she was angry?

'Maybe ridiculous is the wrong word,' she conceded. 'Maybe I'm not being fair. Your dad worries because of what happened to you and your mum, because he knows bad things happen. He brought you to Banksia Bay because it's safe, and it is, but maybe he needs time to see it. I tell you what; why don't you and your dad bring the dogs to the beach this afternoon and watch? When your dad sees how safe it is, then maybe next Saturday or the one after that he'll agree.'

'You think I'm being dumb,' Nick said, sounding goaded.

'I do.' She hugged the dogs and she hugged Bailey. 'But that's your right.'

'Being dumb.'

'Being…safe. But let's change the subject,' she said—and the frustration in his eyes said it was high time she did. 'You and Bailey talk about sailing and let me know if you ever want to join me. Meanwhile, I need to go see Gran. So if you gentlemen could give me a little privacy and if you could take the dogs with you it would be appreciated,' she said, and she smiled at Nick and she kept her smile in place until he'd taken his son and their dogs and let her be.

'Why not?' Bailey demanded as soon as Misty's door was shut.

'If anything happened to your arm…'

He was talking to a six-year-old. He should just say

no and be done with it. What happened to the good old days when a man was master in his own home?

This was Misty's home. Her rules?

'I can wear my brace,' Bailey said, and he slid his hand into his father's. Beguiling as only a six-year-old could be.

'No.'

'Dad…'

'We'll think about it. Later.'

'Okay,' Bailey said. He really was a good kid. There'd been so many things he couldn't do over the last year that he was used to it. 'Can we make Ketchup and Took bacon for breakfast?'

'Yes,'

'Hooray,' Bailey said and sped away, dogs in pursuit.

How much bacon did he have? Enough for dogs?

He could borrow some from Misty.

The way he was feeling… No.

But then he thought of Misty, her chin tilted, defiant, pushing him to the limit.

And he thought of his son.

There'd been so many things Bailey couldn't do over the last year…

What was he doing, adding more?

Define *safe*, he thought, and he thought of Misty in bed with dogs and Bailey.

Misty was safe.

Misty was gorgeous.

The feeling stilled and settled.

Misty was home.

Chapter 8

Misty visited Gran, who was so deeply asleep she couldn't be roused.

Discomfited, worrying about Gran and worrying almost as much about the guys she'd left at home, she made her way to the yacht club. There was no need for her to go home to change. She kept her gear here.

'Hey, Misty, how's the boyfriend?' someone called, and there was a general chuckle.

She didn't flush. She didn't need to, for the words had been a joke. But inside the joke made her flinch. Was it so funny to think Misty could ever have a boyfriend?

It had been four years since she'd had any sort of relationship, she thought, as she fetched her sailing clothes from her locker. She'd been twenty-five. Luke had been her friend from kindergarten. He'd been away to the city, broken his heart and come home to Misty. He'd wanted to marry, settle on his parents' farm and breed babies and cows.

She'd knocked him back. He'd married Laura Buchanan and they had two babies already and four hundred Aberdeen Angus.

Since then… Misty was twenty-nine and for four years she'd lived alone with her scrapbooks and a list. Miss Havisham in the making?

'What's he like?' someone called, and she tugged herself back to the here and now. 'The boyfriend.'

'Wildly romantic,' she threw back, figuring she might as well go along with it. 'I've seen him in his pyjamas. Sexy as.'

She hadn't seen him in his pyjamas. She'd seen him in his boxers. He was indeed sexy.

Let's not go there.

'Woohoo,' someone called. 'Our Misty has a life!'

Only she hadn't. She changed into her yachting gear and the old frustrations surged back.

Nick had kissed her. *Misty has a life?* Maybe she had. If she wanted it, a relationship was beckoning.

But why had he kissed her? He was attracted to her because she was Misty, the safe one.

Luke had broken his heart and come back to her.

To Misty. To safe.

She glanced out at the bay and saw a gentle breeze rippling the water. It was perfect sailing conditions, but she didn't want perfect. She wanted twenty-foot waves, a howling sou-easterly and trouble.

'My turn to win this time,' someone said and it was Di, the local newsagent. At sixty-five, Di was still one of the town's best sailors. She'd represented Australia in the Olympics. She'd travelled around the world honing her skills.

Misty had stayed home and honed hers.

She and Di were competitive enough. In this bay she could often beat her. But if she ever got out of this bay…

Who knew? She certainly didn't.

Don't think about it, she told herself. Concentrate on beating Di.

And not thinking about Nick?

The race didn't start until two. Mostly the yachties sat round the clubhouse talking, but Misty bought a sandwich and launched *Mudlark*. She sailed out to the entrance to the bay—looking for trouble? But conditions outside weren't any different to inside.

No risks today. Safe as houses.

What was wrong with safe? she demanded of herself. Get over it.

Thoroughly unsettled, she sailed her little boat back inside and spent an hour practising, pushing herself so she had *Mudlark* so tuned to the wind she was flying.

Finally, it was time to make her way to the start line. She'd win today.

There was nothing else to aim for.

Oh, for heaven's sake, what was wrong with her? If Gran could hear her now she'd give her a tongue-lashing. What was the point of complaining about something you couldn't change?

What was wrong with settling for dogs and a lovely tenant—a tenant who'd kissed her…?

The boats were tacking backwards and forwards

behind the starting line, trying to gain an edge. There were up to thirty Sharpies who raced each week. The yacht club kept some available for hire, so visitors to the town could join in. That made it more fun; often an out of town yachtie could surprise them. But no out of town yachtie could beat them.

Di had the experience. Misty had the local knowledge. It was Di or Misty, almost every week.

She checked Di's boat. Di was geared up, ready to go.

The starter's gun fired. *Mudlark* flew, streaming across the water, her sails catching the wind at just the right angle.

The wind was in her hair, on her face. She was sailing fast and free. If she couldn't have her list, this was the next best thing.

And Nick? Was he the next best thing?

A boat was edging up on the same tack as *Mudlark*. She saw it out of the corner of her eye and was surprised. She'd expected to be well in front by now.

And then... Startled, she realised it wasn't Di. It was one of the little orange Rentaboats.

Hey, an out-of-towner pushing her. That'd do to keep her mind off things. She tightened the jib, read the wind, tightened still more.

She passed the marker buoy. Brought her round. The Rentaboat was closing in. What the...?

No matter. Just win. Tug those sails in. Go.

Rentaboat was almost to the buoy and, as she caught the wind and sailed back, she passed within ten yards.

'Hey, Miss Lawrence, we're racing you.' The high,

excited yell pierced her concentration and Misty came close to letting go of her stays.

Bailey.

Nick.

'Go faster, Dad, we're catching up,' Bailey yelled and Misty saw Nick grin.

Her heart did this stupid crazy leap.

Nick was racing. Nick and Bailey…

Bailey was crouched in the bow, whooping with excitement, bright with life and wonder. Nick was at the helm, intent, a sailor through and through.

'Miss Lawrence!' Bailey yelled across the water. 'Miss Lawrence, we're going to win.'

Maybe they would. Her jib had slackened. She was tightening, tightening. Of all the…

She and Di were competitors with each other. Occasionally something happened and another local took line honours, but to concede honours to a Rentaboat…

Pride was at stake here.

She tuned and tuned, every sense totally focused on the boat, the water, the wind. But no, that was a lie because overriding everything else was the awareness that Nick was in the next boat.

He'd brought his son sailing.

A risk…

Hardly a risk. They were both wearing life vests; of course they were. They'd not be allowed to race without them. They were surrounded by a fleet of small boats. Even if they capsized, they'd be scooped up so fast there was never a hint of risk

But still…it was a start, Misty thought.

No, she corrected herself. Getting Took had been a start. This was simply the next step.

As finding Ketchup had been her start. Her start of retreating from her list, from her dreams.

What was her next step?

The wind rose, just a little. She should have seen it coming. Maybe she had seen it, but she was away with her lists. The sudden gust caught her unaware, pushed her sideways, dropped her speed.

Nick surged ahead.

'Hurray, we're winning,' Bailey yelled and they would; the finish line was in sight. But then…

Di. Misty hadn't even noticed her coming up on the far side of Nick. Di's Sandpiper edged just ahead. Nosing over the line.

Local pridc was intact. Di first. Nick and Bailey second.

Misty third.

But a win had never felt as good. It felt fantastic. It was as if she'd been granted the world.

Was it silly to feel like this?

Thoroughly disconcerted, she reduced sail, manoeuvred her little boat back to dock and was inordinately pleased to see Nick had trouble. You needed to know the currents around the clubhouse to get in tight. He didn't know the currents and was having to take an extra run.

Di was calling to him, congratulating him over the water. On the dock, Fred, the vet, was watching. Fred's son sailed. Fred usually watched his son but he was watching Nick now, and she remembered Fred's reaction when he'd heard Nick was a painter.

Nick would be painting for Fred's beloved repertory society in no time.

He'd be a local.

That was great. Wasn't it?

Befuddled, conflicted, she pushed her little boat into shore, then tugged her out onto the hard. Nick needed to go further along, to return his Rentaboat. It gave her time to get her thoughts together, so when Bailey came hurtling through the yard gates and whooped towards her she could laugh and swoop him up into her arms and hug him. And smile over his shoulder to his father.

'You beat me.'

'Your mind must have been on other things,' he said, smiling back, and he looked…fantastic. Faded sweatshirt. Jeans rolled up to his knees. Strong, bare legs. Bare feet. Wind-tousled hair.

He was smiling straight into her eyes, and something was catching in her chest.

Your mind must have been on other things. Really? What could they have been?

'We should have warned you,' he said, and she wondered if she was blushing. She felt as if she was blushing. Was it showing? 'I believe Bailey's yell might have distracted you.'

'You really can sail,' she managed.

'It's what I do,' he said softly. 'It's what I love. I just…needed reminding.'

'That it's safe.'

'That it's still possible to have fun. We've forgotten a bit.'

'And now you have a dog and a sailing club,' she

said, a bit more sharply than she intended, and then wondered why she'd snapped. What was wrong with her? She should be pleased for him. She *was* pleased for him. She was delighted that he was starting to loosen up, become part of this community.

But there was something still not right. Something…

'Speaking of dogs… Did you leave them home?'

'What a question,' he said, sounding affronted. He motioned to the clubhouse yard. The dogs were tied under a spreading eucalypt, a water bowl in reach. They were occupied with a bone apiece. A vast bone apiece.

'I didn't do the bones,' he told her. 'But Fred told everyone their story within two minutes of them arriving and your local butcher headed straight back to his shop and brought them one each. Have you ever seen anything happier?'

She hadn't. She felt herself smiling. But then… Tears?

Of all the stupid, emotional…

She did not cry. She didn't. But now…

Dogs with happy endings. Nick and Bailey with happy endings.

And Nick was watching her. Mortification plus. But he wasn't laughing at her. He didn't look like her tears embarrassed him. He lifted his hand and he wiped a tear away before it had the chance to roll down her cheek.

His touch burned. She wanted to catch his hand and hold it against her face—just hold it.

People were watching.

What did it matter? Was this the next step?

'Hey, Nicholas…'

The moment—the danger?—had passed. Fred was bearing down on them, intentions obvious. 'Great sail. Well done. I hear you can paint.'

'Paint?' Nick said cautiously and Misty managed a chuckle as she moved swiftly away.

'Welcome to my world,' she murmured and went to congratulate Di. She hadn't taken his hand, she told herself. She'd stayed self-contained. Good.

But self-contained wasn't actually going to happen. Not if Bailey could help it. She'd taken two steps when he slid his hand into hers.

'When we go home can I come in your car? Dad says we can have fish and chips for tea. Can we eat tea together? The dogs and I would really like it.'

It seemed surly to refuse, so yes, they ate fish and chips together on the beach. Took bounded a mile or more and then settled beside Ketchup in blissful peace. Apart from looking enquiringly to the chips every now and then, both dogs seemed happy.

Ketchup was looking better every day. The initial pinning of the badly fractured leg needed follow-up. There'd be more surgery later on, but for now he was with Took and he'd found a home.

More, he'd found a boy. And boy had found dogs. The three of them were curing each other, Misty thought, as she watched Bailey tease Took with a chip—tease her, tease her, then shriek as Ketchup whipped in from the side to snatch it. While Bailey was expounding indignation, Took wolfed three more.

Bailey giggled, his father chuckled, Misty went to move the chips out of dog range, Nick did the same and somehow Nick's hand was touching hers again.

They glanced at each other. Nick moved the chips. Then he returned to touch again.

And hold.

'It's been a magical day,' he said softly. 'Thanks to Misty.'

'Thanks to Misty not winning, you mean,' she said with what she hoped was dry humour, but he shook his head and suddenly he had both her hands and he was drawing her closer.

'That's not what I mean at all. Misty…'

What was he doing? Was he planning to kiss her? Now?

'Not in front of Bailey,' she breathed. No!

'Not what in front of Bailey?' Nick asked, smiling down into her eyes. 'Not thanking his teacher for giving us a lesson in life?'

'How can I have done that?'

'Easy,' he said. 'By being you.' He tugged her closer. 'Misty…'

'No.'

'You mean you don't want me to kiss you?'

'No!'

The laughter was back in his eyes. Laughter should never leave him for long, she thought. He was meant for smiling.

He was meant for smiling at her?

'You mean no, you don't not want me to kiss you?' he asked, his smile widening. Becoming wicked.

'No!' She had to think of something more intelligent to say. She couldn't think of anything but Nick's smile.

'It's very convoluted,' he complained. 'I'm not sure I get it. So if I pulled you closer…'

'Nick…'

'Bailey, close your eyes,' he said. 'I need to give Miss Lawrence a thank you kiss.'

'She doesn't like 'em slurpy,' Bailey said wisely. 'She tells Ketchup that all the time.'

'Not slurpy,' Nick said. 'Got it.'

'And she hates tongues touching,' he added. 'That happened yesterday after Ketchup chewed the liver treat. She went and washed her mouth out with soap.'

'So no tongue kissing—or no liver treats?'

'Nick…' She was trying to tug away. She was trying to be serious. But his eyes were laughing, full of devilry, daring her. Loving her?

'Miss Lawrence has said I mustn't kiss her in front of you,' Nick told his son, and his eyes weren't leaving hers. He was making love to her with his eyes, she thought. How did that happen?

'I mean it,' she whispered.

'So can you take Took down and feed the rest of the chips to the seagulls?'

'Why? It's okay to watch.'

'What would the kids at school say if they saw you kissing a girl?' his father asked.

Bailey considered. 'I guess they'd giggle. And Natalie would say, "Kissie kissie". I think.'

'Exactly,' his father said. 'Miss Lawrence is really scared of giggling and she's even more scared of kissie kissie. So, unless you go away, I can't kiss her.'

'You can't kiss me anyway,' Misty managed and his eyes suddenly lost their laughter.

'Really?'

And how was a girl to respond to that?

'I don't…'

'Know?' he said. 'There's only one answer to that. Bailey, down to the water right now or there's no fish and chips on the beach until the next blue moon. Right?' And then, as Bailey giggled, and he and his dog headed towards the seagulls on the shoreline, he pulled her closer still. 'Ready or not…'

And he kissed her.

Second kiss.

Better.

He knew what he wanted.

His parents considered him insane for being a risk-taker. He'd sworn risk-taking would end.

Was it a risk to believe he was falling in love in little more than a week? Was it a risk to want this woman?

It had been a risk to think he was in love with Isabelle. More—it had been calamity. But this was no risk.

This was Misty. A safe harbour after the storm. A woman to come home to.

She wasn't pulling back. Her lips would feel warm, he thought. Full and generous. Loving and reassuring.

But then his mouth met hers and instead of warmth there was…more. Sizzle. Heat. Want.

Instead of kissing her, he found he was being kissed.

There was nothing safe about this kiss. It asked much more than it told, but it told so much. It told that this woman wanted him, ached for him, came alive at his touch.

It told him that she wanted him as much as he wanted her—and more.

Just a kiss…

Not just a kiss. He was holding a woman in his arms and he was making her feel loved, desired. He knew it because the same thing was happening to him. The awfulness of the last twelve months was slipping away. More—the pain of a failing marriage, the knowledge that he was always walking a tightrope, slipped and faded to nothing, and all there was left was Misty.

He was deepening the kiss and she was as hungry as he was, as desperate to be close. Her hands tugged him closer. Closer still… She was moulding to him and her breathing was almost like part of him.

He wanted her so much…

He was on the beach with two dogs and his son.

Ketchup was nosing between them. Misty's hands were…pushing? She wanted to stop?

They should stop.

Who moved first? He didn't know; all he knew was that they were somehow apart and Misty was looking at him with eyes that were dazed, confused, lost.

'Misty…' Her look touched something deep within. Was she afraid?

She'd wanted him as much as he wanted her. Hadn't she?

Her look changed, the smile returned, but he knew he'd seen it.

'What is it?' he asked, but her smile settled back

to the confidence, the certainty he knew. The impudent teasing that he somehow suspected was a mask.

'Entirely inappropriate, that's what it is,' she retorted. 'For me to kiss the parent of one of my students.'

Her student was whooping back to them now, trying to beat Took, who was practically dawdling. 'Can I come back now?' Bailey demanded.

'Yes,' Nick told him. 'And you're not to tell anyone.' His eyes didn't leave Misty's. 'That I kissed Miss Lawrence.'

'Why not?'

'People will tease us,' Nick said and Bailey considered and decided the explanation was reasonable.

'Like saying "kissie kissie".'

'Exactly. And then I wouldn't be able to kiss Miss Lawrence again.'

'I think you need to call me Misty,' she said, no longer looking at him. 'Bailey, when we're on our own, would you call me Misty? Could you remember to call me Miss Lawrence at school?'

'Sure,' Bailey said. 'Do you think you'll marry Dad?'

What sort of question was that?

It was a reminder that fantasy had gone far enough. It was time for reality to kick in.

'Um...no,' Misty managed and the schoolteacher part of her took charge. 'Kissing someone doesn't mean you have to marry them.'

'But it means you like them.'

'Yes,' she admitted, carefully not looking at him. She could feel colour surge from her toes to the tips of her ears. 'But I gave you a kiss goodnight last night. That doesn't mean I'll marry you.'

'It wasn't a kiss like the one you gave Dad.' Bailey sounded satisfied, like things were going according to plan. She cast him a suspicious look—and then turned the same one on his father.

'Have you guys been discussing kissing me?'

'No,' Nick said, but the way he looked…

'Has your father said he wants to kiss me?' she demanded of Bailey and Bailey looked cautiously at his father and then at Misty. Truth and loyalty were wavering.

'I'm your teacher,' Misty said, hauling her blush under control enough to sound stern. 'You don't tell fibs to your teacher.'

'Dad just told you a fib,' Bailey confessed, virtuous.

'Hey,' Nick said. 'Bailey…'

'So you have been talking about me?'

'I saw you kissing in the laundry,' Bailey said. 'I was sort of…up. But I hardly looked.' He grinned. 'But I saw Dad kiss you and later I asked if it was nice to kiss a girl and he said it depends on the girl. And then he said it was very, very nice to kiss you. So I asked if he was going to kiss you again and he said as soon as he possibly can. And tonight he did. Dad, was it okay?'

'Yes,' said Nick.

Misty glared at him. 'You planned…'

'I merely took advantage of an opportunity,' Nick said, trying to look innocent. 'What's wrong with that?'

'How many times do you have to kiss each other before you get married?' Bailey asked.

'Hundreds,' Misty said and then, at the gleam of laughter in Nick's eyes, she added a fast rejoinder. 'So that's why I'm never kissing your father again.'

'Really?' Nick asked and suddenly the laughter was gone.

'R…really.'

'It wasn't just a kiss,' he said softly. 'You know it was much more.'

'It was just a kiss. I'm your landlady.'

'I'm not asking for a reduction in the rent.'

'I'm thinking of putting it up.' She started clearing things, trying to be busy, doing anything but look at him.

'Why the fear?' Nick asked and she shook her head.

'No fear. You're the one who wants to be safe.'

'Hey, we went sailing.'

'I won't be safe,' she muttered.

He frowned. 'What sort of statement is that?'

'Safe as Houses Misty. That's me. Didn't you know? Isn't that why you kissed me? Now, if you'll excuse me, I need to go say goodnight to Gran.'

He was questioning her with his eyes, gently probing parts of her she had no intention of exposing. 'Misty, your Gran's been in a coma for months.'

'And I still need to say goodnight to her,' she snapped.

'Of course. I'm sorry. I'd never imply otherwise. You love her. It's one of the things…'

'Don't,' she said, panicking. 'Nick, please, don't. I need to go.'

'It wasn't just a kiss, Misty,' he said gently, and

he rose and took the picnic basket from her and set it down on the sand before she could object. 'Was it?'

And there was only one answer to that. 'No.'

'Then let's not get our knickers in a knot,' he said and his sexy, seductive, heart-stopping smile was back. It was crooked, twisted and gorgeous, as if he was mocking, but there was no mocking about it. His smile was real and wonderful and it turned her knees to jelly.

'Bailey's going too fast for us,' he said. 'There's no rush. There's no need to panic. But still, it wasn't just a kiss. We both know it.' He took her hands and tugged her to him, only he didn't kiss her this time, at least not properly. He kissed her lightly on the tip of her nose.

'Let's take this slowly,' he said. 'We won't mess this up by rushing. But maybe we both know it could be something wonderful. If we play it right—it could be home for both of us.'

Misty took the dogs with her because she wanted to talk to someone. She left Nick and Bailey sitting on the beach, and they had the sense to let her be.

As they should.

'Because they're my tenants,' she told Ketchup as she carried him. 'I need to be separate.'

But Took was bouncing along beside her. Took was Bailey's dog. Ketchup was her dog.

To separate the two would be cruel.

It felt a little like that now. She was aware of Nick and Bailey watching as she walked away. She was leaving Nick. She was leaving his laughing eyes, his sudden flashes of intuitive sympathy, his sheer arrant sexiness.

'See, that's what I can't resist,' she told Ketchup as she changed out of her sandy clothes to go to the hospital. 'He makes my toes curl but he just thinks I'm safe. If I give into him…if I dissolve like he wants me to dissolve, then I get to stay here for ever. In this house. Mother to Bailey.'

Wife to Nick?

'Maybe I want that,' she said. Ketchup was lying on her bed watching her while Took roamed the bedroom looking for anything deserving of a good sniff. 'Banksia Bay's fabulous, and so's this house. It's the best place in the world.'

As if in response, Took leaped onto the bed and curled up beside Ketchup. Misty looked down at them. Her two dogs, curled on her bed, happy, hopefully for the rest of their lives.

But… There was a scar running the length of Took's face from an unknown awfulness. Ketchup's leg was fixed tight in its brace.

'You guys have had adventures,' she whispered. 'Now you've come home, but I've never left.'

Don't think about it, she told herself. Take your scrapbooks and burn them.

Nicholas had kissed her and he'd touched something deep within. To risk losing what he promised…

For scrapbooks?

The kiss had felt amazing. Her body had responded in ways she'd never felt before.

'I'm a lucky girl,' she told the dogs. 'Yes, I should burn the scrapbooks.'

But she didn't. She slung her bag over her shoulder and she went to see Gran instead.

* * *

'Do you want to marry Misty?'

Nick had left enough time for Misty to change and go to the hospital. He was aware he was rushing things. Risking things. Now Bailey tucked his hand into his father's as they set off towards the house and he asked his most important question.

Did he want to marry Misty?

'I've already been married,' he said cautiously. 'It was dreadful when Mama was killed. It takes time for a man to be ready to marry again.'

'Yeah, but we sailed again.'

'So we did.'

'And it was awesome.'

'It was.'

'You marrying Misty would be awesome.'

Would it?

It wasn't his head telling him yes. It was every nerve in his body.

But he wouldn't rush it. He couldn't rush it. There were things he didn't understand.

She didn't want safe?

She must. To come home… He longed for it with all his heart.

And to come home to Misty…

Home and Misty. More and more, the images merged to become the same thing.

Chapter 9

How had they become a couple in the eyes of the town? It had just…happened. There was little gossip, no snide rumours of the Frank variety. There was simply acceptance of the fact that Nick was sharing Misty's house, he was an eligible widower and Bailey needed a mother.

'And he's rich!' Louise, the Grade Five teacher, did an Internet search and discovered a great deal more information than Misty knew. 'He can demand whatever he wants for his designs,' she informed Misty, awed. 'People are queueing for him to work for them. If I'd realised what we had here I'd have kicked Dan and the kids out of the house and invited him home myself. You're so lucky.'

That was the consensus. Misty was popular in the town. A lonely childhood with two ailing, elderly grandparents made the locals regard her with sympathy. They knew of her dream to travel, and they knew she couldn't. This seemed a wonderful solution.

Especially since Nick was just…there. Wherever Misty was.

'So tell me what sort of steak you like for dinner,' he'd ask as he collected Bailey from school, making no secret of the fact that they were eating together. Well, why wouldn't they? The dogs and Bailey insisted the door dividing the house stayed open. Nick was enjoying cooking—'Something I've never been able to try'—and it seemed churlish to eat TV dinners while the most tantalizing smells drifted from the other side.

They settled into a routine. After dinner they'd take the dogs to the beach. They carried Ketchup to the hard sand, set him down, and he sniffed the smells and limped a little way while Bailey and Took bounced and whooped around him.

Then Nick put Bailey to bed while Misty went back to say goodnight to Gran—whose sleep seemed to be growing deeper and deeper—and when she came home Nick was always on the veranda watching for her.

He worked solidly through the day—she knew he did for he showed her his plans—but he always put his work aside to wait for her. So she'd turn into the drive and Nick would be in his rocker, beer in hand. The dogs were on the steps. Bailey was sleeping just beyond.

It was seductive in its sweetness. Like the call of the siren…

Sometimes she'd resist. She did have work to do. When that happened Nick simply smiled and let her go. But, more and more, she'd weaken and sit on the veranda with him. No, she didn't drink cocoa but it was a near thing. He'd talk about the boat he was working on. He'd ask about her day. And then…as the night stretched out, maybe he'd mention a place he'd been to and she couldn't help but ask for details. So he'd tell her. Things he'd done. Places he'd been.

She was living her adventures vicariously, she thought. Nick had had adventures for her.

And then the moon would rise over the horizon and she'd realise the time and she'd rise…

And he'd rise with her and always, now, he'd kiss her. That was okay, for kissing Nick was starting to seem as natural as breathing. It seemed right and wonderful—and after a month she thought it seemed as if he'd always been a part of her life. And part of Banksia Bay.

He was painting for the repertory society. He was repairing the lifeboat at the yacht club. He was making friends all over town.

And her friends were starting to plan her future.

'You know Doreen's mother's coming from England next term,' Louise said thoughtfully one school lunchtime. 'Doreen would love to get a bit of casual teaching while her mum's here to mind the kids. If you and Nick were wondering when to take a honeymoon…'

Whoa. She tossed a chalkboard duster at Louise. Louise ducked and laughed but Misty suspected she'd go away and plant the same idea in Nick's head.

So what? She should be pleased. Nick warmed parts of her she hadn't known were cold. He held her and he made her feel every inch a woman.

She should embrace this new direction with everything she possessed. She knew she should.

But then Nick would tell her about watching the sunset over the Sahara, or Bailey would say, 'You remember that humungous waterfall we walked under where there was a whole room behind?'

Or Nick would see a picture in the paper and say, 'Bailey, do you remember this? Your mother and I took you there...'

And she'd wait until they'd gone to bed and she'd check the Internet and see what they'd been referring to. The dogs would lie on her feet, a wonderful warm comfort, like a hot-water bottle. Loving her. Holding her safe.

Holding her here.

'So when do you think he'll pop the question?' Louise demanded as term end grew closer, and she blushed and said,

'He hasn't even... I mean we're not...'

'You mean you haven't slept with him yet?' Her friend threw up her hands in mock horror. 'What's keeping you, girl?'

Nothing. Everything. Louise got another duster thrown at her and Misty went to lay the situation before Gran.

'I love him,' she told Gran and wondered why it didn't feel as splendid as it sounded.

Maybe it was sadness that was making her feel ambivalent about this wonderful direction her life was taking. For Gran didn't respond; there was no longer any way she could pretend she did. Her hands didn't move now when Ketchup lay on the bed. There was no response at all.

Oh, Gran…

If she didn't have Nick…

But she did have Nick. She'd go home from the hospital and Nick would hold her, knowing intuitively that things were bad. She'd sink into his embrace and he'd hold her for as long as she needed to be held. He'd kiss her, deeply, lovingly, but he never pushed. He'd prop her into a rocker and make her dinner and threaten her with cocoa if she didn't eat it.

He and Bailey would make her smile again.

What more could a girl want?

'Are you sure he hasn't asked?' Louise demanded a week later.

She shook her head, exasperated. 'No.'

'He looks like a man who's proposed. And been accepted.'

'How could I miss a proposal?'

'You're not encouraging him.' Louise glared. 'Get proactive. Jump his bones. Get pregnant!'

'Oi!'

'He's a hot-blooded male. There must be something holding him back.'

She knew there was. It was her reluctance. He sensed it and he wouldn't push.

All she had to do was smile. All she had to do was accept what he was offering.

She would, she thought. She must.

And then Gran…

Five in the morning was the witching hour, the hour when defences were down, when everything seemed at its worst. For some reason she woke. She felt strange. Empty.

Something was wrong. She threw back the covers and the phone rang.

Gran.

'She's dead.' She barely knew if she'd said it out loud. She was in the hall, standing by the phone, staring at nothing. And then Nick was there, holding her, kissing her hair, just holding.

'I… I need to go.'

'Of course you do. Put something warm on,' he said, and while she dressed—her fingers didn't work so well—she heard him on the phone. Then someone was at the front door. There was a short bark from Ketchup, quickly silenced, and she went out to find Louise in the hall.

Louise's husband farmed the neighbouring property, and Louise's son was in the same grade as Bailey. Louise and Misty often swapped classes, so Bailey already knew Louise well.

She hugged Misty now, tight. 'Oh, Misty, love, she was a lovely lady, your gran, she'll be missed. Nick says he's going to the hospital with you, so we've agreed that I'll stay here until Bailey wakes. Then

I'll scoop him home with me. Is it okay if I tell him what's happened?'

'It's okay,' she said numbly.

'And it's Saturday so there's no pressure,' Louise said. 'If Bailey's okay with it, maybe he can have a sleepover. That'll leave you to get on with things. But we can talk later. You'll be wanting to get to the hospital. Give her a kiss goodbye from me,' she told Misty and she hugged her again and propelled her out of the door.

Nick held her as they walked to the car. She shivered in the dark and moved closer. She'd known this was coming. It wasn't a shock. But…

'She's all I've had for so long.'

'I wish I'd met her,' Nick said. 'Your gran raised you to be who you are. She must have been wonderful.'

She huddled into the passenger seat while Nick drove and she thought of his words. They were a comfort.

And Nick had known Gran. He lived in Gran's house. He walked on the beach Gran loved. He cooked from her recipe books. And once… She'd needed to stay back late at school. It had been late before she'd made it to the hospital—something she hated. Gran probably no longer knew she came every day but there was a chance…

So she'd rushed in, feeling dreadful, to find Nick beside the bed with Bailey curled up beside him.

Nick was reading aloud, *Anne of Green Gables*, Gran's favourite book of all time. It wouldn't be hard to guess it, for the book had been lying on the bedside table, practically disintegrating with age.

She'd stopped short and Nick had smiled at her, but fleetingly, and he hadn't stopped reading until he reached the end of the chapter.

'I guess that's all we have time for tonight, Mrs Lawrence,' he'd said as he drew to a close. 'Misty'll take over now. Bailey and I will leave you while she says goodnight.'

Who knew what Gran had been able to understand, but Nick had read to her, and for now it felt right that he take her into the hospital to say goodbye.

'Thank you,' she told him as he drove.

'It is my very great honour,' he said. 'This is a privilege.'

The next few days passed in a blur. Too many people, too much organization, too great a bruise on her heart to take in that Gran finally wasn't here. If she'd had to do this by herself…

She didn't. Nick was with her every step of the way. That first night she clung and he held her. If Nick had carried her to his bed she would have gone. But…

'I don't want you to come to me in grief,' he said softly. 'I'll hold you until you sleep.'

'You're stronger than I am.' She tried for a chuckle. 'If you think I can lie beside you and sleep…'

'Okay, maybe it's not possible,' he said and tugged her tight and kissed her, strong, warm, solid. 'So separate bedrooms still.'

'Nick…'

'No,' he said, almost sternly. 'I want all of you, Misty. When you come to me it's not to be because you're raw and vulnerable. It's because you want me.'

'I do want you.'

'For the right reasons?' He set her back, tilted her chin and his smile was rueful. 'Loving you is taking all my strength but I won't go back on what I promised. I won't rush you.'

He was stronger than she was. There was nothing she wanted more than to lie with him, to find peace in his body, to find her home…

And she knew, as he turned away, that he sensed it. That she was torn.

There was still a part of her that wasn't his.

She and Gran had a contact point for her mother—a solicitor in London. A postcard had arrived about five years ago, adding an email address, 'In case anything ever happens'. She emailed her mother the morning Gran died. She left messages with the solicitor but she heard nothing.

So what was new? She went about the funeral arrangements and she could only feel thankful that Nick was with her. He didn't interfere. The decisions were hers to make, but he was just…there. His presence meant that at the end of a gruelling time with the funeral director she could stand in Nick's arms and let his strength and his warmth comfort her. She wasn't alone.

The funeral was huge—Gran had been truly loved. Misty sat in the front pew, and who cared what people thought, Nick sat beside her.

She spoke at the ceremony, for who else was to speak for Gran? When she choked at the end, it was Nick who rose and held her.

This was the end of a life well lived. She couldn't be too sad that Gran was finally gone. But what did make her desperately sad…

Where was her mother?

She remembered her grandfather's death, terrifyingly sudden, her grandmother devastated.

'But your mother will come home now,' Gran had whispered, her voice cracked with anguish, and Misty knew she was searching for something that would lighten this awful grief.

'I expect she will,' she said, but of course she didn't.

So why should she come now?

If Nick hadn't been here…

All through that long day, as neighbours came, hugged her, comforted her, Nick was beside her, ready to step in, ready to say the right thing, ready to touch her hand, to make sure she knew he was there for her.

The locals responded to it. Nick had been here for little more than a month, yet already he was treated as one of them. He was Misty's partner. Misty's man.

If he wanted to marry her she'd say yes, she thought, as the day faded to dusk. It might not be the right thing to think on this day but it steadied her. She had Nick and Bailey and two dogs and a house, and a job she loved and a town full of people who loved her.

Her house was full of food and drink, full of people who'd loved Gran. There was laughter and stories and tears, all about Gran.

'I keep thinking about Paris,' someone said—it was an old lady Misty scarcely recognised. And then she did. This was Marigold, her grandmother's bridesmaid. She remembered Marigold visiting them when she'd been a child. Marigold lived in Melbourne now, with her daughter. That she'd come so far to say goodbye to her friend made her want to cry.

'Paris?'

'Before we were married,' Marigold said. 'Your grandmother and I scraped enough to buy tickets on a ship and just went. Our parents were horrified. Oh, the fun… Not a bean between us. We got jobs waitressing. We taught each other French. We had such adventures. The night we both got bedbugs… There were two lovely English boys who let us use their room. They slept on the floor so we could have clean mattresses but the scandal when Madame found out where we'd slept; you'd have thought we were worse than bedbugs.'

Her old face wrinkled, torn between laughter and tears. 'Such a good friend. Such memories. Memories to last a lifetime.'

'Gran went to Paris?'

'She never let me tell you,' Marigold said. 'She told your mother and look what happened.' Then she glanced at Nick with the unqualified appreciation of a very old lady for a piece of eye candy. 'I can tell you now, though,' she said. 'You wouldn't leave this to racket around the world like your mother. This is lovely.'

For some reason, Misty was finding it hard not to cry. Why now, when she'd held it together all day? 'I…'

'Misty's had enough,' Nick, interceding gently. 'Today's been huge. If you'll excuse her…'

'That's right; you look after her,' Marigold said approvingly. 'She's a good girl, our Misty. She always does the right thing.'

* * *

The crowd left. Nick started clearing the mess but he shooed Misty to bed. The dogs were on her bed, warm and comforting, but she felt cold.

Gran had gone to Paris?

And then…the sounds of a car arriving. She glanced at her bedside table—eleven o'clock? What? Bailey had wanted to stay with Natalie tonight. Was something wrong? Had Natalie's parents brought him home?

She heard a car door banging. Nick's greeting was cautious—not the greeting he'd give Bailey. She heard a woman's voice, raised in sharp query.

'Who are you? What are you doing in my house?'

She knew that voice.

It was her mother.

It took her five minutes to get her face in order; to get her thoughts in order, to get dressed and calm enough to face her mother. By that time, Grace was already in the kitchen, drinking coffee, dragging on a cigarette.

She looked older, Misty thought, but then why wouldn't she? How long since she'd seen her? Ten years?

She was wearing tight jeans and black boots to above her knees. The boots were stilettos, their heels digging into the worn wooden floor. She was too thin. Her hair was black—definitely not what Misty remembered. It was pulled up into a too-tight knot and tied with a brilliant scarf that dragged the colour from her face.

This was a new look mother. Grace had a new look

every time she saw her. Not so hard when she left years between visits.

She saw Misty in the doorway, stubbed her cigarette out and rose to embrace her. 'Misty. Sweetheart. You look awful.'

'Mum.' The word was hard to say.

Nick was standing beside the stove, silently watchful. He'd obviously made Grace coffee. He motioned to the kettle but Misty shook her head.

Her mother was here.

'Why have you come?' she asked, maybe not tactfully, but the emotions of the last few days had left her raw and unable to do anything but react instinctively.

'I was in Australia, darling, when the lawyer contacted me. In Perth.' Her mother sat down again and lit another cigarette. 'Wasn't that lucky?'

'How long have you been in Australia?'

'About a year.' A careless wave of the cigarette. Took had emerged from the bedroom to check out this new arrival. The cigarette came within inches of her nose and Took retreated.

Misty felt like doing the same.

A year…

'I let you know about Gran's strokes,' she said. 'I contacted the lawyer every month saying how ill she was.'

'Yes, but there was nothing I could do. Hospitals are not my scene. It was bad enough with Dad.'

'You only visited Grandpa for ten minutes. Once.'

'Don't you get preachy, miss,' her mother said tartly. 'I'm here now.'

'Not for the funeral. They're not your scene, either?'

Nick said nothing. He stood silent, wary.

'No,' her mother said. 'They're not. I can't pretend grief for someone I hardly knew. But I'm here now.' She glanced at Nick, considering. 'You two aren't in my bedroom, are you?'

'No.' Her mother's bedroom was on her side of the house. Beside hers.

'Excellent. No one told me you had a man.'

'I don't have a man. Nick's my tenant.'

'Some tenant.' She yawned. 'Such a long flight. I had to take a cheap seat. Did you know Fivkin and I have split? So boring. The money…you have no idea. But now…' She glanced around the kitchen thoughtfully and Misty suddenly knew exactly why she was here.

'I don't know any Fivkin,' she said, playing for time.

'Lovely man. Oh, we did such things. But now…' Her mother's face hardened. 'Some chit. He married her. Married! And the paltry amount he settled on me makes me feel ill. But that's okay. I'm fine. I've been checking out real estate prices here. We'll make a killing.'

'We?'

'Well, you and I,' Grace said, smiling tenderly at her daughter. 'The lawyer said I may need to give you a portion. You have been doing the caring, after all.'

It took only this. All of a sudden, Misty wanted to be ill. Badly.

'Leave it,' Nick said, and suddenly he was no longer on the sidelines. He was by Misty's side, holding her, his anger vibrating as a tangible thing. 'This is not the time.'

'To speak of money?' Her mother rose, too. 'I suppose you think I'm insensitive. It's just that I need to sort it and get away again. I've been stuck in Perth for too long. I hate keeping still. I talked to Mum years ago about selling this place but she wouldn't. Now...'

'Is there a will?' Nick asked. He was almost holding Misty up.

'I...yes,' Misty said.

'Whatever it says, it doesn't matter,' Grace told her. 'I'm the only daughter. Misty inherits after I go.'

'Misty's going to bed,' Nick said, cutting across her with brutal protectiveness. 'We'll talk this through in the morning.'

'We?'

'You fight Misty, you fight me,' he said.

'I'm sure Misty doesn't want to fight. She's a good girl.'

She *was* going to be ill. Seriously. If she stayed here...

'We're going,' Nick said, ushering her through the door. 'Look after yourself, Grace. Misty's had a terrible few days and she's exhausted. I need to look after your daughter, and I will.'

She'd thought she was shivering before. Now... She couldn't stop. Her whole body shook. Nick held her and swore. Or she thought he swore. She didn't actually recognise the words but he kept right on until finally what he was saying cut through her shock and misery.

He was definitely cursing—but not in English.

She let it be for a while, letting the string of invective wash over her, finding it weirdly comforting. Being held by Nick and listening to…

'Russian?' she managed at last, and he said a few more carefully chosen terms of obvious invective.

Distracted, she pulled away. 'What are you saying?'

'What do you think I'm saying?'

'Swearing?'

'A nice boy like me?'

It was impossible to keep shaking when he was smiling. 'A nice boy like you,' she said, and she found herself smiling back. 'Definitely swearing.'

He tugged her back again, into his arms. Against his heart. 'Don't stop me,' he said. 'Otherwise I'm going to have to slug your mother and it's already been a black day. Ending up in jail might put the cap on it.' He waited until she was nestled against him again. He rested his chin on her hair and swore again.

'What is that?' she managed.

'Something a good girl shouldn't listen to.'

She choked. 'Language?'

'Tajikistan,' he said. 'It has the best cusses. Uzbekistan's good and so's Peru. Mozambique's not bad and Kazakhstan adds variety but, when I'm really against it, good old Tajikistan comes up trumps every time. Tonight's definitely a Tajikistan night.'

'That's my yurt territory.'

'Yurts and swear words. A truly excellent country.'

How could you not smile at yurts and Tajikistan swear words? She was almost forced to chuckle. Oh, but Grace…'She's appalling,' she whispered.

'She is appalling. Is there a will?'

'Yes, but…'

'Leaving her the house?'

'Leaving me the house.'

'You want me to evict her tonight? It'd be my pleasure.'

'No.'

'I could set the dogs on her,' he said thoughtfully, and once again shock and sadness gave way to laughter.

'Right. And they'd evict her how?'

'Wind,' he said. 'If you're in a small enclosed place they can clear a room at twenty paces. All we do is ease them into her room and lock the door.'

She smiled again, but absently. 'She'll win,' she said. 'She has the right.'

'To this house? No, she doesn't. But it's okay, Misty. I'll manage this. This is our home.'

Our home.

The words had been swirling round for weeks. Our home.

He held her tight and let the silence soak in his words.

Our home.

Her home and his. And Bailey's and Ketchup's and Took's.

Home.

'It's okay,' he said again, and he stroked her hair and then he kissed her, first on the top of her head and then on her nose—and then more deeply on her mouth. He was tilting her face, holding her to him, but with no pressure. She could step away at any time.

The night was far too bleak to step away.

Nick. What would this day have been without him?

He loved her and she knew it. This man could make her smile when her world was shattered. How lucky was she that he was here?

She wanted him.

And, with that, everything else fell away. The sadness, the shock, the anger. There was only Nicholas, holding her, loving her.

There was only Nick.

'Can you take me to your bed?' she whispered and she felt his body still.

'Misty…'

'My mother will be sleeping next door. I don't want to sleep so close. Please… Nick, tonight I want to sleep with you.'

'I can't…' he said and she knew exactly what he was thinking. He couldn't hold her all night and take it no further.

'Neither can I,' she whispered and somewhere a chuckle came; somehow laughter was reasserting itself. 'Not any more. I want you, I need you and unless you don't have condoms…'

'I have condoms.' He sounded dazed. 'You think I'd enter a house you were in without condoms?'

'I do like a man who's prepared.'

'Misty…'

'You've been wonderful,' she said, but suddenly he was holding her at arm's length.

'No,' he said, suddenly harsh. 'Not that. I'm not accepting an offering, Misty. Do you want me?'

'I…yes.' There was nothing else to say.

'Then this is mutual lovemaking, or not at all. I

want you more than life itself, but I won't take you as thanks.'

'I do want you.'

'For love? This needs to be an act of love, Misty, or no matter that it'll tear me in two, it's separate beds. You've had an appalling day. Is this shock and grief talking? Or something else? Something deeper.'

Something deeper?

Her world was changing. It had changed when Gran died, she thought, and it had changed again when her mother walked in. But now… Something was emerging she wasn't aware she had. Herself. Misty. She had rights, she thought. This was her life.

And Nicholas was her man?

She took his hand, lifting it, resting it against her cheek. He let her be, not moving, letting her make her own declaration as to what she wanted. The back of his hand was against her cheek. She loved the feel of it. The strength.

Nicholas.

She did want. She ran her fingers across his face, a wondrous exploration, never letting her eyes move from his.

'Definitely deeper,' she whispered. 'I need to be kissed. More, I need to be loved, and I need to be loved by you.'

He gazed down at her for a long moment. He smiled, that magical heart-twisting smile—and then he kissed her.

Magically, his mouth was merging with hers. His hands were holding her face, brushing her cheeks with his lovely long fingers, loving her.

Loving her with his mouth.

The awfulness of the day disappeared as the kiss deepened, then deepened still more. She clung to him, aching to be held, aching to lose herself in love. Nicholas…

But he wasn't completely done with her. Not yet. He moved back then, just a little, and his eyes were dark with love and desire.

'Misty, love, are you sure?'

She smiled at that, for she'd never been so sure of anything in her life. This moment. Nicholas.

'Yes.'

Definitely yes.

And the word was no sooner formed before she was being kissed again, lifted, held, claimed. Holding her in his arms as if she were a featherweight. A man triumphant with his woman.

'My bedroom,' he said, and she hardly recognised his voice. It was shaken with passion and desire. It was deep and husky and so sexy she wanted to melt.

But not here. Not yet. He walked to the door, still carrying her. Paused. Listened.

They heard a clatter in the kitchen—Grace was still there, then. They could make their way through the darkened passage, through the dividing door, then into Nick's side of the house.

Nick's bedroom was vast. The bed was a big four-poster with too much bedding and too many pillows. It was a bed made for more than one man.

It was a bed made for a man and a woman, and she wanted to be in that bed.

Nick was kissing her as he carried her. Then he was

kissing her as he set her down on the bed. As he undid the buttons of her blouse. As he held her and held her and held her, closer and still closer.

She closed her eyes, aching with sensual pleasure. His fingers were tracing the contours of her body, her breasts. Each tiny movement sent shivers of wonder from top to toe.

She clung to him as he kissed her, holding him, glorying in the strength of him, the sheer masculinity, the wonder of his body. This day had seemed unreal. Now she wanted reassurance that this was happening in truth.

Her blouse was gone, and so was her bra. Nick was still clothed, but she could feel the strength of him underneath. In a moment she'd attack the buttons of his shirt, she thought. In a moment. When her body had space between trying to absorb the sensations she was feeling.

They had all the night. They had all the time in the world.

'I think I love you, Nicholas Holt,' she told him. 'Is that scary?'

He pulled away at that, holding her at arm's length. 'You think you love me?' he queried.

'I guess I know.'

'That's very good news.' His voice was grave, serious, husky with passion. 'For I know I love you. I'd marry you tomorrow. I will marry you tomorrow.'

Tomorrow.

The word gave her pause. Tomorrow. Grace. The worries that crowded in.

Nick sensed her withdrawal. He cursed in Tajik. 'Hey, Misty, don't look like that.'

'Tomorrow's tomorrow,' she murmured. 'Can we just take this night?'

A flicker of doubt crossed his face, and she smoothed it away with her fingers. 'No,' she said. 'This is not some one-night stand. I'm not saying that. I'm saying I do love you. I want you. Whether I want to marry you tomorrow…'

'It could be the day after.'

'It could,' she said and chuckled and tugged him close because she didn't want him to see doubt. She didn't want anything to interfere with tonight.

For tonight there was only Nick.

He still had clothes on.

'Not fair,' she said, and started slowly unbuttoning. He was hers, gift packaged, and she was going to take her own sweet time unwrapping.

Only maybe not. For, as she was concentrating—or trying to concentrate—on buttons, he was kissing her. Slowly, sensuously, achingly beautiful. Her neck, her lips, her eyelids.

She felt herself arch up to him and felt his fingers cup the smooth contours of her breasts, tracing the nipples, just touching, feather-soft, making her gasp with need and love and heat.

The night was magic. The moon was full outside, sending ribbons of silver over the ocean, the ribbons finding their way into the bedroom, across the bed, giving two lovers all the light they needed.

Only she had to get these buttons off!

She ripped.

'Uh oh,' he said.

'Was that a good shirt?'

'My best.'

'Sorry,' she said and her mouth found his nipples and suddenly any discussion of the ripped shirt was put aside.

He was hers, she thought. One loving gesture and she had him, putty in her hands. Or in her mouth.

His breathing was ragged, harsh, as her fingers found his belt, unfastened, unzipped. She could hear his breathing deepening. She kissed his neck, tasting the salt of him.

He'd marry her. Her Nick.

Her fingers sought and found. Explored.

Loved.

Enough. One ragged gasp and he surrendered—or not. His hands caught hers, locked them behind her, and suddenly she was his again, and it was she who was surrendering. He kissed each breast in turn, tantalizing, teasing. Savouring. Their heated bodies moulded together.

Skin to skin.

Their mouths were joined again. Of course. It was as if this was their centre—where they needed to be.

Or maybe… Another centre beckoned. His hands were below her waist and she felt her jeans slipping.

As everything else slipped. Doubts. Sadness. Anger.

This night…this time… It was a watershed. Somehow, what was happening right now was firming who she was. A woman who knew what she wanted.

She wanted Nick, and wondrously he wanted her right back. How cool—how magical—how right!

But…

'Wait,' he said, in a voice she no longer recognised. 'Wait, my love.'

She must, but it nearly killed her to wait, until he'd done what he needed to do to keep them safe.

But then there was nothing keeping them apart. The night was theirs.

Outside, the world was waiting but for now, for this night, for this moment, there was only each other.

They were lying against each other, their bodies curved against each other, skin against skin. She'd never felt like this. She'd never dreamed she could feel like this.

A rain of kisses was being bestowed on her neck, her breasts, her belly, while his magical hands caressed and caressed and caressed. The heat…

The French windows were open. The warm night air did its own caressing, and the soft murmur of the surf was more romantic than any violin. She could vaguely hear the distant chatter of the ring-tailed possums who skittered along the eaves. She'd never felt so alive and so aware and so…beautiful?

But…hot? Oh, these kisses. The sounds of the night were receding, giving way to a murmur in her ears that was starting to grow.

He was kissing her low, loving her body, his tongue doing crazy, wondrous things… Amazing things.

'Nick!'

'Hey,' he growled and chuckled his pleasure and did it again. 'You like?'

Did she like? She arched upward, close to crying, aching with need. He was above her, sliding up again so his dark eyes gleamed down at her in the moonlight. He was loving her with his eyes.

'You want me?' he murmured and what was a girl to say to that?

'Like life itself,' she managed and she held him and tugged him down. Down…

But he wasn't sinking. His arms were sailor's arms, muscled, too strong for her to fight him. He was forcing her to wait. She arched and moaned and he kissed her, deeply, more deeply still. Holding the moment. Savouring what was to come.

'My Misty,' he whispered. 'My heart.'

'I need you. Nick, please…' Her thighs were burning; her body was on fire, but still he resisted. He lowered himself, a little but not enough, just so his chest brushed lightly against her breasts. He kissed her neck, behind her ears, her throat, her eyelids, and all the while his body brushed her breasts, over and back until she thought she'd melt with desire and love and need.

No more. What use would she be to this world if she melted into a puddle of aching need, right here on the bed? She took his shoulders and tugged, fierce with want, strong with need, and she rose to meet him.

And he was there.

Her love.

Her Nick.

Her body took rhythm from his. He was reaching so deep inside her, to the point where love and desire and need melted into one and she felt as if she were dissolving, dissolving, flying.

The night and the moonlight and the sounds of the sea, the grief of the day, the shock of the night, the luxury of this bed, the feel of this man's body… There was no separate sensation. No separate thought.

There was only her love.

And when finally they lay back, exhausted, as his arms cradled her and she moulded to his body and she felt his heartbeat, she knew her safe haven—her home—was much more than it had ever seemed.

Nick wanted to marry her. It was a tiny thought at the edge of all the consciousness she had left, but it felt lovely.

Their bodies could merge over and over. She could lie with this man for the rest of her life. She could help him raise his son, a little boy she loved already.

Wife and mother…

It felt… It felt…

'Like a miracle,' Nick said and he kissed her softly, languorously, lovingly. 'My Misty. At last I've come safe home.'

Safe home.

They were the last words she heard as she drifted into sleep.

Safe home.

Chapter 10

Misty stirred, stretched, opened her eyes. Sunbeams were streaming through the windows, falling across the rainbow quilt on the bed. Morning?

She'd slept spooned in the curve of Nick's body. Now she could no longer feel him. Oh, but she was so warm. Sated. She rolled over to find him. The grief she'd felt for Gran had eased, backed off, taken its rightful place. She was no longer bereft and grey. Nick…

Nick's side of the bed was empty.

The bedside clock said ten. What was she thinking? Her mother had to be faced. Life had to be faced.

Was Nick out there, facing it for her?

She showered fast, in Nick's bathroom because she didn't want to be caught by her mother, tousled by sleep, fresh from lovemaking. Besides, she liked the smell of Nick's soap. It smelled like Nick. Of course it did. So much for distinctive aroma, she thought wryly. Lemon grass? She'd thought it was testosterone.

She chuckled. Feeling absurdly happy even though Grace was out there—and that was a scary thought—she twisted a towel round her hair, donned Nick's dressing gown—a gorgeous crimson robe that looked as if it had come from somewhere exotic—of course it had come from somewhere exotic—and scuttled along the passage, through to the other side of the house to find fresh clothes.

And then she paused. There were voices coming from the kitchen. Her mother. Nick.

She should dress before she faced her mother, but…

She hesitated. The kitchen door was almost closed, but not quite. If she stood silent, she could hear every word.

Why would she want to?

She did.

'How much?' It was Nick's voice, but it was a tone she hadn't heard before. He sounded harsh and angry, trying, she thought, for control.

And her mother named a sum that made her gasp.

What the…? They were discussing…

She knew suddenly, definitely, what they were discussing. Selling her house.

'It's Misty's home,' Nick said. 'Her grandmother left it to her.'

'Misty's grandmother was my mother. This house is my right. I'll take her to court if I must but I won't need to. Misty will do the right thing. She always has.'

'You mean you expect her to walk away and leave you to do what you want?'

'I mean she'll do what's expected of her.' Her mother sounded scornful. 'You don't know her father. I did. He was a doormat. Misty's the same. Useful, though. She's kept this place looking great.' She could almost sense Grace assessing the place, looking around at the warm wood, at the lovely old furnishings. 'It'll get a good price. Much more than you're offering. So tell me again why I should accept?'

'Because Misty and I wish to live herc. It's our home.'

'You're marrying her?'

'Yes.'

'Well, good for you. So buy it outright. Give me market value. Save your wife the nasty business of the courts. That'd upset her, fighting me in the courts.'

'It would or I wouldn't suggest it,' Nick snapped. 'You know she's a soft option. She's had no experience of the real world.'

'Then pay,' her mother said harshly. 'Of course you can't expose her to the courts. My mother always said she had to be protected. Don't tell her about what you're doing,' she said. 'It'll upset her. And here you are, ready to keep on keeping her safe. Excellent. Nasty thing, reality.'

'I'll get an independent valuation…'

'You'll take my price or I'll see Misty in court.'

She almost burst in on them then. Almost. Right at the last, she pulled back.

And here you are, ready to keep on keeping her safe.

Last night hadn't been about keeping her safe. Last night had been about loving her, pure and simple.

Did loving involve keeping her safe?

Last night she'd been so sure, but now…

She's a soft option. She's had no experience of the real world.

Standing in the passage, listening to her mother produce valuations of like properties, listening to Nick become reasonable, as if what her mother was suggesting was reasonable, suddenly certainty gave way to doubt.

Nick was doing this to protect her. She knew it. So why did it seem so wrong?

Her mother's words…

You don't know her father. I did. He was a doormat. Misty's the same.

Anger came to her aid then. She was no doormat. How could Nick simply accept that as fact?

She's had no experience of the real world.

Nick wasn't going to pay for her house. Hard cold fact. She could go in there right now and tell him so. But something inside her was saying, *think. Get this right before you fly in with temper.*

She backed out of the passage, out of the back door to the veranda. Ketchup and Took were out there in the morning sun, supervising the sea. She sank down beside them and they nosed her hands and wagged their tails.

'Why aren't you in there biting my mother?' she whispered. 'Dogs are supposed to protect their masters.'

But the dogs weren't in the kitchen because they'd found each other. Their security was each other.

As her security was Nick?

The dogs had had their adventures. They'd come home.

They weren't doormats.

Nick had had his adventures. Even Bailey…

She's had no experience of the real world.

Even her grandmother, never telling her she'd been to Paris because Misty had to be protected. Protected from herself?

There was a huge muddle of emotion in her mind but it was getting clearer. She stared out over the bay she'd loved all her life. The dogs nestled against her and the knot of confusion in her heart settled to certainty.

A doormat. Safe.

'You guys don't need me,' she whispered. 'When Gran was alive, when Ketchup needed me, and when I met Nick, my list seemed wrong. Stupid. But maybe it's not stupid. Maybe it's important if Nick and I are to build something. I won't have him spending his life thinking I need to be safe.'

Ketchup whimpered a little and put a paw on her knee. She managed to smile, but she didn't feel like smiling. What she was thinking…? It would hurt, and maybe it would hurt for ever.

'You don't really need me, do you?' she told Ketchup. 'You have Took. What's more, you have Nick and Bailey. You have guys who are in the business of keeping everyone safe. That's what they want to do, so they can stay here and do it.'

Okay. She took a deep breath. She girded her

loins—as much as a girl could in such a bathrobe. She thought of what she had to do first.

'Nick's keeping this place safe. He can keep doing that, only there's no way he's paying my mother for the privilege,' she told the dogs.

She closed her eyes, searching for courage. What she was going to do seemed appalling. Loving Nick last night had made it so much harder.

She thought back to Frank, to her bitter colleague, regretting for all of his life that he'd never left this town.

'I can't do that to Nick,' she whispered. 'I'd try not to mind, and mostly I wouldn't, but every now and then...'

Every now and then she would mind, and it could hurt them all.

She's had no experience of the real world.

So do it now or do it never.

Deep breath. She stood and wrapped Nick's gown more tightly round her.

'Wish me luck, guys,' she whispered. 'Here goes everything.'

Nick had trouble with his own parents. Grace, though, was unbelievable.

She'd dumped her infant daughter on her parents and walked away. Half an hour with her this morning and he understood why. There was nothing she wouldn't do to get her own way.

If he hadn't been here... Misty would be trampled, he thought. Misty was no match for this... He couldn't find words to describe her. Not even Tajikistan had a good one.

'I have good lawyers,' Grace snarled and he faced her with disgust.

Maybe a fight through the courts would give the house to Misty, but the thought of it not succeeding, and the thought of what Misty would go through to claim it…

She might not even try. Misty was a giver, and he loved her for it.

'We need to get this in writing…' he started but he didn't finish. The back door slammed open. Misty.

She was standing in the doorway, his crimson bathrobe all but enveloping her. The towel around her hair was striped orange and yellow. Her eyes matched her outfit. They were flashing fire.

'What do you think you're doing?' she demanded and she was talking to them both.

Grace stubbed her cigarette out in her saucer and smiled at her daughter, a cat-that-got-the-cream smile that made Nick feel ill.

'We're discussing business,' she said sweetly. 'Your man's being very reasonable. There's no need for you to get involved.'

'Nick's not *my man*.'

Uh oh. Nick sensed trouble. Where was the woman who'd melted into his arms last night, who'd surrendered completely, utterly, magically? The look she gave him now was one of disbelief. 'You're offering to buy *my* house. From my mother.'

'We want to live here.'

'So?'

'It's easier, Misty. I'll just pay her and she'll leave.'

'She's leaving anyway,' Misty snapped. 'Grace, get out of my house. Now.' She picked up the ash-filled saucer and dumped it in the bin. 'You light up one more cigarette in this kitchen and I'll have you arrested for trespass.'

'This is my house.' Grace looked as stunned as Nick felt. This wasn't Misty. This was some flaming virago they'd never seen before.

'You left this house when you were eighteen,' Misty told her, cold as ice. 'You came back only when you needed money—or to dump a baby. What gives you the right to walk in now?'

'They're my parents,' Grace hissed. 'This house has always been waiting…'

'For you to sell it the moment they're dead? I don't think so. Gran left me this house, and its contents.'

'I'll contest…'

'Contest away,' Misty snapped and Nick could hear unutterable sadness behind the anger. 'Gran had macular degeneration for the last fifteen years. That's meant she's been almost blind. Since I was sixteen I've been signing cheques, taking care of all the business. Grandpa left Gran well off but almost all her income has been siphoned to you. You've been sending pleading letters. I've read them to her and every time she'd sigh and say, "What shall we do, Misty?" To deny you would have killed her. So I've sent you cheques, over and over, and every single one was documented. You've had far more than the value of this house, yet you couldn't even find it in you to come to her funeral. I don't know what gene you were handed when you were born, but I thank God I didn't inherit it. Gran loved me. She wanted me to have this house and I will.'

'Misty…' Nick started and she turned on him then.

'And don't you even think of being reasonable. You're doing this to protect me? Thank you but I don't need protecting. I've had no experience of the real world? Maybe not, but I'm not going to get it with you protecting me. So I'm telling you both what's going to happen. First, Grace is going to get out. The cheques have stopped. You're on your own, like it or lump it. And Nick, you want a quiet life? That's what you can have because I'm leaving, too. Oh, not for ever, just for twelve months. I have a list to work through and for the first time in my life I'm free. I had Gran but she's dead. I thought I had Ketchup but he has Took and he has you. You and Bailey will love this house. It's safe…as houses.'

She took a deep breath, holding her arms across her breasts as if she needed warmth. He rose to go to her but she backed away. 'No. Please, Nick…' Her anger was fading a little but she seemed determined to hold onto it. 'This is hard but I have to do it. I know it sounds ungrateful, but…it's what I'm going to do. Now, I need to go and get dressed. Grace, when I get back here I don't want to see you. You'll be gone. Nick will be looking after my house—*my house*—but it's my house in absentia.'

They were left looking at each other. Grace looked…old, Nick thought and, despite the shock of Misty's words, he felt a twinge of pity.

Misty hadn't called her Mom or Mama or Mother.

She'd called her Grace. If Bailey ever looked at him as Misty looked at Grace…

She deserved it. She'd been no mother to Misty, but still…

'You'd best go,' he said and Grace looked at him like a wounded dog.

'I don't… I can't. I don't have any money.' It was a defeated whine.

He hesitated. There'd been a resounding crash from Misty's bedroom door. They were safe from her hearing.

Had Misty meant what she said?

Don't think about that now. Just get rid of Grace. Without Misty knowing?

Definitely without Misty knowing.

He tugged out his chequebook and wrote, and handed over a cheque. Grace stared down at it, stunned.

'I want the value of the house.'

'And instead I'm giving you your plane fare back to Perth and enough for approximately six months' rent. If Misty finds out I've done it I'll cancel the cheque. It's the last you'll get off us, Grace, so I suggest you take it and leave.'

'Us?' She dragged herself to her feet and regarded him with loathing. 'It didn't sound to me like there's any *us*. She sounds like she's leaving.'

'That's up to us,' he said evenly. 'But you're leaving first.'

Misty found him on the veranda, in his normal place, in his rocker, dogs at his feet. She was feeling ill.

She'd yelled at him. He didn't deserve to be yelled at.

'I'm sorry,' she said quickly before he could rise. 'That was dreadful. I sounded like I was a witch. You were only trying to help.'

'I'd like to help,' he said. 'You know I want to marry you.' He rose and came towards her. 'I'll protect you in any way I can.

'But I don't want to be protected. Nick, I'm sorry, but I don't want to marry you. Or…not yet.'

His face stilled. He'd taken her hands but she wouldn't let her fingers curl around his. She mustn't.

'I've never taken a risk in my life,' she said.

'That's why I love you.'

'You see, that's what I'm afraid of. I won't be loved because I'm safe.'

That he didn't understand was obvious. 'I don't love you just because you're safe,' he told her. 'I love you because you're beautiful and warm and big-hearted and fun and…'

'And safe. I'm someone to share a rocker with.'

'Misty…'

'It's okay,' she said, feeling unutterably weary. She didn't want to say this. It would be so easy to sink into the rocker beside him, to wait until Bailey came home, to live happily ever after.

Was there something of Grace inside her? Some heartlessness?

No. She felt cold and fearful and sad, but she knew she was doing the right thing. If she didn't go now… She'd seen what bitterness could do.

'If you still want me in a year…' she said.

'A year?'

'I think I can do most of my list in a year.'

'What list?'

'It's a dream,' she said. 'I've had it since I was little. To fly away, to see something other than this town. Occasionally, when I was little, Grace used to send postcards, from one exotic place after another.'

'You were jealous of Grace?'

That was easy. 'I never was. Sometimes I even felt sorry for her. She'd fly in and make Gran cry and Gran would say the house was empty without her. But I kept thinking…why would you want to make Gran cry? That would have made me ill. I couldn't. Until now.'

His face was expressionless. 'So now you'll leave?'

'What's holding me here?'

'Us. Bailey and me.'

She closed her eyes. There was such a depth of meaning in the words—so much. He didn't understand. For her to walk away… To hurt him…

'See, that's the problem,' she said, as gently as she could. 'I'm falling so in love with you that I never want to hurt you. It's borderline now—that I never want to leave. As I could never leave Gran. For a while there I couldn't even leave Ketchup. But I must. Just for a year. Nick, can you try and understand?'

'Understand what? What do you want to do for a year?'

'Adventures,' she said promptly. 'I want to balloon over Paris at dawn. I want to roll down heather-covered hills in Scotland and get bitten by midges. I want to go white-water rafting in the Rockies…'

But she'd already lost him. 'You don't know what

you're talking about,' he said coldly, flatly. 'You have everything you need here. It's…'

'Safe,' she threw at him. 'Tell me, if you didn't think I was safe, would you seriously consider marrying me?'

'No, but…'

'There you are, then.'

'But I have Bailey to consider.'

'You're not considering Bailey. You're choosing a wife for yourself. To choose me because top of your list of requirements is safe… Good old dependable Misty, cute as, we'll stay in her lovely house and if anything threatens her like a nasty, mean mother then we'll drive her away; we'll protect Misty because she's little and cute and can't protect herself.'

'This is overreacting.'

'Like paying for a house without even asking me?' she said incredulously. 'I guess I should be grateful, but I'm sorry, I'm not. You see, I want to be independent. Nick, I can't cling to you before I see if I can manage without anything to cling to. I need a year.'

'To go white-water rafting in the Rockies.'

'Yes.'

'You're just like Isabelle.' It was a harsh, cold accusation that left her winded.

She didn't answer. She couldn't. Was she just like Isabelle? Would she put a child's life at risk when she didn't need to?

If he thought that, then there was nothing to defend. He wanted her to marry him and he didn't know the first thing about her.

She looked at him and her heart twisted. How easy

would it be to fall into his arms, say sorry, it had all been a mistake and she wanted nothing more than to stay here with him, with Bailey, with Ketchup and Took, for ever and ever?

But he was looking at her with such anger.

Last night meant so much to her. It meant everything. But in a sense it was last night that had given her the courage to do this. For last night she'd accepted that she wanted to spend her life with this man, and she also knew that he deserved all she could give.

All or nothing. She would not marry him feeling like she did right now—knowing she'd dissolve into him and he'd make her safer, safer. She'd fought to get him onto a yacht. Every tiny risk would be a fight, but it'd be a fight to do what she already had now, and not what she dreamed of.

She couldn't let go of her dreams and marry him. She'd end up bitter and resentful.

She's had no experience of the real world.

It was a line to remember. It was a line to make her go.

'I will not end up in this rocker before I'm thirty,' she said, and suddenly she kicked the rocker with a ferocity that frightened them all. Took yelped and headed down the steps with her tail behind her legs. Ketchup yelped and cowered and cringed behind Nick's legs.

'Enough,' she said wearily. 'Sorry, guys. Sorry to you all. I know you're all very happy here. I hope you'll stay here and be safe and happy while I'm away. And if at the end of twelve months…'

'You expect us to wait for you?' Nick's voice was so

cold she cringed. But she'd known this was the risk—the likely outcome. She had to face it.

'Can I ask whatever you do that you'll take care of Ketchup and Took?'

'Misty, after last night…' he said explosively and she nodded sadly.

'Yes. Last night was magic. It made me see how close I am to giving in.'

'Then give in.'

'I won't be married because I'm the opposite of Isabelle,' she said, and she knew it for the truth, the bottom line she couldn't back away from. 'You figure it out, Nick. I think I love you but I'm me. I'm me, lists and all.'

Chapter 11

'When I suggested we get a relief teacher next term I thought you might use the time off for a honeymoon. Not to leave.' Louise was practically beside herself. 'What happened? We were all so sure. A honeymoon with Nick… Oh, Misty, why not?'

'Because our honeymoon would be at Madge Pilkington's Bed and Breakfast out on Banksia Ridge, with tea and scones, a nice dip in the pool every day and bed at nine. We might watch a bit of telly. Wildlife documentaries, maybe, but no lions hunting zebras for us. Nothing to put our blood pressure up.'

'You're nuts,' her friend said frankly. 'Nicholas Holt would put my blood pressure up all on his own.'

'Not if he can help it,' she said. 'Safe and sedate R Us, our Nick.'

'So you're definitely leaving?'

'I'm leaving.'

'Natalie's mother says he wants to marry you.'

'How would Natalie's mother know?'

'Does he?'

'He doesn't want to marry me,' she said. 'He wants to marry who he thinks I am. But, if I'm not careful, that's who I'll be and I suspect I'd hate her.'

'I don't understand.'

'You know something?' Misty muttered. 'Neither do I. But all I know is that I've fallen in love with him. He deserves everything I'm capable of giving and I don't know what that capability is. I have to leave to find out.'

'For ever?'

'For a year,' she said. 'I've taken a year's leave of absence. I'm not rich enough to walk away for ever. Nor do I want to.'

'He won't wait. You can't expect him to.'

'No,' she said bleakly. 'I can't expect him to.'

'Why is she going away?'

It was about the twentieth time Bailey had asked the question and it never got easier.

'Because her gran's died and she needs a holiday. Because we're here to look after the dogs.'

'We could all go on a holiday.'

'Misty wants to be by herself.'

But did she? He didn't know. He hadn't asked.

He wasn't going to ask. There was no way he was taking Bailey white-water rafting in the Rockies.

'We could go sailing,' Bailey said, verging on tears. 'All of us together.'

'You and I will go sailing. Next Saturday.'

'Misty's leaving on Friday.'

'Then we'll miss her very much,' Nick said as firmly as he could. 'But it's what she wants to do and we can't stop her.'

Friday. At eight Louise was collecting her to drive her to the airport. At dawn Nick went outside and found her crouched on the veranda, hugging two dogs.

'Hi,' he said and she turned to face him and he saw she'd been crying. 'Misty…'

'Hay fever,' she muttered, burying her face in Ketchup's coat. 'I'm allergic to dogs. How lucky I'm leaving.'

'Stay.'

'No.'

'Misty, we love you,' he said, feeling helpless. 'Both of us do. No, all of us,' he added, seeing the two dogs wuffle against her. 'This is craziness.'

'It's not craziness,' she said and swiped her cheeks with the back of her hand. 'It's what I need to do. I'm not Isabelle, Nick, no matter what you think, but I have my reasons. Instead of hating me for what I'm doing… I wish, oh, I wish you'd try to see who I really am.'

'I know who you are.'

'No, you don't,' she said and rose and brushed past him, heading for the door. 'You see what you want to see, and that's not me.'

'So who are you?'

'Heaven knows,' she said bluntly. 'I'm heading off into the unknown to find out.'

Nick watched her go.

He watched until Louise's car was out of sight.

Then he walked inside and slammed the door so hard it fell off its hinges.

Great. Something to do.

Something to do to stop him following her and dragging her back any way he knew how.

Misty was staring down at the receding vision of Sydney and all she could think of was what she'd left behind. What she'd given up.

'But I'm not giving it up,' she muttered. 'I'm leaving for a year. It'll be there waiting for me when I get back.'

'Nick won't be there,' she reminded herself. 'That's up to Nick.'

Oh, but what a risk. She sniffed before she could help herself and the man in the next seat handed over a wad of tissues.

'My wife does this every time we fly,' he said. 'So I come prepared. She's not with me this time but she sobbed at the airport. Leaving family then, are you, love?'

'Sort of.' It was all she could manage.

'He'll be there when you get back,' the man said comfortably. 'If he has any sense.'

'That's just the problem,' she told him. 'He has too much sense.'

'So what will we do without her?'

What, indeed? Move? The idea had appeal—to shift out of this house where he'd thought he had his life sorted. Only he had two dogs, and Bailey loved his new school, and to move out now…

They'd move before she came home, he decided. If she came home. She'd probably meet someone white-water rafting. Or kill herself in the process.

'Why do you keep looking angry?'

'I'm not angry.'

'So what will we do?'

It was Sunday afternoon. They'd had a whole forty-eight hours without her. It was raining.

Even the dogs were miserable.

Nick stared round the kitchen, looking for inspiration. 'Maybe we can cook,' he said. 'I've never tried a chocolate cake. You want to try?'

'It'd be better if Misty was here,' Bailey said, stubborn.

'Yes, but Misty's not here.' He headed for the recipe shelf and tugged out a few likely books. 'One of these…'

But then he was caught. There was a pile of scrapbooks wedged behind the recipes. One came out along with Mrs Beeton's *Family Cookery*.

It was a scrapbook, pasted with pictures. All sorts of pictures.

On the front in childish writing…

'Misty Lawrence. My Dreams, Book One.'

It didn't quite come up to expectations. Flying over Paris at dawn…

For a start, it was loud. It hadn't looked loud in the pictures. The brochures had made it look still and dreamlike, floating weightlessly above the Seine, maybe sipping a glass of champagne, eating the odd luscious strawberry.

She was cold. Champagne didn't cut it. If she wanted anything it was hot cocoa—where was Nick and his rocker now?—but she was too busy gripping the sides of the basket to even think about drinking or eating. The roar of the gas was making her ears ring. It was so windy… It had been a little windy before they'd started but had promised to settle, but a front had unexpectedly turned. So now they were being hit by gusts which, as well as making the ride bumpy and not calm at all, were also blowing them way off course.

Mind, she couldn't see their course. All she could see was a sea of cloud. The guy in charge was looking worried, barking instructions into his radio, most of which seemed to be about the impossibility of finding a bus to get his passengers back from who knew where they were going to land.

There were three couples in the basket and Misty. The couples were holding each other, giggling, keeping each other warm.

She was clinging to the basket, telling herself, 'Number One on my list, okay, not great, but now I'll get to wander down the Left Bank and take a barge down the Seine and buy Lily of the Valley on the first of May.'

Alone. She glanced across at the giggling couples who were holding each other rather than the basket.

Get a grip, she told herself. This was her list. She'd waited almost thirty years for it.

A month of Paris. Then the Dordogne. The great chateaux of Burgundy.

And then cruising the Greek Islands. It'd be fantastic—if she could just hold on for another hour and she didn't freeze to death or burst her eardrums. And maybe the clouds would part for a little so she could see Paris.

She must have started these lists when she was Bailey's age. They had all the scrapbooks out now, spread across Misty's kitchen table. Every night they seemed to be drifting back to Misty's side of the house to read her scrapbooks.

But, in truth, it wasn't just to read her scrapbooks. It felt better here—on Misty's side.

The dogs seemed more settled in Misty's kitchen. They slept by the stove, snuggled against each other, but every time there was a noise their heads came up and they looked towards the door with hope.

No Misty, and their heads sagged again.

How can they have fallen in love with her in so little time? Nick thought, but it was a stupid question. He knew the answer.

He had. And he was still falling…

They were reading the scrapbooks instead of bedtime stories. There was so much…

She'd been an ordered child, neat and methodical. The first couple of scrapbooks were exotic photographs cut from old women's magazines, and the occasional postcard. Some of the postcards had lost their glue and were loose. They were tattered at the edges as if they'd been read over and over. As he and Bailey flipped the pages it was impossible not to read their simple messages:

In Morocco. Oh, guys, you should be here. I feel so sorry for you, stuck in Banksia Bay.
Grace.

He thought of an eight-year-old receiving this from her mother, and he thought of going out and cancelling Grace's cheque. He couldn't. It would have been long cashed. Grace was gone.

Misty was gone.

'I wish she was here,' Bailey said, over and over. He leafed through to the third scrapbook. 'This place is number one on her list.'

Her list…

They'd found it now, carefully typed, annotated, researched. What she'd done was take her piles of scrapbooks and divided them into twelve to make her list.

He went from scrapbooks to list, then back to scrapbooks. Pictures, pictures, pictures. And then, later, articles, research pieces, names of travel companies.

A child's hand turning into a woman's hand.

These were dreams, a lone child living with ailing grandparents, using her scrapbooks to escape to a world where her mother lived. Her mother didn't want her, but to know a little of her world… To dream of a world outside Banksia Bay…

I feel so sorry for you, stuck in Banksia Bay...

She'd been raised with that message ringing in her head.

Bailey found the scrapbooks entrancing but, as Nick worked his way slowly through them, he found them more than entrancing.

He began to see what he'd done.

He'd asked her to give up her dreams.

'Twelve months,' she'd said. 'I just want twelve months.' He hadn't given them to her. He'd reacted with anger.

'You're just like Isabelle.'

It had been said in an instinctive reaction when he hadn't got his way. Yes, it was born of his need to protect Bailey, but it had been unfair and untrue. He thought of Misty's face when he'd said it and he felt appalling.

'We miss her,' Bailey said, looking at pages linked to the item at the top of her list, at the advertisements for hot air ballooning over Paris, at the lists of castles on the Dordogne, at photographs of a tiny chateau hotel at Sarlat, at underground cellars, miles and miles of cellars where they kept the world's great Burgundies. Paris in springtime. France. 'She'll be there now,' he said. 'Is hot air ballooning dangerous?'

Yes, was his instinctive response. After the terrors Bailey had been exposed to…

But he knew it wasn't.

'No,' he told his son. 'It can be uncomfortable. Often noisy.'

'It doesn't look noisy,' Bailey said doubtfully.

'The gas burners are really loud.'

'I don't think Misty likes noise. Do you think we should ring her and tell her not to do it?'

He picked up the list and read it. Drinking Kir at sunset on the Left Bank. Wandering through the Louvre. Standing on top of the Arc de Triomphe and watching the crazy traffic underneath.

What was this? Hiring a motor scooter and riding

round the Arc de Triomphe? Should he ring and tell her how crazy that was?

No.

He thought of her sailing, wearing a life vest. He and Bailey had watched her from the clubhouse before the race, practising and practising. Pushing herself to the limit, but her little boat was fine.

He'd accused her of being just like Isabelle. Was he mad?

'I think Misty wants to find out all by herself,' he said, and he knew part of it was true—she did want to find out—but the rest...

Bailey went to bed and he returned to Misty's side of the house—with scrapbooks. Misty was here on these pages, a girl's dreams followed by a woman's serious commitment.

He'd given her a choice. Himself and his son—or her dreams. Would he want her to give this up?

He'd asked her to.

What to do?

He had clients arriving in Banksia Bay now. His international clients were talking to him about their boats, about their dreams. They were finding out where he was based and saying, 'You know what? We'll come talk to you in person.'

They loved it. Banksia Bay was beautiful. He never had to leave.

Bailey was safe.

But these scrapbooks...

Her list...

Twelve months.

The dogs sighed. They lay at his feet but they looked at the door.

'She'll be back in a year,' he told them.

But if there's someone else in her balloon…some guy who sees what Misty really is…how beautiful…

How could they not? He flicked through the list, thinking if she found someone to do these with her…

It was an amazing list.

He hadn't done some of the stuff on this list.

Bailey was asleep. Here. Safe. But maybe… maybe…

He read the list again. Slowly. Thoughtfully.

This was not Isabelle.

Maybe dreams were made to be shared?

He turned to the dogs, considering. It was his responsibility to care for these two.

Kennels?

No. He knew where they'd come from. If he and Bailey were to be free…

'Sorry, guys, but I think tomorrow morning we need to go see Fred.'

Fred the vet.

She'd been away for six weeks. She was loving every minute of it. Sort of.

Number three on her list was cruising the Greek islands. It'd be magic. She'd pinned pictures up on her study wall at home. Whitewashed villas with blue-painted windows. Caiques bobbing at anchor. Greek fishermen stripped to the waist, hauling in their nets. Santorini, Mykonos, the Cyclades islands. It was all before her.

She climbed off the bus at the harbour in Athens. Her boat was due to leave in two hours.

Two emotions…

After so much planning, it was impossible not to feel exhilarated as dreams became real.

It was also impossible to block the thought that back home was Nick. Nick and Bailey and Ketchup and Took, learning to live in Banksia Bay without her.

She couldn't think about them now. She mustn't. To follow her dreams with regret—what sort of compromise was that? She lifted her back pack and trudged down to the departure point, telling herself firmly to think ahead.

But the boat at anchor wasn't what she'd expected. In the pamphlets it had been shown as a graceful old schooner, wooden planking, sails, lovely.

The boat before her was huge, white, fibreglass. There were tourists filing up the gangplank already. Many tourists. This was far bigger than she'd imagined.

Her heart sank—but she was getting used to this. Adjusting dreams to fit reality. She would *not* be disappointed. She'd looked forward to this for so long. Sailing on the Aegean…

But still… No sails. So many tourists.

A hand on her shoulder.

'It's not the same as your pictures. Maybe we can offer you an alternative?

She almost jumped out of her skin.

She whirled—and he was there.

'We came to find you,' Nick said before she could even kick-start her heart. 'Me and Bailey.' He smiled down at her, a smile that made her heart stop even trying to kick-start—and he put on the voice of a spruiker, the guys who pushed tourists to change their minds.

'Madam wishes to sail the Greek islands? On this?' He gestured contemptuously to the fibreglass cruiser. 'My *Mahelkee* is a much smaller boat, but she's infinitely more beautiful. There's four aboard now. A crew of four, whose only wish is to keep madam happy. You come with us, madam, and we will make you happy. You come with us, madam, and we intend to make you happy for the rest of your life.'

Chapter 12

You didn't travel alone for long without learning to avoid spruikers. Misty was very good at saying, 'No, thank you,' and walking away without looking back.

But this was some spruiker.

For a start, he wasn't alone. He was working as one of a pair. For as well as Nick with his heart-stopping smile, there was also Bailey. Bailey wasn't smiling. He was a little behind his father, gazing up at her as if he wasn't quite sure he still knew her. Anxious. Pleading?

Nick. Bailey.

How to get her heart beating like it should again? She wasn't sure she could.

'H… How…?' she managed. 'How did…?'

'Lots of work,' Nick said. He'd removed his hand from her shoulder. He was no longer touching her. He was just…smiling. If she wanted to back away and head up the gangplank to her cruiser, she still could.

Turn away? A girl would be mad.

'W…work?' she managed. 'You've worked to get here?'

'We just got on an aeroplane,' Bailey said from behind his father. 'It was easy.'

'So no work.'

'We would have worked if we had to,' Nick said. Virtuous. 'To reach you. And I had to make a whole lot of phone calls.'

'Dad slept on the aeroplane,' Bailey said.

'First class, huh,' she said and somehow she managed a smile.

'Of course,' Nick said, and his smile deepened and strengthened, a caress all by itself. 'If it's to reach you, then only the best will do.'

'Nick…'

'We have your list.' Bailey was clutching his father's hand but his eyes were on Misty. Desperately anxious. 'Dad and I have your list. We want to do it, too. If you let us.'

There was a statement to take a girl's breath away. *We want to do it, too...*

'I believe I've made a mistake,' Nick said gravely. Around them, passengers were streaming up onto the gangplank. They were having to divert around this couple and child, plus one very large backpack. Misty didn't notice. 'I believe I made the biggest mistake of my life. I'm hoping… Bailey and I are hoping…that it's not too late to fix it.'

She was having trouble breathing. 'I don't know what you mean,' she whispered.

'We mean your list is part of you,' Nick said, and still he didn't touch her. He was holding back, leaving her be, outlining the facts and allowing her space to absorb. 'After you left, Bailey and I read your scrap-books.'

'You read...'

'We hope you don't mind.'

'No, but...'

'But they're part of who you are,' he said. 'Part of the whole. Misty, we tried to love only the part of you that I wanted. That was so dumb it doesn't bear think-ing of. I'm hoping against hope that it's not too late to let me repair the damage. I'm hoping it's not too late to tell you that I love all of you, without reservations. That Bailey and I fell in love with Misty the school-teacher, Misty the dog-lover, Misty the sailor. But we want more. We want Misty the traveller. Misty the ad-venturer.' He hesitated. 'And... And Misty, my wife?'

'Oh, Nick...'

'And Misty the mother,' Bailey piped up from be-hind. 'When we talked about this at home... Dad, you said Misty the mother. You said let's come over here and see if we can make Misty love us. Let's come over here and see if we can get Misty to teach me how to make scrapbooks. But I've already started,' he said proudly. 'I have a picture of a motorbike on the first page.'

'A motorbike,' Misty said faintly. 'Aren't they dan-gerous?'

'Yes,' Bailey said, peeping a smile. 'And they're noisy. Like balloons.'

She smiled back. She wasn't sure how she managed to smile. She believed there were tears slipping down her cheeks.

Tears? Who felt like crying now?

'We have a tour mapped out,' Nick said. He reached a hand towards her and then pulled it back again. As if he was afraid to touch—as if she might turn and flee if he did. 'Santorini, Mykonos, the Cyclades Islands.'

'They're the ones on your list but Dad says we can do more,' Bailey said. 'Cos *Mahelkee* is a smaller boat. She can go into lots of places big boats can't go. Dad showed me on the Internet—there's beaches and beaches and beaches. There's even places where Ketchup and Took can get off. They can't get off here because of…qu… Dad, what is it?'

'Quarantine,' Nick said, his eyes not leaving Misty's face. 'We had a friend sail *Mahelkee* here, and Ketchup and Took flew with us. Fred's given them every inoculation they need. If they stay on the boat when there's any restrictions then they can go with us wherever we want.'

'You've brought the dogs?'

'Family,' he said diffidently. 'They didn't want to stay at home.'

'You've brought two stray dogs to Greece?'

'Their inoculations will cover them for almost every place on your list. There's a couple of places they can't go, but Rose and Bill will look after them then.'

'Rose and Bill?'

'Isabelle's parents,' he said, and there was a tension in his voice that said he wasn't sure if he was stepping over some invisible line with this. 'They've been desperate to help since Isabelle died. They love Bailey. We've sort of… I've sort of backed off from them, but they're lovely people. They're Bailey's grandparents. I know they'll like you.'

'And they have a really big boat,' Bailey said. 'So they can look after Took and Ketchup every time we go and have adventures and then we can come back and get them. And Took's even learned to swim. Dad went swimming yesterday and Took jumped right in and swam as well—and they already know how to use their sand tray.'

'How long have you been here?' she asked faintly.

'Four days,' Nick said. 'Waiting for you.'

'Four days…'

'We'll wait for a year if we must. If you really want to do your list alone. Only we'd very much like to do it with you.'

'I want to see snow buntings,' Bailey said.

Oh, help. She was really crying now. She was crying and crying, and an elderly woman cast her a sideways look and stopped.

'Are you okay, dear?' she said. 'Is this man annoying you? Can I get my husband to carry your bags aboard?'

'I…' She had to pull herself together. Somehow. She sniffed and sniffed again. 'I'm fine,' she managed. 'I'm really fine. This gentleman's not annoying me at all. In fact…' She took a deep breath. Regrouped. Cast a last look at a big white fibreglass boat that was no longer about to carry her to her dreams.

'In fact, I might have found someone to carry my bags for me,' she managed, and she smiled. And then she smiled and smiled, and before the elderly lady knew what hit her she reached out and hugged her. 'But thank you for offering. I love it that you offered your husband, but I believe I might just have found my own.'

'You mean you'll let us join you?' Nick asked and the whole world held its breath.

Her world settled. Her heart started beating again. She was standing before the man she loved with all her heart, and her list was waiting.

'Why, yes,' she said as he reached for her and beside her an extremely astonished elderly lady started to smile as well. 'Why, yes, I believe I will.'

Sunrise.

Bailey was still in bed, deeply asleep. He'd had a really big day yesterday, trudging gamely up the sides of the hills of Tulloch. He'd seen snow buntings. He'd giggled and run and been every inch the child he should be.

He seemed younger now than he'd been twelve months ago. That was great. It was how it should be. He was confident and happy. If he woke now, he had his dogs on his bed and the lovely lady who ran their bed and breakfast overlooking the loch would reassure him that Dad and Misty would soon be home.

But not yet. Bailey might have seen a snow bunting but Misty wanted to hear them, and there wasn't a lot of listening to be had with a chattering seven-year-old. So they'd crept away at dawn, rugged up, because even in summer the Highlands could be cool and misty.

They walked side by side up the scree, sometimes

hand in hand, steadying each other, sometimes coming close, hugging, then clambering the tricky bits apart… and then coming together again as they intended coming together for the rest of their lives.

They reached the point the landlady had suggested. They sank into a bed of heather—not so soft as Misty had imagined—she did need to keep adjusting these dreams—and they watched the sun rise over the distant peaks.

In silence. Apart from the snow buntings.

It was the best…

Where had she read the words… *'It's not how many breaths you take; it's how often your breath is taken away'?*

Her breath was taken away now. She was lying in heather on a Scottish hillside, listening to the birds she'd read about for so long, beside the man she loved.

Her husband.

They'd married in Greece, on the Isle of Lindos. In an ancient temple overlooking the Aegean Sea. Lindos hadn't been on her list but there'd been a few wonderful additions to her list and there were more to come.

'Does this place come up to scratch?' Nick asked her as the sun rose higher and the tangerine blush faded to the cool, clear grey of the day. 'Can we put a tick beside this one?'

'Yep,' she said and rolled happily into his arms. 'Yes, we can. Definitely a tick. Or maybe a scratch is a better description. Oh, Nick, I love you.'

'I love you, too,' he said and he kissed her long and wondrously and they clung and held—two lovers finding their dreams together. 'You want to go back to bed?' he asked as the kiss finally ended and she knew by the passion in his voice what he wanted—what they both wanted right now.

'Wuss,' she said. 'Just because heather's a bit scratchy.'

'A lot scratchy. Double bed back at the house. Pillows. More pillows. Lovely, soft quilt.'

'Take your coat off,' she ordered. 'Heather. More heather. Lovely soft coat.'

'Wicked woman. Someone might see.'

'We're the only people in the world,' she said and kissed him again. 'Don't you know?'

'We're not, you know,' he said and held her close. 'Misty, it's almost time we went home.'

Home. Banksia Bay. It was waiting for them, a lovely place to come home to.

But maybe not for ever. They'd leave and leave again, she thought. But for now...maybe they did need a bit of stability.

Banksia Bay was a good place to have a baby. Twelve weeks to go... She put her hand on her tummy and she felt her baby move, and she thought life couldn't get any better than it was right now.

'I'm thinking we should get another dog,' Nick said and she pushed herself up on her elbows and looked down at him. Dark and lean and dangerous. Wickedly laughing.

Her Nick.

'Why would we get another dog?'

'I've been thinking...'

'Thinking's risky.'

'Yes, but...' He tugged her down and kissed her

nose. ‘Ketchup and Took…in a way they brought us together.’

‘I guess they did.’

‘So to bring this new little person into the family…’

‘We need another dog?’

‘A pound dog,’ he said in satisfaction. ‘One who needs a home.’

‘We’d have to extend the sand tray on *Mahelkee*.’

‘I’m a marine architect,’ he said smugly. ‘Bigger sand tray? I can handle that.’

‘Baby first,’ she said. ‘Dogs need attention.’

‘Home first,’ he said, unbuttoning her coat with delicious, languorous ease. ‘Banksia Bay.’

‘For now,’ she said and kissed him and kissed him again, as she intended to kiss him for the rest of her life. ‘Banksia Bay’s our base. Somewhere Bailey can go to school, where we can work, where we can recoup for the next adventure. But home? Home’s where the heart is. Home’s number thirteen or number fourteen on our list. Home’s wherever we are, my love. Home is where I am, right now.’

* * * * *

Tamara Owens is supposed to be finding the person stealing from her father. But when she meets prime suspect Flint Collins—and his new charge, Diamond—she can't bear to pull away, despite her tragic past. Will Flint be able to look past her lies to make them a family by Christmas?

Read on for a sneak preview of the next book in The Daycare Chronicles, An Unexpected Christmas Baby *by* USA TODAY *bestselling author Tara Taylor Quinn.*

How hadn't he heard her first knock?

And then she saw the carrier on the chair next to him. He'd been rocking it.

"What on earth are you doing to that baby?" she exclaimed, nothing in mind but to rescue the child in obvious distress.

"Damned if I know," he said loudly enough to be heard over the noise. "I fed her, burped her, changed her. I've done everything they said to do, but she won't stop crying."

Tamara was already unbuckling the strap that held the crying infant in her seat. She was so tiny! Couldn't have been more than a few days old. There were no tears on her cheeks.

"There's nothing poking her. I checked," Collins said, not interfering as she lifted the baby from the seat, careful to support the little head.

It wasn't until that warm weight settled against her that Tamara realized what she'd done. She was holding a baby. Something she couldn't do.

She was going to pay. With a hellacious nightmare at the very least.

The baby's cries had stopped as soon as Tamara picked her up.

"What did you do?" Collins was there, practically touching her, he was standing so close.

"Nothing. I picked her up."

"There must've been some problem with the seat, after all..." He'd tossed the infant head support on the desk and was removing the washable cover.

"I'm guessing she just wanted to be held," Tamara said. What the hell was she doing?

Tearless crying generally meant anger, not physical distress.

And why did Flint Collins have a baby in his office?

She had to put the child down. But couldn't until he put the seat back together. The newborn's eyes were closed and she hiccuped and then sighed.

Clenching her lips for a second, Tamara looked away. "Babies need to be held almost as much as they need to be fed," she told him while she tried to understand what was going on.

He was checking the foam beneath the seat cover and the straps, too. He was fairly distraught himself.

Not what she would've predicted from a hard-core businessman possibly stealing from her father.

"Who is she?" she asked, figuring it was best to start at the bottom and work her way up to exposing him for the thief he probably was.

He straightened. Stared at the baby in her arms, his brown eyes softening and yet giving away a hint of what looked like fear at the same time. In that second she wished like hell that her father was wrong and Collins wouldn't turn out to be the one who was stealing from Owens Investments.